ANAHUAC

ANAHUAC

A TEXAS STORY

William D. Darling

Cover Illustration Copyright Canned Peas Productions, LLC., Austin, Texas
Cover design by Ashley Ferguson

ISBN-13: 978-1974645404
ISBN-13: 1974645401

For Diane Miller, whose friendship
and gracious support will never be forgotten.

Author's Note

By the time William B. (Buck) Travis reached Anahuac, a seaport village located in the Mexican province of Tejas in 1831, he'd failed at most everything he had ever tried. Behind in Alabama he'd left a wife and children, an insolvent newspaper enterprise, and suffocating debt. The young lawyer sought to start a law practice in this ragged village located at the top of Trinity Bay in what is modern-day Texas.

The Mexican government hoped that Anahuac would serve as a gateway to the riches in the rugged interior of Tejas. The government's lofty aspirations for the seaport were reflected in the name they gave it: Anahuac, an Aztec word that referred to the ancient core of Mexico. The American immigrants, now called Texicans, anglicized the pronunciation to "Anna whack".

Travis was one of a large number of immigrants from the United States who were running from one unpleasant circumstance or another. The Mexican government initially welcomed these immigrants to help settle the isolated and barbarous land that was Tejas. However, the government had neither foreseen the prickly nature of its invited guests nor their penchant for evading Mexican law. Unhinged by the immigrants' belligerence, the Mexican government issued the Law of April 6, 1830 that sought to close Tejas to future American immigration.

To that end, Commander Juan Bradburn, a Kentuckian by birth but Mexican by allegiance, had sailed into the nascent port of Anahuac in 1830 with a contingent of soldiers, including convicts conscripted to serve in the Mexican Army. It would have been difficult for Bradburn to be any more disliked by the Texicans. His unsavory command wasn't his only problem. After the Texicans assisted Bradburn in the construction of Fort Anahuac, he refused to pay them for their labor and supplies.

Buck Travis found himself in Bradburn's world. It wasn't long before Travis and Bradburn butted heads. The dispute started over a runaway slave. Travis represented a land owner from Louisiana whose slave had found sanctuary in Fort Anahuac. Mexican law did not recognize slavery. Bradburn properly refused Travis' demand for the slave's return. One thing led to another and Bradburn incarcerated Buck Travis and Patrick Jack, his law partner. The conditions at Fort Anahuac were so rudimentary that the law partners were jailed in a filthy brick kiln. The arrest of the law partners was but one of a series of conflicts between the Texicans and Mexican authorities.

After Bradburn refused to release Travis and his partner, a group of armed Texicans marched to Anahuac to secure their freedom. Texicans were ready to rebel at any real or imagined provocation by the Mexican government. A violent conflict erupted between a Texican Militia and the Mexican soldiers at Fort Anahuac on June 10, 1832. Ultimately, negotiations between the Texicans and the Mexican Army led to the release of the lawyers and the dismissal of Bradburn. After his release, Travis became an even more zealous revolutionary. In 1836 that zeal led Travis to San Antonio as the commander of the ill-fated Alamo. Travis penned his famous "victory or death" letter shortly before the Alamo was overrun, etching his name in Texas history forever.

Anahuac never attained prominence. The isolated village drowsed through the nineteenth and twentieth centuries as a ranching and fishing community. While Anahuac slumbered, the city of Houston, located across the bay, became a center of world commerce. Only a few broken bricks remain to mark the location of Fort Anahuac.

☆☆☆

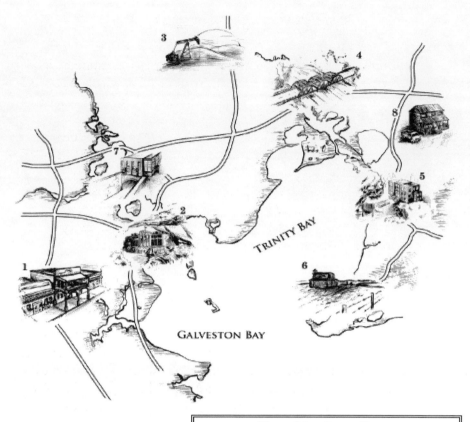

Map of Anahuac, Texas

1. La Porte Texas
2. Morgan's Point, Bay Villa
3. Barbers Hill
4. Trinity River
5. Anahuac Courthouse & Fort Anahuac Park
6. Sarita Jo's Ranch
7. Baytown Tunnel
8. Little Harry's Ranch

PROLOGUE

SARITA JO FRANKLIN

Sarita Jo Franklin stared out at Palmetto Ranch as it shimmered in the numbing afternoon heat of a late August day in 1972. The isolated spread was 12,530 acres of pastures, fields and bayous located at Smith's Point on the shore of Galveston Bay. Palmetto was the way Texas used to be.

Sarita Jo leaned heavily on the silver knob of her wooden cane with both hands. In earlier times she had crisscrossed the ranch in total control of her kingdom, sitting tall and strong astride Big Sandy. It had been an afternoon like this one three years earlier when Big Sandy stumbled in the wet, gumbo-like soil after an afternoon rain shower. Sarita's aching hip and a pronounced limp were lingering reminders of the fall, but the memory of her pistol shot to Big Sandy's head to end his misery hurt her worse.

Sarita Jo tired quickly in the afternoon heat and made her way to a rocker on her large screened porch. She was proud that she had kept the ranch going through droughts, floods and declining beef prices. The days of large independent cattle ranches in Texas had begun to wane as they were replaced by massive feed lots. But in the end it was government meddling that had finally done her in. The ranch had been in full swing until three large white vans from the Immigration and Naturalization Service showed up to take away the six hands and their families who had worked and lived on the ranch for years. Without the illegals, there was no way Sarita could sustain her cattle operations.

Sarita was sure it had been her brother, Elvin "Lard" Franklin, who had tipped off the INS. He wanted what he called "my ranch" back. Lard had originally owned half of Palmetto, but he pissed away so much money gambling and whoring down in Villa Acuna in Mexico that Sarita Jo had managed to buy his half by paying off the bookies in Houston and giving Lard enough to buy a small place close to High Island. In a case of blind, dumb luck, the oil-producing salt dome at High Island spread further than anyone thought. Lard was back in the money, and in no time he was back to his old ways, but this time there was no chance he could outspend his surprising new-found oil fortune. He couldn't outlive it, either. His liver quit, taking the rest of him with it.

Sarita Jo might have had to sell Palmetto except for a secret only a few people knew. Sarita Jo Franklin, the able rancher, was a wizard at forecasting agricultural markets. She made a fortune buying and selling pork bellies and the like.

From her seat on the porch she was left to only remember the fields as they had been when they teemed with cattle, horses and crops. On a small table next to her chair were a bottle of bourbon and a small pitcher of branch water, medication to ease her pain. Before her fall she had rarely taken a drink.

Her three-story wood frame ranch house had stood since 1858. The house sat on a circular half-mile wide hill that rose but seven feet above the flat coastal plain that surrounded it. More bump than hill, the elevated ground allowed the mansion to survive the wrath of hurricanes. For three days after Hurricane Carla in 1961, the house appeared to be a ship crossing the bay until the waters receded.

Her grandfather, along with eight black men without say in the matter, had built the home on the tiny rise. The slaves had cut ancient oaks from the forests that stood at the far end of the ranch. Fine bricks made from native clay fired in a kiln in Anahuac were used to buttress the foundation. The kiln had fallen into disuse shortly thereafter. The bricks were now crumbling from the relentless humidity. While both the house and Sarita still retained hints of grandness, their best days were behind them.

She was sipping her medicine when she saw the fine dust cloud rising from the shell road leading to the ranch house. Sarita's lug of a nephew, Cletus "Clete" Franklin, her last blood relative, had telephoned her a few days earlier to announce he was going to stop by for "a friendly chat." She shuddered to think what the idiot child of her dead brother had in mind.

The fine dust swirled behind Clete's pickup as he barreled recklessly toward her. The truck slid to a stop in front of the house and the dust cloud momentarily caught up with the truck, obscuring it. Clete swung open the door of the cab and stood on the running board as the dust cloud swirled about him.

"Auntie Jo!" Clete hollered as if there were some love not already lost between them. He clomped up the steps with a big grin on his face.

"Mind if I have a drink?" he said. Without waiting for an answer he helped himself to the bottle of bourbon on the table. "It's too hot out here; let's go into the kitchen so I can get a glass."

"It's hotter in the kitchen," Sarita said.

Clete disappeared into the house, the slap of the screen door closing behind him his only response. Sarita used her cane to pull herself up from her chair. By the time she made it to the kitchen Clete had poured himself

2

three fingers. He was seated at the kitchen table as if he owned the place. None of this suited Sarita, no sir, not one damned bit.

"I'll get right to it. You're too old to be sitting out here on this ranch by yourself. I've talked to the people at Big Pine Nursing Home in Beaumont. They can take good care of you. You just deed me the ranch and I'll make sure you'll have plenty of money to take care of you for the rest of your life."

Sarita Jo Franklin looked over the top of her glasses and in a chilled voice said, "Clete, I'm only sixty-one years old. What in the blue blazes would I do in a nursing home? If your daddy was still alive he'd help me whip your goddamned ass for such foolishness."

Actually, Sarita was fairly sure if Lard had still been alive he would have helped Clete load her in the truck to haul her away to the death house in Beaumont. Clete was like his father—sorry as dog shit.

It wasn't about the money. It was about hard work and its reward. Sarita had persevered when others had not. She had been given much and she had given much of her life to preserve it. Sarita never married. There had been suitors, but only one had turned her head. He had been perfect, but fate intervened in their love affair. When he was wrenched from her arms, she accepted no more. The isolation of Palmetto and the hard work required left little time for the folderol that passed for courtship.

"Aunt Sarita, you can't keep living here. I don't care how old you are. You're too stove up to take care of yourself. Nobody but me even knows you're alive. I'm the only one who cares about you," Clete said unconvincingly.

"Wait here," she commanded. When Sarita returned to the table she held the old pistol that her grandfather had worn when he settled the land. It hadn't worked in fifty years, but Clete didn't know that. She put the pistol on the table in front of her. Sarita said nothing.

"What'd you go and get that for, Sarita?"

"Clete, this discussion is over. I'm not going anywhere, but you are. Now git!" she said as if she were shooing away a stray dog.

Clete sat for a moment and then shot out of his chair knocking it backward behind him onto the kitchen floor. If his intent was to startle her, it failed. Sarita sat calmly looking down at the gun.

"You'll be sorry; some alligator is going to crawl in here and have your sorry ass for supper if he can stomach it. You're going to die out here and no one cares."

"Run along boy before you get something you don't want."

3

Clete stepped back and his foot tangled in the chair. He grabbed the table as he struggled to catch his balance. The pistol slid off the table and hit the floor. Clete grabbed it and pointed it at Sarita. "I ought to kill you right now. My daddy always said you were trouble and selfish, too."

Sarita knew she wasn't going to be killed by a bullet from a broken gun. She rose from her chair and said, "Git, I said, now git."

Clete exploded with rage and threw the gun across the room. As he stormed out he shouted all manner of threat. After he was gone Sarita was sad, but not because of the fight. Sarita was sad she hadn't brought one of her working pistols to the table so she could've shot him.

It was getting late and the sun was going down. As was Sarita's custom, she ate a peanut butter sandwich and poured herself another stiff bourbon, but without the branch water. She picked up her little turquoise transistor radio and hobbled back to the porch to look at the stars and find radio stations far away from her struggles on the ranch. The frogs and cicadas were serenading and the sky was clear. She'd never had time to worry about what would happen to the ranch when she was dead. She was too busy staying in control. Now she recognized her death would mean Clete would inherit the ranch if she didn't write a will to prevent it. All of her work and sacrifice would be for nothing. The reality staggered her and she had no answer.

Sarita turned the tiny dial on the radio until a hypnotic voice floated melodically out of the speaker. Not even the scratchy static of a distant station could distract Sarita's fascination.

"Do you have what you need? I'll say it again. Do you have what you need to get into heaven? Do you have money, but not love? Do you have money and no family? You can't take it with you. Yooou might not know, but I know what you need to do. You can make sure the Randall Clay Prayer Hour stays on the air. Can you help me assure God's works are done here on earth? God rewards those who make sure his word is spread. All you have to do is send your check to the Reverend Randall Clay Prayer Hour at P.O. Box 823, Hope, Arkansas." Randall Clay managed to turn the town's name of Hope into a three-syllable word.

Reverend Randall repeated the address over and again. "Now get up and get a pen or pencil and write this down." He repeated the address. "I know there is someone special out there who is wondering if this is the right thing to do. God knows you're thinking about it. He told me straight out right before I came on the air. Don't you disappoint him! He won't disappoint you. May Gaaaaawd's grace be upon you. Once again that's P.O. Box …"

Sarita Jo Franklin stared down at the little radio after the sermon ended, lost in the enormity of the moment. She was not religious and not even sure whether God existed. But the visit from Clete, her aching hip, and the uncertainty about what would happen to the ranch after she was gone was upon her with a vengeance. Sarita had thought she was indestructible, but now she knew different.

Sarita walked into the house, repeating "P.O. Box 823, Hope Arkansas, P.O. Box 823." She rummaged through the roll top desk for a box of Palmetto ranch stationery and a fresh sheet of carbon paper. Carefully she aligned the carbon paper between the white sheet of stationery and a thin sheet of onion skin paper for Clete's copy. Satisfied they were aligned, she rolled the sheets into her ancient typewriter. She struck the keys of the manual typewriter forcefully to assure that the carbon paper left a clear image on Clete's onion skin copy. The rhythmic slapping of the typewriter's keys comforted her as she typed a letter to the Reverend Randall Clay.

On the bottom of Clete's copy she hand-wrote a note. "You are no better than your daddy!" When she sealed the two envelopes she felt better. There was just enough time for one more drink before she went to bed. Tomorrow Sarita Jo would fire up the old Chevy truck and drive into Anahuac to the post office. The sooner she and Reverend Randall Clay met up, the better it would be.

CHAPTER ONE

"You want me to whaaat?" Wells Wilson croaked into the telephone.

It was a mistake to call his home before noon, but I had to get moving.

Wells was silent for a moment and then growled, "Jim Ward, is that you?"

"Yeah, Wells, it's me and it's before eleven. I've got to get all of the arrangements made. We need to get business cards printed and such."

Wells drew a slow deliberate breath, then exhaled loudly. "Why in the hell would I want to practice law?"

"We need to do something productive with our lives."

"Do I have to wear a tie?" Wells said with more than a hint of alarm.

"Well of course, we're lawyers."

"This is just plain crazy, Jim. I have more money than God. Why in the hell do I want a job?"

"It's not a job, it's a profession. Look, we might even help our fellow man," I laughed.

"Let's meet at the club at three. Maybe after a few drinks this will make sense."

The Houston Yacht Club was not an unusual destination for us. "Wells, I've got a better idea. Meet me at that two-story office building with all of the wrought iron work on Main Street in La Porte at three. That's where we are going to office. Cooper and I bought it yesterday." The directions were more than adequate; La Porte was a small town, a distant suburb of Houston, with most of its commerce located on a single broad street that bisected its residential neighborhoods.

"You've finally said something I can deal with. I thought we'd have to office in Houston in one of those silly brass and glass places. This way we're only seven minutes from the club. This might work, but it's still crazy."

"It *would* be crazy if Cooper's dad wasn't giving us the Fair News Corporation business. Most law firms don't start out with a multi-million dollar first client. I finally had to do it. You know Taylor Faircloth, he doesn't recognize "no" as an answer."

There was an uncomfortable pause. Then Wells said, "There is something I have to tell you." The next pause was even longer and when Wells spoke it sounded like an apology

"I promised my wife that if I ever practiced law she could have her name on the door."

6

"You have a wife?"

"Yes."

"And she's a lawyer?"

"Well, it's 1972 after all!" Wells said with a laugh.

I didn't know which revelation was more surprising. When I attended law school in the mid-1960s, there was hardly a woman in sight except the undergraduates who studied in our law library hoping to get a Mrs. degree. It never occurred to me to wonder why.

"Nice lady, more of a friend than a wife. She lives in Manhattan and works for the US Attorney's Office."

Wells and I had been friends for several years. I knew he made regular trips to New York, but I assumed that it had to do with all of the testamentary trusts created by his parents' wills. Their deaths in a plane crash in Mexico had left a young *cum laude* graduate of the Harvard Law School with more money than the treasuries of many small countries.

"Uh, where did you meet her?" I had no idea where else to start.

"Harvard Law School."

Flabbergasted, I blurted, "I didn't even know that women could go there! Would she move here?"

"Well, I hope not. We do better at a distance." Wells chuckled.

The import of the telephone call was clear. My wife had to hear this news. Cooper had warned me not to involve Wells in my law practice, but I didn't want to be a solo practitioner. Now the firm had three partners before it was even off the ground.

I dialed Cooper's office in Baytown where she reigned as managing editor of the Fair News Corporation. Its eleven successful newspapers were located throughout rural towns in East Texas. Cooper's poised executive assistant answered.

"Ms. Faircloth's office," she said.

Cooper was one of the new breed of woman that insisted on keeping her maiden name after marriage. It just wasn't right.

"Hi Claudia, it's Jim. Is Cooper there?"

"I'll check to see if she's here."

That was another thing that annoyed me. Claudia was just outside her boss's office door. Cooper was either there or she wasn't. There was a silence and then Cooper answered.

"Hey, what do you need? I am up against deadlines right now."

"We need to talk about Wells and the practice."

"What's up?"

"A lawyer wife for one thing."

"I don't have time for riddles."

"Wells has a wife who is a lawyer and he won't be a partner unless she is part of the practice. She lives in New York City. He never told me about her."

"That's impossible," Cooper said.

"It might be impossible, but it's a fact. She is going to fly into Houston on Thursday. Wells wants to take us all out on his yacht Friday afternoon and then have dinner at the club."

"This is a big mistake."

"Can you go?"

"You know I can't just take off." Her tone was the one she used when she was the most aggravated. There was a silence. "Oh, all right, but I think this is all a mistake."

"I'm not worried. She probably won't even want to come when she sees La Porte, Texas."

"Gotta go."

Her voice sounded like she wanted to scold me further, but the deadlines weren't going away. I was going to tell her I hoped it was one of Wells' pranks. He might be punishing me because I had called him too early in the morning. But she had hung up.

The fantasy that it was a prank dissolved three days later. Cooper and I stood at the end of a long dock at the Houston Yacht Club watching Wells tinkering with the rigging of his yacht, *Remembrances*. It was shortly before noon when Cooper and I loudly repeated our usual and quite unnecessary request to Captain Wilson.

"Permission to come aboard?"

Wells' head rose up from the deck and with a comical hand salute, he said, "Permission granted!"

At that moment a woman's beautiful face framed in thick blond hair emerged up the galley way stairs from below deck. A brisk breeze off Galveston Bay lifted her hair into a flaxen swirl about her face. She was managing a tray full of martinis. She handed the tray to Wells and strode toward Cooper and me—all six feet of her. She was a force of nature, the tallest, most graceful woman I had ever seen.

"Welcome aboard," she said in a lilting British accent and held out her hand. "I'm Aurora."

Aurora had celebrity presence. I was lost in the wonderment about the accent when I realized that her handshake was crushing my hand. Cooper looked as flabbergasted as I by what we would soon call the "Aurora Borealis" treatment. Aurora simply shimmered with energy.

Wells laughed as he held the tray of dry martinis high over his head. It was as if he were celebrating a victory in the America's Cup. His grin made clear that he enjoyed watching Aurora's performance and our reactions to her. What I couldn't understand was how this couple, or non-couple, had come to be. The afternoon sail made one thing as clear as the vodka. Aurora was a serious person, intent on becoming our partner.

"I need to get into private practice. I like the experience that I'm getting in federal court, but I have higher expectations." This gal was all business.

"What do you want to do in private practice?" I asked.

"Use the connections that I have made in New York and around the world to start an admiralty practice."

"Don't the big firms in downtown Houston have a choke hold on whatever admiralty business there is down here? I thought it was mainly controlled by the big New York firms," I said.

"I have friends in international shipping. They say they don't trust these big-firm Texas lawyers. They trust me."

I wasn't sure what to say. A small-time firm with giant clients sounded great. I couldn't imagine it would work, but it didn't matter, really. I wanted Wells as my partner. He was moneyed, connected, and most importantly, he was my friend. It didn't matter if we had to take on his beautiful, high-flying, big-talking wife. "It doesn't matter" became a mantra that trumped all else.

At supper that evening Aurora had ordered the wine. After dinner she asked the waiter for a cigar. The whole evening had centered on her stories of London, New York and Paris. Cooper and I spent most of the evening exchanging glances. Cooper's glances were openly hostile.

Cooper and I were silent until we were back on Morgan's Point. Cooper's frustration flooded out of her. "I hope you know what you're doing. That woman is simply too much."

Clearly, she felt threatened by Aurora. Cooper was used to being the only powerful woman in the room. She had held her tongue until she was on home soil.

"She's going to be all right. I'll talk to Wells and make sure she stays in her place."

9

"You're naïve and you don't know anything about women. She'll have you for lunch if you don't watch out."

She was right of course. I had proven many times in my life that women were a total mystery. "I'll watch out." I said hopefully.

"Well, you'd better; this is your law firm."

The conversation was closed, but I was disquieted. Who had a woman partner? Maybe I hadn't thought this through, but I was sure Wells could control his wife. Then there was another disquieting thought. You mean like you control Cooper?

CHAPTER TWO

The agitation of a vague nervous dream hung on, even as my eyes struggled to open. Some critical pleading due in some nameless case in some unknown court had not been timely filed. A judge railed at me that I'd committed malpractice. Any lawyer can tell you it's their worst nightmare. The sun was still below the horizon and the bedroom was pitch black.

I rolled over and my hands fruitlessly searched for Cooper in the darkness. I longed to touch her. The sound of the toilet flushing in our master bathroom stopped my search. My wife was always an early riser. There was not going to be love-making this morning. As I lay, disappointed, a jolt of electricity darted through me. It wasn't just the day after Labor Day. Today I was opening my law practice.

The first months of 1972 had been filled with chaos. I'd escaped from the prosecutorial disaster of convicting the wrong man for a robbery and survived an accident that left Wells Wilson and me swimming for our lives in the Houston Ship Channel. If that wasn't enough, my wife had wrongly suspected that I was having an affair with a local TV reporter. Fortunately, Providence had intervened at a critical moment and I felt I could truthfully say that Cooper's suspicions were unfounded.

Because I was his son-in-law, Taylor Faircloth had tried to hire me as the general counsel for Fair News Corporation when I graduated from law school. It was a heady offer and a solid job. I had seen myself at sixty-five, stooped from sitting behind a desk my whole career, doing nothing exciting. A shudder had run up my spine. I wanted Taylor's respect, but that didn't seem possible if I was just another of his employees. I wanted to do what real lawyers do. I wanted to be a trial lawyer. So I took a job with the DA's office in Houston.

Since moving to Bay Villa in 1966, I'd lived the life of a wealthy man. Marrying into money was like winning the lottery—more luck than effort. I had the trappings of wealth, but everyone knew that the money was Taylor Faircloth's doing, not mine. I could have most anything I wanted, but I had to say "may I" to make it happen. I had worked my way through college. Cooper understood it was difficult for me to marry into the Faircloth fortune. I'm not saying I hadn't enjoyed the ride, but in reality it had sometimes bruised my manhood. I would erase some of that bruising today. My law practice would be my ticket to my own money and success.

"Jim Ward, are you awake?" Cooper asked through the bathroom door.

"Yes, but now I prefer to be known as Jim Ward, famous trial lawyer," I said. I dreamed that Cooper would someday proudly write about my success in her newspapers.

"Great, let's get some breakfast. I have to get over to Baytown for a staff meeting and then go to a meeting somewhere else. I can't even remember where."

A blinding light flooded the bedroom as she opened the bathroom door. She was already dressed. Backlit in the bathroom light she looked powerful, attractive, and in control. I loved her so.

"I've got something for you downstairs. I hope you're going to love it."

She was skilled at gift-giving. Cooper had a sense about what people liked. I threw on a robe and followed her down the grand staircase. When we got to the breakfast table her gift was sitting in my chair.

"Beautiful," I said as I pulled the soft leather briefcase close to my face. The smell of its fine Italian leather intoxicated me. My initials were stamped on the case in gold.

"My old briefcase was pretty well shot."

Cooper looked up at me with a smile.

"I wanted my man to look good in court," she said between sips of coffee.

"Now I will," I said as I slid into my seat.

"I'll see you tonight." Cooper rose from the table. She kissed me on the cheek and was gone.

She left so quickly that I sat for a second wondering, should I go after her? Did I say thank you? I love you?

Before I could do anything Cooper's head popped back around the corner of the door. "Good luck on your practice. Not that you need luck. Well, maybe you do need some luck with the Wilsons on your team. Go knock them dead." Always the phantom, she was on the move.

Jerome Jefferson, the glue that held Bay Villa together, raced in from the kitchen as Cooper disappeared. "Is she gone? I wanted to know if she still wanted fish for dinner. That woman is always in such a hurry."

The sound of Cooper's car racing up the driveway answered his question.

"I'm sure fish is fine. I'd wait till you see the whites of her eyes before you put it in the oven."

"That's a fact," he said. "You want eggs this morning?"

"Just toast. I have to get to work."

12

Cooper Faircloth and I had married in college. It had been almost ten years. Our lives were in a steady pattern. Some might have called it a rut. It wasn't like we had discussed any of it. I had a feeling that the introduction of a private law practice might go a long way toward changing the direction of our marriage. I just wasn't sure which way that might be. One thing was certain; if we saw any less of each other we wouldn't be seeing each other at all.

I ate the toast as I went upstairs. I had two trial suits that I liked. Today was special. Setting a tone with my staff was important. The custom-made light wool navy blue seemed the strongest. I dressed carefully making sure that my red power tie was neatly tied in a Windsor knot and centered in my collar. There was a growing anxiety about the day. Saying I was in private practice sounded nice. Succeeding in private practice was another thing. Financially there wasn't much chance I would fail. Taylor had a world of business ventures that always needed law work. That wasn't the success I craved. My success would be measured in jury cases won.

Jerome met me as I was about to drive away. He presented me with a gift, a pressed monogramed handkerchief. He handed it to me like a medal of honor. "Man's got to have a proper hankie. You never know when you'll need one."

I started to laugh it off assuming he meant it for me to use it to blow my nose, but then I realized it was a genuine and charming gesture.

"Thanks, I really appreciate it," I said. Jerome looked pleased.

I made a production of placing it in my front jacket pocket.

"Good luck, Mister Jim."

I cocked my head and gave him a sideways glance of disapproval.

"I mean, Jim."

"Thanks Jerome. I may need to bend your ear sometimes about things, if that's all right. This is tough. I don't know how it will go, but I'm excited."

"Be my pleasure…Jim."

My new law office was no more than five minutes away. When I arrived there I would be in a new world. I wanted to forget the last year, at least most of it. I'd looked forward to this morning for a month. Now that it was here I fought to stay focused.

My car slid into my parking space in front of my building. My heart raced briefly at the thought of what lay ahead. There was hardly another car on the street. I climbed out of my car, took two deep breaths, and stared at the ground. When I had expelled the second breath, my anxiety passed. I looked up at the two-story brick building. It stood out. There was a grand balcony, finished with an antique wrought iron rail, on the second floor, more suited for New Orleans than La Porte, Texas. My eyes locked on the sturdy black wooden sign attached to the front of the building. Its golden lettering glistened in the sharp angle of the morning sun:

Wilson, Wilson and Ward
Attorneys-at-Law

I had two partners and I hoped Cooper's fears about them were not realized. Now filled with a pleasant excitement I reached for the front door. The door swung open before my hand could grasp the door handle. Alice Ann Glass thrust a steaming cup of coffee out the door. My new secretary was making points with me even before I could get inside the building. I expected to spend a leisurely morning arranging my desk, drinking some coffee and contemplating my next steps.

Alice Ann looked worried. "Mr. Faircloth is in your office," she said in a stage whisper. "He was standing on the porch when I got here at seven-thirty."

All expectations of a leisurely morning evaporated. I should have known that Taylor Faircloth would pull this. Oil man, publisher, and political king-maker were but a few of his titles. His most important title to me was father-in-law. Taylor was a man in perpetual motion, notorious for his ambush interviews when he was a young reporter.

"Thanks," I said, trying to sound like I was in charge. I don't know that anyone, especially me, was buying it. I took a sip of the hot coffee and walked to my office. I could see Taylor reading a document as he waited.

"Did you drive over from Houston this morning?" I wanted to know if Taylor had slipped into Bay Villa after I went to sleep the night before and left before I awoke. He spent most of his time in his rented suite at the Rice Hotel in Houston after the death of Electra, his beloved wife of thirty years. Sometimes I was surprised to find him drinking coffee at the breakfast table at Bay Villa when I came downstairs. He had given Bay Villa to Cooper, but it didn't guarantee our privacy or even a courtesy call before he showed up.

Taylor continued to look at the document he was reading and said, "Like to get an early start Jim, never learned how to sleep much." He never answered a question directly. He was using this encounter as a teaching moment. Clearly his new lawyer hadn't met Taylor's expectation. Any fanciful thoughts about how our business relationship would be conducted were quickly disappearing.

"I didn't have any appointments. I mean, its eight o'clock," I protested. Taylor finally looked up from the document. His face clearly communicated "not good enough!"

"I'm running a newspaper chain, an oil production company and five other businesses. I get an early start every day. There are many people who depend on me to provide them employment. I need the people that work for me to get in early and work hard," Taylor said. There was no mirth in his tone.

This was the moment to make it clear that I didn't work for him. I was his lawyer, independent, my own man. This was the time to set him straight. I was about to open my mouth to do just that when Taylor began to speak.

"That little British girl knows what it takes to represent me. I never thought much about having a woman lawyer before, but she was here when I got here. She thinks this letter I got from the Texas Railroad Commission is bullshit, but of course that's what I'm here to see you about."

Aurora was here at seven-thirty? I didn't know how to respond. There was a moment of anger, then fear, and finally resignation. I did work for him and he was making it clear that there were other lawyers in the world. I might be his son-in-law, but I was going to do things his way if I was to remain his lawyer. None of it felt right, but what could I do?

"It won't happen again" out of my mouth before I could stop it.

Taylor shoved the Notice of Violation complaint from the Railroad Commission across my desk. It alleged that one of his oil companies had failed to plug an abandoned oil well.

"I never owned this crummy little well. This is the work of a slick operator out of Louisiana. He's done it before. Look at the signature on the records. He didn't even try to make the signature look like mine. Make this go away," he commanded.

"I've got this." I said, my head still spinning from what had just transpired.

Taylor made a noise as he rose from his chair and headed out the door. It was not a word really. It was only a dismissive grunt like my grandfather used to give me when I was a boy.

After Taylor left it was clear that I needed to set things straight. I was the boss. I walked into the well-organized work hub where the secretaries were busy organizing their spaces. I walked to Alice Ann's desk. Her head

15

was down. She never saw me coming. "Look, you have to keep people out of my office when I'm not here." She looked up with a pained expression. I could see the other secretaries were freaked out by my tone. Before I could get another sentence out I realized this was a bad idea. Alice Ann was an experienced secretary that I'd been lucky to steal away from a large Houston firm. I needed her and she didn't need me. Alice Ann knew how a law firm should work

I took a breath before I spoke again. It only took that breath to realize that I wasn't pissed at her. Taylor did as Taylor wanted. Alice Ann couldn't have stopped him if she'd tried. But it wasn't only Taylor that pissed me off. My new woman partner had undercut me with my biggest and, at that point, only client.

In reality, most of my anger was reserved for me. When I left the district attorney's office there was a small farewell at the strip club across the street. Most of my now-former colleagues had simply wished me well, shaken my hand and ignored me for the rest of the evening. Once a man left the office he was no longer a part of the team—a respected alumnus, yes, but still an outsider. A few made it clear they wished I would take them with me. But at the end of the evening, only Big Ted and I were left to watch the lovely Lila bare her breasts yet one last time. Big Ted was a mentor, sort of a friend and more importantly the guy that had cleaned up the mess I'd made with a robbery case that started my journey to private practice. We'd had a great number of beers and it was time to drive home. Big Ted's mood turned seriously paternal. "Never let your fear of failure make you practice law with people you don't like or work for clients that don't respect what you do."

It hit me full force. I had worked my ass off to become a trial lawyer. What I did was valuable. Taylor had disrespected my role as an attorney. He had always treated me with respect as his son-in-law. He had told me from the beginning that he was going to teach me how to run his business empire. That early conversation had been awkward for me since his offer presupposed that his daughter and my wife, Cooper wasn't suited for the task. Taylor valued his fortune and he was only doing what he thought necessary to protect it. This dual role I had now assumed would easily lead to confusion. Taylor had disrupted my office, caused me to lose my temper with my secretary, and damaged my self-respect. All in my first minute as a private practice lawyer. How I was going to deal with this dual role without causing a family riff was a complete mystery to me.

I thought Alice Ann was going to cry. I handed her my white monogramed hankie so carefully pressed by Jerome. She was too experienced to cry. She handed the hankie back without comment. My tone and the hankie had been a mistake. How many had I already made this morning? Private practice was going to be far more difficult than my structured world back in the District Attorney's Office. If I was going to regain control, I had to start by mending fences with Alice Ann.

"Not your fault," I said quietly as Aurora and Well's secretaries stared down at their desks wondering if working at this firm had been a good idea. Alice Ann looked at me, searching my face to see if I was serious. "It's not your fault," I repeated. "We'll lock my door in the future. He can sit in the waiting room like our other clients." My next stop would be Aurora's office.

Aurora had been wrong to counsel Taylor. He was not her client. Maybe they did things like that in New York City, but I would not tolerate it.

She was on the telephone with one of her New York clients and waved me away without looking up from her desk. It wasn't a dismissive wave; it just said, "I'm concentrating and this is going to take a while."

I went back into my office to wait for Aurora's call to end. I sat behind my desk for the first time, without the pressure of Taylor Faircloth's condemnations. I was tired and I was less than an hour into private practice. The clock said 8:50. Was it really going to be this hard? Alice Ann knocked on my door.

"Come in."

"I'm sorry."

"It's done, it wasn't your fault. Is the conference room ready for our ten o'clock partners' meeting?"

"Yes, but that's why I came in. Mr. Wilson called and said he's running late."

In that moment of painful clarity I realized it really *was* going to be this hard.

CHAPTER THREE

No partners' meeting meant there was no binding agreement between the partners. In the first hour of my new practice Aurora had tried to poach my father-in-law's business and Wells was nowhere to be found. Was there going be a second day of Wilson, Wilson and Ward? I knew what I was getting when I asked Wells to join me in a partnership. Cooper's dire warnings reverberated around my brain. There had never been an expectation that Wells would actually be involved in the day-to-day practice of law. I was only hoping to give my well-heeled but rudderless friend a purpose for his life.

We had both sworn off drink after Wells drove us off the Lynchburg Ferry. In Wells' case, he did not drink while he was in the hospital overnight for observation. I had abstained for at least a week. But in my mind it was Aurora who had changed everything. The clear delineation of women's roles in the DA's office had left no ambiguity as to what they did. The only woman lawyer in that office had handled child support enforcement cases. The men had assumed this was appropriate work for a woman. The rest of the women staffers typed, filed and brought us coffee. I didn't see me asking Aurora to fetch me anything.

There were more complications than my confusion over Aurora's role. She was Wells' wife. She was also a one-third partner in the firm, or at least I assumed we were all equal partners. If she and Wells voted together they could control the firm. In my rush to get things done I hadn't thought like a lawyer. My focus for the month after Wells, Aurora and I had agreed to form a partnership had been filled with buying furniture, remodeling my building, and hiring staff. There were no classes in law firm economics in law school. The three of us had never run a business. We were all operating on assumptions. We would have been furious if one of our clients had operated this way.

Our meeting in the conference room had been scheduled for ten o'clock, to hash out the particulars. It was 10:45 on our first morning and one-third of the partnership had not darkened the door. I just hoped Wells wasn't drunk when he got to the office. One of the problems with our partnership was that we all had money. I guess in my case I had *access* to money. Being Taylor Faircloth's son-in-law had many advantages.

I stood behind my desk wondering what to do next. Aurora was still on the telephone. There was a loud commotion toward the front of the building. When I came out of my office to see what was happening I was met by Wells Wilson and a full complement of servers carrying cases of champagne and enough food to feed half of La Porte.

"Upstairs, upstairs!" he shouted, his finger pointing the way to the upstairs conference room and our law library. He was flanked by a large number of people whom I assumed he had enlisted on the street to join what I now could see was our grand opening party. There were a policeman, the pharmacist, two preachers and at least a dozen workers who had been repaving the road in front of our building.

Wells carried an open and nearly empty bottle of champagne. The folly of letting our practice open without some kind of understanding had come home to roost.

Aurora emerged from her office and was as flummoxed as I. There was little to do but adjourn to the second floor. Wells led the way as the grand marshal. I followed him. A mariachi band was behind me strumming guitars and singing their way up the stairs. They were followed by a man carrying a frozen margarita machine. I started looking for one of the bottles of champagne. I had no idea what to do other than join the party.

Wells was clearly in his element and I was seeing this side of him for the first time. Our time together had almost always been on his yacht or in the bar of the yacht club. I saw him as a withdrawn fellow with few friends who drank for a living. But there he was in the middle of half of the owners of commercial businesses in downtown La Porte, regaling them with stories and singing with the mariachi band. He had a good voice and was singing in fluent Spanish.

In the initial melee I had missed one thing. The person who was managing all of the wait staff was Jerome Jefferson, the man who had handed me my clean white hankie as I left Bay Villa.

I made my way to Jerome through the crowd that had grown so large that the fire marshal would have shut the party down if he had not just had his second frozen margarita.

"Did you know about the party this morning?"

"No, sir. Mister Wells called me two hours ago and told me he had bit off more than he could chew without my help."

Jerome handled our household. Cooper's travels between the newspapers of the Fair News Corporation and my trial schedule in the DA's office would have prevented us from living in Bay Villa. The place was overwhelming and a maintenance nightmare. Jerome was smart, resourceful and loyal.

"Thanks for coming," I said as yet another group of shopkeepers and assorted locals made their way up the stairs.

After an hour and a half there was a lull in the party. The mariachis had taken a break. Many of the now-drunken shopkeepers had made their way back to their businesses. The two preachers who had been shanghaied off the street by Wells had returned to their churches. The most notable departure had been the twelve workmen who were repaving the street in front of the office. The general contractor responsible for the job had appeared and sent them back to work. This proved to be a big mistake and the next day the hung-over group ripped up their work from the previous day and repaved the mess they'd made. I got to know the contractor well during his three-drink stay and he said he'd be back in a few days to talk about some legal work he needed done. It was at the height of the lull that Wells said, "I want to make a little speech."

I'd had experience with Wells making a speech at my wedding when he was drunk so I rushed to his side.

Before Wells could start his speech, I said, "Thank you all for coming, and feel free to stay as long as you like. We look forward to meeting you all in the coming days." Wells wandered away to get another margarita.

Surveying the diminishing crowd, I hoped they would soon leave. For me, drinking early in the day was normally reserved for weekends on Wells' boat. Ronda our receptionist came to the top of the stairs and waved for me to come with her. She was the only one downstairs working.

I followed her down the stairs to where we could hear each other.

"There's a man on the telephone. He says he's from Arkansas. He says it's urgent."

I knew no one in Arkansas. I couldn't imagine who was interrupting our party from there. Ronda transferred the call to my office. The voice on the other end of the telephone spoke rapidly in a New York accent.

"Slow down, slow down, I can't understand what you're saying."

"I'm sorry, it's just so unthinkable, Mr. Ward. My name is Maurice Marrow. I'm calling you on behalf of the Reverend Randall Clay. I am Reverend Clay's business manager. He is being held there in Texas in the sheriff's office in Ana-hoo-hac. He says they are questioning him about a murder. He needs a lawyer."

"Wait a minute," I said. I knew plenty of Texas towns with strange sounding names, but Ana-hoo-hac was not one of them. "Where is this town you're talking about?"

"It's a little town in Chambers County. It's the Chambers County sheriff who arrested him."

Chambers County was across Galveston Bay from Morgan's Point. Only one town in the county was larger than a village and its name was Anahuac. "Here in Texas it's pronounced Anna-whack." I said.

"I don't care what you call it," Marrow said. "Reverend Clay needs a lawyer. He says he's sure that they don't mean to hold him. You have to know Randall; he's a bit of a showman. Sometimes his oratory gets the better of him."

"I'm going to put my secretary on the telephone. Anahuac has to be at least forty miles away by car and I need to get over there before he says anything," I said as I reached for my new briefcase. "Alice Ann is going to take some information from you."

I was so excited about the prospect of a murder case, I was on the road before I realized I didn't actually know how to get to Anahuac. I checked the map in my glove compartment to find that the trip was incredibly circuitous over, under and around multiple waterways. Tabb's Bay, Cedar Bayou and the Trinity River were the major obstacles I would have to cross to reach Anahuac. The town wasn't that far from La Porte as the crow flies, but since I wasn't a crow it was forty-five miles or so.

Then, as I breezed under the Houston Ship Channel in the two-lane Baytown Tunnel, another important thought hit me. I'd never asked Marrow if he had any money. An instant shot of soberness flooded my brain. I could get tangled up in this case, not get paid, and be forced by the judge to try a murder case. I had seen plenty of that in Houston where eager young lawyers took on cases on the promise of "I'll pay you tomorrow." The lawyers waited too long hoping to be paid and then had been forced to try the case by judges interested only in moving their dockets.

It would be the following day when I returned to the office before I had full understanding of my great good fortune to hire a legal secretary who knew what she was doing. Alice Ann didn't only take down information for the file when I put her on the telephone. She had Maurice Morrow wire $25,000 into the firm's bank account as a nonrefundable retainer before I had crossed the Chambers County line. Alice Ann had brought in almost three times her annual salary in one day. I sent her flowers. When I told Cooper about my flowers gesture she shook her head and said "dumbass." I handed Alice Ann a hundred dollar bonus the next day.

CHAPTER FOUR

The trip around the outskirts of Baytown on Texas State Highway 146 was a blur as thoughts of the day intermingled with the thrill of my first case. The adrenaline rush of Marrow's telephone call removed much of the glaze of the three margaritas. Clarity of thought now allowed another question to cross my mind. What kind of preacher has a business manager?

I knew I was getting close when I reached the Trinity River. The river lost its momentum as the lands flattened near the bay. The one river became several. The result was a massive swamp as the river ended its journey into Trinity Bay. There was nothing besides a road sign for Anahuac when I finally reached the exit. By now, it had been close to an hour and a half since I left my office. The Lord only knew to what my client had admitted while I was driving. But once I was off of the interstate, only nine miles of pine and hardwood forest separated me from the Chambers County Courthouse.

The outskirts of Anahuac were a rambling collection of small marine and auto repair shops side by side with residences, some in advanced stages of decay. Some of the homes had randomly scattered mobile homes on the properties. Many of the mobile homes had long exceeded their useful lives. Their rotten carcasses sat side by side with rusting cars, forlorn and forsaken waiting for collapse. Amongst the shabbiness of the mobile homes an occasional upscale brick home disharmoniously appeared along the banks of Lake Anahuac.

I turned right off of the two-lane blacktop toward Anahuac proper. There was little sign of civilization for a mile or so. The road turned where the waters of Lake Anahuac entered Trinity Bay and the village came into view.

The business district was situated around the typical Texas courthouse square, a rambling assortment of wooden and brick buildings mostly from the late nineteenth century. The three-story Courthouse was at such variance with the other structures in the village that I simply stopped my car in the empty street to look at it. It was by far the largest structure within forty miles of Anahuac.

The limestone skin of the courthouse was pocked with impressions of shells of creatures that had lived in a shallow sea. The stark Depression-era architecture was blunt, square and cold, but the building was something solid on this spit of land surrounded by water in almost every direction.

A metal sign on the corner pointed to Fort Anahuac three blocks away. I made a mental note to follow up when I had time. I knew nothing about it, but I imagined that it was like something out of an old Western movie.

The sheriff's office was located on the third floor of the courthouse. For the first time I felt a tiny rush of anxiety. I had never before represented a defendant in a criminal case. Six years in the DA's office had prepared me for everything but the reality that it was now *me* against the State; the tables were turned.

I jogged up the stairs into the courthouse. Any interrogation had to be cut off. Inside were the familiar smells of wood paneling, stale cigar smoke and moldy wallpaper. I didn't wait for the elevator. I was out of breath after the climb to the sheriff's spartan offices. Three desks cluttered with newspapers and coffee cups were crammed behind a small table that I assumed must be a reception desk. The waiting room was empty.

The two closed doors in the office had opaque windows; "Sheriff Leonard Staunton" was neatly painted on one. The fading paint indicated that it had been there a long time. The other window said "Interrogation Room." That seemed intimidating enough. I heard the sound of muffled voices behind the door. Presuming my client was being grilled by the sheriff, I knocked on the door.

"What!?" The word hurtled out through the door in a deeply bass and thoroughly threatening voice.

My assumption proved right. The door swung open and a tall, muscular man in his mid-fifties wearing a brown, tailored sheriff's uniform stood in the doorway. Sharp creases gave his uniform a military look. A large white cowboy hat was on his head. If his intent was to project a dangerous persona, he had succeeded. He stared down at me with cool contempt.

"I'm sorry to interrupt, but I'm Jim Ward, counsel for Reverend Clay. Is he being interrogated in this room?"

"We're almost through talking to him." With that he closed the door.

"No sir," I said firmly through the door. "I'm his counsel and I am advising him to answer no more questions."

There was silence from the room for a moment and then I heard a different, reassuring baritone voice with a decidedly southern accent call out. "It's all right, Mr. Ward. These gentlemen are only doing their jobs. I'm just helping them with their investigation. I'm sure they mean me no harm."

Marrow's fears were real. Reverend Randall Clay needed a lawyer.

"Reverend Clay, it is imperative that you stop talking to these gentlemen until you have consulted with me. If you want to talk to them after we consult then that's fine, but please indulge me on this point."

23

"If you want to talk to your lawyer that's fine; we won't be talking to you anymore if that's the case. We'll just file murder charges on you. This is your chance to clear yourself." The words reverberated within the room.

"Don't believe that," I shouted back through the door to a client that I had never seen. "They are going to file charges regardless of what you say."

Apparently even Reverend Clay understood the truth of that statement.

"Gentlemen, I regret to say that I have to follow the advice of my counsel, no matter how foolish it may sound."

With that the door opened and three sullen-looking deputies brushed by me, scowling. The sheriff was the last to leave the room. He passed me with a smirk that said I'd just screwed up. He didn't offer a handshake.

"He's all yours, he's told us enough. Old Sparky is going to stop the bullshit coming out of this asshole's mouth."

Old Sparky was the electric chair at the state penitentiary in Huntsville. I took a deep breath and walked into the conference room. There sat the Very Reverend Randall Clay in all of his glory. Curly black hair topped his large round face. He was slightly overweight, but it was hidden well by his tailored dark green suit. The suit was made of a shiny material known as sharkskin. I made a mental note—get him in a new suit before anyone else in Anahuac sees him. They might mistake him for a pimp. He looked to be about forty years old.

Rather than greet me, the Reverend sat with his head down, silently praying. I didn't want to interrupt him, but we had work to do. He would have plenty of time to pray later. Abruptly he turned his face to the ceiling and raised a clenched right hand. He extended his index finger dramatically to the ceiling and said, "Thy will be done." Then his head bowed again and he silently mouthed the rest of his prayer before offering a robust "amen."

He turned his face to me and rose from his chair smiling as if *he* were trying to comfort *me*. His head cocked slightly sideways and he nodded at me with a look a preacher might give to the bereaved at a funeral. He was in full showman mode.

I was tempted to query him about whether he thought this was all God's will, but he spoke first.

"Mr. Ward, did someone from my office call you?"

"Your business manager called me."

"Mr. Marrow is such a good Christian man and my dear friend."

Getting information quickly could make the difference between a successful defense and disaster. As I took my yellow pad out of my briefcase, there was a sharp rap on the glass of the door. Before I could answer, the door opened and the sheriff filled the doorway. I could see his deputies bunched up behind him.

"Randall Clay, you are under arrest for the murder of Sarita Jo Franklin in the first degree."

One of the deputies began reciting the Miranda warning. The rest of the group barged into the room, as if they had cornered two bank robbers. One of the deputies actually had his hand on his gun. I was glad it was still holstered.

"I'm consulting with my client!" I shouted, fighting to control my temper.

"Visiting hours tomorrow afternoon are between two and four o'clock. You can talk then. We have work to do." said the Mirandizing deputy.

"This is outrageous," I was losing the battle with my emotions. "You're depriving this man of his constitutional right to counsel."

"So what?" Sheriff Staunton said. The look on his face assured me that he thought no one on earth could challenge him.

In that moment, I knew he hoped that I would try to stop him. As I stared into his frightening countenance I heard Reverend Clay say, "I'm not resisting you." The deputies had jerked him out of his chair and were handcuffing him. I took a step to follow them out the door, but Sheriff Staunton stood in my way. As the deputies shoved Clay toward the door he turned to me and whispered, "The letter, get the letter."

CHAPTER FIVE

After the deputies hustled Reverend Clay out the door, Sheriff Staunton gave me a provocative smile. He was taunting me and I had no power over him, at least for now. He turned his back to me and followed his deputies as they strong-armed Reverend Clay down the hall to the elevator. I followed the sheriff at a prudent distance. As the elevator door was closing I shouted to the Reverend, "I'll be back tomorrow."

I stood, impotent to stop what was happening. Lawyering from the other side of the docket was full of challenges unknown to me. As an assistant district attorney, the cases arrived in neat file folders full of narrative statements, affidavits, confessions and an indictment. The contents of the file had been created by professional law enforcement officers trained to tell a story on paper. Rarely were my hands dirtied with the messy work of arrest and interrogation.

The actions of Sheriff Staunton and his deputies exposed me to a system of justice that I thought only existed in the heads of whining defense lawyers. There was nothing more to do this night but to get in my car and head home to the comfort of Bay Villa.

Early September had brought no coolness to the evening. As I walked to my car, the air was heavy with humidity and the smell of sulphur that was riding across the Gulf of Mexico on an east wind. A plant in nearby Louisiana was refining another of the earth's subterranean bounties produced from salt domes along the Gulf Coast.

The streets of Anahuac were absolutely empty. It was getting dark. No substantial lights came from the few businesses around the courthouse square. I was uneasy about what might be happening to my client in whatever served as a jail in the bowels of the courthouse. Genuine fear for my client's safety engendered an overwhelming urge to go back inside the courthouse, but I didn't know what I could do.

When I reached my car, I stopped and looked back at the limestone house of justice that was built to protect the citizens of Chambers County. The chaos of Reverend Clay's arrest had unhinged me. My helplessness had overwhelmed my ability to think like a lawyer.

The preacher's whispered message came back to me. What letter was he talking about? How did it affect the case? Who had the letter? God help us if the sheriff had it and it was exculpatory. I doubted if I would ever see it. Thinking like a lawyer gave me comfort. This first encounter with law enforcement as a defense lawyer had momentarily knocked me off my game. I knew I couldn't let this mistake recur.

As I drove off into the darkness of Chambers County I considered Clay's prayer that "...thy will be done on earth..." I wondered if I were the one being arrested if I would be so sanguine if I thought it was God's will. My suspicion that all of the things that happen on the earth are God's fault had been with me for years. I sped along a dark road lined with forests of impenetrable pine trees back to Interstate 10 and home. I struggled to find a silver lining in my first day in private practice. I had survived and would be back to fight again tomorrow. It was the best I could do.

Out of the darkness came a memory that thrust me into a white hot summer's day on a prairie in Kansas. Had all of that been God's will? Two drowned little girls lay in front of me. Then I heard the voice that had haunted me since that day.

"Why didn't you save me?"

Why didn't God help me save them? The fear that I couldn't save Reverend Clay shot through me. I felt a cold sweat on my brow. For a moment, I wondered if this whole idea of private practice had been a mistake.

Only when I crossed the murky waters of Cedar Bayou on Highway 146 and was back in Harris County did I begin to gain control of my emotions. My thoughts refocused on the responsibility of what I had just taken on. Thinking like a lawyer again allowed me to begin planning for the defense of a man whose alleged crime could buy him a one-way ticket to hell strapped to Old Sparky. The only thing I knew about him was his name, his show business appearance and a cryptic whisper about a letter. I was lost in thought about the future of the Reverend's defense as I pulled into La Porte. Suddenly flashing red lights erupted from behind me. It was the end to a perfect day.

The police car's headlights and flashing red lights formed a lethal combination. I could see little. I knew sudden movements could be lethal if a police officer felt threatened. I carefully retrieved my billfold from my coat pocket and rolled down my window.

"License and registration," the officer said as a command that left no question he was in charge at this moment. He was nestled against my car behind the driver's window to protect himself from sudden attack by a driver. His flashlight had fairly blinded me.

"I'm going to reach into my glove box for my vehicle registration. I don't have a weapon," I said, handing him my license. As I reached carefully into for the glove box the officer started laughing.

"Jim, I didn't know it was you. Sorry for the drama," he said.

When he lowered his flashlight, I could see it was Clayton Ward, a Harris County sheriff's deputy. We were not related, but we had joked about sharing a name when I was an assistant district attorney in Harris County.

"By the way, you were doing 70 in a 45 mile an hour zone. You OK to drive?"

"Clayton, it's been one long day. I was only trying to get home. Sorry, I'll tone it down." I wondered if the smell of stale margaritas was still on my breath.

"No problem. Take it easy." Clayton folded up his ticket book.

I was about to roll up my window when a car I recognized blasted by us. Clayton looked at it with concern.

"Don't worry, Clayton. That's my wife Cooper. It looks like she had a long day too." I flashed my lights at her to get her attention, but she never slowed down. I drove after her just under the speed limit.

Cooper was already inside when I arrived. Jerome, whose day had been as long as ours, was talking to her in the living room.

"There you are!" Cooper greeted me.

"You know I just saved you?

"What do you mean?"

"You'd have gotten a ticket if I hadn't been talking to the sheriff's deputy."

"That was you?"

"Yes, thank goodness I knew him."

"Thank goodness I knew you," Cooper said with a tired laugh.

"Jerome, are you sending us traffic scofflaws to bed without supper?" I asked.

"Oh no, I have it all ready for you. I didn't expect either of you to be here early."

We adjourned to the main dining room. Jerome seemed to have a sixth sense about our comings and goings. I couldn't imagine life without him. There was a time when I first came to Morgan's Point and Bay Villa that I couldn't have imagined a life like this at all. Now it all seemed ordinary.

Jerome disappeared back to his quarters leaving Cooper and me to our conversation. Our work schedules had ordained that conversation would be limited. They almost never occurred when we weren't both exhausted. Yet, when I examined our lives I saw us as the lucky ones. I couldn't imagine those simple lives that most people lived without the excitement that was the fuel of our daily existence.

"Okay, tell me all about your first day in private practice. Was it full of dull stuff like sharpening your pencils?" Cooper said.

"Yeah, that was pretty much it," I said with a sigh. It was close to eight-thirty. I couldn't imagine how many pencils she thought the job required. It rocked me to hear her dismissive tone. It usually preceded a long story about what she thought was interesting about her day.

Our conversations were often full of moments when it seemed there was an unspoken competition. Why were we trying to impress each other? It was confusing and tonight it seemed pointless. I had struggled since my youth with a vague sense that I didn't measure up to the standards of some secret committee that was judging me. Their standards were high and no matter how much I accomplished, their approbation eluded me. Taylor had never been effusive in his praise of Cooper and perhaps that was her problem, too. Fatigue had frazzled my concentration and I barely heard Cooper say, "What do you think?"

"About what?" I said wearily.

"About the hostages!" she said, knowing I hadn't been listening.

"What hostages?" I responded.

"The Israeli Olympic Team members have been kidnapped by Arabs."

"Are they still pissed off about the Six-Day War?"

"Jim, it's a lot deeper than that. Don't you know anything about the Middle East?"

"Not really. I mean I know it's got sand and oil and the Arabs don't like Israel, but not much more than that."

"I think you better start learning about it. Daddy says World War III will be fought there. Most of the gasoline that we burn in our cars comes from their oil. I've got people doing a research piece. We have to start learning where Qatar, Syria, Iran and Iraq are on a map. They may be players in our future. I'm going in early tomorrow."

I suppose if my job was to decide what news was important enough to print in a newspaper it would all seem important. While I was busy living my life, Cooper was flooded with stories that impacted millions of lives. Viet Nam, Charles Manson, and a million others filled her days.

"Sensory overload," I demurred. "We normal folks can't keep up with all this stuff you know about."

"Well, you should."

There was a momentary lull in her conversation and I said softly, "I picked up a murder case today."

"Oh yeah, where?"

"Anahuac."

"The Sarita Jo Franklin case?"

"Yes, how…" I started to ask how she knew, but as vice president of the Fair News Corporation it was her job to know these things. Her father had installed her as the titular head of the company and its eleven East Texas newspapers upon graduation from the University of Texas. There were some who questioned whether she was ready for such a position. They should have understood: she was Taylor Faircloth's daughter. She was more than ready, even if some of the editors of the newspapers were not ready for a woman boss.

"I've assigned a reporter to cover this thing. Sarita Jo was a larger than life character. The case is going to be big. Tell me about your client!"

"I don't want to talk about it right now. I don't know much about him."

"Well, even off the record?"

The idea that we were having such a conversation struck me as funny. The day got the best of me and I started laughing.

Cooper frowned, not understanding the irony behind my mirth. In a single day, I had pissed off Taylor *and* Cooper Faircloth. I wondered if anyone had ever done that and survived. As we walked up the grand staircase to our bedroom, I wondered if I would.

CHAPTER SIX

Cooper and I undressed, kissed good night and retreated to our separate sides of the four-poster. Sleep eluded me. Physically exhausted, I still couldn't slow my mind. Taylor, Aurora, Alice Ann, Wells, Maurice Marrow, Sheriff Staunton and last, but not least, the Right Reverend Randall Clay invaded my brain. Each played a significant role in my insomnia. I hadn't settled anything today. After an hour of grappling with worries of day one, physical exhaustion won.

The next morning, I woke to the sound of thunder over Galveston Bay. A tropical storm in the Gulf of Mexico was threatening Houston. Cooper was already out of bed and dressed. She leaned over and kissed me.

"I love you!" Occasionally she surprised me and I loved it. She was already heading down stairs and I hollered back, "I love you too." I thought she was gone, but she suddenly returned.

"They killed them all!" were the only words she spoke before she was gone again.

It took me a moment to understand she was talking about the Israelis. I was saddened, but Cooper published stories about an unending parade of calamities each week. By the time she was home tonight there would be new tragedies to report. In Cooper's world, there was never time to grieve for long.

I had to go by the office. Would the mariachis still be there? If Wells was involved you could never tell. I dressed quickly. Jerome had prepared my breakfast for me. A silver warmer covered my food. It struck me again that I had become used to living in what seemed at times to be a 1930s movie. I finished tying my tie and lifted the silver cover. It was my favorite, creamed eggs and bacon. I thought I was alone, but Jerome appeared from nowhere.

"Is there anything else I can get you?"

"No thanks, I'm on the run. I have to go by my office before I go to Anahuac."

"Will you be here tonight for supper?"

"Normally I would just say yes, but after yesterday I'd have to say maybe. I'll call if I am going to be late."

"Mrs. Ward will be late. She told me no later than eight."

My eyes followed him as he walked back to the kitchen. It was just after six in the morning. It was dark outside and yet he was dressed impeccably. Not only that, but he knew more about my wife's comings and goings than I did.

I ate breakfast and was in my car in a flash. I wanted go by the office to retrieve my messages from the afternoon before. I had a long drive to Anahuac before me. The pink colored message slips were on Alice Ann's desk firmly secured on a sharp pointed spindle. There were several messages from judges whose campaigns were supported financially at election time by Taylor. There was another call from my representative from West Publishing Company wanting to sell me more law books.

I was just about to leave when I noticed the Notice of Violation that Taylor had brought me the day before. I did the unthinkable. I left the complaint and a note on Aurora's desk. The note asked, "Can you please take care of this?"

Anahuac had not changed since the night before. There were a few pickup trucks around the courthouse square, but I could see that the pace of life was significantly slower than I had grown used to in Houston. As I drove around the square I realized that I didn't even know the name of the district attorney for Chambers County.

The listing of county officials on the first floor produced the name I needed. It was a famous one: Lindell Washington II. I knew it must be the son of the former US Senator from the town of Liberty located about 40 miles to the north of Anahuac. Lindell Washington had been a senator from Texas in the 1950s. Upon being defeated for reelection, he became a Republican in his last six weeks in office. Since there hadn't been a Republican in office in Texas since the 1860s, it made him an item of great consternation and concern from the likes of Lyndon Johnson and other state leaders of the Democrat Party.

The second floor was empty when I approached the DA's office. It seemed abandoned. I opened the door to see an office about one-third the size of the sheriff's office where I had been the day before. A secretary, whose face was buried in a romance novel, was seated behind a desk in the lobby. She looked surprised to see anyone. "May I help you?"

"I'm Jim Ward. I'm an attorney and I represent Reverend Randall Clay. I was hoping that Mr. Washington could give me a few minutes to talk about the case."

"He's upstairs with the sheriff right now, but you're welcome to wait. He's been up there since early this morning. I'm sure it won't be too long."

"Thanks, I wasn't sure whether Mr. Washington lived in Chambers County."

The secretary laughed and said, "Oh no, Mr. Washington lives in Liberty County. He's the district attorney for the judicial district that includes Liberty and Chambers Counties. Since we have so few residents over here in Chambers, the legislature just lumped us together."

Apparently being the son of a Republican was not politically fatal in this area of Texas. The secretary had exhausted her interest in conversation with me and went back to reading the romance novel. Occasionally she looked up and smiled at me. It was uncomfortable.

After fifteen minutes the door opened and Lindell II walked in whistling "Moon River." He gave me a cursory glance and said, "Any messages?" to his secretary.

"No sir, this gentleman---Mr. Ward is waiting to see you."

Without asking me why I wanted to see him or shaking my hand, Lindell II turned and walked into his office. After he sat down behind his desk he looked out and said, "Come on in."

I extended my hand and said, "I'm Jim Ward from La Porte. I'm here representing Reverend Randall Clay. He's in your jail. I wanted to see if you and I could work out bail."

Lindell II slowly extended his hand across the table. It was a ploy that worked. It left me uncomfortably standing before him. After a languid shake of my hand Lindell II said, "I know who you are, Mr. Ward. Sheriff Staunton told me all about you this morning. I'm sorry to say, Mr. Ward, your trip here has wasted your time. I'm not agreeing to any bail for this charlatan. We don't like people coming in from out of state to murder people and cheat their heirs out of their inheritance. Sarita Jo Franklin might have been a little strange, but she sure didn't deserve to get shot. It'll just be a mute point if you file for bail."

I started to ask if he meant a moot point, but Lindell II was now in a tirade about the lawless element in the country and how the moral majority was going to straighten out the problem with long prison sentences. He concluded his rant with the chilling statement, "We'll be giving you a notice that we will seek the death penalty."

"Reverend Clay is not the kind of person capable of the crime of murder. This is way out of line. You are aware that the Supreme Court has suspended the death penalty while it considers a pending appeal."

"That's their problem. I'm sure they'll come to their senses by the time we get to trial on this one. Then we'll just have to let a jury of the good citizens of Chambers County decide that."

All I could do was shake my head and mouth, "Bullshit."

Lindell II smirked and said, "There's an examining trial set in a couple of weeks. You can waive it now and save yourself the trouble of coming over here. My judge isn't going to let this guy see the light of day before trial." As he finished talking he stood up, trying to get me to leave.

I held my ground. "Reverend Clay told me to get a letter. I assume it was in his room at Miss Franklin's. Do you have a letter in his personal property?"

"Don't know anything about any letter. See you next month at the examining trial."

I left Lindell II's office with a sickening knot in my stomach. I didn't know what was going on, but my instincts told me that it was nothing that was helping Reverend Clay.

One of my jobs in my early days as a prosecutor was to negotiate the jail cases. Jailed men and woman without lawyers were anxious to get out of the hot, stinky hell hole that was the Harris County jail. No one caged without air-conditioning in a world of metal doors slamming, homemade knives, people yelling, and angry underpaid guards would feel differently. I didn't look forward to telling the Reverend the bad news that this would be his life until trial.

The jailer led me into a secure area off the booking area. The familiar stench of a jail enveloped me as he led me into a cramped metal cage that passed as the attorney consultation room. The heat of a Texas summer had not abated and the cage was an oven. The deputy closed the door while he went to retrieve Reverend Clay. An instant wave of claustrophobia rolled over me. I closed my eyes and struggled to control my breathing. I opened my eyes when I heard the metal door opening again.

There stood the shackled Reverend Randall Clay with the same consoling smile from the night before. Otherwise his appearance was totally different. A garish orange jail uniform had replaced his tailored suit. The heat of the jail and a steady flow of perspiration had reduced his hair to an oily, matted mess. I might not have recognized him if not for his smile. I couldn't explain it, but I felt consoled. Before I could speak the Reverend was speaking.

"Oh Mr. Ward, I have prayed all night. God has shown me his plan and a glorious one it is, indeed."

I stood to shake his hand. Sweat rolled down my forehead. Not the cold sweat I had felt the night before as I drove back to Bay Villa. I was representing a man who had God on his side. I couldn't wait to hear how God wanted me to defend this case. Before I could ask the Reverend about God's plan for the defense, he had begun talking again.

"God's plan sent the Apostle Paul and Silas to prison to show his majesty and to preach to the lost." He annotated the verse. "Acts 16: 16-40. My short time in this prison has shown me that there are many souls to be saved here. My time here won't be wasted."

I assumed this was what it felt like to listen to one of his broadcasts. Who quotes scripture while sitting in an orange jumpsuit? "Did your God give you any plan for your defense?" I said, unable to dampen my disdain.

"Mr. Ward, I didn't pray about that. I assumed that you would take care of the defense," he said without the slightest concern.

I would have laughed except for the fact that the DA was going for the death penalty. This was serious business and I had a client who was either delusional or talking directly to God. Since God wasn't talking to me, I needed to get started on finding out about his plan for the case.

"What was that about a letter you told me to get last night? The DA told me that he doesn't know anything about a letter."

"Oh my, that does complicate things a bit."

Even Reverend Clay's mellifluous tone couldn't make this turn of events sound positive.

"Start from the beginning. We'll get to the letter in due course. How did you end up here in Chambers County to start with?" I asked. If I didn't control the interview I suspected the Reverend would preach a sermon rather than help me with his defense.

"It all started with the letter from that dear departed woman, Sarita Jo Franklin." He actually looked up at the top of the cage and pointed to the heavens. A beneficent smile crossed his face. "She was moved by one of my sermons. What I mean is that God moved her. I'm just His messenger."

I was beginning to wish I had taken this case on an hourly fee basis. There seemed to be no end to Reverend Randall's puffery. A preacher with a for-profit entity seemed strange. They all took advantage of tax-exempt status.

I had to get back into the present. My mind was wandering and the Reverend was still talking.

"The radio message that day was dictated to me by God. I was going to talk about the evils of adultery, but clear as a bell, I heard God say 'no Randall, there's a woman out there who is lonely and needs to lay down her burden of money and redeem her family's past sins.'"

"Wait a minute; you want me to tell a jury that God sent you to Sarita Jo Franklin."

"Oh my, no, His messages are never that specific. I mean, well, there was this one time…"

He stopped talking when he saw my face had taken on an unmistakable look of frustration and impatience.

"I mean no." Reverend Randall restarted. "He didn't tell me anything about her. Only that I was to deliver the message."

"Like what kind of message?"

A trance-like appearance took over his face. His voice grew deeper, louder and more melodic. I could see why he was one of the up and coming radio evangelists in the South.

"Do you have money, but not God? Have the sins of you and your family sentenced you to a life of isolation and loneliness?" the Reverend articulated in a way both calm and urgent. This guy was good. I felt like I needed to give him a hallelujah or at least an amen.

When he stopped preaching he looked satisfied. I wasn't sure about what. We were still in a cage in the Chambers County jail.

"She sent me a letter to come to Texas to fetch her fortune for God. It was a miracle, really. The signal from the radio station in Little Rock that carries God's message is not very strong. God must have strengthened the signal for us that night. She was frightened. She said her nephew, I think his name was Clete, who owns 2000 acres close to her place had come over earlier that day and threatened to move her to a nursing home. He was after her place. I don't know if this is true, but her letter says she sent him packing with her grandfather's old Civil War pistol."

"That's all in the letter?" I said.

"Of course, it is four pages long."

"Did you bring it with you to Texas?"

"It was in the bedroom where I was staying at her house."

"I think the sheriff has it and is hiding it."

"Why would he do such a thing?"

"I have no idea. Did you make a copy of it?

"Mr. Marrow has been after me to let him buy one of these new Xerox copying machines, but it didn't seem necessary. We have so many

36

people who are in need of our ministry our old mimeograph machine works for most things. I thought we should use that money to buy additional radio time.

I would have thought him silly, but I had been confronted with the same question when I was outfitting the office. Lawyers have always lived in a world of carbon paper. The world has operated for eons without Xerox and I was not sure it wasn't a fad. Cooper's newspaper in Baytown had one and I assumed we'd just use hers if some extraordinary event required it. "Tell me what else is in the letter," I said, still wondering about buying a copier.

"I'm trying to remember the important parts. She said in the letter that her whole family was gone except her nephew. Apparently alcohol had killed most of them. You know alcohol is such a tool of the devil."

I could tell him a thing or two about that. The night Wells drove us off the bow of the Lynchburg Ferry into the Houston Ship Channel we'd had a devil's ration of his swill. I fought to focus on the Reverend. The DA's office had never required me to listen too much to anyone except when I was in trial. Adrenaline kept my focus then. The Reverend was back on what he remembered about the letter.

"She was sure that the fact her great-grandfather owned slaves had cursed her family. She wanted to give her ranch to God as penance. I'm afraid she really did it to spite her nephew. That's why she took me to her lawyer here in Anahuac last week to deed the property to me. She kept a life estate in the ranch so she could live out her days there."

"Wait a minute. You have the deed to Sarita Jo's ranch? Who's the lawyer that drew up the deed?"

"Harrison Chambers. Sarita told me his family has been here since the beginning."

I only knew of Harrison Chambers through tales that were told about him in lawyer circles. He was mid-forties, eccentric, a history buff, and extremely independent. His wealth had come from a large ranch he inherited at a place called High Island. It was so named for the salt dome that had created a significant bump of a hill near the center of the ranch. Except for the oil the salt dome had trapped, he would have probably just been another rancher trying to eke out a living raising cattle on the swampy grasses that grew around the hill. Instead, he was a Harvard-educated oddity in a county filled with ranchers and rice farmers. He lived at another ranch he owned in Wallisville. He had been one of Wells' classmates in law school.

"Did he record the deed here at the courthouse?"

37

"Why yes, after we finished signing the papers we walked directly from his office to the county clerk's office and filed the deed."

This was an amazing piece of news, but the Reverend wasn't quite through.

"She made me the sole beneficiary of her will. There is a fortune in stocks and bonds that our ministries will be able to use for God's glory."

Things were beginning to crystallize for me. There was a fortune involved in this case. I was already pretty sure that I would find the dearly departed had written her nephew out of her will. I wondered how much Clete Franklin knew of this. If he didn't, he was in for a hell of a surprise. Then Lindell II's words came back to me. "We don't like people coming in from out of state to murder people and *cheat their heirs out of their inheritance.*" Clete damn well did know about the transfer, but how?

"Did you tell anyone about the transaction?" I asked not knowing whether yes or no was the answer I hoped for. If the answer was no there might not be anyone else that was a candidate to take Reverend Clay's place in this fetid hole of a jail.

"I told Mr. Marrow. I thought my business manager needed to know why I was staying down in Texas."

"Did Miss Franklin tell anyone?"

"Clete Franklin got a copy of the letter that she sent me. She said she wanted him to know he couldn't push her around."

I felt like I had been through a day of trial and we hadn't even gotten to what happened to Sarita Jo. What I'd heard so far had me worrying that my first case could go south. A radio preacher from Arkansas whose manner was a bit too show business for my taste, a sudden change of ownership of a ranch and the disinheritance of the only living blood relative of Sarita Jo Franklin weren't the facts I would have chosen for my first criminal defense. Like my law professor said, "You don't make the facts, you inherit them." The facts I had inherited were pretty bleak. I was hopeful that our conversation about the murder itself would make my life easier.

We were about thirty minutes into the interview and I was beginning to understand that Reverend Randall Clay was not an idiot or a religious nut. Clay was lucid, clear and thoughtful. "Well-oriented in all spheres" was the way the psychiatrist we used back in the Harris County District Attorney's office would have described him. The Reverend was sane, but clearly operating in some parallel universe from mine. No question he understood the charge and why I was there.

If he was bothered by his wrongful incarceration, he didn't show it. I was depressed just sitting here in this cage and I was going home to Bay Villa when our interview was through. His tone was upbeat. There was a perpetual smile on his face. Before we went further I wanted to understand why. I didn't want to get blindsided at some future moment by a defect in his reasoning.

"I don't get it. Aren't you worried about the fix you're in? You seem so calm."

"There is no profit in worrying about tomorrow. The price of worry about tomorrow is the loss of today. God only gives us today for sure. Only he knows what his plan is for your tomorrow. Why would you waste today on regrets for yesterday and fears of tomorrow? Yesterday and tomorrow are beyond your control. Besides, God came to me in a dream last night and gave me his plan for me. Like Paul and Silas, I am to preach God's word to these lost souls in this prison."

My formative religious education had only warned me about not being a wayward teenager. After I had gone to college there had been no more church in my life. I knew a bit about Paul. Silas was a mystery man.

"You mean you're happy to be here? You do realize that you are likely to be tried for murder and could be sentenced to death." I was beginning to question whether he was 'well oriented' after all.

"If that's God's will for me, I have no complaint. He is the potter upon whose wheel I was created. Does the potter not have the right to discard the bowl he created?"

"I don't know; I'm a lawyer, not a prophet."

"Ah, Jim, you could be if you only listened closely. God is always speaking to us. It is we who have no ears for him."

"Reverend Clay, with all due respect—if I'm going to help you get out of here alive, you need to stop preaching and pay attention to your defense. I can't get distracted by the mission that you think God's given you."

He shrugged his shoulders and said, "As you wish. I will help you the best I can. You have your role and I won't interfere with it."

"So you drove here from Hope, Arkansas to meet with Sarita Jo?"

"I arrived here one week ago today."

"The Wednesday before Labor Day?"

"Yes. I received her letter and gave her a call. When I arrived in Anahuac there were still twenty miles to her place. Her big white house sits on a broad hill that is higher than the prairie. Quite a place, I remember thinking as I approached it. The house is three stories."

"So you talked to her by telephone, jumped in your car and drove straight to her house?"

"God's ministry can be brought to his people only if there is money to spread his word. I saw this as an opportunity to bring his glory to many. I don't apologize."

"I'm only weighing your story as a juror might."

He smiled broadly and said with vigor, "I'll leave my actions to the judgment of God."

"Well, a jury in Chambers County is going to have a hand in it, too."

"That's why he sent me you."

I was about to lose my temper. My presence was at the behest of this guy's business manager and a $25,000 retainer. I didn't remember a call from God. The Reverend was wearing me out. I fell back on a technique that lawyers use to keep testimony moving. "What happened next?"

"You mean after I got to her house?"

"Yes," I groaned, wondering if my blood pressure was going to burst a vessel.

"I pulled up in her driveway at about four o'clock in the afternoon. There was no answer for a long time after I knocked on the front door. Before she finally opened the door, she shouted, 'Cletus, if that's you. I'm warning you to get off my property!'"

"What was her tone of voice? Did she sound scared, or mad or what?"

"She sounded aggravated. I told her who I was and I held my Bible up so she'd know for sure it was me. She opened the door just a crack and peeked out. She said I was younger than she thought I'd be and she was glad she didn't just shoot through the door. She thought I was her nephew coming to try to take her to that nursing home. I believe she might have been drinking."

"Was she drunk?"

"No, but I could smell the alcohol. You know, I had my own problems with the devil's brew ten years ago. I can really smell it now. She had an old pistol in her hand."

"What happened next?"

"She took me into the parlor and offered me some iced tea. She offered me something stronger, but I told her ice tea would be fine."

"What did she drink?"

"It could have been tea, but I suspect it was bourbon."

"What happened next?" I was writing notes to myself as fast as I could. No one was going to provide me with a neatly typed rendition of his statement like I got when I was prosecutor.

"She began talking about how her great-granddad had settled the property in 1858. How he had built the house over a two-year period. A hurricane had come after great-granddaddy and his slaves had been working on it for five months, and it washed away all their work and his cattle. She said he started over with the big foundation so the first floor was high above where the water had come. He restarted his cattle herd and became successful. She said he would ferry them over to Galveston Island to sell them.

"It was all quite interesting. She took me out on her screened-in porch on the back of the house to show me where my message revealed Christ to her. She showed me the little turquoise transistor radio she was listening to when she heard God's call. She said, 'This little radio is my only friend.' I was touched. It is really isolated out there. She said she never married because she was too busy running the ranch."

"Was she still drinking?"

"No, she seemed content after we began to talk, and I told her of our work with the poor and those plagued by alcohol. She seemed relieved I was there. That lady didn't need to be in a nursing home. She was lonely, not senile. Every once in a while, she would say, 'Cletus used to be such a nice boy. I don't know what happened to him.'"

"Did you talk about the transfer of the ranch and the stocks and bonds?"

"No, I asked her if we could pray together. At first, she seemed reluctant. She said, 'It's been awhile.'"

"What did you pray about?"

"I prayed for peace and health for Miss Franklin, for her being able to forgive her nephew and for the mission of the Reverend Clay Prayer Hour."

"Why did you pray for your radio show?"

"That it might prosper and grow strong enough to broadcast throughout the whole of the USA. Maybe even TV!"

Just when I was starting to be lulled to sleep by this guy's melodic tones he would say something that rocked me back into reality. What would a jury think if they heard that prayer?

"I guess you might say your prayer was answered more quickly than anyone could imagine."

"I try to console myself that Miss Franklin is with Jesus now. If I'd known that her gift to God would have resulted in this tragedy, I would never have come here. But sometimes God's plan is not the easiest to understand.

"What happened after the prayer?" I asked. Even if he wasn't worried, I was going to have to sell a jury his story.

"We ate a light supper. I guess you'd call peanut butter sandwiches a light supper. After dinner, we went back on the screened-in porch and she tried to pick up my program. Mr. Marrow said he would replay old sermons while I was gone. Unfortunately, the reception was poor and after a while we gave up and went to bed."

"Together?"

"Not in the same room! Dear God, Mr. Ward, I am not some barbarian."

"I have to ask. The prosecutor will, if just to plant the seed."

"The next day she called Mr. Chambers and made an appointment to meet with him on Friday in his office in Anahuac. After she finished the call we drove around Smith's Point and High Island. After that we took the Bolivar Ferry across to Galveston Island and had supper at the Balinese Room. It was a lovely view of the Gulf of Mexico. We drove back to the ferry and returned to her house. We went to bed, in our *separate* rooms!"

"So when did you go to see Mr. Chambers?"

"The next morning, we drove into Anahuac to Mr. Chambers' office. He's a prickly sort. He asked me lots of questions. I mean, I realize he needed to know whether I was legitimate, but he was intense. Finally, Miss Franklin snapped at him. 'Mr. Chambers, do you think I'm senile?' Mr. Chambers said he didn't and Miss Franklin said, 'Then let's get on with this.' We left his office and drove back to the ranch. Late that afternoon we went back and he had prepared the papers. I never knew a lawyer to work so quickly. We signed them and we all went to the courthouse to record the deeds with the county clerk. The clerk asked, 'Does Clete know about this?' Miss Franklin told the clerk it was none of her damned business."

"So there was someone besides Miss Franklin, you and Mr. Chambers who knew about the deed.

"Well, I guess so."

"And of course, the deed is public record after it's filed."

"Then I suppose it wasn't much of a secret after we filed it."

"What happened after that?"

"Nothing much until I heard an argument downstairs in the house the next morning about eight o'clock. I had just stepped out of the shower and was about to dress. I couldn't make out what was being said, but it clearly was Miss Franklin and a man's voice. I heard her shout, "No!" and then there was a shot. I wasn't sure what to do. I had to put on some clothes."

The choice he made almost made me laugh--his modesty before all else?

"When I got downstairs, Miss Franklin was on the floor, mostly dead I think. She never spoke. My God, you can't imagine the blood. I ran to the front door and saw a truck far down the road, driving away."

Actually, I *could* imagine. I had been called to the site of a few ongoing murder investigations while I was a prosecutor. Four quarts of blood congealing on a floor is ghastly. The first time had been the worst. It had never gotten much better.

"I called for an ambulance. It took forty-five minutes for it to arrive. A sheriff's deputy was there in about fifteen minutes. I was busy trying to help Miss Franklin when he arrived. I was covered in her blood.

"What happened when the deputy arrived?

"He told me to stop messing with her, that she was dead. He asked me 'Why'd you do it?' I told him about the intruder. He seemed agitated and mad at me. It never occurred to me that he didn't believe me."

"Did he read you your rights or say you were under arrest?"

"No, when the Sheriff and the other deputies arrived they said for me to go onto the screened-in porch and sit in the swing. They searched the whole inside of the house and around the outside."

"Did they tell you anything?"

"They just said, 'Get in the car; we're going back to Anahuac so we can get a statement from you.'"

"Not 'you're under arrest' or 'will you voluntarily come with us?' Did they read you your rights? Did they ever say, 'You're free to go if you want?'"

"No, it's like I told you. They just told me to get in the car. I wanted to help."

"Did you ever say you were going of you own free will?"

"I didn't have to say anything. They escorted me to one of the deputy's cars and put me in the back seat. I didn't really think about it much."

"You weren't handcuffed, searched or questioned at the house?"

43

"No, I was only searched later, when they arrested me at the sheriff's office. I did ask if I could use Miss Franklin's phone to call my business manager to tell him I might be late getting back to Arkansas. Maurice wasn't there, but my secretary said she would let Maurice know to get me a lawyer. She kept telling me to not say anything. I feel silly now that my secretary was smarter than I was. I just thought they would understand that I was a man of the cloth."

"Did they question you on the way to the sheriff's office?"

"One of the officers kept saying something like, 'It takes a sorry prick to kill an old lady for her money.' I couldn't understand why they were so belligerent. I kept saying there was an intruder and they needed to be looking for him."

"Did you tell them about the gift?"

"I didn't think I was a suspect at Miss Franklin's house. When we got to the sheriff's office I told them everything about the will and the deed and that I didn't see anybody when Miss Franklin was killed."

"Tell me about the interview in the conference room."

"When we got to the conference room in the sheriff's office, they were vulgar and one kept shouting that he had a mind to whip my ass. I was terrified. Fortunately there was this one deputy who was quite nice. His name was Zeke. He kept making the others leave the room to calm down. Zeke told me he was my friend and believed my story and all I needed to do was tell him what really happened so he could keep me from being beaten. He said there was a witness that knew what happened, so I might as well come clean. When I told him I'd told the truth before, Zeke got mad and told me that he couldn't help me. He said 'God better help you when I let these other guys back in.' I didn't know what to do and I was really afraid they might kill me. The others came back in and they were really mad. They called me all kinds of names."

"Mutt & Jeff," I said shaking my head.

"What?"

"They Mutt and Jeffed you. One officer pretends to be your friend. He acts like he is protecting you from the officers who are acting tough. A lot of defendants really want to confess to get it off their conscience. The deputy who plays the part of your friend gets you to let down your guard. I've seen a defendant confess to his 'friend' then get mad at him because he told the others. I am amazed how many times I've seen it work."

"You got there right after they had come back into the room. I was sure they were going to beat me. Then like one of God's angels I heard your voice coming through the door."

So there it all was. An isolated pre-Civil War plantation, an out-of-town preacher, no witnesses, and a shitpile of money. To top it off, a preacher had just called me, the Sinner-in-Chief, an angel. It was just your average run of the mill first case. I had taken thirty pages of notes.

"Is your business manager coming to town? Do you have a wife or other family?"

"I don't have any immediate family. Mr. Marrow is my mentor and closest friend. I know he'll be here soon."

"Have him call me when he arrives. Look, this is tough. I have to begin sorting things out. I have to meet with Mr. Chambers. You may not see me for a few days."

"Oh, Brother Ward, you worry too much. I will be about the Lord's work here. I trust I'll see you when God thinks it's necessary."

I didn't know whether to laugh or cry. I didn't have time for either; a man's life was at stake, whether he was worried about it or not.

CHAPTER SEVEN

I hesitated for a moment before I pushed a button mounted on the interview table. The faded button looked like something for an ancient doorbell. Before I left I wanted to make sure I'd covered everything that might be important. There was one more thing.

"Where was Mr. Marrow while you were staying at Sarita Jo's place?"

"I don't know for sure. I assume he was in Arkansas. Why do you ask?"

"Because the prosecutor might ask you where he was," I said as I scribbled a note to ask Marrow.

With that I was through and I pushed the button. The deputy returned and shackled the Reverend.

"Is that really necessary?" I asked the jailer.

"Sheriff's orders," the jailer said without emotion. "I just do what I'm told."

As Clay was led away to his cell, he turned back slightly and attempted a waist-high goodbye with his shackled hands. His omnipresent smile was still plastered on his face. I felt a sadness that I didn't expect. Emotions other than anger rarely intruded on my days as a prosecutor. The might and majesty of the State cloaked me with a righteous indignation against the defendants whom I prosecuted. The numbing numbers of cases and endless wrongs to right allowed me no time to contemplate the alternative to guilt.

This was different. I saw a man whom I now believed had been falsely accused. The suffocating responsibility to right that wrong lay with me. Reverend Clay seemed hell-bent on his delusional thoughts that God had some plan for him behind bars. If I lost this case, the inmates at the Huntsville penitentiary would become the Reverend's congregation. These conversations with the Reverend reopened a fear in me that had begun long ago. God made his own son climb on a cross. He wouldn't lift a finger to help me save two little girls from drowning in a Kansas farm pond. I wasn't holding my breath that he gave a damn about Reverend Clay or me.

I assumed that practicing law as a defense lawyer would be much as it had been in the DA's office. The conveyer belt of cases that had flowed by my desk left little time to develop a real connection with any of the victims, witnesses or defendants. My fear was that Reverend Clay could be executed or at best rot in a prison the rest of his life. The terror of losing was always present when I was a prosecutor. The terror related to my ego. Now there

46

was the added pressure that if I didn't do my job well an innocent man might die.

A more terrifying thought crossed my mind. What if Reverend Clay was right that God had a plan for him, but the plan was that another innocent—in this case, Reverend Clay—must die? Injustice was one thing at a distance. It was quite another when the injustice was punishing a man across a table from you.

On the drive back to Morgan's Point, I pondered the chaos that had been the past few days. I wondered what had been going on in my office. I wanted Wells to help me arrange a meeting with Harrison Chambers about his legal work for Sarita Jo and Reverend Clay. I wondered if Aurora had been able to get anything done on Taylor's case at the Railroad Commission. I needed to meet with the Reverend's business manager. Then there was that other minor detail; the creation of a partnership agreement. In short, I had a plate full of mundane administrative responsibilities that gave me no joy.

There was another responsibility that required my attention. Cooper Faircloth and I had been married for nearly ten years. Our courtship and marriage had always seemed different from those of college classmates. Certainly there was romantic love, but for my part, I thought we shared a strong attraction to the other's intellect. Some had mistaken that element of our relationship as a kind of a business arrangement. Cooper never needed money. Taylor Faircloth's fortune, accumulated in oil, newspapers and political capital, would have made any business arrangement between Cooper and me laughable. I had come to the marriage as a broke college student. There was nothing wrong with our marriage that some together time couldn't cure. How and when that was going to happen was as big a mystery to me as I suspected it was to Cooper.

As I sped away from Anahuac, the late afternoon had grown quite dark. The tropical storm still far off shore in the Gulf of Mexico had sent increasing lines of rain ashore all day. A potent squall suddenly reduced the visibility to a few feet on the long bridge over the Trinity River. The wind shook my 1972 Lincoln Continental. The Lincoln was a gift from Cooper on our ninth wedding anniversary. The Alfa Romeo that I had longed for since seeing *The Graduate* six years earlier was out of the question. "I'm not having you drive down Interstate 10 at seventy miles an hour in a paper sack," she said, closing the discussion. A large gust of wind shook the Lincoln once again and I had to agree that she had probably been right. An Alfa would have fit in the trunk of this sturdily-made American car. Safe or not, I could still see Dustin Hoffman driving that red Alfa across the Bay Bridge with Simon and Garfunkel's music urging his character, Ben, on to find his true love and meaning in his life.

I summoned all of my faculties to stay alert as I splashed across the bridge, now flooded with rainwater. The heavy Lincoln plowed through puddles that would have swamped the Alfa. I leaned forward toward the windshield to improve my vision. An oil truck laden with crude oil was suddenly in front of me. The truck's bright red tail lights appeared at the last minute and I braked solidly, just missing his rear end. The squall passed as suddenly as it came and small patches of blue sky broke around the angry clouds over the Gulf. The interstate was nearly flooded and large puddles threatened to hydroplane the Lincoln. It was heavy and solid and stayed its course toward Bay Villa and Cooper. I fought to stay focused but Simon and Garfunkel had taken control of my thoughts. I was thirty years old and driving a Lincoln Continental. Was this what I had hoped for? A light melancholy edged over me as I wondered about whatever happened to Ben and his true love. The melancholy grew heavier as I wondered what ever happened to me.

Nine years of marriage had produced no heir for the Faircloth fortune. Cooper ignored Taylor's insistence for a child. When his campaign had led nowhere, Taylor had raged at Cooper. "We need an heir. Is something wrong with Jim?" When she told me I was outraged, but what was I going to do? Invite him into our bedroom?

The truth was she had no wish for children. I still couldn't imagine she could get away with it. Every young couple we knew had at least two children. I wanted a family, but Cooper was careful about the birth control pills. We were getting to an age that a child could be a disruption neither of us could handle.

I wondered how my first college sweetheart, Chinky Mason, handled her life. In 1961 Chinky had abruptly broken off our relationship, immediately become pregnant, and married. Her husband was killed in an accident. I lost touch with her until she suddenly showed up in Houston in 1968. Hired as a television crime reporter for Channel 2, she covered the courthouse where I was a prosecutor. She was successfully juggling her job and raising a son.

Chinky reemerged at a time when Cooper was totally occupied with the newspapers. I felt ignored. There is no greater threat to a marriage than a husband with unresolved feelings for a former lover and a sense of abandonment by his wife. Chinky and I had nearly rekindled our love affair

48

late one afternoon in a quiet felony jury room. Fate intervened and nothing much had happened. I mean there was no actual sex, but I guess that was open to interpretation. Cooper had her suspicions about us and issued a dire warning to both Chinky and me. It was a threat well heeded by us. I wondered how life would have been different for me if I had married Chinky.

Simon and Garfunkel kept throbbing in my brain, urging me on to Bay Villa to find my true love, my wife. I turned off I-10 without even realizing it. I drove down Highway 146 toward home without a thought about where I was going. I was too busy wondering what life would have been like if I could have had the Alfa.

CHAPTER EIGHT

By the time I got back to La Porte it was early evening. The festering tropical storm visited its next squall line on the coast of Texas as my headlights played off the large wrought iron gate at the entrance to Bay Villa. The horizontal rain overwhelmed my windshield wipers and I could only inch my way up the horseshoe-shaped driveway to the front door of the rectangular mansion. The rain obscured the lights shining through the mansion's first floor windows, giving no hint of the magnificence inside.

Governor Ross Sterling built the home in the 1920's after amassing a fortune in the oil business. He grew up on the family farm near Anahuac on Double Bayou. He was no stranger to the havoc that the tropical storms that roared off the Gulf of Mexico could wreak. Ross Sterling left nothing to chance when he built a mansion of concrete on the shore of Galveston Bay. No hurricane would wash his masterpiece away.

The front door of the mansion swung open as the Lincoln crept to a halt. Surprisingly, there was only a small *porte-cochère* to shelter the entryway. Jerome emerged with a giant umbrella. The umbrella only made it a foot or two out of the door before it was inverted and blown out of Jerome's hand. Expediency demanded that I run for it. The gusting winds almost took me down. Cooper and Jerome were still standing in the doorway as I bolted through.

"That was fun," I said as I slid to a stop on the marble floor. Puddles formed all about me.

"Thank God you're here," Cooper gasped. "Do you know how hard the wind is blowing out there?" She answered before I could. "Fifty miles an hour and getting worse."

"I didn't know. I've just seen more rain than we used to get in San Antonio in two years."

"We're lucky," Cooper said as Jerome returned with a towel and a mop to dry the floor. "This could have been worse than Hurricane Carla. It's turning away from the coast—it'll be gone by tomorrow. I called the sheriff's office in Anahuac to be sure you were OK when I saw how bad it was. They're a grumpy bunch. What did you do to them? They acted like they didn't know you and finally they admitted that you were gone."

"Yeah, I'm not high on their list of favorite lawyers. I'm not sure it's just me; I think it's my client. I need a Scotch."

"Chivas or Glenmorangie?" Jerome asked.

After all these years, I was still not comfortable with the idea that I couldn't pour my own drink. I mean, I could, but Jerome always acted embarrassed if I did. He was always there with a meal, a clean shirt or a drink.

"Chivas, neat, four fingers," I said, "It's been a long day. I'll be back downstairs in a minute. I'm drenched."

"Jerome, I'll have a drink, too. Scotch and soda, lots of ice," Cooper said as I slogged up the stairs.

"Jim, meet me in the library," Cooper called, as I reached the top of the stairs. "I want to hear all about your preacher!"

"Attorney-client privilege," I said as I disappeared into our bedroom. I was laughing, but it was serious business. Her job was to print news. My job was to defend a client. Anything I told her could open the door to my confidential conversations with Reverend Clay. It was a game to her. Her business life was spent aggressively probing, snooping and exposing. Now, as a defense lawyer, my life would be devoted to obfuscation, diversion and excusing bad behavior. In Reverend Clay's case it was different. Getting to the facts about what happened on Smith's Point was crucial to saving him. Right now, however, I had to put on dry clothes and go downstairs to face the press.

A bolt of lightning illuminated Galveston Bay as I reached the bottom of the stairs. The immediate roar of thunder reverberated through the house. The wind whistling around the eaves added to the sense that the fury of nature was in charge. It was comforting to know that this would pass soon. We had escaped with a near miss of a hurricane that had now swerved back out into the Gulf toward Louisiana. As I reached the library there was a bolt of lightning that must have struck a lightning rod on the roof of the house. The lights flickered and went out. The library was dark, then bathed with the sudden flashes of lightning. Cooper was seated in one of two large leather chairs. Our drinks were on two side tables beside the chairs.

"Be careful!" Cooper called out of the darkness.

The strobe light effect of the lightning made the scene dreamlike. One second I could see her and the next she and Bay Villa were gone.

Another voice floated out of the darkness. "I have some oil lamps, I'll be right there."

There was no end to Jerome's surprises. In a moment, the room was lighted with the pleasant glow of two aged lamps.

"There is an old generator in the basement. It still works. I'll start it up," Jerome said as if this were a routine part of the day.

"I fancy the lamps," Cooper said.

Without response Jerome was gone to the bowels of Bay Villa to again produce light. The oil lamps softened the sharp edges of the room and the mood. We were now standing together in the middle of the library. The lamps cast a golden aura around us. I was sure Cooper was going to grill me about my client, but I was met with a surprise.

"I love you," she said, in the golden glow.

Her declaration caught me by surprise. I was deeply in love with Cooper. Our chaotic lives distracted us from our love life. This storm, however, had created a rare moment when the physical world vanished. My armor assembled to parry her grilling about my client retreated. Every care in my head evaporated. In that moment there was only us. Lightning flashed revealing Cooper's smiling face and I was struck with that strange sweet aching feeling in my stomach that I had felt the first time she kissed me on the steps of Kinsolving Dormitory at the University of Texas.

"I love you, too." My response was heartfelt, not the obligatory responses that husbands and wives sometimes give each other. I was glad the Lincoln had brought me home safely.

We embraced with the kind of sudden passion that is overwhelming. This was real and unexpected. We needed to reconnect. This was a great woman who had chosen me as her husband. Our lives were complicated, but in this moment, in this embrace the essence of our love filled the room. We stepped back from our embrace in the mottled light holding hands waist high. We looked each other straight in the eye in silent reaffirmation of our love. Our fingers slid slowly apart as our hands parted. I wasn't certain we had ever had such a moment even at our wedding. Cooper breathed deeply and whispered my name. If Jerome had not been there we would have made love on the carpet.

I took her hand again in the darkness and we retreated to two large leather chairs.

"How's it been going for you?" I asked.

"Hectic, but fun. Honestly, I think I'm hitting my stride with the editors of the papers." Her face was animated as she warmed to the subject. "I'm trying to fire some of the old closet segregationists. I've hired new blood. There is a hope. Television has reached all of East Texas, so there's some competition for advertisers now that we never faced. It's shocking how many of these local merchants want to see themselves on television. But people will always want to hold their newspaper in their hands. We're going to do fine."

"No, Cooper, how are *you* doing?" I asked softly.

She seemed stumped by my question. In the glow of the lamp I saw a look of consternation on her face. It was as if my question wasn't relevant to her life. I understood. I seldom had time to assess how I was doing. This moment was as golden as the lights that illuminated the room. We had a chance to slow down, to consider things, and to be Cooper and Jim once again. The room was silent as she examined my question, even as the thunder and lightning raged outside the window.

"Can I get back to you on that?" she said. I was glad she hadn't asked me the same question. I had no answer either.

"Cooper, you're going to have to slow down. You're running all over East Texas, fighting with your editors and trying to get the truth printed. You get home exhausted and you're gone before I have a chance to say hello."

"Do you think private practice isn't going to do the same to you? You haven't even been in practice for two days and look what you've been doing. Really, tell me how to slow down and I'll do it. Daddy left me in charge of all this. I can't let him down," she said resolutely.

If it had been a cross-examination, I would have said she nailed me. This was the first honest discussion we'd had time for in a long time. This was a critical moment in our relationship. I was pondering how to change her life and giving no thought to mine. It felt like one of the critical moments in a trial when you have the opportunity to change the direction it's going to the good if only you can say the right thing. My brain switched to trial mode and was operating at warp speed. As I desperately searched for the answer there was a blinding surge of light through the room. The generator had kicked on and the harsh edges of the room were back.

"I don't know, but we've got to work on it," I said as I drank the last two fingers of the Chivas.

"We'll work on it together," she said as we stood to go upstairs to bed. In the glow, dinner was forgotten.

We were two young adults in love. We had everything one could materially want, but we wanted more. We wanted each other and we were going to work on planning our lives together. Cooper began unbuttoning her blouse as we hurried up the grand staircase to the master bedroom. When we were inside the bedroom we laughed as we thrashed at each other's buttons. She was smothering my face with soft kisses as I struggled with her bra. It was an art I had never mastered. We had not made love for at least two weeks. There was an urgency that demanded gratification.

"You are so going to love this! Cosmo had an article about how to please your man. I have been practicing the "silken swirl" for a week—I mean in my office, alone, of course."

"The silken, what?"

"Lie down Jim and quit talking for a change," Cooper rolled over onto the bed.

My excitement was profound. Quickly I realized that a woman's tongue can do things to a man that will cause him to forget his name.

"What do you think?" she said proudly.

I could only gurgle a monosyllabic response before I was on top of her. Nine years of marriage had honed our bedroom skills, and Cooper's enthusiasm was contagious. I struggled to wait for her, but it wasn't necessary. Cooper's excitement over the silken swirl escapade had driven her to a jubilant orgasm. I joined her in my own ecstatic howl that was probably heard in La Porte. My only hope was that Jerome was still in the basement.

The stresses of life were momentarily forgotten and we caressed for several minutes. Exhausted we went to sleep in each other's arms, safe from the storm that was now retreating offshore to pound Louisiana.

CHAPTER NINE

The next morning broke with shafts of sunshine darting through the cloud remnants of the storm. Bay Villa was a fortress that could have withstood a hurricane. Morgan's Point had been spared, but the people in the Cajun country lowlands of southern Louisiana were not. The arcing shore of the Gulf of Mexico serves as a sort of watery box canyon for tropical storms. Once in the Gulf, there is little chance that a storm's fury will not cause suffering somewhere. This time it was the hard-working, fun-loving citizens of the swampy Louisiana coastline.

Cooper and I were on the portico of Bay Villa drinking our first cups of coffee as the sun rose above Galveston Bay. The sky was clearing, but the bay's water, now a sandy brown, was pitching wildly in the aftermath of the storm. We scarcely took note of it. We were giggling and talking as if we were newlyweds. There had been a sexual storm in our marital bed the night before. The mention of the "silken swirl" had produced gales of laughter. The old saying "it's an ill wind that blows no good" seemed never truer. The storm in our bed had begun a conversation between us that was solely about us. It was the first time in a long time.

"Maybe we should take a vacation and talk about things," Cooper said as a question.

"When was the last time we took one?"

"There was that time we were in New York for a week."

"But that was a publishers' convention."

"Well, we went to the fiesta in San Antonio for the Night in Old San Antonio celebration."

"That was just one night and we were trying to buy the *San Antonio Express*."

"We went to the bar convention in Dallas."

"Yeah, but I was speaking to the criminal law section of the bar." I tried to make it better. "Well, living here is like a vacation."

I knew we had stumbled on to a realization that was truly frightening. We were certifiable workaholics. There was no twelve-step support group for that. Work was a national passion. Why couldn't we stop running and take a vacation? Cooper was rich and we were childless. I was painfully aware that our twenties were now in the rearview mirror. Surely we could take control of our lives at least to some modest degree. Even criminals took vacations.

"Call the travel agent over in Baytown and see where we could go. Maybe the Caribbean?" I suggested.

"I'll ask our travel editor. He's always going places for free. I'll bet he can fix us up."

"I can't wait to hear what you find out," I said as I checked the time. "Yikes, I've got to get to my office. I have no idea what's going on there. I bet I have a spindle full of telephone calls." Reverend Clay was back in my head. I was anxious to meet with his business manager. The idea of a vacation now seemed like a vague aspiration, but certainly not a reality.

"I better get going. The damage this storm is doing will be a big story. I need to coordinate how we handle it."

Jerome picked up our breakfast dishes and said, "I'd better go down to the boat house to check on the boat. Those waves are really banging hard against the bulkhead." We all gazed down to the water and it was apparent he was right.

"It would be good to have a boat if we ever get time to use it" I said, trying to be funny. It wasn't funny. It was an indictment of our lives. Cooper and I bolted for the door. It was just another day.

The short drive down Bay Ridge Boulevard to La Porte was filled with small limbs from pine trees. A few diseased pines had fallen, but the road was clear. The large oak trees that lined the road had fared well. The tenacity of the strands of Spanish moss that clung to their branches amazed me. The Point had been through this many times. Weathering storms was nothing new.

My drive to the office felt like it was my first day again. The partners Wilson and I needed to talk. I was thinking about how to arrange the partnership so they couldn't outvote me.

The large Cadillac sitting in front of my office jolted me out of my ethical debate with myself. For a moment, I thought that Taylor was waiting for me. The Arkansas plates on the car told me a different story. The man standing on my office porch smoking a cigar could only be the Reverend's business manager, Maurice Marrow. I pulled up next to the Cadillac and sat in my car for a moment, sizing him up as if he were a witness I was about to cross-examine.

Over six-feet-two inches, heavy, and slippery were my first impressions. Late forties, balding and wearing glasses so thick they magnified his dark eyes to an outrageous extent. He looked Eastern European and reminded me of a Mafia accountant I had once prosecuted. He stared cautiously at me as I sat in my car. I was appalled when he snubbed out the cigar on my porch rail. He casually tossed the cigar butt over the rail into the small, newly planted bushes. The glint from a large diamond cuff link flashed from his sleeve as he released the cigar. The serious look frozen on his face made clear he was all business. God's work was up to Reverend Clay. We eyed each other warily as I walked up the steps of the office.

"Mr. Ward?" he said with an extended right hand adorned with a large diamond pinkie ring.

"Mr. Marrow?" I responded as I extended my hand.

We had barely finished our confirming nods before Marrow said, "We've got to get him out of jail."

"Let's go inside. This is very complicated," I said. Alice Ann was busy shuffling papers at her desk.

"Good morning, Mr. Ward," she said as she stood up. "Coffee?"

"Yes, please. This is Mr. Marrow, Alice Ann. I believe you talked to him on the telephone."

"Yes, of course, Mr. Marrow. Welcome, would you like coffee?"

"With some bourbon," he responded.

"Certainly," Alice Ann said as if it was a routine request. With Wells as a partner, it might have been.

"Oh no ma'am." Marrow chuckled. "I don't drink anymore, but it did seem like a good idea for a minute."

"Black coffee, no sugar?"

"Yes, please," Marrow answered in an accent that sounded very much New York to me. But then again, any accent that wasn't Texan sounded like New York to me.

We sat in my office making small talk about the storm as we waited for the coffee. "Mind if I smoke?" Marrow asked as he took a cigar out of his coat pocket.

"No, here's an ash tray," I said as I pushed it across the desk. I had never been tempted by tobacco, but since I was in the small minority of people I had long been used to others smoking. He carefully clipped one end of the cigar with an ornate double guillotine cutter. The flame from his lighter fired the other end of the cigar. He drew heavily on the cigar and it produced a colossal cloud of smoke. He took the cigar from his mouth, held it out and admired it. As he looked at the cigar he said, "Who do we need to pay off?" The words did not sound new to his lips. He put the cigar in his mouth and inhaled its smoke lovingly.

"There is no one to pay off." I said. "Let's start from the beginning. I need to know about you and Reverend Clay." Mr. Marrow had essentially disappeared in the smoke of his cigar.

"Not much to tell about me. I was a theatrical agent in New York for 15 years. I'm a drunk. Most of us are. It's an occupational hazard. I moved to Arkansas to get away from my life in the theatre game. I joined AA and met Reverend Clay." He talked so fast that I fought to understand him.

"Reverend Clay was in Alcoholics Anonymous?"

"He's in AA—he hit a bit of a rough patch. He was a wildly popular associate preacher at a large church in Memphis. There was a young woman that came for counseling about her marriage. Well, one thing led to another and he got fired. His wife left him. He was basically run out of Tennessee. That's when he found a new religion in the bottle. He had no money. He couldn't stay in Tennessee. Randall had to move in with his sister in Hope, Arkansas. I moved there about the same time. I thought I might disappear there. A few people in New York were looking for me. The money I still had that I hadn't sent offshore was all but gone, so it wouldn't have done them any good if they found me. Unfortunately, some of those looking for me didn't care so much about the money as finding me, if you know what I mean."

"This sounds pretty bleak. I guess things changed for the better." I wasn't sure I wanted to hear how all that happened. This case was tough enough.

"I believe his listeners want to give him money, but some are so senile they send in a check for a million dollars, but they don't have thirty cents in the bank. For some reason Randall was on fire about this letter from Miss Franklin. 'I feel God's hand in this,' he said. There was no stopping him. The next thing I know is he calls from Texas and says he is on his way to jail. I called a lawyer in Anahuac out of the telephone book. He said he didn't do criminal defense. He gave me your name. He said you were a young hotshot trial lawyer fresh out of the big-city DA's office."

"Look, the letter from Miss Franklin has disappeared. The Reverend is at risk of being convicted, if for no other reason than he's an out-of-state con man. That shouldn't be enough, but juries have bought worse theories."

"Can we get him out of jail? I need him back in Arkansas."

"They're going to ask for the death penalty. He's not going anywhere."

"My God, this is worse than I realized. I thought the death penalty was banned by the Supreme Court."

"Effectively it was, in June. Texas has to adopt statutory criteria to guide a jury in making a decision to impose the death penalty. The legislature hasn't done that yet. If we can't get this case dismissed, we want it tried while the state has no ability to impose a death sentence."

"What are you going to do?"

"Ask my partner who is a former federal prosecutor to help me on this. This is not a one-man job. If you will excuse me, I'm going to see if she is here."

I had no idea how that got out of my mouth. Why was I bringing Aurora into this defense, even if she had been a prosecutor in New York? I knew it was the right thing to do, that's why.

"Certainly, Mr. Ward. I need him home."

"Plus, we're going to need a bigger nonrefundable retainer. Say another twenty-five thousand."

"No problem."

"I'll be back in a second. You can write the check now, if you don't mind."

"Don't mind at all," Marrow said, patting his coat pocket. "I set up the ministries as a for-profit company. None of the contributions are tax deductible. Randall tells them that he does it to keep the government out of religion. They eat it up. Even Randall thinks it's God's will that we keep the godless government out of God's business. Just get him off."

I left the room shaking my head. If it had been a non-profit they couldn't have taken out donated money to pay for a criminal defense. Talk about "trust me." I knocked on Aurora's closed door. A brusque "Yeah?" barked through the door.

"You got a minute?" I asked as I opened her door slightly and peered in. I was still wondering what was leading me to do this.

"That's about what I've got."

"You want to ride second on this murder case?"

Aurora looked up with a smile that answered the question.

"You bet!" she said in her British accent.

"You're going to have to practice your Texas accent. This case ain't in Manhattan."

"No problem, partner," she said in a fractured Texas drawl and with a gleam in her eye.

"Come in my office and meet the Reverend Clay's business manager. We need to get started."

The smell of cigar smoke had filled our entire office. My office looked as if it was on fire when I opened the door. The money man was preparing to light another cigar. He had his back to us when we entered the room. He stood as we entered.

"Aurora Wilson, meet Mr. Maurice Marrow."

Aurora was in the process of extending her hand to Mr. Marrow when she froze in her tracks.

"Sol?" she laughed. "Sol Friedman?"

Mr. Marrow looked as if he had seen a ghost. "Miss Wilson, I had no idea you were here in Texas. It's so good to see you again."

The silence in the room was palpable. Three people stood in the smoked-filled room alternating looks of incredulity at each other. The silence was broken when Aurora asked, "You still in Arkansas?" She said it with a wry smile.

"Yes I am. I'm surprised you knew that."

"US Marshal had a slip of the tongue. I'm not supposed to know. How'd you get mixed up in this mess? You know it's a condition of the witness protection agreement that you not promote any theatrical events."

"I'm strictly a business manager of a religious organization. I know the rules."

I stood thunderstruck. What in the hell was going on here? Maurice Marrow was Sol Friedman?

"Ah, can somebody fill me in?" I asked. "How do you guys know each other?"

Aurora looked at Marrow and he nodded his head.

"Sol was involved in the promotion of a Broadway show. He had several extremely interesting friends."

"Ex-friends," Marrow interrupted.

"Ex-friends," Aurora continued. "They promoted a lot of people out of money for a show that never opened. The money disappeared and the investors were more than disappointed. Unfortunately for Sol, one of the investors was a politically-connected guy who came to the US Attorney for Manhattan and filed a complaint."

"So, Mr. Marrow, uh, Sol turned over on his interesting ex-friends and testified for the government about some of their criminal activities in return for immunity."

"Bingo," Sol said with a smile. "I knew we were hiring the right guy to defend Randall."

"This isn't good news. I had planned to call you to the stand to back up Reverend Clay's story that he was invited to meet with Sarita Jo Franklin. What is your legal name?"

"Maurice Marrow. It's all legal. The record of my name change is a sealed court record, new social security number and even a new birth certificate. Only a few people know who I am except the US Marshals that placed me in Hope and now, Miss Wilson."

"I'm Mrs. Wilson. I used Miss when I was in New York."

"I guess we all have stage names," Marrow laughed.

I'd tried a lot of cases in the DA's office. I had learned to listen intently to witnesses as they spilled out their stories in the hall outside of the courtroom moments before a trial started. I had the steely concentration it took to listen to boring testimony for days on end. Drop your pen, reach in your brief case for a yellow pad or drift for a second and you may miss something monumental. With all of that, I was struggling to keep up with the conversation about Mr. Marrow's hidden past. Fortunately, Aurora seemed on top of it.

"Jim, we can work all this out later. I assume you didn't work with the witness protection program in state court. I can give you the details. I think we will be fine to put Sol, excuse me, Mr. Marrow on the stand," Aurora said, sounding as if I had just been demoted to second chair in this trial.

It didn't get any better when Marrow pulled hard on the cigar, spewed out a lethal cloud of cigar smoke, and said, "I'm relieved to have a New Yorker to help save Randall. These cowboys will never know what hit 'em."

I had never competed with a woman in business before. I might have swatted away a pesky male trying to poach a case out from under me. It wasn't like I didn't have plenty of experience with a strong woman. Cooper was tough as nails, but we slept together. She couldn't take a choice case away from me anymore than I could try to publish a newspaper.

Though I wanted to take charge, this witness protection stuff was not something we dealt with at the state level. There were embedded legal questions that I couldn't answer. I saw the check for $25,000 written on the Radio Hour LP sitting on my desk and was relieved. At least we were getting paid. I realized that my mind had wandered away from the conversation between Marrow and Aurora. I heard her say, "I think that's all we need for today. We'll call you when we need you to come back. I'll do everything I can to get the prosecutor to back off the death penalty."

We all stood up and shook hands. I watched as Marrow walked out of my office still talking to Aurora and realized that she was a blessing, but she came with a hefty price. I realized that Marrow hadn't even said goodbye

to me. It was all so confusing, and worst of all, I knew it was only the
beginning.

CHAPTER TEN

The next morning I was in the office by seven. I wanted to show Taylor that I was just as hard-working as he. If he was waiting for me, he'd just have to get used to the fact that this wasn't a twenty-four hour law office. If he wasn't, I'd get some work done. The Railroad Commission complaint was an immediate issue. When I left it on Aurora's desk the day before I wondered how it would sit with her. I shouldn't have worried. A dismissal of the action was waiting on my desk. How did she do it? No matter how she did it, I suspected it would not go unnoticed by Taylor.

I left my cup of hot coffee on my desk and wandered over to Aurora's office. Her office was spare. I had hung my law degree, Texas Bar license and an original LeRoy Neiman sailing picture on my wall. She had displayed no professional certificates. Instead she had a large black and white photo of the Manhattan skyline. A pen set from the Justice Department was in the center of her desk. She seemed supremely confident in herself. I needed props. She was behind her desk reading a federal statute.

"How'd you do it?" I asked as I lightly knocked on her open door.

"Apparently Taylor Faircloth is one important man," she said with a measure of deference. "All I did was tell the railroad commission staffer that the case involved Taylor and he told me that he would call me back. He did, but the dismissal was faxed two minutes before he called. He told me to extend the commission's apologies for the inconvenience. I'm guessing that this was a test by Taylor. He could have made the call himself."

"He is a wonder, but so are you. Thanks for the help. You want to give him the good news?'

"This can be our little secret. He's your father-in-law. You call him."

I had tried to play Aurora a little. I wanted her on my side if there were partnership issues. Instead she played me. She was a force of nature.

The day went quickly. There could be no partners' meeting. Wells was nowhere in sight. There were a million administrative things to do and I wanted no part of any of them. I was the managing partner by default. It was a little after four when my telephone rang. Alice Ann excitedly announced, "That Channel 2 reporter is on the telephone for you."

"Who is it?" I had no question as to the identity of the caller, but Alice Ann didn't need to know that.

"Chinky Mason."

A sense of panic settled over me. I knew this day would come. If Chinky was calling about my case I was successful. I knew I would have to tell Cooper about the call. How I was going to tell her was not clear at that moment.

"Put her on," I said, trying to sound calm.

"Jim Ward," I said formally.

"Chinky Mason here on official business. You have a few minutes for me?"

"Always."

The banter that followed was strained and contrived.

"I guess you know why I'm calling," she said.

"Not a clue," I responded. No need to take her bait.

"Well, congratulations. I hear you got the Reverend or not-so-Reverend Randall Clay. I can't imagine you have something sexier than his case over there in repentance land."

"Seriously, what's not to like about La Porte? Not much traffic and all the refinery air you can breathe. Throw in a whiff or two of the natural gas odorizing plant from Baytown and you can't live without it." My weak attempt at humor was to deflect any more conversation about the location of my practice. Somebody with my experience and connections should have been in a brass and glass building in the heart of Houston. Staying clear of Chinky Mason was the primary condition of my probation.

"You're going to get cancer."

"Smells like money," I said using the slogan that politicians and businessmen of the area liked to say.

"Seriously, I'm shooting a story on your boy. We're doing a whole series on the case. It's just too juicy to miss. If you want, I'll interview you in front of the courthouse tomorrow in Anahuac. Just like old times, big interview, no tough questions. Come on now, you know you love it. You know my angle—ex-DA saves the day in hillbilly heaven. I can see your baby blue eyes sparkling in the country sun."

I did love it. The camera and I had become great friends while I was a prosecutor. I won't deny that the bright lights turned me on when I won. But, and it was a very big but, I wasn't going unless Cooper knew about it. "I need a kitchen pass," I blurted.

"Of course you do."

I didn't know whether that was a crack or not. "What time...I mean, if I can come?"

"How about ten in the morning?"

"I'll call you if it's a no go. I'm sure Cooper will understand. She might even come with me."

"Tomorrow," she said and she was gone.

After the call, I fought to purge my mind of Chinky and our love affair. I was happy that the silliness in the jury room had gone no further. Chinky had everything a man could want. Smart, beautiful, rich and now sober, she was the complete package. Fortunately, I already had that in Cooper. I had been foolish to risk my marriage.

That evening I sat with Jerome while we waited for Cooper to return from somewhere in East Texas. I had gotten to the point that I didn't even ask where she was going.

"What do you make of this Black Power thing? Do you think it's helping your people?"

Jerome looked at me with an expression that confirmed his old school discomfort with discussing race with me. At that moment, we heard Cooper's car door slam. Jerome was on his feet heading to the kitchen.

When she came inside Cooper was like a wild woman. She had fired one of the editors and Taylor had coerced her into to hiring him back.

"I don't know why I even try to do my job. That editor should have been fired years ago. Daddy just protects him because he's near retirement. I hate it."

Jerome had two fingers of fine scotch in a large glass. He always knew what she needed.

She took the glass and eyed it lovingly for a second. Then she exploded. "Shit, I was supposed to be in Baytown for a meeting tonight. She threw her head back and downed the scotch like an old newspaperman. As she headed back for the front door she said over her shoulder, "I don't know when I'll be back. Don't wait up, Jim."

As she sped away I remembered that I needed approval to do the interview with Chinky. Cooper was out of sight by the time I got to the door.

"Oh my, how that girl does take after her daddy," Jerome said.

"Yeah, she does. I don't know how to fix it."

"I don't think it can be fixed. It's just the way they are."

Jerome was right. I closed the door and wondered when I could talk to Cooper about the interview. Cooper never watched Chinky's segment of the news anyway. Maybe it would be just as well not to bother her.

CHAPTER ELEVEN

I had no idea what time it was when Cooper came home from her forgotten meeting. Her arrival in the bedroom was heralded by an almost inaudible muttering that she reserved for matters and stories that agitated her the most. I remembered through the haze of sleep that there had been a major city council meeting that night about taxes and the refinery, but I was too sleepy to get much further. The sounds of her brushing her teeth were the last thing I heard as I drifted back to sleep secure in the knowledge there was no need to trouble her with the news of my interview with Chinky Mason in Anahuac. It was all on the up and up and she wasn't going to see it anyway. Clearly, the perceived atrocity the city council had committed would have her fully engaged in righting that wrong in the morning.

It was hardly light when I awoke. Surprisingly, Cooper was still in bed. I lay still, debating which of my trial suits would look best on television. I lay on my back assessing the case of brown v. blue. Cooper's hands were suddenly caressing me and blood flooded my penis. Nighttime was for love-making, mostly because of newspaper deadlines, travel and such. The feel of her hands on me caused me to postpone my decision concerning the suit matter. In the faint light, I could see that she was naked. Cooper as the aggressor and morning sex were unusual, but I had no complaint. She rolled her naked body on top of me and she kissed me so passionately that all thought ceased in my brain. Sex had been great since the night of the storm. She was on top of me and she was in complete control.

"Go ahead, big fellow," Cooper whispered from above me as she rhythmically moved her body. I was surprised. Cooper was not a woman who usually missed out on an orgasm.

"You sure?"

"Yes, you go," she commanded.

I enjoyed our simultaneous orgasms that brought unrestrained shouts of joy.

I assumed it must be some woman thing that made today different and gave in to the euphoria that today was only mine. Finished, I relaxed savoring the moment. Cooper lay on top of me breathing deeply. When I opened my eyes to kiss her, I saw her face was only two inches from mine. She looked like we were about to have a serious talk.

"Spoken to Chinky lately?" she asked in a manner that sounded as if it were a question one routinely asked after sex.

Sometimes coincidence provides a good explanation for strange things. I knew instantly this was no coincidence.

"She called me yesterday about doing an interview in Anahuac today. I was going to ask you about it this morning. What do you think?'

"Jim, what you do is your business," she said

As I lay there wishing I were in the dentist's chair, I knew her statement wasn't even marginally true.

"Well, this would be great exposure for the practice. I was thinking about taking Aurora with me." I was desperately trying to save my ass and my marriage as I blurted, "I mean, what do you think?"

Cooper abruptly rolled off of me and lay on her back. "If you want Chinky you should go be with her."

"What do you...?" I had started down the road to hell. I knew damned well what she meant. "Oh, for God's sake, Cooper, I don't want Chinky. She was a college girlfriend." I stared at the ceiling. "We would never have made it as a married couple."

"You slept with her; don't you want to sleep with her again?"

What can a man do with such a question? Even if "no" is truthful, it won't mean much unless the woman who asked it is only anxious for your confirmation. A moment of reflection before answering would have been the most deadly of answers.

"No!" I said as I put my face directly over hers. "Now let's go get breakfast.

Through a forced smile she said, "All right, I want to trust you, but, well I *know* what happened before.

There was no purpose in continuing the discussion. "I love you," I said as I kissed her fingers. "Let's get some coffee." I wanted out of this bedroom before this conversation turned for the worse, although I wasn't really sure how it could.

Breakfast was subdued until I said, "Why don't you come with me?"

"No, I'll take a pass on that. You're a big boy; I trust you'll handle it appropriately. Besides, I told Chinky at the council meeting last night that it was okay."

A lesser man might have spit out the coffee he had in his mouth. Thousands of hours in trial had conditioned me to hear horrible news without showing a jury my dismay. I calmly swallowed the coffee and said, "It's probably a good time to get Aurora some publicity. Maybe she can do the interview." It was one of those "moving duck" moments: on the surface I was sailing along calmly, below the surface I was paddling like hell. I shuddered at the conversation that must have transpired between my wife and my former lover. Neither was a shrinking violet.

"I doubt Chinky has any real interest in Aurora," Cooper said.

When you make your living with your words it is hard to find moments to be silent. This train wreck of a conversation might wreck my marriage. For once in my life there was a silence that I didn't rush to fill.

After breakfast I headed to the office. Aurora would be startled to know that she might be the subject of a television story this day. There was no need to worry. She came to work each day dressed as if Chet Huntley and David Brinkley might show up in her office. Visions of a conversation between Cooper and Chinky played in an endless loop in my brain. Would Chinky tell me truthfully what they talked about? I surely wasn't going to ask Cooper about it. I never wanted to talk about this with her again. This bonanza of professional publicity had become a rope around my personal neck.

I pulled into my parking space in front of the law office and sat trying to sort things out. A rough-edged shard from a childhood conversation with my grandfather interrupted the endless loop.

"Be a man about it, boy," he'd said, frustrated that I had been stung by his criticism.

"Be a man!" I commanded out loud. Looking at my face in the car's rear view mirror, doubt whispered insinuations. "Be a man, indeed," I repeated softly.

I was in a tight spot. When the day was through I needed to be sure that Cooper was pleased with how I handled it. I also needed to please a powerful television reporter with a juicy story that would help her career and mine. It was then that it struck me that if Chinky were just another male reporter there wouldn't be sex involved. Sex, that great muddler of relationships, was the culprit. Aurora could solve all of my problems, if she only would. All I needed was for my woman partner to be a chaperone. There was a perfect irony in the solution. I needed Aurora, the force of nature, to help me with the other two strong women in my life.

CHAPTER TWELVE

My blood ran cold when I looked in Aurora's office. She wasn't in. Had my perfect plan gone awry so soon? In the quiet of the early morning I could hear water running. It was the shower that Wells had insisted that we include in the office. I had no idea why we had one, but someone was using it. My fondest hope was that it was my putative chaperone.

I sat in Aurora's office waiting and hoping. After the shower stopped I heard the whine of a hairdryer from the shower room. After ten minutes Aurora appeared at the door of her office still brushing out her hair. She was dressed impeccably in a pantsuit that I understood was the new uniform for women lawyers. Her blond hair really was stunning.

"Are you living here now?" I quipped.

"No, I was jogging."

"Jogging?"

"Running, exercising, you know. You don't jog?"

"No, the thought never crossed my mind."

"It's really popular in Manhattan. People are running around Central Park in rain, sleet and snow. I ran by your house this morning around five-thirty. You need to buy some of these jogging shoes. You need bug spray though. The damned mosquitoes will eat you alive if you don't wear it."

There was little time to explore this jogging thing. Chinky was probably pulling out of Houston headed for Anahuac as we spoke. If Aurora had not been my partner I would have approached her cautiously just as I would any woman whom I was asking to help me solve a problem with my wife. The beauty of this situation was that I could treat her like a man. I was asking her to help me, one partner to another.

"Look, I've got a personal problem. If we're really going to be partners we have to help each other with personal stuff sometimes. Chinky Mason is a television crime reporter and she wants to interview me about the Sarita Jo Franklin murder this morning."

"Terrific, the firm could use the publicity."

"Yeah, I agree but there's a…a complication."

"You've been sleeping with her," she said, as a smile broadened across her face.

"No, but she was a college sweetheart. It's all kind of complicated."

"You want me to go to Anahuac?"

"Can you…will you please?"

"I would love to get out of the office. The shipping world is under control or at least the part I'm responsible for at this moment."

"You're a life saver. Can you be ready to go in fifteen minutes?"

"Sure, but I have to finish my hair."

Just when I was sure that Aurora was like any male partner that woman thing had popped up again. Having a woman partner wasn't any easier than any other man and woman relationship but it was saving my backside right now and I couldn't have been happier.

Aurora spruced up her hair in twelve minutes. She looked like a movie star, albeit a tall one. She was athletic, trim and beautiful. She and Wells made a beautiful couple.

"Let's take my car, it needs some highway miles," she said as we walked into the parking lot.

"I've never been in a 911 before," I said. She revved the engine. The yellow Porsche made beautiful sounds unheard from American cars.

"I'm still mad at you boys for sinking the Jag."

"I was only a passenger."

"At least you saved Wells' life."

"Do you believe in predestination? It was just not our day to die."

"Wells won't talk about it. What happened?"

"Wells tried to drive across the ship channel. We only made it to the end of the ferry boat. Alcohol may have played a role in the accident."

"It was my favorite car. I don't even think they make the XKSS model anymore."

"It's a better car than boat. We're more careful now."

"I'd hope so."

"I'd like an Alfa, but Cooper won't let me have one."

"Why on earth do you want an Alfa Romeo--you can't keep them running."

"It looks really sporty." I didn't want to admit my obsession with *The Graduate*.

"That boat of a car you drive could probably cross the Ship Channel," she said, and I felt a crazy embarrassment to be driving the Lincoln.

The Porsche raced away from our office and I wondered if I was still protected from the traffic laws in Harris County. The g-forces produced an exhilaration that I had never known. We buzzed under the Houston Ship Channel in the Baytown Tunnel and the reverberations of the engine off the tunnel walls sounded like a symphony. Bright sunlight momentarily blinded

70

us as we exited the tunnel. On the left side of the road, Wells' white mansion shone brightly from across Crystal Bay as the sun bathed it in the morning light. Next to the road on the right was a group of oil wells with their pump jacks still producing oil after almost fifty years.

"How do you like living over there?" I asked.

Aurora ignored my question and asked, "Why did they drill those wells in the water?"

"They didn't. They were drilled on dry land. They pumped so much oil out of the sands that the land subsided until the bay covered it. Ross Sterling drilled the wells."

"The guy that built your house?"

"Among other things. He built Humble Oil too. How do you like being back home in Texas?"

"Texas has never been my home. Wells kept asking me to come down here, but I like New York."

"Why'd you come now?"

"I think Wellsy needs me."

I stared straight ahead at the road for a moment. I'd never heard him called Wellsy. It sounded like she was talking about a little boy. This conversation made me uncomfortable. She was right that Wells needed a hand in getting his directionless life in order. The partnership in the law firm had been my way of offering help. The impromptu grand opening party erased any illusions that it had been an effective fix. Aurora had cracked open a door that led into their private lives. Did I really want to see Wells' problems this clearly?

"I'm sure he needs you. I'm glad you're here."

Aurora's response was to drive faster. The conversation stopped in place and I wondered if she was asking for my help. We both loved Wells, but my friend had grown-up problems that I had no idea how to address. As we reached the Trinity River Bridge, the garish bright red Channel 2 station wagon that Chinky had dubbed the "Red Rover" came into view. Aurora passed the lumbering wagon on the two-lane narrow bridge at 100 miles an hour. She tooted the distinctive Porsche horn. I could see Chinky sitting in the passenger seat as we blew by them.

"That's your girl, right?"

"That's Chinky; she's not 'my girl.'"

"Well, used to be your girl."

"Yeah."

"I can't wait to meet her," Aurora said and slowed the Porsche to eighty miles an hour. The pavement, broken apart by so many oil tanker trucks, bounced the small car about the road. The Lincoln could have handled it better. We reached the turnoff to Anahuac and I said, "I think you better watch your speed in here. These county Mounties would love nothing more than to put my ass in jail. This is an isolated place. This sheriff runs his own show." Aurora nodded and slowed the car to the speed limit.

As we drove up to the courthouse, I realized that the Porsche made a clear statement that "you folks aren't from around these parts" in ways that made me wince. This had been a bad idea. The Red Rover was going to get enough attention on its own. Managing the publicity surrounding a case had never been my responsibility. I stood beside the Porsche in the humid September air and scanned the courthouse square for signs of life. There were none.

Chinky and the Red Rover were not far behind. The incongruous scene of the beautiful yellow Porsche and the garish red station wagon was a sight to behold. I had no doubt it was a first, here in the middle of God's country. The good news was that these people worked for a living. There were a few old timers shooting the breeze on benches around the entrance to the courthouse, but beyond that we were in the clear. The Red Rover parked next to Aurora and me.

I watched Chinky as she got out of the Red Rover. She stretched her arms in front of her and God, did she look terrific. Bringing a chaperone to this party had been an excellent move. Aurora unwound herself out of the Porsche and Chinky's eyes focused on her.

"Welcome to God's country," I said to no one in particular.

Chinky's eyes slowly turned to me and a familiar smile broke out on her face.

"This is better than I thought," Chinky said as she surveyed the scene.

"It's somebody's slice of heaven," I responded, but Chinky was distracted as she got an eye full of Aurora striding purposefully toward her. Watching Chinky experience the Aurora Borealis treatment was entertaining. But I had no doubt that Chinky was up to the challenge.

"Chinky, it's so good to meet you. Jim has told me so many good things about you," Aurora said as her powerful right hand engulfed Chinky's.

"I'm sure he has," Chinky said, looking up into Aurora's eyes. "I'm sure he has." She repeated, turning her gaze to me.

"Are you a lawyer?" Chinky asked Aurora as their hands parted.

72

"I'm Jim's partner. My husband Wells is our other partner."

"Are you going to help Jim try this case?"

"We hadn't discussed it yet, but I am a former assistant US attorney from Manhattan. I think I could be of help."

After our meeting with Mr. Marrow in my office I realized that Aurora had worked herself into my first big case and there wasn't much I was going to be able to say about it.

"Jim, I'm proud of you. I had no idea that you were so forward thinking about women lawyers."

Chinky's compliment caught me by surprise since I was busy trying to figure out how to put Aurora back in her role as chaperone. "Ah, yeah, I really am pleased to have a partner who is a woman."

"You know, I've wanted to do a series on women who are making it in various professions these days. Aurora, you would be the perfect person to lead off the series. Let's get together next week in Houston and you can fill me in on the terrible struggle you've had to become a partner in a law firm."

"I'd be delighted. I mean, I'd be delighted if Jim's okay with it."

All eyes were now on me. "Great," I said. This was not going the way I'd hoped. I had the honor of breaking the gender line in Harris County. My colleagues would no doubt erect a statute of me in front of the Harris County Courthouse.

CHAPTER THIRTEEN

"Jim, you stand over here," Chinky said as she set up the establishing shot that would include the courthouse in the background. "Let's have you and Aurora walking up the sidewalk and onto the stairs into the building. We'll cut away and do the interview on the stairs. This is only a preliminary interview so it isn't going to be very long."

"You want Aurora in the shot?"

"Well yeah, that makes sense. We can interview you both at the same time. It will be great to get some answers with Aurora's accent, don't you think?"

"She doesn't know that much about the case. What are you going to ask her?"

"I want the women's angle on this. The station has a high male demographic. We're trying to increase our women's viewership. You know, get them out of the kitchen during the news so we can sell some women's products."

"You're not going to ask her which brand of deodorant she wears, are you?"

"Now, Jim," Aurora intervened. "I think she wants to get the woman's perspective on being in a courtroom. They interviewed me on local New York City television about that very thing."

"Exactly, Jim. I want to show that women have a place in the courtroom."

Wild thoughts filled my head. If I said that women shouldn't be trying cases, these two new best buddies would fry my ass. Chinky's cameraman was standing to the side trying to hold back laughter. My predicament was not lost on any of the four of us.

"That would be fine," I said. This damn women's thing had been funny when it didn't involve me. How in the hell had I ended up standing on the street in Anahuac, Texas trying to make sure that Channel 2 could sell feminine hygiene products?

Chinky positioned us on the sidewalk to get the best light. As we stood there preparing to do our walk up the sidewalk, a terrifying thought crossed my mind. Six feet of Aurora standing in four inch heels made me look like I was a midget. My driver's license said five feet-eleven, but I had fudged that by an inch. My humiliation would be complete.

"We're rolling, start walking," Chinky commanded. The camera was set up in the middle of the street.

74

There was nothing to do but accept my fate. Naturally, as a gentleman I had to be on the street side of the sidewalk. I couldn't wait to see that visual on the news later tonight. As we started up the stairs, Chinky said, "Stop!" I managed to get one of my feet on the stair above where Aurora had stopped.

"I'm going to interview each of you separately so Jim, you come down and I'll talk to Aurora first."

I stood behind the cameraman who was repositioning his camera. Chinky and Aurora laughed and carried on as if they were sorority sisters. Aurora had a way of doing that. Chinky had overcome a world of alcohol problems to be standing there at all. I'd grown to like the sober Chinky. But there was no denying that drunken Chinky had been a hell of a lot of fun in college. Now she was strong and sure of herself and winning awards.

Aurora threw her head back and laughed enthusiastically. I didn't hear what Chinky had said, but Aurora said, "I can do that."

I watched as she stepped out of her heels and stood a stair step below Chinky to set up the shot. The ease with which it happened made me wonder what would have happened if I'd ask her to do the same thing. Chinky and Aurora were now on an equal footing. The cameraman moved his camera closer to them and Chinky nodded.

"Looks good," the cameraman said.

"I won't ask you your name," Chinky said. "I'll introduce you in a voice-over. Are you ready, Aurora?"

"Absolutely."

"Great. Roll the tape."

Aurora stood calmly as if she had been on television all of her life. The whine of the battery on the large video camera broke the silence around the courthouse. The camera lights shone brightly on Aurora.

Chinky led with, "Do you expect this case to be tried?"

"It's way too early to know that. Reverend Clay has not even been indicted."

"How is Reverend Clay holding up?"

"Quite well. He is a man who knows God's justice will ultimately prevail in this terrible tragedy."

Chinky stood silently for a moment and then said, "Perfect. You know, as long as you are standing here let's do a few shots of you in front of the entrance to the courthouse. I can use those when we do your expanded interview for "The New Professional Women" series. I just came up with that name. How's that sound, Jim?"

"Great," I said wondering if there was still time for Chinky to do my interview. I was feeling like the first victim of the "good ol' girls" network. Chinky, Aurora and the cameraman moved about the stairs in front of the courthouse, getting a good variety of shots to edit. After ten minutes, they were finally through.

"O.K. Jim, are you ready?" Chinky said.

"Absolutely," I said, mimicking Aurora. I was afraid after I said it that I hadn't adequately disguised my annoyance with being a supporting cast member for the new *Aurora Wilson Show*.

"Let's just stand where Aurora and I did."

"Sure, do you want me to take off my shoes?"

"Oh no, we're fine," Chinky said so matter-of-factly.

Now I was making jokes at my own expense. There was nothing left to do but stand still and endure it like a man.

The tape rolled and Chinky's first question was, "How does it feel to be on the other side of the docket after a career as a prosecutor?"

"I'm pleased that I can bring my experience and talents to protect a man we feel has been wrongly accused."

Her second question was, "How do you think having a woman trying this case with you will affect the outcome?"

"My partner is an experienced criminal trial lawyer. How could that be a bad thing?"

Chinky stood silently. I assumed she was contemplating her next question, but then she said, "That's all we need."

The lights on the camera were off and I was full of questions about what had just happened to me. Chinky answered my question.

"It occurs to me that it would be good to get comments from you and maybe some judges' comments about women in the courtroom. You wouldn't mind stopping by the studio after I interview Aurora, would you?"

I shook my head to indicate no. I wasn't sure what "no" meant. The day had taken on a surreal tone I'd never seen coming. My chaperone was about to become the star of the show and the darling of all these women running around spouting stuff about women's lib. I was the guy who started it all. Jim Ward, the great emancipator.

CHAPTER FOURTEEN

"That went well," Aurora said as we walked back to her car.

"Absolutely," I said in a tortured British accent.

"You're not mad, are you? I was only trying to help."

"Cut the bullshit, Aurora. You know exactly who you were trying to help."

"Now, Jim, I'll back off if that will make *you* happy."

Aurora had played her cards well. There was no set of facts that would let me stop her now. I fantasized about a telephone call to Chinky from the Harris County Bar Association that informed her that the men of the bar had met and determined that it was neither in the best interests of justice or women to allow women lawyers near a jury trial. Since I'd never tried a case against a woman I had no idea what it would be like. My mind conjured a vision of a woman lawyer sobbing to get her way with a judge after he ruled against her. The thought of it confirmed my suspicions of how it would be. It chilled my soul.

"I'm good," I said. "We're partners in a law firm. Success of one partner is a success for the partnership. I just hope you and your new friend Chinky will give me some air time after I win this case."

"Jim," she said as she chided me in that seemingly gentle way that women use to shame men into being reasonable.

"I mean it," I said. "Please remember the little people whose heads you stepped on to get to the top."

Aurora frowned at me. "OK, you win, I was a bitch. Are you happy now?"

"Yes."

"What are we going to do now?" Aurora asked.

"Let's go on a picnic."

She was clearly caught off guard by my suggestion. "It's a pretty day and visiting hours are not until two. Let's buy some sandwiches and go see what this Fort Anahuac State Park is all about."

A smile drifted across Aurora's face as she cocked her head. "It'll be like going to Central Park at lunch."

"Don't look for any carriages."

"Right," she said in a very British sort of way.

Finding food was not simple. There was one small grocery that also sold bait and fishing licenses. We settled on Slim Jims, fried pork rinds and a bottle of white wine.

"What are these things?" Aurora asked when we were back in her car.

"The staples of the rural Texan diet. Well, maybe not the wine."

She eyed the assorted buffet and repeated, "Right. I think I'll drink my lunch today. There is a cork screw in the glove box."

Really, we were both celebrating. We'd been interviewed on television by a hotshot reporter, we had a picnic feast in hand, and Fort Anahuac awaited our review.

"Where's the fort?" Aurora asked as we entered the park.

"I've never been here. It must not be too far. Maybe it's over in those trees."

The park was located on a bluff above a narrow waterway that led out into Trinity Bay. There were picnic tables, swings, and barbeque pits, but no fort. An elaborate metal marker erected by a local lawyer soon told us the story.

"It's a story as old as Texas," I said to Aurora.

"How so?"

"The sign says the Texicans tore down the fort and stole all of the timber and bricks back after the Revolution."

"The American Revolution?"

"No, the Texas Revolution. It happened in 1836. The American immigrants ran the Mexicans out of Texas.

"You colonists always were a bloodthirsty lot."

"We don't take kindly to irritation."

"No fort?" Aurora confirmed.

"There is no fort, just some bricks from the foundation. There are the remains of a brick kiln over there by the trees. It says that William Travis practiced law here in Anahuac. The Mexican commander threw him in jail."

"Who is this fellow Travis?"

"He was the commander at the Alamo."

"Is he some Texas hero?"

"He is. I can't imagine what it must have been like here practicing law in 1832."

"From your description of what's going on here it sounds like nothing much has changed."

We picked a table that was on the edge of the bluff. There was a mishmash of flora and fauna before us. Open water, then stands of reeds and then more open water made it clear that the land before us was transitional between land and sea. Blue herons patrolled the shallows and a multitude of fast-flying, small, blue-winged teal darted about. Nothing impeded our view to the waters of the open bay that lay a mile or so away.

We had forgotten to buy cups, so we took turns pulling long sips of the truly bad wine directly out of the bottle. The Slim Jims and pork rinds lay unopened. A soft breeze blew over us and the sun was shaded by puffy white clouds. All seemed right with the world.

"I want to thank you," Aurora said as we watched a blue heron gulp down a small fish.

"For what?"

"For one thing, allowing me to be your partner. You have no idea what it's like having an obsession to accomplish something and be denied that opportunity because you're a woman. I wanted to be like my father."

"I wanted to be a football star, but all I got was a busted leg."

"But, Jim, don't you see the difference? You got the opportunity to break a leg. All I'm asking for is that opportunity."

The wine had taken its toll on me or I was getting soft. Aurora's plea made sense to me.

"So you want a chance to fail?"

"I want the same chance as you have, to win or lose."

I looked out at the wildlife drama playing in front of me and pondered the significance of her plea. Out in the water it was simple. The only way you measured success was if you were alive to fight and mate for another day. Some humans live their whole lives in a world as primitive as that. Aurora and I were blessed. We took living and living well for granted, and yet we had some primal need to fight. What were we trying to prove? The quiet of the park was broken by the sound of two seagulls arguing over lunch.

"Your father was a diplomat?"

"He worked in embassies."

Her tone sounded as if there was some mystery about his job.

"You mean like James Bond?"

"No, nothing quite so dramatic. He was a legal affairs officer for years until he and Wells' father went into business together. My father knew many important people around the world. The shipping industry is a small world actually. Wells and his family would come to visit us when Daddy was posted to the embassy in Mexico City. Wells and I got on well, maybe a little too well. He got me pregnant when we were teenagers. We were married and then I lost the baby. We never saw any reason to get divorced. I think he loves me. I know I love him. I hope we can get him back."

79

The wine had clearly gotten to Aurora. In thirty seconds, the mystery of their marriage was at least on the table for inspection.

"Wells said you met at Harvard."

Aurora laughed and shook her head negatively. "Wells doesn't like to talk about those times before Harvard."

The story wasn't complete and I wondered if I'd ever know the rest. I didn't know what to say. Her vulnerability surprised me and it scared me too. It wasn't the type of conversation I would have expected with a law partner. I looked at my watch and it was nearly two-fifteen. "We'd better get to the jail if we're going to talk to the Reverend." It was time to sober up and be lawyers again.

"This was fun," Aurora said.

"Are you ready to get your hands dirty in a Texas courtroom?"

"Absolutely."

"This case makes me nervous. We aren't in a place where the normal rules of engagement apply. This sheriff doesn't strike me as a fellow who will take kindly if we are successful in walking the Reverend out of the courthouse. I need all the help I can get."

Aurora gave me a smile that acknowledged my offer. I wondered if I would regret my magnanimity when the wine wore off.

There was a familiar car in front of the courthouse when we arrived. "That's Sol's car," Aurora said. "I hope he's not up to no good. I didn't tell you, but there's a rough edge to this guy. His file is sealed, but he isn't just an accountant who didn't get his hands dirty. We had to hold our noses to put him in the witness protection program.

"Great," I said. I wondered how many more times I would say that word today.

CHAPTER FIFTEEN

"He's already got a visitor," the jailer growled. We had disturbed his reading of *Field & Stream*. Unless you've been in jail or worked around one you might not understand why everybody is pissed off all the time. Prisoners hate guards, guards hate prisoners and jail is, well, penal. I wondered if anyone but the severely twisted or terminally dedicated to public service could say they'd found their dream job as a jailer.

"I'm...ah we're Reverend Clay's lawyers. Can you tell the Reverend we need to see him immediately?"

My request was met with a tight-lipped frown. "Give it five minutes. Personal visitors only get thirty minutes. His visitor has been in there twenty-five." During our short conversation, the jailer kept staring at Aurora as if he wanted to ask her something. Finally he could stand it no more. "So you're a lawyer?" He made no attempt to hide his incredulity.

"She is," I said firmly. "She's my partner."

"I'll be." He shook his head slowly. He said it as if he had discovered a new sub species of human. His reaction probably didn't surprise Aurora. The jailer once again buried his head in the magazine. Aurora and I found seats on a hard metal bench under a large picture of Richard Nixon.

Five minutes later the jailer opened a drawer and took out a large key ring with two heavy keys. With great effort, he hoisted himself up as if gravity had been doubled around his chair. He left the metal door ajar and we could hear the clanging of another metal door and muffled conversation. Mr. Marrow, an unlit cigar in his mouth, preceded the jailer into the waiting area. He seemed genuinely surprised to see us.

"Mrs. Wilson...Mr. Ward, I'm glad you're here. Randall will be so happy to see you."

When we first met, I had forgotten to ask Maurice Marrow, aka Sol Friedman, where he was the morning that Sarita Jo had unexpectedly passed. Aurora's news that Sol wasn't necessarily the tame accountant type he'd tried to sell me had triggered a healthy skepticism about both him and the Reverend.

"We need to talk," I said in my sternest tone. It was time to treat this guy in a way he would respect.

"Certainly, would you like to talk now?"

"We need to talk to the Reverend. Call me tomorrow. There are some loose ends we need to clear up."

"I'll call you in the afternoon. I have an important meeting in the morning."

Marrow bowed graciously to Aurora and nodded to me as he walked away. There was just something about that guy that I didn't like. He turned before he walked out of the waiting area. He lit his cigar, looked back with a creepy smile and was gone. My dual-named friend was slick, but this wasn't my first rodeo. It obviously wasn't his either.

"Okay, you two—any guns or weapons?"

"No," I said.

"I've a can of mace in my purse," said Aurora. I gave her a sideward glance.

"What?" I asked.

"I lived in Manhattan," Aurora said, laughing.

The jailer gave us a dirty look and said, "Hand it over. You can't have that in there."

After disarming Aurora, the jailer led us back to the consultation cell. The heat was suffocating and the air reeked with all manner of human aromas. The wine we enjoyed for lunch didn't seem like such a good idea now.

"These conditions are outrageous," Aurora whispered to me. The jailer overheard her and said, "What's the matter, afraid you're going to ruin your hairdo?"

"Let it go," I whispered back to Aurora.

"Now I see why so many defendants who are charged in both state and federal court offenses want to go to federal prison," Aurora said, not whispering.

"We're not running some Club Fed here," the jailer said.

"Let it go," I repeated as the jailer stopped walking and looked back at us, ready for trouble. Aurora's silence ended the impasse and we were inside the cell with Reverend Clay. He stood when Aurora entered the cell and said, "You must be Mrs. Wilson. Mr. Marrow told me that you were going to help me."

"I'm glad to meet you, Reverend Clay," Aurora said.

I wondered how much Marrow had told Reverend Clay about why he knew Aurora. The relationship between Clay and Marrow had bothered me from the beginning. In fact, there were a lot of things bothering me at this point. Regaining control over my law practice and my murder case was my first priority. Aurora might be a great help, but she wasn't going to take over this case without a fight from me.

"Reverend Clay, we have a lot of work to get done. I want to reassure you that I am the lead attorney on your case. Mrs. Wilson is a skilled criminal trial lawyer and she will be assisting me in your defense. Aurora, please take notes of our conversation today." I looked directly at Aurora. She smiled a tight-lipped smile but made no protest. Clay nodded his understanding.

I was pleased that I was the man in charge. Maybe I had made some progress.

"We're over here primarily to give a television interview to the press about your case. We want to put a spotlight on Anahuac to make sure that we get a fair trial."

"Actually, that is what Mr. Marrow and I were discussing. There are a few of my listeners who have contacted the radio station that carries my messages. They want to come south to Anahuac to set up a vigil."

"My God, what kind of vigil?" I couldn't hide my alarm.

"Please respect the name of our Creator," Clay said with a frown. "Listen, many of my listeners are farm folk. When they get their crops in, they go south in their campers for the winter to places like south Texas. Mr. Marrow recorded a message from me a few minutes ago so that I could urge them to come to Anahuac."

"Great," I said for what seemed like the thousandth time that day. "We don't want to stir up animosity in this town by having a bunch of outsiders coming in and setting up a…vigil."

"I don't know, Jim. Maybe it will create more interest in the story and we can make the sheriff play fair," Aurora said. "I mean it's your call, but I'm just saying…"

"How many people might come?" I asked.

"I have a few thousand listeners. They're pretty loyal to me."

"You know this could blow up in our face if there is any trouble between your people and the locals. There is only one small motel in town. Where would they all stay?" I asked.

"Mr. Marrow says there is a state park near the courthouse called Fort Anahuac. There are acres and acres for my people to pitch tents and park their campers. We might set it up as a tent revival. We could hire the local evangelical preachers to fill in until I get out."

"Your business manager needs to talk with your lawyers about things like this. If the people on the jury pool are mad at your followers they could take it out on you," I said with a growing annoyance. We had absolutely no control over these two.

"My followers will be welcomed with open arms, if it is God's will." Clay spoke in a tone that sounded like a rebuke.

"Reverend Clay, with all due respect, didn't Jesus say something like 'Render unto Caesar what is Caesar's and unto God what is God's?' Is it unreasonable to assume that being charged with a crime on earth would fall into the Caesar realm?"

"I view my work here as God's work. It is God's destiny for me that his majesty be revealed in this manner."

Aurora straightened up in her chair and said, "Reverend Clay, I hope you'll be careful that you are not starting to believe in your own divinity."

"Your point is well taken. My faith tells me that there is so much more to this matter…"

"Excuse me, Reverend Clay, but this is not a 'matter,' it's a goddamned murder charge. Is Marrow telling you these things or is it God?" I said it as strongly as I could without raising my voice.

Clay winced at my blasphemy, but didn't respond to it. "My faith is my faith. I can't explain it. God gives me comfort in trying times. Jesus does not fail me."

How do you reason with a man whose reality is in a dimension different from your own?

"If God's plan is that you should listen to your lawyers and you don't, then that's on you. We have advised you appropriately. I'm considering having you examined by a psychiatrist. It's not that I believe you don't know right from wrong, but I need you to cooperate with us if we're going to defend you. My experience is that God helps those that help themselves."

"There's no need for that. God's plan is flawless. God will guide the two of you. You'll see."

I looked over at Aurora. She was dutifully taking notes. She looked up and shrugged her shoulders.

"Reverend Clay, I think we are going to call it a day. There is an examining trial set for ten days from now. It is designed to determine whether there is enough evidence to hold you until a grand jury can review your case. I want to go forward with it even though I'm sure the justice of the peace that conducts it will bind you over to the grand jury. I want to have it so we can get a look at the state's evidence. It's a minimal standard that the state has to prove. Don't get your hopes up. Even if the judge found there

84

wasn't enough evidence to hold you, the DA could still get you indicted. A district attorney can indict a lamppost if he wants."

"I understand," he said. "God wants me to do my work and you to do yours."

As Aurora and I walked down the front steps of the courthouse where we had been interviewed by Chinky that morning, Aurora said, "I think you do need to have him examined. He may not meet the *McNaughton* test of not knowing the difference between right or wrong, but his grandiose ideas about a direct pipeline to God give me concern."

"What if he *does* talk to God? What if we *are* part of a plan?"

"Has he made a convert of you?" Aurora said with a speck of alarm.

"No, I'm just saying that I'm not sure what we do with a diagnosis that he knows right from wrong, but has delusions of grandeur. If this town is like most rural towns, you better not mess with God. A jury may want to fry him if they think he is a blasphemer. It's only going to help him if the shrink says he doesn't know right from wrong."

"I guess until we know more we'll just have to hope that he's right. It would make our job easier if we are part of some divine plan!"

"I hope that God lets the jury in on the plan," I said, as Aurora started the Porsche.

The sun had fallen in the west sufficiently that it flashed like a strobe light through the slash pine forest along the road back to the Interstate. The distraction did not deter Aurora's lead-footed ways. On the way to Anahuac she'd voiced concerns about Wells. I certainly knew he needed help. If Aurora had a plan to save him from himself I wanted to be on the team. "How can I help Wells?" I asked.

"He has to moderate the drinking for one thing. You two get together and it's like you are in competition to see how much gin you can drink."

"It sounds like you think I'm part of the problem, not the solution."

"You had good intentions, asking him to be a partner in the law firm, but it's making him crazy. He doesn't want to let you down. He's never had a job in his life. All he has to do is deposit huge checks from his trust income. He'd do anything for you. He thinks you saved his life at the ferry. We need to take the pressure off him and ease him into this. He's brilliant, but alcohol has muddled his life."

I sat quietly, staring down the highway. Aurora had opened my eyes about my friend in a way that scared me. Wells and I blew off steam on his sailboat. Drinking was part of it. If I were going to help, there would need to be changes that might alter our relationship. "Let's have a partnership meeting tomorrow. Can you get him there by noon?"

"I will," Aurora said, sounding like she had just taken a vow.

CHAPTER SIXTEEN

Chinky had disappointed me. She was clearly more interested in promoting Aurora's career than mine. Reverend Clay was a handful, although I suspected he was Marrow's pawn. The worst of it was the lunch of cheap wine. I had an epic headache. My car lights played off the high gate in front of Bay Villa in the late twilight. It was good to be home. Surely Cooper would be happy with the news that Aurora chaperoned me. For the moment, there was a bottle of scotch in the bar that had my name on it. A little hair of the dog would cure my hangover.

I was surprised to see Cooper's car. There was much I needed to tell her. The alliance of Aurora and Chinky was delicate. Cooper was already skeptical about Aurora, and Wells too, for that matter. The key to Cooper's happiness and consequently mine lay with my ability to assure her that her trust in me was well placed.

"Well, how was your day?" Cooper asked as I walked through the front door.

I was surprised to see her waiting in the front hall. "It was eventful and productive," I said.

"I've been watching your performance on the six o'clock news, what there was of it." I thought Cooper never watched Chinky.

"Well, today's interview was just preliminary. When we get closer to trial I'll have more to say."

"I see that Aurora found a venue to be the star of the day."

"That was Chinky's doing." Better to blame Chinky, who was already on Cooper's shit list. I couldn't afford to have Aurora on that list if we were going to be everyday law partners. "I've got Aurora squared up and working for me now." It was a boast that would have brought a scoff from even a simpleton. Cooper was no simpleton.

"Laughable," she said with a flip of her hair as she walked away.

"Everything is going to be fine. Aurora and I had a talk. She took notes today," I said as I followed after Cooper.

Cooper wheeled so quickly on the marble floor that she momentarily lost her balance. It was then I smelled the scotch and saw the half empty bottle on the hall table. "Chinky is already promoting Aurora for an interview next week about professional women and their difficulties. I wonder if she will call me."

"She should, but well…"

"Oh yeah, that bitch would rather run over me with a bulldozer than interview me."

"You don't need to be on her television show. Everybody knows you."

"Wrong, everybody knows Taylor Faircloth. I suppose soon enough they will all know my husband's law partner, too."

I walked to where she stood, frantic that I'd done something to cause this tantrum. Cooper was always calm, even when she was furious with me. "What's wrong, Cooper? There's got to be something else bothering you."

To my astonishment, Cooper burst out crying. I held her close as she cried for only the second time since I'd known her. The scotch glass fell to the tile floor. Shards of shattered heavy crystal showered the floor. Cooper's body shuddered as she fought to catch her breath between uncontrolled sobs.

"Daddy says he might sell the newspapers. He says there's an offer."

"He won't do it," I said. "It's in his blood and he knows it's in yours. I'll talk to him."

Whatever happened to those quiet nights when I came home from the DA's office? No worries about partners, clients, or the next day. For the first time, it occurred to me that money and fame came with a hefty price tag. All of my fantasies had ended with "happily ever after." If Taylor sold the newspapers, he would give up his bully pulpit to educate the world about hard work and its reward. There was something else going on here, and I was damned well going to find out about it tomorrow.

I did everything I could to console Cooper through dinner. I kept repeating my promise to make it right for her. Cooper had poured her life and soul into the newspapers of Fair News Corporation. Life after Fair News for Cooper was not something that either of us had ever considered. Cooper never drank to excess. Tonight had been an exception. I helped her up the grand staircase to our bedroom.

"Thank you for being so strong for me," she slurred as I tucked the covers up under her neck. "I hate to involve you in this, but Daddy just wouldn't listen to reason."

"Go to sleep, my love. I'm on the case now. You can count on me."

I walked back down stairs to the dining room. Jerome was cleaning up the dishes.

"I don't know what Taylor's trying to accomplish selling the Fair News Corporation. He's trained Cooper to take it over since she was thirteen."

"The man always has his reasons. Sometimes Mr. Faircloth has *his* reasons that might not suit anybody else."

Suddenly, the realization that I had projected a healthy part of the practice income from Fair News Corporation came as a gut punch. Watching Cooper's distress had blinded me to my own predicament. Taylor had always been good to me, but my suspicion was growing that I was being drawn into one of Taylor's snares. Most people never saw them coming. I only wished I knew what his motivation might be.

CHAPTER SEVENTEEN

I turned the alarm off an hour before it was set to go off. Cooper was sleeping. I slid out of bed and put on a robe and house shoes. I closed the bedroom door before going downstairs to the library where we had an office. Taylor was going to get a bit of his own medicine today. The clock said 5:52 a.m. I sat in a high back leather office chair, composing my thoughts. Early on, it had been hard for me to remember that Taylor Faircloth was only a man. He seemed invincible, but his life story was full of tough times. The death of a sister, and growing up in poverty were a few of his difficulties before he became wealthy. Yet, he had moved forward with steady resolve. In some respects, I guess my awe of him was fueled by my own difficulties in overcoming the tragedy in Kansas.

This morning, before the sun rose, I was being called upon to stand up to this man who was threatening to take away my wife's soul and a major part of my law firm's income. My wife was relying on me to do battle with her father who controlled all things around him and never accepted no as an answer. I looked at the telephone and hesitated. In that moment of doubt, I saw that nothing about "being a man" was ever easy. But I had to try. Even if I failed to change Taylor's mind, I had to try. My wife was depending on me.

The telephone only rang twice before Taylor answered. "Yeahlo." His rising inflection made his voice sound like it was midday.

"Taylor, its Jim. Have a minute?"

"Ah, Jim, it's good to talk to you so early. Up and at 'em before six. Glad my lawyer is on the job."

He was patronizing me and for an instant I almost exploded. Trying jury trials had taught me restraint in the face of provocation. Nothing worked better than giving it right back.

"Glad to see my client is up and at 'em so early. Got a full day today?"

"Every day is full around here," he bragged.

"As your lawyer, I thought it would be a good idea to check in with a client who apparently is negotiating to sell a major asset of his empire without talking to his attorney."

There have been few silent moments in my life I relished more than this one. Taylor was used to controlling the battlefield and I had just launched a sneak attack.

"Well, we're only talking right now."

I drew in a deep breath and forged ahead. "It doesn't make sense as I see it, either financially or personally. Politicians fear you because of your newspapers. Sure, you can give money to influence campaigns, but you'll just be buying political ads in somebody else's newspaper. As your lawyer, I need to be involved in these types of discussions from the beginning."

His voice was level and cold. "I did all right before you came along to represent me."

"Times have changed. You can't do business on a napkin in Texas anymore."

"It worked pretty well for those Southwest Airline boys. Thank you for that advice. I'll take it under consideration," he said with a distant tone that I'd never heard from him.

"Do you mind telling me why you're doing this?"

"It's simple, really. The newspaper business is going to fade. Politicians are more interested in listening to the troublemakers than those of us that create jobs. More people are getting their news from the television. Newspapers are always running behind in the news cycle. Costs of employees keep going up, and I don't have an heir to run the business after Cooper."

I swear I heard it that he had no "air." There was a moment when I thought he was telling me he was sick. Then the enormity of what he said struck.

"This is about grandchildren?"

"Partially."

"Bullshit, Taylor. This is blackmail. You're willing to take away the only thing that gives your daughter purpose in order to make her bear a child? Goddamn it, do you think I don't want children? I do. But I respect my wife's decisions and I think you should, too."

The fury came out of me before there was thought. In the past, I had buried my own wish, again and again, to have children. Taylor and I were on the same side, but his method was too rough, even for me.

It was the only time I had ever heard him stutter. "I...I always let her do what she wanted. I never knew she'd rather edit newspapers than give me an heir. I mean we're only in preliminary discussions," he said as his voice softened.

"Don't do this to her. She can't handle it and it won't end well. I'll talk to you later. I've got to try to pry my wife off the wall right now."

"They're only preliminary discussions," he repeated.

"I will call you later. Goodbye."

"All right, talk to you later."

91

I sat in disbelief. First that he would think this was an okay strategy, and second that he thought it would work. At the same time, there was a part of me that agreed with him.

"I'm sorry for all the craziness last night," she said as she stood in the doorway of the library. I was still lost in the battle I'd just had with Taylor.

"You mean for being human?" I answered, trying to lighten the moment. I wondered what she'd heard.

"I guess I never thought much about you wanting children. I'm sorry." Clearly she had heard most of the conversation. "Don't be mad at Daddy. He always fights hard for what he wants. I don't think he appreciated that this time he was dealing with family."

"It's not his business."

"You and I think that way but he looks at all of it as his business. Tell him to sell the papers if he wants. I own enough stock in Fair News Corporation now that it will allow me to start my own newspaper."

Taylor Faircloth's daughter just showed she was tougher than any son could have ever been. Was she really calling his bluff?

"Do you mean that?"

"I do. Daddy's idea of newspapers is frozen in time. This is the seventies and it's all beginning to change. I can put out a better paper than I'm editing now. You've shown me that you're on my side."

"But you heard me say that I want children."

"I did and I don't know what to say," she said still standing in the doorway. She was holding onto the door with both of her hands.

"At least tell me why you don't want children."

"It's complicated. Every day I go to work and a parade of tragedies drifts across my desk. There is so much death, so much suffering and injustice."

"Come on, Cooper, there has to be something else. Life's full of risks, but there are rewards too. We can protect a child better than most. It's your decision and you don't have to give me a reason. However, you owe it to yourself to understand the honest reason why you want our bloodlines to stop. I hope it's something other than fear. You're tougher than that. Either way, you decide. I've always got your back."

Cooper stood at the door still firmly gripping it with both hands. The moment was so painful, so *permanent*. There were no answers that would satisfy us or her father.

"Tell him to sell the papers," she repeated and closed the door.

Taylor Faircloth was a legendary poker player at the Petroleum Clubs of Houston and Beaumont. He'd once bluffed a card shark into folding a hand full of aces and eights for a $30,000 pot. He had what some might call a psychic ability to look inside people's souls to see what frightened them. He buffaloed opponents with a casual gesture, an off-the-cuff remark, or a simple smile. It didn't matter whether it was cards, an oil deal, or a debate over politics. I reached for the telephone to call Taylor Faircloth's hand. If he was bluffing about selling the newspapers, Cooper Faircloth had called his bluff. My bet was that Taylor was about to fold his hand. I took little joy in Cooper's victory. Taylor and I were playing the same hand.

Lawyers have to guard against representing a client when that client's interests conflict with another of the lawyer's clients. Fair News Corporation, my client, was owned by Taylor and Cooper. Taylor was using strong-arm tactics on the minority shareholder to force her into having a baby. I wanted Taylor to win, but I wondered where I'd be living if I joined sides with him. The financial interests might best be served by selling, but, in the end, there was already enough money to last us a lifetime. Our personal interests collided with our fiscal interests. I wanted to build a law practice I could call my own. Fair News Corporation business would make that a cinch. Cooper loved running the newspapers. The money from a sale wasn't going to replace her passion. Then there was the heir thing. That hurt me the most as I dialed Taylor's number.

"Yeahlo," he said with his usual impatience.

"Sir, I talked to my wife." It was the first time I had ever addressed him as "Sir." The same could be said for referencing his daughter as "my wife." If it had been a poker game he would have raised me right there. "She says to sell the newspapers if that's what you think is best. Should I come to Houston to get started reviewing their offer?"

Taylor breathed heavily into the telephone for a few seconds. It was unnerving and I desperately wanted to say, "Sir, please hold the telephone. I'll rush her upstairs and impregnate her."

"I'll call you later. The more I look at their offer the more it looks like a silly deal that doesn't solve the other issue or lack of issue," he said making a joke that only a lawyer could love.

CHAPTER EIGHTEEN

By 6:38 in the morning, I'd put out the first fire of the day. Taylor had given me some great advice when I told him I was going to start my practice.

"Make a 'to-do' list. Every morning, arrange it with the things you don't want to do the most on the top of the list. Do them first. With the worst out of the way, the rest of the day is a breeze."

I had taken care of number one on my list that morning. Having a partners' meeting to work out an agreement was second on the list. If Aurora could get Wells to the office sober by noon, we might have number two worked out by 1 p.m. I wasn't looking forward to the meeting. Marrow had called to say he was coming in that afternoon. I needed to find out his whereabouts the morning that Sarita was killed. It would be a big surprise if he told me anything I could believe. Nevertheless, I had to ask.

Cooper was subdued at breakfast. She received the news that Taylor wasn't sounding serious about a sale with gratitude. She waited until breakfast was almost over before she said, "Do you hate me? I never wanted to be a mother. I told you that in the beginning."

She had always said she didn't want kids. I couldn't imagine that she wouldn't change her mind. But today it was clear; she wasn't going the mommy track at Fair News.

"I love you. If you do change your mind and want kids, I stand ready to serve."

What was I going to say? Random, unwanted children were nature's unpleasant joke before the pill. Chinky's unplanned pregnancy wasn't going to happen to Cooper, no matter how hard I tried. I had a vague feeling that we would be revisiting this question regularly until menopause set in or Taylor died. I didn't believe that he could make demands from the great beyond, although if anyone could it would be Taylor Faircloth.

Friday had never looked so good. If it weren't for a slight apprehension about the partners' meeting, I would have been relaxed for the first time since Tuesday morning before Taylor's surprise invasion. He had been in Houston at five fifty-seven this morning and I was fairly comfortable that I could finally "sharpen my pencils," as Cooper had put it.

I was proud of the way we had laid out the office. A large reception desk stood at the entrance. Cooper had found it in an antique shop and it gave us the appearance of being an old, established law firm. Behind the reception desk hung a large oil painting that Taylor had loaned us from his extensive collection of the work of a new Austin artist, G. Harvey. The painting depicted Congress Avenue in Austin on a rainy day from an earlier time, when men wearing yellow slickers and trail coats rode horses.

The opposite wall was decorated with a large photograph of Galveston Bay taken from the roof top garden of Bay Villa by one of the photographers from the Baytown paper. By sheer chance, Wells' yacht *Remembrances*, with its spinnaker fully extended, was in the center of the picture. I wondered if Wells had noticed the picture yet.

There were six expensive high-backed upholstered chairs that I didn't think were comfortable. Cooper and some decorator she knew from the Montrose area in Houston outvoted me on that purchase. The decorator added a genius touch by lighting the room with table lamps and track lighting. The table lamps gave the room a subdued tone. Most people in a lawyer's waiting room don't need to be hyper-stimulated. The track lighting illuminated the painting and the receptionist's desk. All in all, it was a dramatic entrance that could have been in an uptown Houston law office.

The door out of the reception area led into a large rectangular space where we had set up six attorney offices, three large and three small. We were confident that we would be expanding. There were secretarial desks outside each office. The back-office activities were actually done in a back office. Upstairs—the scene of the grand opening party—was the large conference room and an extensive law library.

The decorator had gone wild in the lawyers' offices. Rich paneling covered the walls and expensive oriental rugs accented the hardwood floors. I kept saying, "Who's going to pay for all of this?" Cooper always gave me a look that let me know it was obvious. It all still made me nervous.

There was an unexpected surprise in the build-out of our law offices. Up until then, my adult life had been lived without a sense of place. Cooper was in the middle of the build-out, as if we were building her office. The friction wasn't apparent at first. I was so used to a Faircloth answer for every question that Cooper's infuriating need to control every paint color and wood stain had seemed normal. But then Cooper and her decorator told me that my idea for a book case was too "simple." The friction had appeared over something without any importance at all. How else do most marital disagreements start? This unexpected battle began with the utterance of a single word.

"No!" I'd said.

Sure, I lived in a real mansion, but Bay Villa was Taylor's and I guess now Cooper's, although neither of them felt I needed to know the ownership particulars of the home I stayed in. My building's solid brick exterior, solid hardwood floors, and ornate balcony gave me a place where I had a sense of me, a sense of *mine*. Why couldn't I have one thing that was mine? I had a car, a home, a yacht club membership, yet it was all Faircloth money. I didn't want to be a welcome guest. I needed a sense of place.

The decorator was appalled and gave Cooper a dramatically pained glance. No words were necessary to convey, "Oh, you poor dear. How do you live with this person?"

Cooper gave him a shrug of her shoulders and turned to me. "Don't you think that Mr. Richard's idea would make it look more regal?"

"I don't need regal. I need a place to put the latest Southwestern Reporter Advance Sheets."

In the end it was a victory, albeit minor. Mr. Richard and Cooper won the rest of the war, but I retired victorious in the knowledge that every time I looked at the Advance Sheets to preview the most recent cases decided by the Texas Appellate Courts, there would be no silver eagles staring at me from the top of the bookcase.

CHAPTER NINETEEN

Never trust your life to a lawyer who likes to do administrative work. There are perfectly good lawyers who are blessed with the ability to administer a law firm and draft stellar business contracts. There are other lawyers whose obdurate determination better suits them for the arena of criminal litigation. One hour into my job as chief administrator of Wilson, Wilson and Ward, I realized that I was better suited to litigation. Thank God Alice Ann came to the rescue.

"Why are you spending your time on this? You've got better things to do."

She was right, of course. "Please escort me to the front door. I have to let me go."

"I've done this forever. I actually enjoy it," she said with a smile that told me it was true.

"Your first job is to call the liquor store. It looks like the grand opening wiped us out."

"I will and thank you for the raise," she said.

I'm pretty well educated, but I had no idea what she was talking about. Cooper's 'dumb ass' comment flashed through my brain. This time I wasn't a dumb ass. "Is two hundred-fifty a month enough?"

"Three hundred-fifty would be better," she said.

"Done deal, take all of this paperwork off my desk, call the liquor store, and I will get to practicing law."

I fidgeted rearranging my desk for an hour while trying to figure out what I should be doing. In my time with the DA's office we were usually drinking somewhere if we weren't in court. Fortunately, at ten-thirty, I heard Wells talking to his secretary. My door was open and I heard him say he was here for a meeting. I assumed that he was early for the partnership meeting. It was a chance for me to say hello and test his sobriety. I stepped out of my office.

"Hey, you're early for the partners meeting," I said.

Before he could answer his secretary said, "The candidate and his group are here. They're in the conference room upstairs."

"What candidate?" I asked, assuming that my partner had set off to hire new people before we could even get a partnership document.

"Dolph Briscoe is here to talk about his campaign for governor. The Republicans are giving him a race. He's an honest guy, but he's from a little town called Uvalde. He's not a household name. He's probably the last Democrat I'll ever vote for," Wells said. He was sober.

"How much is the ante to this poker game?" I asked cautiously.

"Five thousand."

"Five thousand! I can buy a new Porsche for that."

"Oh, come on. I'll give you five and you give it to him. You won't even have to ask Cooper."

"Isn't that illegal?"

"Hell, I don't think anything is illegal in Texas politics."

"I better call Cooper. I don't know if Taylor is supporting this guy. After Briscoe beat Taylor's guy in the Democrat primary election, Taylor hasn't said much."

"Come meet him. You don't have to give him anything now." He led the way up the stairway.

The candidate had company. Three heavy hitters from Houston were with him. One was Mark Andrews, a lawyer only slightly older than I. I knew Andrews from the Houston Young Lawyers Association. The other two were oilmen who were part of Taylor's cadre of political friends.

The candidate looked as if he would rather be back at his ranch in Uvalde. He flashed a smile that betrayed the weariness and boredom of the endless campaign. His handshake was strong and all business.

Andrews said, "First I want to say that we are pleased that you want to join us, Jim." Andrews turned to Briscoe and said, "Jim is Taylor Faircloth's son-in-law."

"Taylor's a good man," Briscoe said as he eyed me and then looked quizzically at Andrews.

Andrews continued. "Wells didn't tell me that the two of you are partners when he agreed to meet us today, but it's a pleasant surprise you're here. I know you fellows are busy, so let's get to it."

It was reassuring that two of Taylor's close allies were on the Briscoe team. Henry Grover, the Republican candidate, had made inroads into the oil community, not so much because of its dissatisfaction with Briscoe's candidacy, but more out of utter frustration with the left-drifting state Democrat Party. As a conservative Democrat, Briscoe was becoming a vanishing breed.

Briscoe made a short, canned speech. Wells didn't hesitate when Briscoe finished. With great formality, Wells said, "Mr. Briscoe, I'm honored to write out this check for five thousand dollars. You boys feel free to call on me if you need more."

There was a moment of silence as Wells wrote the check. The sound of the check ripping out of his checkbook filled the room. He handed the check to Andrews.

"Wells, I knew your father. He was a fine man. I want you to know that you can call on me at any time." Briscoe said.

It was intoxicating. Taylor always controlled everything political in our house. The thought of the fifty thousand dollars in the Wilson, Wilson and Ward bank account crossed my mind. I wanted to be a part of this excitement. I had made some serious money this week. "Mr. Briscoe, I too would be honored to be on your team." I reached into my coat pocket for my checkbook and once again the room was silent. I wrote a five-thousand dollar check and handed it to Andrews.

Briscoe looked me directly in the eye and I had never felt such an adrenaline high. I had given my money to a political candidate of *my* choice.

"I want to thank you, Jim. I didn't expect you to be here today. We'd love to have Taylor on our team too. I was disappointed when he told me had committed to Grover. Maybe when he hears about this contribution he'll change his mind. Thank you so much."

If Briscoe had sucker punched me in the gut the moment would have been complete. Taylor was backing a Republican? He'd never said a word about it. If Cooper knew, she wasn't talking. I'd just put my big-boy britches on without knowing what I was doing. So be it, I thought. It's time to live my life. There were two things I had to do when Briscoe left our office. The first was to get a firm check from bookkeeping for five thousand dollars to cover the hot check I'd just written to the next governor of Texas, and the other was to call Cooper to warn her of the political breech in the Faircloth household before she heard about it from somebody else.

There was a moment when Cooper's telephone was ringing that I wanted to hang up. Did I have to ask for permission to spend my own money? Cooper's secretary answered with her usual "I'll see if she is here" routine.

"What's up?" Cooper said when she came on the phone.

"I may have done something that might upset your dad."

"Like what?"

"I just wrote a check to Dolph Briscoe's campaign. I didn't know he was supporting Grover."

"Dad's sitting right here. I'll let you tell him."

There was a shuffling of the telephone on their end and I heard Cooper whisper something indiscernible. "Hey Jim, what's up?" he said as if he knew nothing. I was prepared to be lambasted. Taylor and I had not started off the day well.

"I didn't know you were visiting this morning."

"I had a meeting with a fellow." Taylor always had a meeting with "some" fellow so it didn't mean anything.

"I gave some money to Dolph Briscoe's campaign this morning. I didn't know about you and Grover until after I handed over the check."

There was dead air for no more than two seconds, but it was enough time for me to brace myself.

"That's great; I'm planning to give him some money at the end of the campaign. Briscoe is a straight shooter. I want him to sweat for the money."

"But what about Grover?"

"He got his money. This race is going to be close. The Republicans have a foothold. It's going to be a way of life in the future, money to both sides."

"Before you give Briscoe his campaign money, can I tell them I persuaded you to contribute?"

"I knew you had good political sense from the beginning." Taylor was referencing the first time we met at a John Connally fund raiser at the Beaumont Petroleum Club. It seemed so long ago.

"Don't forget," I said.

"I need him to get on board with a couple of little things. I'll keep you in the loop. You'll be my 'inside' guy with Briscoe. This is perfect."

Things couldn't be going any better. Even when I screwed up I was successful. Now it was time for the partnership meeting. Could my luck hold? In fact, it did. Wells was clearly sober. Aurora was charming and agreeable and I was relieved. The meeting lasted all of five minutes. We agreed that we were equal partners, but every major decision would require unanimity. I announced that I had named Alice Ann the Office Administrator of the firm and we were adjourned. These were wealthy people. The money wasn't important. In an hour Marrow would be here and I was beginning to get the idea he was in Chambers County when Sarita Jo was killed. Exploring his whereabouts was the real important business of the day.

CHAPTER TWENTY

Marrow was on time and happy. He was whistling a Broadway show tune whose name escaped me as he entered my office. He'd had a meeting with a fellow that morning. I wondered who he knew in this area that could make him so giddy.

"What's this about a prayer vigil?" I asked before his butt hit the seat. He smiled as he lit up his cigar.

"Reverend Clay has a faithful group of followers. They are flooding the radio station with requests for information. There are a few who want to travel to Anahuac to show him support."

"You're turning the trial into a destination vacation?"

"They are coming because he gives them hope of salvation. They believe in him. They don't want to lose him."

"But the trial is not until at least November."

"Well, there are several of his followers whose crops are already in and they go somewhere warm for the winter. I had Randall mention in a recorded message that Anahuac would be a good place for them to visit this year."

"It's fraught with danger," I said.

"Life is fraught with danger. He couldn't be in a much more difficult spot. What would you have us do? We can't let this sheriff railroad him to the electric chair for something he didn't do. I spent my life around Broadway. Publicity is good. If you want to assure a fair trial, generate all the publicity you can. Shine a light on 'em. I saw on the news that Aurora…and you got off to a good start."

"My concern is that the locals could get cross-ways with his followers," I said, trying to stifle my angst over Aurora's high-jacking of the publicity train the day before.

"Let me handle that part. I have orchestrated lots of events. Believe me, this is *going* to be an event."

"Okay, but keep it legal and keep me in the loop."

"You bet I will."

"Has anyone from the sheriff's office asked to interview you?"

"No, why would they."

"Take a guess."

"You mean because of the bequest?"

"You think? Come on, Marrow. You could be a suspect here. I can't believe they haven't talked to you. Where were you on the morning that Sarita Jo was killed?"

"I was driving to Anahuac. When Randall called me on Friday after Miss Franklin signed her will and had the deed recorded, I thought I better get down there. I started driving late on Labor Day. I went to an AA meeting in Hope, Arkansas on Labor Day morning. Holidays are tough for us drunks. I slept in my car in Tyler, Texas Monday night. I stopped in Lufkin Tuesday morning and called my office to make sure Randall was still in Anahuac. They told me I better call the sheriff's office because Randall was in jail."

"Can you verify where you were when you called the sheriff's office?"

"It was a pay phone in a gas station in Lufkin. It was a Texaco station, I think. It cost me a dollar and five cents to call, as I remember it."

"So there is no way to verify where you were after your AA meeting?"

"I guess now that I think about it, no. Say, is Mrs. Wilson going to join us?"

"Why? Do you need to confess something to her?"

"No, I just wanted to make sure that she's involved at every step."

"She's never tried a murder case, you know."

"I have confidence in you. Don't get the idea that I think a woman can handle this case by herself, no, not even Mrs. Wilson could do that. I just believe that she can be of great assistance to you."

I nodded my agreement with his assessment and dialed Aurora's extension. She answered in her usual clipped manner, "Aurora Wilson."

"Can you join Mr. Marrow and me?"

"Be right there," she said. I still had the telephone in my hand when she came through the door.

"Mr. Marrow has requested that you be involved at every step of this case. Understand one thing—he doesn't have a verifiable alibi for the time that Sarita Jo was killed."

"That doesn't sound good, Maurice. Has anybody from the sheriff's office asked to talk to you?"

"As I told Mr. Ward, I was driving to Texas and no, no one has asked to talk to me."

"I know you roughed up an associate of your investors who tried to strong-arm you in New York. Please tell me you're not involved in this murder."

"Even if I was, I couldn't tell you. You two are not my lawyers. I have some business I need to take care of. If there is nothing else to discuss, I will be running along."

He wasn't our client. If he confessed, he had no attorney-client confidentiality to protect his statements from disclosure by us. "Okay, but you agree that you'll call me if the district attorney or the sheriff wants to talk to you. You need a lawyer if you meet with them."

"I've been around the block a few times. I know that."

"I guess that's all I have. Aurora, is there anything else?"

"No, but don't you fuck with us, Sol," she snapped.

"You mean Maurice?"

"Just don't fuck with us," she repeated. Her British accent made it all seem so formal.

"Never," he said.

When he left, the pungent odor of his cigar lingered. There was also a whiff of suspicion that much more was going on here than either Aurora or I might ever know.

Aurora shook her head. "He's slippery. We would have buried him in prison, but he was the only witness who could nail some really bad people. I don't know what to make of this."

"Don't like him, don't trust him," I said.

"Are we going to have an examining trial?" Aurora asked.

"Yes, I think I'd better call the DA right now and make sure he doesn't try to say we waived it. It's set for September 22." I dialed the DA's office. Lindell II took my call.

"I want to make sure that we are still set for that examining trial. I think the judge might give us bail on such a flimsy case."

"I'm glad you called. The grand jury meets next Friday. I'm taking the case to them then. We won't need an examining trial after the Reverend is indicted. You can take up bail with Judge Hope."

"That's chicken shit. What's wrong? Afraid to give us a look at what a sorry-ass case you have?"

"You want Reverend Clay to testify before the grand jury? If it's such a sorry-ass case, I'm happy to have the grand jury hear his testimony," Lindell II said. It was really a taunt. There was nothing I could do. I'd hoped to get a free look at his case. He was going to screw us out of the chance.

"Maybe I will put him in the grand jury room, I'll let you know," I said, with no intention of giving the DA a free shot at the good Reverend.

"Let me know. I promise we'll talk real nice to him before the grand jury."

There was no way I would do that. The defendant can appear, but his counsel must stay outside the grand jury room. The defendant can come outside and consult with his lawyer, but Lindell II could ask him anything he wanted and his answers would be admissible at trial. It would be nuts to put Clay before them.

"You know I'm not going to let him testify."

"Wish you would," he said and hung up without saying goodbye.

Being annoying was all part of the game that litigators play. I have to admit that Lindell II was pretty annoying. So it was game on. I knew there was no chance that Randall Clay could avoid indictment. Even so there is always that vague longing to be surprised. In some respects, it was a relief. We knew where we stood and now I had to decide how to craft the defense. One thing I knew for a fact was that it was Friday afternoon and I was tired. Bay Villa's roof top garden and its full bar cried out its siren song to me. Eighteen-year-old scotch would help soothe my nerves and I could forget all of this for a while.

CHAPTER TWENTY-ONE

Monday morning of my second week in private practice came without the hysteria that seemed to dog every moment of my first week. This was a morning to drink a bit of coffee and contemplate how we were going to defend Clay. The calm before the storm was welcome.

My limited exposure to Lindell II didn't make me think he was any great shakes as a trial lawyer. As quickly as the thought entered my head, I sent it packing. Overconfidence was a trap for the unwary. More than one slick big-city lawyer had been waylaid by an unassuming country-boy prosecutor. His astute move had eliminated my opportunity to have a free look at his case. We were going to get only one shot at the state's witnesses.

Since Lindell II didn't have an eyewitness to the shooting, this was a circumstantial evidence case. The state has the burden of proof beyond a reasonable doubt. Circumstantial evidence cases are proven through inference. Lindell II would demonstrate to the jury that, beyond a reasonable doubt, there was no reasonable hypothesis other than Clay killed Sarita Jo. Circumstantial cases are usually a defense lawyer's best friend. If the jury liked Reverend Clay, we had a chance. If they thought he was lying, we might be dead. If I could find that letter showing Clay had been invited to the ranch and Clete had threatened Sarita Jo, we would have a world of doubt.

Relaxation is an unusual state of being for trial lawyers. Most of the ones I knew were anxious if they weren't in the middle of some uproar. I was beginning to relax so much that it unsettled me. Fortunately, there was a remedy for my relaxation: my telephone rang.

"The district attorney from Chambers County is on the telephone." Alice Ann said. "He seems excited."

"Put him on." There was a click as Alice Ann connected me to Lindell Washington II. "Jim Ward," I said in my deepest voice.

"Ward, what the hell do *you* people think you're doing?"

"What do you mean? I'm here in La Porte drinking coffee."

"Well the sheriff isn't going to put up with you invading Fort Anahuac with this bunch of religious fanatics."

"I have no idea what you're talking about."

"Bullshit! We know you and that Arkansas Jew boy with the New York accent are behind this. We've had our eye on him and we're getting reports from around town that he's up to something."

"You've been invaded by Jews?" I was smiling as I said it. Pricking Lindell II was only for sport. I knew that the first wave of Reverend Clay's army had arrived. I was concerned about what kind of no-good Marrow was nurturing. Then again Marrow was smart enough—or dumb enough—to rip off the Mafia. I hoped he knew what he was doing.

"Don't play dumb. You know who these people are. You better get over here and advise them to get out of town. The sheriff is going to arrest the whole lot of them—you too, if you're part of this. I think he's on the telephone to the Texas Rangers right now."

"I do not know who these people are," I said in my calmest voice, "but just for the sake of argument, what crime have they committed?"

"Riot comes to mind. There are more than seventy of them and we believe they are here to obstruct justice and interfere with government business. That makes it a crime under the riot statute. They may even be homeless. Hell, we don't know what they may try."

"What are they doing now?"

"Well, they've been down there at Fort Anahuac State Park singing hymns all morning. Hell, we can hear them in my office. They're disturbing the peace is what they're doing." Lindell II was beginning to sound frazzled.

"I remember reading in the paper last spring that the city sponsored a crawfish festival. As I recall you had Cajun bands playing there the whole weekend in the park? Did you arrest them?"

"That was different, we invited them."

"Well, I'm sure you did and Anahuac made some money, I assume. Mr. Washington, it sounds like you are going to violate a couple of provisions of the Bill of Rights if you arrest these folks. As I recall from law school, they can assemble peacefully and exercise freedom of religion. That doesn't even take freedom of speech into account. That is, unless you have some different laws over there in Chambers County. Of course, you do what you have to do. I don't represent them so I have no say in trying to stop them. Although I might be interested in taking a lawsuit against you, personally, and the county if you arrest them and violate their constitutional rights and all."

The silence on the telephone thrilled me. "Don't be a prick," Lindell II growled. After another long silence, he repeated in a measured tone, "Don't be a prick, okay?" It sounded like a plea. Was it possible that even Lindell II didn't feel safe from the sheriff's wrath?

"I tell you what I'll do. I'll come over there and see who these people are. Maybe I can help you set up some ground rules. I suspect they're here for the duration of the trial. If I help you, I want you to tell that sheriff of yours that from here on in I can see my client anytime I say. Oh, and another thing, Clay isn't to be shackled just to harass him."

"I thought you said you didn't know who these people were."

"Tell the Sheriff I'll be there in a couple of hours."

I only heard a faint whisper of "you prick" and the telephone went dead.

Three strong women had to hear this news. I was still seething from the lack of television time I'd gotten the week before. Maybe this story would get me some air time. I knew Chinky's number by heart.

"Chinky Mason," she said, using her manufactured Midwest accent.

"Miss Mason, it's Jim Ward. Do you want a story or are you too busy being the new face of women's rights?"

"Don't be such a prick, Jim. What do you have?"

"That's the fourth time in ten minutes I've been called a prick. I'm beginning to like it."

"I'm working against a deadline. I've got no time for telephone sex."

"Okay, an invasion of Fort Anahuac is going on as we speak."

"I give. What's the joke?"

"It's no joke. A band of Reverend Clay's disciples showed up in Anahuac and started a tent revival at the old fort site."

"Delicious," she said as if I'd put a rare New York strip in front of her. "You organize this invasion?"

"No, but I'm headed that way to see what they are doing."

"I'll check it out. It's too far out there for me today. They aren't going anywhere, are they?"

"Not if I can help it. I'll call you when I get back, to fill in the details."

Cooper would kill me if she didn't know about the Fort Anahuac caper. My call to her was short and sweet until she said, "Did you call Chinky?"

"Well, I was thinking about it. I want some airtime for the firm. Chinky can get us business."

"Right," Cooper said and I could tell this situation was always going to be a problem.

The next person that needed to know was Aurora. If she had any background in freedom of assembly or freedom of religion she could helpful. When I finished explaining what was happening, she shook her head.

"I've never dealt with it. But you're in luck. When Wells and I were in law school, he participated in a moot court contest and the issues in the case they argued were similar to what's going on here."

"Can you call him? I need help now."

"He's in his office. I made him research a couple of law issues I have. He likes research, but he would be happy to escape my supervision."

The news was stunning and also welcome. I wondered if Aurora's intervention strategy was to bring Wells into the office.

"Perfect," I said.

Wells was deep in thought when I opened his door. This was a new perspective for me. I saw a former frat boy with a ton of money and a drinking problem. He and I were great friends, but the idea of Wells as a law partner still felt foreign to me.

"You want to go to Anahuac?"

"It's too late to sail there before dark. Tomorrow maybe."

"No, this is work. I hear you are an expert on freedom of assembly and religion."

"I won the moot court competition at Harvard on it. I am *the* expert."

"Come on, I've gotten you sprung from your research job. I'll fill you in on the way." The idea that Wells and I were headed to a potential fight over a constitutional law question in Anahuac was exhilarating. The Wilsons, as they were known about the office, were working out fine.

Now all I had to do was figure out how to manage the very Reverend Randall Clay's army of Christian soldiers, who had captured Fort Anahuac.

CHAPTER TWENTY-TWO

"It's been fifteen years since I won that moot court competition. I'll have to do some research to see if the courts have adjusted their thinking on the right of assembly. Nothing seems nailed down anymore. Earl Warren and those liberals on the Supreme Court have found ways to pervert the constitution to suit their own agenda," Wells complained as we flew along on I-10 toward the turn-off to Anahuac. He was driving the 1972 Jaguar XKE he'd bought to use until he found another Jaguar XKSS. At times, he swung one or both of his hands in the air as if he were directing a symphony.

"It doesn't seem like it would be an everyday kind of case," I said as I tried to concentrate on his legal commentary between glances at his dramatic gesticulations and the erratic path of the car. It was the first time I'd ridden with Wells since the night he had driven us off the Lynchburg Ferry into the Houston Ship Channel. We were both sober this trip, but it didn't seem to improve his driving.

"Those in power don't tolerate dissent willingly. Every constitutional freedom is limited in some way. It cuts both ways. Those on top of the heap today are on the bottom tomorrow. If a majority of a court wants to limit freedom of assembly to squash an unpopular cause, they'd best understand that there will be a time when they'll be looking up from the bottom," Wells said.

"But it's an absolute right guaranteed by the Constitution," I pointed out.

"Ah, my friend, you were educated at a somewhat regional school in this quaint outpost of civilization called Texas. We can't all receive our education at Harvard. Freedom of speech, of the press, of assembly, and to petition the government for redress of grievances have all been restricted in one way or another by court decisions," Wells said in the special imperious voice he used when he was lauding his Harvard degree over my Texas Law School education.

"I know there are limits, but public parks have long been places that people could gather and debate important issues. Just because local law enforcement wants to prevent dissent isn't enough." I added.

"Very noble thoughts my friend, but your man could be executed before you could ever get a freedom of assembly case to the US Supreme Court," Wells said. "Our game plan will be to intimidate and compromise. These two cases are not related."

In my zeal to press a perceived advantage, I had gotten lost in the brambles of legal reality. "You're right, but we can bring some heat on them through Chinky and Cooper. Those local Houston television stations will all follow Chinky's lead. Let's just go see what is happening at the Fort." I wanted Wells to put two hands on the steering wheel.

There was something besides the "riot" that we were racing towards that bothered me. I'd wanted to talk to Wells since the day Aurora and I had picnicked at the Fort.

"There is something that I want to clear up," I said hesitantly.

"What's that?"

"Aurora said she knew you before Harvard."

"We had some history."

His statement shut the door. Was it any of my business how they got together? Wells was staring straight ahead with both hands gripping the wheel, his knuckles white, and this conversation was closed.

Clay's "army" was diverse. They were young people with children, old people, and in between. I had guessed that they would be rural people. What I had not divined was that Reverend Clay's holy army was integrated. A small contingent of blacks had joined the group. The army had gathered in a large open-air picnic pavilion. I could see they were ignoring the show of law enforcement not far from the pavilion. They were singing a hymn and appeared to be as law-abiding a bunch as you could imagine.

All six of the sheriff's patrol cars were amassed about one hundred yards away from the pavilion. They had been joined by two Department of Public Safety cars. The emergency lights were flashing from the tops of all eight vehicles. If it hadn't been potentially serious, I would have laughed. Was the outside world so threatening to the sheriff's universe? As we pulled into the parking lot, I spotted Lindell II. He was packing a shotgun.

Wells and I parked at a distance. We walked up to the law enforcement skirmish line. "Jim Ward and Wells Wilson. We are lawyers and unarmed," I hollered as we walked directly to Lindell II. The sight of an armed district attorney was so incongruous that it produced a deep fear in me. I didn't know the people who were singing about one hundred yards away, but they didn't scare me half as much as those who were there to enforce the law.

"Hey, Lindell." I greeted the shotgun-toting prosecutor in my best Texas accent. I needed the credibility of being from around these parts. I didn't know what might have preceded our appearance at the Fort, but the faces and body language of the assembled lawmen showed that they would love to join in battle with anyone who challenged them.

Lindell II looked relieved that I was there. "Hey, Jim!" he responded and glanced quickly at the sheriff as if to make sure he hadn't overstepped his bounds.

"What do we have here?" I asked.

"They have guns," Lindell said nervously.

"Well, of course they do. We all have guns. Anybody threatening to use them besides you guys?" I looked back toward Wells to see how he was doing. I'd spent the last six years in the DA's office dealing with police every day. I knew that some had a twitchy trigger finger. I worried that Wells might be freaked out by the moment. To my surprise, Wells was over shaking hands with Sheriff Staunton.

"How do you know Wells Wilson?" Lindell II asked.

"He's my law partner."

"Good guy. He throws a big weekend party for law enforcement over at his hunting camp on the bay every year. He flies dealers in from Vegas." Lindell looked around as if he wanted to make sure no one else could hear. He winked at me and said, "We do a bit of gambling."

"He hasn't mentioned any of that to me."

"He's helped some officers who were in financial trouble over here, too. I can't imagine he needed a job."

"It's a profession and you're right, he didn't need a job. Has anybody tried to speak to these assembled folks?"

"We have. They sent that Marrow fellow over. What's his story?"

Ah, if Lindell II only knew his story. For that matter, it would be even better if I knew.

"He's sort of a manager."

"Of what?" Lindell asked.

"The Reverend Randall Clay Prayer Hour." I didn't add LLP. There was no need to complicate things with the truth.

"So his meal ticket is locked up in the county jail," Lindell II said, gesturing at the courthouse. "Kind of strange, this Arkansas Jewish fellow with a New York accent managing a crusade."

"I guess he must have had a come to Jesus moment somewhere along the way."

"Right, and I'm the Pope," Lindell II said.

"Think we ought to check in with the sheriff and Wells?" Wells seemed to have the sheriff's ear, but I wanted to make sure that what he was putting in it was helpful.

As we approached the two men I heard Wells say, "Aw, Leo, I don't think the ATF needs to bother with this. These are country people. They didn't come over here to blow up the jail."

I wasn't sure if I was elated or terrified that Wells had inserted himself in the matter. I had brought him along as my freedom of assembly expert in case I needed any intellectual muscle. I was elated when I heard Sheriff Staunton say, "If you say so Mr. Wilson, but make sure that *you* check 'em out. Tell those coloreds we don't take prisoners if they start shooting."

"Now Leo, we've talked about this. You just call me Wells like we agreed."

"Yes sir," the sheriff said. He gave me a frown.

Wells said, "Jim, you and I need to go talk to some fellow named Maurice over there. He seems to be running the show. There was some concern on the sheriff's part that these people have a bunch of rifles and guns in the gun racks of their trucks. This Maurice fellow may be some kind of outside agitator. Sheriff here says they won't tolerate any civil rights marches. This isn't Mississippi."

"I don't think it's a problem. Maurice Marrow is a business associate of Reverend Clay. He's no threat." I wondered if that last part was true.

Wells and I walked away from the knot of officers who had gathered around us. As we approached the singing army, we could see they had no hymnals. They knew the hymns by heart. I was relieved that we reached the flock without a hail of bullets from the law. Their anxiety worried me. Marrow met us at the edge of the pavilion.

"Come back here, I've got a little motor home rented. Did you bring the television people?"

"We didn't have time to get anyone here," I said. "I tried."

"Oh well, there's plenty of time for the television."

Wells extended his hand and said, "I'm Wells Wilson, Jim's law partner."

Maurice eyed him closely and said, "So you're the lucky one who married Aurora."

"Guilty as charged." Wells lifted his right eyebrow.

"Aurora knew him from New York. I'll fill you in later," I said. "Maurice, we need to be careful. These guys shoot first and let God sort it out later. It's not like New York."

112

"You don't know much about New York," Maurice said with a rueful smile.

"Why are these black people here? Are they protesting something other than Clay's arrest?" I asked.

"Craziest thing, they didn't know Clay was white. They came down to save a black brother. Once they found out he wasn't black, they stayed anyway. This has got the possibility of becoming a great Broadway musical. I wish I wasn't barred."

"Let's stay focused on the present. The sheriff thinks you want to blow up the jail and seize Reverend Clay. I don't know if he really thinks that or he's just getting his excuse set up so he can shoot everyone later," Wells said.

"We need a set of ground rules so they know you are peaceful and law-abiding citizens," I added. "These people are nervous and very skeptical of outsiders. We need to agree to limit the noise and not harass the townspeople."

"Sure, but our goal is to bring attention to Clay's wrongful indictment. We've got to generate a few Broadway theatrics to get the local TV reporters out here," Maurice said.

"Tell them I'm going to write up an agreement tomorrow and take it to the DA for approval. Tell these folks to treat this park as if were their own home—there are limitations on the right of assembly. The important part is to leave room for some activities that gets TV coverage for us," I said.

"I've come up with a name for the encampment. The press will love it," Marrow said as Wells and I turned to leave. "New Jerusalem," he said proudly.

"Catchy," Wells said.

Wells and I walked through the pavilion, and the protesters looked at us warily. Our suits bespoke of authority. "We're on your side," I hollered and was surprised by the sound of my own voice.

"Praise to Jesus Christ our Lord and Savior," "Hallelujah," and a dozen other shouts of praise rang out from the crowd. A tall, skinny young man, no more than twenty years old, with thick black hair leaped on top of one of the picnic tables and shouted, "Join me in our hymn for strength in a foreign land." He began singing the first line of a hymn I'd never heard before, but since I hadn't been in a church since high school that wasn't so strange. It was a moment of high drama as we walked back toward the line of law men crouched behind their cars, with guns drawn as if a war was about to start. I couldn't swear to it, but it looked like some were aiming their pistols at us. We strolled over to Lindell II, who had discarded his shotgun.

"I'm going to draft an agreement to govern this assembly. These are good people here doing what the U.S. Constitution says they can. They are going to be the best temporary citizens Anahuac has ever seen. If there is a problem, Wells or I will meet with the two sides and get it fixed. No shooting, no bombs, and no late-night singing. Are you okay with that?" I was looking right at Sheriff Staunton, even though I was standing in front of Lindell II. It didn't matter because Lindell II was looking at the sheriff too.

"Sheriff, you've got my word on this," Wells said.

With that the sheriff nodded and Lindell II said, "Okay, but I reserve the right to revise your written agreement."

"I'll see you tomorrow. Can we agree to turn the lights off these cars and just have one deputy here? There is no need to scare the citizens of Anahuac."

The sheriff nodded and Lindell II said, "Yes."

We got in Wells' car. He looked at me and said, "Is this what every day is like for you?"

"Damned near," I said. "You know, Wells, none of this would have worked without you here."

A smile erupted across his face. "I haven't done anything meaningful since I won that moot court competition." With that he revved the engine of his Jaguar and we headed home.

"Don't sell yourself short, Wells. You've built a network of contacts that are worth a fortune to our law firm," I said as we sped away from Anahuac.

"Wealth needs the protection of the law. The wealthy sometimes need special protection from themselves. I'm glad to help those folks that help me."

"Special protection?"

"I'm not sure, but I think my dad had a girlfriend. So, say your mother takes a shot at your father and the police have to come and calm her down. They know that she doesn't need to go to jail."

"That actually happened?"

"Only once, shortly before I had to go to Eton."

"So, you give the police money to assure this special protection?"

"No, not just for that. I don't think they make enough. If I have money and can help them and there are times they can help me, like today, then what's the harm?"

I didn't have an answer. My upbringing was in a modest home without an education in England or Harvard. We didn't pay the police for their protection, except with our taxes.

"It makes sense," I said without a clue whether it did or not.

Wells was quiet as he drove. I wondered if I had embarrassed him about his history with Aurora. If we hadn't been close friends I would have never said another word. Wells was usually gabby. "I didn't mean to pry—about Aurora."

"It's complicated. Someday we'll talk," Wells said as he stared straight down the road.

"Will you help me write the ground rules for Clay's army and the sheriff? I don't want to waive any Constitutional rights. I want the draft document to give the impression the sheriff is in control. We'll reserve our ability to exercise our right of free speech. The more the agreement gives the illusion of capitulation, the better. If we need to raise a ruckus, I want the freedom to do so."

"We'll do it when we get back to the office. I don't want to spend the night worrying about it," Wells said with confidence.

There was hope. Before this day Wells would have suggested we finish the day at the Yacht Club. I couldn't wait to get back to Cooper and tell her the news. I so wanted her to be wrong about my decision to make him a partner.

The document Wells drafted was magnificent. I had begun preparing myself for a long night in the office. In the time it took me to position legal pads and pencils to begin the arduous process, he completed the document. It was simple and seemed very reasonable. The first section of the agreement said that the flock would not act unreasonably. The second section outlined the permitted exceptions to the agreement. The exceptions allowed all action permitted under the U.S. Constitution. I couldn't believe that Lindell II was going to buy this willingly, but then again how could he object to the flock's free exercise of their constitutional rights?

CHAPTER TWENTY-THREE

Chinky's show had been airing when Wells and I had returned to our empty office, so I'd left her a message that the second Battle of Anahuac had been averted, but she was missing a hell of a story if she didn't get herself out to Anahuac in the morning. "We're talking a series of national stories. This isn't just a murder case. You'll get a New York gig out of this if you play your cards right. I'll be there in front of the courthouse at ten in the morning. I promise."

If that didn't get her attention, I knew other reporters. I wasn't worried about news coverage any more. My second call was to Cooper. She was at home and I gave her a tease of the issues; civil rights, constitutional law, murder, the mysterious Mr. Marrow, money, and the flock. "Come home," she urged.

"I'm on my way in five minutes. Let's have some wine on the roof garden."

"I'll let Jerome know. I can't wait."

A dream case ripe with notoriety was in my lap. Great story lines involving the racially diverse flock camped out in Fort Anahuac were potentially national news. Huntley and Brinkley bantering about Jim Ward, the brilliant young litigator for the defense could be next. I was standing behind my desk with an electric smile. This was about me, not Cooper, and not Taylor. This was my chance to make my own way. A bright flashing arrow seemed to be directing me to endless success.

Arrogance sheltered me from the reality that my celebrity was funded by the incarceration of an innocent man. My electric smile waned as I thought about the intersection of our destinies in Anahuac. Anahuac—this isolated place on a lonely planet spinning impossibly through the cosmos. Surely this mess we called life must be about more than the accrual of celebrity and wealth. Clay's outrageous claim that he had been brought to the Chambers County Jail by God's plan revisited my mind. Did Clay have some knowledge of a divinity that controlled us all? Had some unseen hand intertwined our destinies for some greater purpose? Surely life wasn't full of love, pain, violence, joy, envy, and greed for no purpose. The infiniteness of these questions was about to shut down my brain. It was just as well; the telephone was ringing.

"Jim Ward," I said absently, still lost in the unanswerable questions.

"Chinky Mason."

Her name jarred me back to my quest for celebrity. "Clay's army has arrived! They have overrun Fort Anahuac," I said with gusto.

"Dear God, is hyperbole your middle name?"

"I was only trying to give you your lead."

"I'll bite, why should I care?"

"Because, there is a battle between good and evil playing out in Anahuac."

"I suppose the role of good is being played by your side in this epic."

"Always."

"What's really going on?"

"About a hundred of Clay's supporters have shown up in Anahuac and they are amassed in tents and campers in Fort Anahuac Park. The authorities in Anahuac are beside themselves." I expected she would understand the story deserved coverage.

"It's a long way out there. I've got the indictment of a Harris County commissioner expected tomorrow."

"Yeah, but this story has a race angle. Clay's army is black and white. They are all sharing accommodations," I said hopefully.

"Really, how's that playing in Chambers County?" Chinky asked with a laugh. "They're not sleeping together, are they?"

"I didn't see any outright miscegenation taking place. The lawmen had their guns drawn for a while, but their guns are back in their holsters now. My people have guns, too."

"Can you hold the shoot-out until I get there? Seriously, I'll be pissed if I get out there and it is a no-big-deal story."

"I have a Broadway producer orchestrating it. I promise something will happen out there tomorrow. No shooting of course. I mean, these folks are motivated but more likely to read scripture to law enforcement than to shoot them. Please come shine a light on rural justice so I get a fair trial."

"I didn't know you were the defendant."

"You know what I mean."

"What time?"

"Ten?"

"It better be good."

"It will be. By the way, how's your son?" I asked, knowing the way to seal the deal was to let her brag about her child.

"He's going through puberty. You're a boy. What else do you have to know? He's discovered girls and they've discovered him. I don't want him repeating my mistakes."

117

"Buy him some rubbers."

"No."

"You'll do him a favor, and yourself."

"Are you going to come over and show him how they work?"

"Thank God for the pill. I've never used one," I said. It wasn't technically true. Cooper and I had used them before we were married, but the idea of providing a child with sex education was unnerving.

"You and I took some stupid chances," she said.

"We were lucky."

"You were lucky," she said. "I got a kid."

What did she mean by that? Two years earlier she had denied that Danny Jr. was mine and I had believed her. Our college breakup and her marriage to Danny Jr.'s father had been dramatically close. We'd had unprotected sex shortly before she married. "Does Danny Jr. look like him?" I asked.

"He doesn't favor Danny or me," she answered.

I realized that Cooper was probably wondering where I was. "I've got to get home. I was supposed to be there ten minutes ago."

"Jim…" She hesitated. "Uh, I'll see you at ten."

She hung up. I was left to my thoughts, but her comment that she "got a kid" kept interrupting. I couldn't solve any of these questions and Cooper was waiting. No matter that the unanswerable questions sent shivers through me, they would just have to wait.

Jerome was walking down the stairs as I raced up to the roof garden. It had been almost forty minutes since I had told Cooper I would be home in five. "She's upstairs," he said. "I think she's tired." That seemed like code for "You are in trouble." Jerome was too much a gentleman to say that directly. I nodded my acknowledgment with a knowing glance.

Cooper stood looking out over Galveston Bay. She was holding a wine glass in one hand and a cigarette in the other. She snubbed the cigarette out on the rail in front of her and said, "I don't do this much, only when I get nervous."

I had never seen her smoke before. "Are you nervous?"

"I was afraid something happened to you. No one answered your direct line when I called."

"I was on the telephone with Chinky. Everybody else had gone home. I left a call for her about the Anahuac situation and she called back.

118

I'm trying to keep the spotlight on the authorities in Anahuac to make sure they know they are being watched."

"That took forty minutes?"

I looked down. The wine bottle on the table was more than half empty.

"Tough day?"

"Don't try your lawyer tactics on me. Answer my question."

"I had to convince her it was worth her time. Come on, is something else going on here?"

"Daddy just won't let this grandchild thing go. He brings it up in front of people at the office."

"I won't have that! He will respect your decision."

"He says you don't agree with me—that you want children. I know this isn't how it worked in the past, but I want my career. Don't any of you men get it?"

"I get it. I've always been on your side. You don't want children, I get it. It's done and over with right here, right now. I will call Taylor again and stop this nonsense once and for all." A surprising sadness settled over me at the finality of it all. I was her champion for a cause I detested.

She looked at me with a mixture of sadness and gratitude. "I'm sorry to put you through this. You know that Daddy means well. He's doing what he thinks is in the family's best interest."

"He's trying to perpetuate the fortune that he spent his life accumulating," I said. "He's scared he'll disappear without a trace if it somehow just slips away. What goddamn difference will it make when the three of us are gone? Why doesn't he give Methodist Hospital a wing or something? That could be his pyramid."

Cooper took a breath and started to say something, but wavered. The confusion of loving her father and hating his demands was written on her face. She was silent for a moment and then, just that quick, turned reporter.

"So what's going on in Anahuac?" she said as if the Taylor conversation had never occurred.

I recounted the story of the standoff at the Fort. My enthusiasm for reporting that Wells had saved the day had withered. I had bigger issues to solve than proving my partnership with Wells had been profitable.

"Ann Taylor lives over there now," Cooper said. "She is our stringer there. I'll get her to cover things. You aren't going to get shot, are you?"

I held up my glass to the heavens and said, "I won't, God willing."

119

CHAPTER TWENTY-FOUR

I wondered if Wells would really be there when I pulled into the office at eight o'clock. To my surprise, the partners were all present. It was the first time I'd felt a sense of us being a firm.

"Are you going too?" I said to Aurora as a greeting.

"Are there television cameras?" she fired back. "I'll be there."

It was now more of a joke between us than a competition. Aurora and I were more alike than different. Motivated, hungry, and aggressive were traits I saw in her that I hoped I had. We were both outsiders in different ways. Aurora, like Cooper and Chinky, was an overachieving woman seeking an equal place at the "men only" table in business. They already had their money. My place at the table seemed borrowed, not earned. Close to ten years in the orb of Taylor Faircloth and his influence had presented me many opportunities to learn and mingle with powerful people. Yet, I felt like I had slipped in uninvited to the party. The irony that Aurora and I were both battling for confirmation that we were worthy in this place was not lost on me.

"You can carry my briefcase," I parried.

Wells seemed amused by our conversation. "Oh girl, can you fetch me some coffee?" he said.

"Did you want cream and sugar?" Alice Ann asked. She had walked up as Wells make his joke.

"Black," Wells said.

"Black for me," I said.

"Two lumps for me," Aurora said.

We moved into my office to wait for Alice Ann to deliver our coffee.

"I hear you have a set of ground rules for the flock," Aurora said.

"Wells wrote a beauty."

"I wanted to make it sound like the flock had agreed to be good boys and girls and yet retain their constitutional right to act up," Wells said proudly.

"And mission accomplished," I added.

"What's the game plan for today?" Aurora asked.

"We have a meeting with Maurice Marrow at the Fort at 9:45 a.m. I'm going to explain the ground rules agreement to him so he can explain it to the Reverend's flock. He says he will have something ready for the television cameras. I want to make sure he doesn't go overboard. We want just enough agitation to get airtime, but not enough to start World War III," I explained.

"Shouldn't you boys get going then?"

Before I could answer, Alice Ann brought coffees. "Anything else?" she asked. "No, I think we're good," I said. She smiled and left us to resume the conversation we thought was finished.

"Yeah, I don't want anything happening over there without our supervision," Wells said. "If the sheriff breaks a head it will make great television. On the other hand, we don't want to get anybody shot."

"You sound like you were a revolutionary in a former life," I laughed.

"I got into to some misguided liberal shit at Harvard. I am in recovery," Wells said with a sheepish grin.

"Are you not coming?" I asked Aurora.

"Somebody has to bill some hours around here. That retainer you got from the Clay case isn't going to carry us too far."

"I appreciate that. I'll tell Chinky you said hello," I said as a jibe.

"She called me last night. We're doing my interview tomorrow in Houston," she said casually with a wry smile.

Her answer reminded me that our relationship was friendly but a competition nonetheless. I was still pissed at Chinky, but glad for the publicity. There was nothing unusual about petty jealousies in law firms. I never dreamed, though, that I would be jealous of a female partner succeeding where I might not.

CHAPTER TWENTY-FIVE

Wells had located another Jaguar XKSS in England shortly after our near tragedy at the Lynchburg Ferry. The car was pricey, but the owner was willing to sell. The ship carrying his replacement vehicle would sail directly over his old Jaguar XKSS now resting at the bottom of the Houston Ship Channel. He talked incessantly about replacing his lost car. It seemed to buoy his spirits. But now that he had accomplished a worthwhile legal task, his talk of the car diminished. Wells was happier than I had ever seen him. Happy or not, we were in a serious fight to save Reverend Randall Clay.

Maurice Marrow was a wild card that scared me. Smart and clearly dangerous, Maurice could make this into a Broadway musical or the second coming of the Alamo. If he went too far, it wouldn't matter what kind of cease fire we negotiated. The sheriff would not be controlled by skillful lawyering. He had to believe he was in charge. Wells and I would have to restrain the Sol in Maurice to keep Reverend Clay's congregation safe. Wells and I were in his temporary car, heading to our meeting with Maurice when he surprised me.

"Do you want me to give the DA the ground rules?" he asked. "I can argue the law with him."

"Have you been drinking?"

"No, I went home last night and had one drink. I had to have one to celebrate. It was crazy; it's the first time since I was in the fourth grade that I just had one."

"I mean today."

"Nada!"

"You give it to him."

A broad grin lit up his face. "I hope he wants to argue that law with me. I'll give him a Harvard beating," Wells said and I truly believed him.

"What do we do with Marrow? I don't want him getting too wild," I said. I wondered if I should tell him about Marrow's past.

"From what Aurora told me, Marrow needs to be cautious," Wells said. "If he isn't, I'll take out an ad in the *New York Times* telling his old friends in New York his new name and address."

"I assume that's against the law," I said, glad to hear Wells knew Marrow's back story.

"I doubt he knows that," Wells said disdainfully.

"Does Harvard teach a class on how to speak with disdain?"

"No, one must be skilled in disdainful discourse to be admitted," Wells said. He smiled, but I doubted he was kidding.

I was getting nervous that I had uncaged the Godzilla of lawyers. A sober Wells might be more than I could handle.

Wells carefully piloted his XKE around the crowded streets in the park and pulled in next to Marrow's rented RV. As we approached, there was a group of men engaged in an intense conversation with Marrow. When we were within earshot of the conversation, I heard a tall man with a long beard say confidently, "Clearly an elder would have to be a man and he would have to believe that the creation was 24 hours, seven days long."

Several of the men were talking at one time and their words blended into babble. In the middle of the group stood an anguished Maurice Marrow holding up both hands. "Gentlemen, gentlemen, we can't organize the church now. Our mission is to gain Reverend Clay's release. There will be time to create a church hierarchy after the trial." Maurice saw Wells and me and reacted as if we were a rescue ship appearing on the horizon. "Tell them, Mr. Ward."

"How would you go on if the Reverend is taken away from you? Squabbles over control of a church without Reverend Clay would be a waste of time," I said.

The small group of men looked at me with universal disappointment. The ephemeral nature of the ministry was lost on them. Their need to control something that didn't exist would have seemed comical if it didn't have the potential of tearing their tent village apart.

"Well, I think until the Reverend is released there needs to be some type of organization. Who will keep us on the right path?" the bearded one said.

"Mr. Marrow," I said.

The bearded man drew near to Marrow's face and said, "But aren't you a *Jew*?"

"By birth, but he has been born again," I said.

Marrow gave me a look that indicated that was news to him, but I had more. "Jesus was a Jew. Could he not lead the church?"

My question was met with silence. Marrow seized on the moment. "I'll lead only until the Reverend returns. He will then decide who should make up the church's hierarchy."

"Gentlemen, we have much to do now. In a few minutes, there will be television cameras here to help us. We must agree that Mr. Marrow will lead. Please excuse us. We need to prepare." I said. The group nodded and drifted away, still fully discussing the future.

After they were gone, Wells looked at Marrow and asked, "What have you got planned?"

"Something simple," Marrow said. "We don't have much control over Randall's people right now. I've paid a guy who owns a vacant lot across from the courthouse to let us organize a little three-hymn inaugural songfest."

"Don't have them march to the lot in a group. We don't have a parade permit. Once they are on private property, there isn't much the sheriff can do," Wells said.

"Okay, that's a minor change. I can swing it." Marrow said. "Will that suit the television people?"

"It's perfect. We need to have someone who is fervent for them to interview," I said. "Somebody with some sense."

"I had Randall's secretary drive down here to help me. She's perfect. The television people won't know she's not just another member of the flock."

"We have a plan. Let me come out of the courthouse before you start singing. I want to make sure we have a deal with the DA," I said.

"I got it." Marrow seemed confident.

Some of Randall's followers had grown curious about what was going on and began gathering close to Marrow's RV. They eyed us closely. Our custom suits seemed out of place in their world of overalls, blue jeans and K-Mart dresses. Wells and I walked through them nodding, but saying nothing. We were on a mission to take the heat off of their presence. Once we had an agreement, we could manage the media coverage without serious fear of bloodshed.

We walked the four blocks to the courthouse. I wanted to have time to mentally prepare for the meeting with Lindell II. The group of want-to-be elders had dissipated my energy. The need to organize and control religion was one of the reasons I usually stayed away. It was hard enough to represent a criminal client. Mediating honorific titles among the members of the flock who sought self-exaltation over servitude was not within my expertise. But right now was about getting a game face on, not about religion.

As we approached the front of the courthouse I saw Chinky and her cameraman getting out of the Red Rover. There was no chance that their presence had been missed.

"Chinky, let's not do any interviews until after Wells and I talk to the DA. Wells here is my law partner," I said as she approached us.

Wells bowed in a broad ceremonial way and I assumed his next move would be to kiss her hand. "Ah Miss Chinky, I'm a big fan. It's so wonderful to meet you." he said.

"Mr. Wilson, your sailing exploits precede you; in particular your attempted crossing of the Houston Ship Channel in the S.S. Jaguar."

"Ill-advised, to say the least!" Wells answered.

Chinky was enchanted. I never understood why Wells was so charming. Perhaps it was because he was tall, blond, and his youthful face, tinged with a few wrinkles, gave the appearance of a vulnerable man in need of a mother.

"We need to get inside and get this deal struck for the flock. See that vacant lot across the street? In about thirty minutes there is going to be a short musical show. You need to shoot it and then we can give you an interview. We have a spokeswoman for the group you want to interview also." I said quickly. I didn't want Lindell II to see us spending too much time with the media.

"Got it," Chinky said.

When Wells and I reached Lindell II's office, Sheriff Staunton was talking to him in the reception area. Lindell looked nervous as he extended his hand. "Let's go in my conference room so we have some room," Lindell said. The sheriff was wearing dark glasses even though the room was not well lighted. For the first time, the sheriff did extend his hand, but only to Wells. "I'm glad you're here, Mr. Wilson," he said.

"Leo," Wells said and nodded. The sheriff took off the glasses and he had piercing blue eyes. The eyes softened his face and I wondered if he realized it.

We sat down in the cramped conference room and there was a momentary silence. Finally, Lindell II said, "It's your meeting." His tone was edgy.

I pushed the agreement that Wells had drafted across the table. They leaned together to read the document. I was fixing to speak when Wells said, "I drafted it."

"You are vouching for this mob?" Sheriff Staunton said to Wells.

"I am," Wells responded.

"I wouldn't agree to this except for your word."

"You have my word," Wells said.

Lindell II looked at the sheriff and the sheriff nodded. Lindell signed the agreement. "Cathy, please come in here," he called to his secretary. She appeared at the door. "Make a couple of copies of this."

Sheriff Staunton looked at Wells and said, "This doesn't mean I'm not going to enforce the law in Chambers County."

"I understand that, Leo. They are God-fearing people; they won't give you any trouble," Wells said, sincerity ringing in his voice. Cathy brought copies of the signed agreement and the meeting was adjourned.

Wells and I were on the stairs down to the street when the first hymn began across the street. The sweet sounds of the hymn washed over the courthouse.

"Let's get the hell out of here," I said to Wells. He laughed and said, "It'll be fine. Leo's not that bad a guy." I rolled my eyes at Wells and we bolted down the stairs.

Across the street were members of the congregation in choir robes divided into two groups. There was a white choir and a black choir. The whites were outfitted in black robes and the blacks were dressed in white ones. There was a small band accompanying the hymn. The rest of the inhabitants of New Jerusalem were standing behind them in the vacant lot. There was a young black girl, no more than fifteen years old in front of the two choirs. Her voice was strong and clear and she led the choirs in the hymn that was only two lines.

"God's will be done? You *will* set him free!" The young girl sang and then the black choir repeated it. The young girl sang it again and the white choir repeated it. The young girl sang and the two choirs repeated it. The hypnotic sound was repeated with a frantic pace. The choirs were animated; they smiled broadly and swayed in unison. The drummer and three guitarists struggled to stay with the choirs. There was more energy in the streets of Anahuac than there'd been since the Texas Revolution. It was impossible to stand still in the face of the music. The first hymn lasted for about ten minutes. By the time it ended, there wasn't a person in what passed for downtown Anahuac who wasn't swaying in the street.

Chinky's cameraman was in the middle of the choirs shooting close-ups. Chinky flashed a smile at me. I knew our case was going to get some major coverage. I looked for Marrow, but he was nowhere in sight. There was uncertain applause from the onlookers who had gathered. Nothing like this had ever happened in Anahuac during their lifetimes.

The young girl bowed and then the band started another gospel riff. "Oh God, deliver the Reverend Clay from this foreign land. Oh Jesus, set him free." The young girl sang and the whole repetitious refrain began again. The two choirs appeared to be in a religious trance. The rhythmic swaying and clapping hands was hypnotic. The second hymn lasted about as long as the first. Some of the townspeople were warily clapping in rhythm with the hymns.

As the band began its riff for the third hymn I turned around to see Sheriff Staunton and Lindell II standing at the door of the courthouse. They were not swaying to the music. They could see the television camera. There was nothing they could do. When the young black girl sang, "Pharaoh set God's chosen people free," the sheriff and Lindell II disappeared back into the courthouse.

When the last hymn ended the choirs and the residents of New Jerusalem began to disperse in groups of five or less in every direction. Some engaged in conversations with town people. It was clear that the locals and the newcomers were cut from the same cloth.

"Well, that was interesting," Chinky said as she and her cameraman set up to do a quick interview with me. "Wells, why don't you get in the shot with Jim? I might have questions for you."

"Aw, I'm not much on publicity. You just go ahead with Jim."

"It's your choice," Chinky said, motioning for the cameraman to set up on me.

"What was the meaning of this demonstration today?" she asked.

"It wasn't a demonstration. It was a musical service to bolster the spirits of a wrongfully-accused man of the cloth. His followers wanted him to know they are here. I'm sure he heard them."

"I understand a grand jury will hear this case on Friday."

"That's what I have been advised. If we could have only gotten a preliminary hearing, I think a magistrate would have set him free. The facts of this case are flawed."

"So you expect him to be indicted?"

"We'll just hope that the good people of Chambers County will see the light when presented the facts."

Chinky turned to the cameraman and nodded. He lowered the camera. "Thanks, I think we have everything we need. I don't know how you did it, but it was show business at its best," Chinky said.

"Thanks for coming. There will be more," I said.

Chinky asked. "Where is the spokeswoman for the group?"

"I'm she." A woman who had stood nearby said.

"Why are you here?" Chinky said as the camera rolled.

127

"You mean here in Anahuac? Your question sounds like an existential investigation," the woman answered. Any mistaken idea that the group was made up of uneducated hillbillies was laid to rest. Marrow's brilliance had struck again.

"Yes, I mean in Anahuac." Chinky laughed as she turned to the cameraman and made a hand gesture to stop the camera. "Let's start again," she said.

When the camera rolled again Randall's secretary said, "A great teacher of the Word is being wrongly held. Everything happens because of God's will. We don't understand why this is happening, but it is not our job to understand, only to accept it. We are in Anahuac to reveal the greater glory of God by supporting his teacher."

Now in a world not made of sound bites Chinky would have continued the interview for hours to investigate a great mystery. But with only one minute and twenty-seconds of airtime, she said, "Terrific, I have what I need."

Marrow was right; Randall's secretary was a good spokesperson. The final cut of Randall's secretary's interview didn't include her existential reference.

Chinky had a deadline to meet. She gave me a wave and was gone. As I watched her go, Cooper's reporter, Ann Taylor, who had been standing near, smiled and said, "Can you give me a moment?"

"Sure, glad to see you again."

"There is something I don't get. These people have descended on our town and they seem to be trying to influence the potential jury pool. Wouldn't you say that is unusual?"

I'd learned the hard way that innocuous agreement with a reporters' statement was an invitation to be misquoted. "No, they are only here to support their spiritual leader," I responded.

"Wouldn't you say that this is some kind of a cult? The Manson family seemed to worship that Manson fellow. Wouldn't you say it's similar?" Ann was clearly looking for a sensational angle and I questioned whether the truth made any difference.

"Good gracious, no," I said in my best Texas twang. "Reverend Clay has given these people comfort in these troubled times. The world is threatened by drugged-out hippies and civil disobedience. Reverend Clay soothes the fears of his flock. They are part of the silent majority. Their leader has been wrongly accused. That's why they're here."

"Well, thanks for your time. It will be interesting to see how this plays out."

"Thanks, Ann, say hello to your husband for me."

It was done and Wells and I walked back to the Fort to retrieve his car. I wanted to talk to Marrow before we left. The choir robes were a touch I couldn't believe. We found Marrow back at his RV.

I was laughing when I asked, "Where did you get the robes?"

"I borrowed them from a preacher here in town. I hired him to preach to the congregation tonight. He threw the choir robes in for free," Marrow said with a wry smile that seemed to say that he knew more than anyone around him.

"Amazing," I said. "Well, I need to let the Reverend know they are going to indict him on Friday. Anything you want me to tell him?"

"I already told him about the indictment. One of the jailers is sympathetic to Randall. He told me and I told Randall when I visited him yesterday."

"I guess that does it then," I said. "Wells and I will get back over to the office and start working on the defense."

"I've got it covered here," Marrow said firmly.

"Don't do anything without calling me," I demanded.

"Never," he said.

As we walked to his car Wells whispered, "Do you trust him?"

A negative shake of my head and tightlipped smile was my only response.

That night Chinky's segment was all about Reverend Randall Clay. The piece started with Chinky doing a voice-over that included the fact that the Reverend had called the sheriff's office for help and that there was no confession, all information Wells and I provided in a memo we gave her. The gospel singing played well and the fervent choirs looked honest. Chinky hadn't bothered to talk to Lindell II. It was as favorable a piece as I could have hoped for.

The next day, when Ann Taylor's story ran in the Baytown paper it was not as rosy. I had failed to take into consideration that Ann was writing from the perspective of an Anahuac resident. She did run my comment, but had clearly spent a great deal of time with Lindell II. He had filled her story with innuendo and fabrication. Lindell II might as well have written the story.

I called Cooper the minute I saw it. "What the hell is this? Can't I get a favorable story in my own newspaper?"

"I'm sorry. The editor never showed it to me. I guess Ann was only trying to give the story a local flavor."

"This freedom of the press thing is going too far. I don't want those lies of the DA printed," I raged.

"Do you know for sure they are lies?"

"I need my version of the truth printed. I'm trying to win a case. Don't bother to ask her to interview me again. I don't need that kind of help."

"I have to be careful how we cover your cases. We don't want to show outright bias."

"Why?" I asked.

"I'll see you at home," she said. It felt like outright treason. There was no chance to respond. She hung up.

CHAPTER TWENTY-SIX

I spent the week distracted by the inevitability of Reverend Clay's indictment. A district judge picks grand juries from voters who are reputable and usually reliable. By reliable, I mean they are not likely to challenge the recommendation of the district attorney. An indictment is not evidence of guilt. It is only an allegation. The secret grand jury proceedings are behind closed doors and orchestrated by the district attorney. The rules of evidence don't apply. The defense is not required to present evidence and normally is foolish to try. Even if a grand jury did not indict or "no billed" as it is called, another grand jury could be empaneled and asked to revisit the case. In short, there is no chance of a no bill.

It was Friday, the grand jury was empaneled, and I stayed close to my office. There was no reason to drive to Anahuac. At 11 o'clock, my telephone rang. "It's Lindell II," Alice Ann said.

"Put him on." I took a deep breath, knowing the outcome of the call. "Jim Ward" I said full of resignation.

"This is Lindell Washington. The grand jury has indicted your client on first degree murder. I guess that's no surprise to you. I'm ready to try my case right now. You want to set an arraignment next week? The judge is in town and can accommodate us. Of course, if you want to waive arraignment and plead guilty, I'm always ready to offer the death penalty as a plea bargain."

"Well, when it's anything over life, I never agree without consulting my client. The death penalty statute in Texas is unconstitutional. I think we'll see the judge next week. How about a reasonable bail? You could get all those folks at the Fort to go home."

"We like having your client where he is. I won't agree to bail. Besides, I've become fond of the singing."

"Are you going to show me your file?"

"I don't want you saying I hid anything from you. You can have access to everything I've got."

"There's a letter out there that I know was at the crime scene. Somebody has or at least had that letter. You still not find it?"

"No letter in my file," Lindell II said with a chuckle.

"If I find a letter, somebody is going to jail or losing their law license. There is exculpatory evidence as to my client in that letter that points the finger to Sarita Jo's nephew," I said.

"It won't be me going to jail. I've never seen any letter and nobody in the sheriff's office knows of one either. Let's agree to the arraignment on Tuesday of next week, say, 10:30?"

"I'll see you there," I said.

The game was on. The grand jury indictment ended any fantasy that the case wouldn't go to trial. Under normal circumstances, it is common for a defense lawyer to postpone cases in hopes that evidence or witnesses will disappear. With my client in jail and little likelihood we were going to find the letter that Clay claimed he'd received, there wasn't much profit in delay.

It was arraignment day for Reverend Clay. The drive to Anahuac annoyed me since I could damn near see the courthouse from Bay Villa. As the crow flies, it was no more than seven or eight miles. But I wasn't a crow; hence I was in the office at 7:30 that morning preparing to get underway. I wanted to spend some time talking with Reverend Clay before the arraignment. There was a heavy fog and the streetlights in front of the building glowed vaguely through the murkiness.

The lights in Aurora's office were on. I stuck my head into her office to see what she was doing. She was on the telephone. Life in New York City was already humming. She was negotiating a deal for a jobber who had hired her to handle his Texas business. He dealt in providing grains to mills. Aurora's tone was all business. It had taken me a while to get used to her directness. When I had commented on her tone with her clients in her first days with us, she had made it very clear that's how it was.

"In Manhattan, we don't have time to screw around with all this chit-chat business that you Texans do. I don't see how you get anything done down here."

I went into my office to get my file and collect my thoughts about dealing with how business was conducted in Anahuac. It had not taken me long to understand that Chambers County was not Houston, Texas. When I worked in the Houston district attorney's office I had certain latitude to work out pleas and dismiss bad cases. A lawyer friend had told me about the first time he'd appeared on behalf of a criminal client in Anahuac. He asked Lindell II if he would agree to probation. Lindell looked at him like he was crazy.

"What'd the sheriff say?" Lindell had asked.

"I didn't talk to him, you're the DA," my friend said, trying to grasp what was going on.

"He makes the decisions on case disposition in Chambers County. I just follow whatever his decisions are."

It took me a while to fathom that this was the way old Texas had operated. When traveling judges left town to go onto the next county, the sheriff was the law. He was the fellow that put the cuffs on criminals. He was the one that handled disputes between neighbors. In short, the sheriff was the man that kept the county under control. You didn't want to cross him. I thought back to my grandfather who had been the constable of a small town in Kansas. He was the law in that town. Now, I understood completely why I had to talk to the sheriff.

Lost in my thoughts I hardly heard Aurora's question. She had wrapped up her call and now stood at my door.

"I assume you want me to go with you to Anahuac this morning for the Reverend's arraignment?"

"Yes," I said. "I'm just going to get a trial setting since the DA insists it's a death penalty case. He's delusional if he thinks this case can be tried in contravention of the Supreme Courts findings about the Texas death penalty statute."

"I can draft a brief on it if you like," Aurora said.

"That's what I need. I'm sure this is only a bluff."

As we walked up the steps of the Chambers County Courthouse it occurred to me that I should introduce Aurora and myself to the district judge. We stopped by his office and he welcomed us in. Aurora had a way of facilitating lots of things. Her persona oozed out of her as easily as melting butter.

"Judge Hope, I'm Jim Ward, counsel for Reverend Clay and I want to introduce you to my partner Aurora Wilson." I hesitated for a second. She was my partner, but I had never had to acknowledge it professionally. I wasn't sure how my having a woman partner would be received.

The judge sat quietly for a moment. He looked at his desk and then abruptly snapped his head up. "I don't assume that you intend to appear before this court this morning, do you. Mrs. Wilson?"

"Well, I thought I would sit at counsel table during the arraignment your honor. I was just ..."

"*No!*", the judge said, "because I want to tell you right now that I've heard tell that some of those women lawyers in Houston have tried to waltz into District Court without proper attire. These pantsuits aren't going to cut it in Chambers County. I expect women lawyers to come to court in a dress. No sir, not going to have any pantsuits in my court."

Aurora was calm and cool. "Well certainly I meant no disrespect to this court." She said almost passively. "The judges in New York are allowing them as proper attire. I certainly understand local rules of court may be *different* in different places."

She broadly enunciated the second "different" in such a way that it made clear her thoughts about rural Texas judges. I knew it was time to get her to leave.

"Judge, I want to thank you for seeing us. Mrs. Wilson will certainly be properly attired if she appears before this court."

"Just stay behind the bar today and it will be fine," Judge Hope said with a polite tone, but a look that was not the same. It was clear that the idea of women lawyers and particularly women lawyers in pantsuits was not sweeping the Chambers County courts.

"Certainly, your honor, I will comply with *the court's* rules." Aurora said with an edge that I was used to hearing from her, but doubted that the district judge of Chambers County would tolerate long.

When we got outside the judge's chambers, I was about to make a funny remark about the encounter when Aurora interrupted me with a stage whisper filled with anger. "Don't you ever speak for me. I can fight my own judge battles. I'm a lawyer, damn it."

It was the second time that Aurora let me see that she was capable of human feelings. Her face showed no hint of her over-the-top persona, no unrestrained bravado and certainly not the aura that that she used as a suit of armor. No, this was a real human, woman by chance and lawyer by choice, fighting to make it in a world where men still made all of the rules.

If it hadn't been for Cooper's daily narrative of abuses from the editors of her daddy's newspapers, I might have laughed it off. But the hurdles that Cooper was facing made it real. For the first time, I realized that Cooper's complaints were not simply my spouse bitching about her job.

I looked at Aurora and nodded my head. "I couldn't agree more."

Now I had a dilemma. Aurora was perfectly in the right to be inside the bar with the rest of the attorneys. What could I do? To have her sit with me at counsel table during the arraignment of our client was guaranteed to set off a war with Judge Hope. I wasn't afraid to fight a war with the judge, but there were the client's interests to protect. An angry district judge could do us a bunch of damage without committing the kind of error that could get him reversed.

"Do you want to sit with me at counsel table? I'm willing to push this if you want," I said, hoping the answer was no. I didn't want to explain to Reverend Clay that we were pissing off the judge who held his life in his hands over whether my co-counsel was appropriately attired.

"No, you go ahead and talk to your client. I have an errand to run," she said with a gleam in her eye.

"Don't get into trouble. I don't know that I can save you."

"Don't worry. I know what I'm doing."

Surprisingly, Reverend Clay walked into the cell unshackled. Even though I had demanded it, I didn't expect it. Clay was talking and laughing with his jailer. Zeke, the same jailer who had been a total jerk the first time I came to see Clay. Clay and I shook hands. After the jailer was gone I asked, "How'd that happen?"

"Zeke has seen the light."

"The light?"

"There was a moment when he was hitting me and then a great light filled my cell. I saw it and I know he did too."

"Hitting you?"

"When I was first arrested, the deputies would hit me for no reason at all. Zeke said the sheriff ordered it. The light may have been lightning flashing through the window. I never heard thunder. I was praying while he was hitting me in the stomach. He stopped, looked at me and claimed the spirit was upon him. He begged for forgiveness and asked if I would baptize him. He converted on the spot. It was about the most powerful thing I've ever seen."

"Why didn't you tell me about this?"

"They said it would be worse if I complained. I trusted that God would fix it."

I sat quietly, trying to fathom what had happened and what to possibly do about it. The jailer was converted and not hitting Clay. If I complained he would be fired and someone new would show up to beat Clay.

"What do you want me to do about this?" I asked.

"There is no need to do anything. Zeke is protecting me from harm. He's a part of my group of seekers now. I am at peace with what happened."

"Don't hide anything else from me," I said with force behind my voice.

"I'm in God's hands here. He will protect me."

"Don't you think maybe he sent *me* to protect you?"

"I have no question that he sent you to me and me to you."

His answer stopped my investigation. I couldn't go further. The subject of arraignment was why I was here, not predestination.

"Do you understand what an arraignment is?"

"Not exactly."

"The DA presents you with the indictment. We will waive reading of the indictment because it is a formality. The judge will ask you for your plea. It is 'not guilty,' of course. I've filed a motion for bail to be set. It won't happen. You are here until we try the case. I assume you want to move as quickly as we can."

"Yes, I worry for my flock. They must get back to their farms."

Reverend Clay was either the most selfless individual I'd come across or self-deluded. This man was in hell and he only thought of others. I felt small and selfish. I'd thought of the Reverend's case as a ticket to fame and my own fortune. But I was not committed to self-flagellation and I certainly didn't have the time. It was 10:30.

"You ready for your arraignment?" I asked.

Clay looked at me and bowed his head. "Jesus, please be with Jim as he helps your faithful servant to throw off these chains," he said.

"Amen" I said. It was the only word that came to mind. To my knowledge no one had ever prayed for me out loud.

It was 10:40 when Judge Hope graced us with his presence. The clerk called Reverend Clay's case and I walked to the counsel table. Reverend Clay was brought from the holding cell in shackles. Clearly Zeke's largess could not be visible to the sheriff. Clay's garish orange jumpsuit gave him a clownish appearance. At that moment, I heard the swish of the door swinging open at the rear of the courtroom. Judge Hope's eyes were fixed intently on the door. His face reflected emotions that alternated between anger and bemusement.

I turned to find my co-counsel now dressed in what could only be called a flowered muumuu. It clearly didn't fit. It didn't even cover her knees. Aurora walked through the swinging wooden gate that separated the gallery from the counsel tables and sat down beside me without a word, staring ahead.

Judge Hope stared at her for a moment and then said, "Mr. Ward I see you have a co-counsel in this case. Would you introduce her to the court?"

"Yes your honor, for the record, Reverend Clay will also be represented by Aurora Wilson.

The judge now laughing said, "And for the record, let it be reported that I liked the pantsuit better."

You didn't want to trifle with Aurora Wilson. She had made her point and I could tell the judge liked her, or at least her spunk.

I couldn't wait to get out of the courtroom to find out how she got the dress. There was not a clothing store in town.

"Mr. Ward, does your client waive reading of the indictment?"

"He does your honor."

"How does he plead?"

Reverend Clay stood as nobly as a man in an orange jumpsuit could muster and said forcefully, "As God is my witness, not guilty."

"We would request that a reasonable bail be set in this matter. The defendant is a respected man of the clergy," I said.

"He *is* from Arkansas, your honor," Lindell II said sarcastically.

"With all due respect to his eminence, he is charged with murder. I don't see how I can grant bail to a murderer, excuse me, an alleged murderer from out-of-state. Now if he were from around here it might be different. But you aren't, Reverend Clay," Judge Hope said. I was beginning to wonder if I should rename him "No Hope."

"Your honor, we would request that we be granted a speedy trial. There is no reason for this case to languish on the court's docket." I figured that this case wasn't getting any better with age.

"Lindell, you have any objection?"

"I have no objection, your honor. I would be happy to send the Reverend over to Huntsville. He could say grace to the inmates before Thanksgiving Dinner."

Judge Hope looked over the top of his glasses and gave Lindell a frown. "Now, Mr. Washington, you and I have talked about this before. We are on the record here. There is no reason for these extraneous remarks."

"I'm sorry, your honor," Lindell II said, but he clearly wasn't repentant.

"Counsel has indicated that he is willing to turn over his file for inspection. We would request that his offer be restated for the record," I said. There was no discovery available under Texas law in criminal cases. Trial by ambush was common. Lindell's file would contain the sheriff's report of his investigation. I didn't expect anything spectacular, but I needed to see what was written.

"I have so agreed. I'll make him a copy," Lindell II said.

"So ordered, what's a good date we can dispose of this matter?" Judge Hope asked.

I quickly replied, "We can be ready for trial November 13th, the week before Thanksgiving."

"We can be ready, your honor," Lindell II said.

"I will set the case for trial for November 13th. Motions, if any, will be heard on the Friday before. Is there anything else that requires the Court's attention at this time?" Judge Hope asked.

"The State is telling me that, contrary to the United States Supreme Court decision declaring the Texas death penalty statute unconstitutional, he intends to give notice that the State will seek the death penalty." I said.

"Well you can't do that. I'll not allow a case to proceed in contravention of the Supreme Court, although I don't know what's going on with Earl Warren these days. You're not going to try that, are you, Lindell?"

"No, your honor."

His admission that he was bluffing took pressure off of the case even though life in the Texas penitentiary was no bargain.

"Anything else?" Judge Hope said.

"Nothing more, your honor." Lindell II said. I shook my head no and we were done.

"We are adjourned." Judge Hope lightly tapped his gavel on its wooden sound block.

I looked at Reverend Clay. "I have asked my partner, Wells Wilson, to set up a meeting with Harrison Chambers to discuss the documents he drafted for Sarita Jo. I will report the outcome of that meeting. I don't expect him to be hostile to us since he did draft them."

"Mr. Chambers seemed like a very nice man. He did argue a bit with Miss Franklin, but he did as she said," Reverend Clay confirmed. Zeke came to his side and was all business as he shackled Clay for his trip back to the dungeon. I swear I saw him wink at Clay as he scowled menacingly. Clay smiled at me and was led away.

After Clay was gone, I looked at Aurora with a faux frown. "I don't approve, but it looks like you got away with it. How'd you do it?"

"I went to the county clerk's office and traded my pantsuit to one of the assistant clerks. She said she had read about pantsuits and she couldn't wait to get it home and alter it so she could wear it to work tomorrow. The pants were at least twelve inches too long. It was a sight to see. She must be a hell of a seamstress.

"You mean you traded your designer pantsuit for this K-Mart dress?"

"Don't you love it? Yes, now let's get out of here before anyone else sees me."

"I think Chinky is outside to interview you. We'll see how she likes you in this dress." I grinned.

Aurora eyed me. "Right," she said and headed for the door.

As we drove back to La Porte, I began a hard look at how the case would be tried. One of the unknowns was the potential testimony of Harrison Chambers. He'd drafted documents. He was stuck as far as Sarita Jo's mental competency--he shouldn't have drafted the documents if he questioned her mental state. It was important with a quick trial that I knew exactly what he planned to say.

"Will you ask Wells to set up a meeting with Chambers? He'll respond to Wells. He might not give me the time of day."

"Why not let me call him? He was always pestering me in law school to go out with him," Aurora said.

I had forgotten that he was Aurora's classmate, too. "Did you go out with him?"

"Heavens no, he was from Texas. That made him geographically undesirable and he had a disgusting personality. Then there was that one other thing, I was already married. Of course Wells and I never told anyone. I told you it was complicated." She shut down the cross examination.

"You and Wells work it out. Maybe we will all go over there together. It'll be like a Harvard reunion, class of '58. You can all tell me what a dumbass I am for not having an Ivy League degree."

"We are a superior breed, you know, even among the Ivy League schools," Aurora said with a grin.

"Just set up the fucking meeting, okay?"

"Well now that you said it so politely, I'll get right on it."

I was shocked at my language. Even if Aurora was a partner, it was not language I would use with women. I knew that the stress of trial preparation had started. The orneriness that it takes to be a trial lawyer sometimes knows no boundaries. Wives, children, friends and law partners could be the recipients of this brooding, misplaced anger.

"Sorry," I said.

Aurora was smiling and staring down the road. I wondered if she felt it yet.

CHAPTER TWENTY-SEVEN

It was almost five the next afternoon. Aurora and I were sitting in my office talking about the trial. I was ready for some good news or a drink or both. Wells delivered both. He walked into my office with three glasses of Scotch on a tray.

"I got a return call from Harrison Chambers. I don't think he's too excited about having to testify. He says the DA is all over him to say Sarita was coerced by Reverend Clay," Wells said.

"He's really in a box," I said. "He can't say Sarita Jo wasn't competent to make the gift because he gets into trouble. I wonder if Lindell II is trying to set him up to speculate that she was threatened and too scared to not sign the papers."

"It still wouldn't help him much. He has a duty to an elderly client to investigate the circumstances surrounding such a large financial transaction," Aurora added.

"So, did he agree to talk to us?" I asked.

Wells smiled as he said, "Harrison doesn't want to piss anybody off at this point. Clete Franklin has hired a big time legal malpractice lawyer. He's alleging that Sarita Jo was mentally incompetent to make a will or sign a deed. Clete will get it all if he can prove it in court. Not just that, Clete could get damages from Harry."

"What I know of her she would have pistol-whipped Little Harry if he hadn't done what she wanted. Chambers says he'll see us tomorrow at his Wallisville ranch. At least we don't have to drive to High Island. I think we should take the will contest on a contingent fee basis. We could take forty percent if Clay gets the money. Of course, if we lose, we have all the costs and nothing to show for it," I said.

"Let's talk to Marrow tomorrow and get his testimony squared up and then we can get a signature on a contingent fee contract with the Reverend, since he stands to inherit Sarita Jo's ranch," Wells added.

"It sounds good to me. If we win the criminal case I'm sure we win the will contest. No lawyer is going to want to spend the money to try the civil case if Clay is acquitted," I said.

"I'll put an engagement letter together for Clay to sign. We'll get it done after we visit with Little Harry," Wells replied.

"Who should go?" I asked.

"I don't dare send Aurora by herself. Little Harry was always stalking her at Harvard," Wells said without mirth.

"Oh, he was not. He doesn't even come to my…ah, chin."

"Well, he was always looking at your chest."

The conversation amused me. It also reminded me once again of the smallness of the world. Had some invisible force out there thrown all of us together for some purpose? If not, these random coincidences made no sense to me. Then again, who was I to expect life to make sense?

"We will all go. This is an important meeting. I don't want to miss anything." I said.

Aurora looked at Wells in a way I interpreted as seeking permission. Wells looked as if he was pleased. Their complex relationship continued to fascinate me. Watching Wells, Aurora and a lawyer I now knew as "Little Harry" would provide an amusing sideshow to an otherwise serious meeting.

"Shall we tell him 10:30?" I asked. "Tell Little Harry I look forward to meeting him."

Wells laughed and Aurora frowned. "Boys!" she scolded.

"Right," I taunted her.

"Bugger."

The WW&W team was bonding. We were in a battle for the freedom of Reverend Clay and a piece of Sarita Jo's estate if Clay signed the engagement letter. It felt good to be on a team again.

We drove the Lincoln to Harrison Chambers' Wallisville ranch since the Wilsons' cars had only two seats. "Should we ride in the back seat?" Aurora asked.

"You're used to riding in limos in New York. I'm only here to serve," I said with a smart ass look on my face.

"I'll ride shotgun. Aurora. You're in the back seat," Wells said. Aurora slid into the backseat behind Wells and we were off to see Little Harry. As we drove down Highway 146, Wells said, "This guy is smart; don't underestimate him. He is vertically challenged and has a fully developed 'little man' complex, but don't be fooled. He was on the Law Review with me. He's in a tough spot. Let's assure him we're on his side."

"Who should do the talking?" I asked. There was a stillness that surprised me. Neither of the Wilsons stepped up.

"Me?" I said after the silence grew heavy. There was no immediate response.

"Yeah," Wells finally said.

"Right," Aurora said.

Clearly there was more history here than the Wilsons had shared. The task was to nail down Little Harry's testimony, not to learn Wilson family secrets. If I played this right it would be simple. Little Harry was under pressure to defend an action that had implications for his financial and professional well-being. Lawyers are always on the edge of this type of disaster. Clients are constantly pissed at their lawyers for recommending actions in the client's best interest but not consistent with what the client wants to do. I knew we would hear that Chambers had tried to talk her out of the gift. The truthfulness of the rest of his answers was what we were trying to ascertain. He could shade his answers in ways that would hurt Reverend Clay without lying. Hearing that he wasn't dumb gave me chills.

The Chambers ranch was a mile off of I-10. We drove through an open gate and the Lincoln's tires rumbled across a cattle guard. Two large dogs emerged from behind the house and began a 200-yard sprint to meet us. Cattle grazed on both sides of the road. The barking dogs scattered them. The dogs ran by us and then fell in behind the Lincoln continuing their barking. Their annoying yapping was an unwelcome herald of our arrival.

A short man in a tan suit stood on the front porch of the imposing 100-year-old house with a shotgun across his arms. As the Lincoln came to a stop the dogs were jumping on the side of the car. Harrison Chambers fired one shot and the dogs yipped and ran back behind the house.

"Oh, for God's sake, can you Texans not simply leash your dogs?" Aurora said in disgust, keeping her voice low enough I could barely hear her.

"Well, I've lived in Texas all my life and that's a first for me," I said.

"Little Harry did that for Aurora," Wells said with more than a touch of annoyance.

Harrison Chambers leaned the shotgun next to the front door. He walked toward the car like the aggressive Banty Rooster that used to chase me around my grandfather's barnyard. As Little Harry swaggered toward the car, his lips were drawn tight like he was going to start swinging at someone. There was nothing welcoming about his demeanor. If he hadn't put the shotgun down and been no taller than his five feet-six at best, I might have gotten back into the car. Chambers eyed me and then Wells and then he caught a glimpse of Aurora. Chambers' demeanor turned on a dime. A broad smile creased his face and he straightened to his full five-feet-something.

The three of us stood frozen beside the car, Wells beside the passenger door with his right hand extended for a handshake. Chambers walked past Wells as if he didn't exist.

"Aurora, Wells didn't tell me you were coming," Harry said with a deep voice that seemed to have come from someone else.

"I wouldn't have missed it," she said in a controlled but friendly voice.

"I never thought I'd see you again." It was almost a whisper. He recovered and walked over to where I stood. His face had taken on a more professional look as he stuck his right hand out. "You must be Taylor Faircloth's son-in-law."

"Well, I prefer to think of myself as Jim Ward."

Chambers ignored my comment and continued pumping my hand. "Jim Ward," he said as if he was examining it from afar. Wells continued to stand by the passenger door of the car, his hands now folded in front of him.

"Let's go up to the porch. My maid's got some fresh coffee on," Harry said without acknowledging Wells.

Aurora took Wells' hand and tugged him toward the porch. I could see her whispering in his ear as she moved him forward. This meeting was so much tenser than I could have imagined. There is nothing worse than the anguish a man feels in his heart for the woman who got away. The impossible illusions the anguished one contrives about the lost woman only make the anguish worse. I wasn't sure that was what we were dealing with here, but it sure looked like it. It could be a problem or a gift. If Aurora Wilson was the imaginary perfect woman of Harry's dreams, it was dicey. There was only one person on the porch who knew how to deal with it.

"Your ranch is beautiful. I'm so glad to finally see it." Aurora said, still holding Wells' hand. "I didn't know that Wells and I lived so close to you."

"You could have seen it anytime you wanted," Harry said cryptically. "You need to see the High Island ranch sometime." He looked for a reaction. When he heard none, he added, "It's full of oil wells. That's why I live here."

When Aurora didn't respond, Harry looked disappointed. I could only imagine that she had been asked to come to Texas while the three of them were at Harvard. Wells was totally passive as he sat between Aurora and Harry.

Aurora took the lead. "We know you're an important, busy man. I don't see how you're able to manage a ranch and a law practice. I'll get right to it. We know that you did a thorough job of examining Sarita Jo Franklin's competency before you agreed to draft the documents for the gift and life estate. We know you are far too smart to have not questioned your client

143

closely about such a precipitous action. You'd known her for years and would have detected if she was being coerced, wouldn't you?" Without waiting for a response, she continued, "In short, she asked you to draft documents that accomplished her goals. You did your job, nothing more, nothing less. If you'd had the slightest doubt about any of this, you would have refused to draft the paper. Does that sum it all up?"

I'm sure that Harry had heard bits and pieces of what Aurora, the most perfect woman, had said, but he was staring at her with a small puppy's hope of approval. He took a deep breath and with a look of resignation said, "That sums it up."

"We don't want to take any more of your time. I'd like to draft a sworn statement for you to sign to that effect. I'll bring it out tomorrow if that is all right with you," Aurora said.

"I'm not going to sign a sworn statement unless I have some time to study it closely. There's a lot at stake. But you bring it out tomorrow and I'll consider it. It may take some time for me to get comfortable with the language you draft." Harry said, still looking at Aurora.

I jumped out of my rocking chair. One thing I'd learned in court was that once you have what you want, don't hang around and take a chance the judge will change his mind. "Thank you very much. Aurora will be by tomorrow." As the words hung in the air the maid opened the front door with fresh coffee. "Sorry, but we have to be going; no time for coffee today."

I was trying to escape without alarming Harry, but there was nothing to worry about. He had taken Aurora's hand and was talking to her earnestly about something. She extricated her hand and Wells thrust his right hand into Harry's now empty hand. "It's great to see you again, Harrison." Wells said and Harry looked angry again.

On my way to the car, I shouted, "Come on guys, we have to get back for that meeting in La Porte." The situation that was developing on the porch between Chambers and Wells was toxic to our case. My shouting broke the moment and Wells and Aurora scurried to the car.

My last image of the house in my rearview mirror was a love sick little Harry looking longingly at the car and a confused maid standing with a silver service full of fresh coffee. As the Lincoln sped away from the house, the hounds from hell again chased us to see if they could kill us before we reached the gate. I never heard more from either Wells or Aurora about the bitterness between Wells and Little Harry. I surmised that the relationship between Wells and Aurora was more deeply emotional and less for convenience than I could have ever guessed. Wells and Aurora's relationship was a mystery that was always interesting, but it was like a black hole, no light escaped.

We drove toward Marrow's RV with our contingent fee contract in hand.

Marrow was sitting under an awning suspended from the side of his RV. A cloud of cigar smoke swirled around him. Somehow he had gotten a telephone line installed in the RV. Its long cord allowed him to take it to the picnic table. He was in a hard negotiation of some kind. His New York edge was intimidating even when I wasn't the target of it.

"Yeah, yeah, yeah," he said rapidly. "Just do it. We need that building now." He hung up.

"Gentlemen and lady, welcome to the arm pit of America," Marrow said.

"I take it the ambience of the Texas Gulf Coast has run thin," I said.

"It's the goddamn mosquitoes and heat and humidity and nothing to do here that's killing me. So, any chance we can get him out on bail?"

"Nope, we're stuck until trial."

"What brings you here to my slice of paradise?"

"The will and life estate deed is going to be contested by Clete Franklin," I said.

"So you want to represent us on it and do it on a contingency fee, right?" Marrow said.

"Yes, how did you know?"

"Looks like an easy and quick big score. You won't have to work for it if you win the criminal case. I'm not a neophyte to the world of lawyers. Forty percent net of expenses if it's tried and thirty-five percent of it if it's not?"

"Seems fair," I said.

"Well it's not fair, but it will give you an incentive to win, so maybe it's best for Reverend Clay and me."

"We need his signature."

"I have his business Power of Attorney. You don't need to bother him."

"Good by me until I see him next time. Not that I don't trust you Mr. Marrow, but you know how it is," I said.

"That pains me, Mr. Ward," Marrow said, his cigar squeezed tightly in his mouth. He managed a smile that said he would have been disappointed if I did trust him.

145

The camp had taken on a look of permanence. There were signs that the black congregation and the white congregation had begun integrating their daily lives. For the time and the place, it was extraordinary. We rejoiced on our way back to La Porte. We had struck a blow for financial security. All we had to do was win.

I had been back in my office for two hours when there was rapping on my door.

"Mind if I come in?" Aurora said.

"The door's now open." I said.

"Here is the statement I want Harry to sign."

I read the statement and it was essentially what she had reeled off to him on his porch. "It looks good to me. Are you OK with going back out to see him alone?"

"You want him to sign it?"

"Yes"

"Then let me do it. Wells is fine. He trusts me. Can you imagine that Chihuahua and me in a clinch? I'd bust his teeth out."

"I want the statement signed," I responded. The rest of the visual was too rife with repulsion to consider.

"I'll get it tomorrow," she said. And that's what she did.

CHAPTER TWENTY-EIGHT

The next afternoon when Aurora laid the signed statement on my desk, she said, "I asked him if he remembered anything about a letter. He said it might have been mentioned. He won't testify about it unless he can refresh his memory about it from his file notes. He said he'd call me after he looks at them."

"I can't believe I didn't think of that."

"The meeting on the porch was a bit chaotic. Don't be too hard on yourself."

"If he will testify about it, we could be home free."

"Don't get your hopes up. I didn't sleep with him."

"Thanks for sharing that with me."

"Right."

"Do you have a minute to look at this autopsy report with me?"

"I do."

I pitched the autopsy report across my desk to her. It had been performed by a contract medical examiner from Harris County. I'd worked with her on several cases. Aurora dissected the report with a slow and thorough manner that impressed me. She honed in on the one thing that seemed out of the ordinary.

"Deep powder burns on her right hand. The killer was so close to her she grabbed the gun. She knew the killer?"

"Maybe or maybe it was someone she surprised in the house."

"Did you notice that it was a .22 caliber bullet? It struck her rib and then did the Cha Cha around most of her internal organs. She bled out pretty quickly. It wasn't a professional hit like I see in New York," Aurora said, "They use heavier caliber guns."

"Yeah, but say you're connected and you want to make it look like an amateur burglary? You wouldn't need an elephant gun to kill an old lady. Maybe a Saturday Night Special is a weapon of choice," I responded.

"You're talking about Marrow now, right?" she asked.

"The question of the day--where was our good friend Marrow at the moment of truth? I tried to pin him down, but he responded with a paper-thin alibi."

"It could have been the nephew. He might have tried to get her to rescind the documents and it all went badly. I doubt he really wanted to kill her. He had to know that once she was dead, the gift and life estate passed fully to Reverend Clay."

"Our dear Reverend Clay was in the house," I said. He claims he was upstairs taking a shower when it happened. If he and Marrow are bad guys it could have been the two of them."

"Confusion is our friend in a circumstantial case. All we need is to introduce a pinch of reasonable doubt. We can free him if the facts could lead to a reasonable conclusion that someone other than Reverend Clay did it. I'll give some thought as to how to work it. I don't want Marrow's name in the case if we can help it. There is too much risk," Aurora said.

"Once a jury starts thinking that Marrow had something to do with it, we're dead. They would assume that Clay was in on it too. I'm not sure there is enough for an appeals court to uphold a conviction, but I don't want to ever get there," I said.

After Aurora left, I thought about Marrow and his relationship with Reverend Clay. Clay seemed so trusting and their history in AA had bonded them. I could see how this clever East Coast gangster could have manipulated the Reverend. On the other hand, maybe Reverend Randall Clay was a con man himself. It could be that he'd conned himself. Was he really willing to kill to spread God's word? That didn't seem reasonable given that Reverend Clay chose to stay in the house after Sarita Jo was dead. A guilty man would have fled to collect his property as her beneficiary. Finally, I dismissed all of the speculation because it wasn't my job to judge my client. My job was to provide him with a defense. God would have to sort it out if I sprung Clay and he was guilty.

The end of the workday could not come soon enough. The word had spread in the local criminal community that there was an ex-assistant DA in town. Several felony theft defendants had shown up seeking representation. Thievery was not an uncommon vocation in the area. I turned some of the work over to a defense lawyer in Baytown who was not particular about his clients. The financial benefit of being Taylor Faircloth's son-in-law was allowing me to be picky.

It was 7:30 in the evening. "Enough," I said. Alice Ann opened my door at the same time and said, "Mr. Ward, you ought to go home now. I'm sure your wife would like to see you sometime."

"Thank you, Alice Ann, I think I will."

I closed the file folder I was working on and left the building. It was the middle of October and the air was cooler and dryer than it had been in six months. Fall in La Porte was not chilly, but at least it was in the low 80s. A band was playing on the deck of the community center at Sylvan Beach as

I drove toward Morgan's Point. It was a weeknight and I wondered what it was about. Life in La Porte was so foreign compared to my life on Morgan's Point; they were completely different worlds. The Point was isolated from the hubbub of Highway 146 and the tank trucks hauling crude oil and products to and from the refineries. Morgan's Point was still wild. There were a few older homes along the bay front, but essentially it was covered with forests that held deer, foxes and armadillos. It was my sanctuary, my private park. I assumed that it would be like that forever. When you were in Taylor Faircloth's world, assumptions about forever were never safe.

Cooper was already home when I pulled through the gate to Bay Villa. Her car was a welcome sight. Taylor Faircloth's car was also parked in front of the house. It was a common occurrence, but not one I welcomed tonight. Cooper, Taylor and Jerome met me at the front door.

"Daddy's got some big news."

"I need a drink. Can we talk about it on the portico? It's so nice out here tonight," I said.

"Should I open the last bottle of the Chateau Bouilde 1962?" Jerome said.

"I'd like that," Taylor said. He seemed to be glowing with excitement.

The idea that there was "big news" had my attention. Taylor was involved in so many big deals that the idea that one was worthy of one of the best bottles of wine in the cellar must be *big*.

After we had sat down on the portico, commanding a view of the bay and the ship channel there was a moment of pause. Taylor was relishing his news and was a master of commanding a room. Finally, I said, "O.K. you two. What's going on?"

Cooper said, "Daddy has …"

Taylor interrupted her and continued, "I have cut a deal with the Port of Houston to buy that worthless tract of land on the other side of the Point."

"Everybody said he was stupid for buying that land, but it was on the ship channel, Daddy always knew it would pan out," Cooper said proudly.

"Wait a minute," I said because the news was spilling out faster than I could understand. "What does the Port of Houston want with Morgan's Point?"

"The future of shipping cargo is going to be in containers that can be preloaded with products so that they can be off-loaded from ships directly onto trucks and railcars. It eliminates the longshoremen. These container ships are too big to travel all the way up the channel."

"How do they unload all of these containers?" I asked.

"With huge permanent cranes." Taylor said proudly.

"Isn't that going to mess up Morgan's Point?" I said with apprehension.

"No!" Taylor said emphatically. He sat looking at me as if I had asked a stupid question.

I started to disagree, but before I could, Taylor said, "Well, people will get used to it. Besides, it means jobs and money to La Porte.

"I guess as a resident of Morgan's Point, I was hoping it would stay wild."

"Don't be silly. Jim, the Point has always been poised for this kind of success. I need you to get right on the papers whenever their lawyers get them to me. Look at it this way; you'll make a lot of money for your firm. Best of all our family is set for generations. Future Faircloths will never have to worry about money."

Cooper gave me a glance that said that the elephant in the room had never gone away. There was already money enough for the generations that would never come unless Cooper bore a child. The responsibility for the distribution of great wealth weighed heavily on Taylor's shoulders. He'd planned for everything except a daughter who wouldn't procreate.

I now knew one thing for sure. Cooper and I would not spend the rest of our days at Bay Villa. Unending fleets of container ships would soon disgorge their cargoes twenty-four hours a day onto convoys of tractor trailer trucks. Morgan's Point, once the sylvan summer retreat for Houston's wealthy, would disappear as so many other handsome natural areas had before. Rather than swoon at the prospect of losing Morgan's Point to progress, I suspected those Houston elites would have marveled at the crafty deal that Taylor had made. Bay Villa was huge and aging, but it had become home to me.

As Jerome delivered wine that had rested in the cellar ten years just for this moment, I felt a profound sadness. But as the wine of financial success filled our glasses a larger part of me was filled with concern about what a future away from Bay Villa might hold. We hoisted our crystal glasses full of the fermented grapes of a noble vintage. The glasses clinked in a toast to Taylor's latest coup. As we tipped our glasses to drink, there was a collective gasp. The Chateau Bouilde, the pride of Bordeaux, had turned to vinegar.

CHAPTER TWENTY-NINE

In late October, thunderstorms preceded the first cool front of the year. Rain clouds swirled over the bay, tossing the shallow waters to and fro. When the rain broke, a hint of fall moderated the high temperatures into the mid-80s. There were fantasies of wearing new fall sweaters and coats, but that was at least a full month away. As I drove down Bayfront Boulevard, there were a few hardwoods whose leaves showed signs of turning various shades of yellow. November 13th would be upon us in a hurry.

My concern about finalizing Reverend Clay's trial preparation had progressed to full-fledged anxiety. It was not that the case was so complicated to try. In fact, it was the sheer simplicity of it that worried me. Lindell II had provided a sparse witness list of only four people that included Sheriff Leonard Staunton, Carolyn Fisk, M.D. Medical Examiner, Harrison Chambers, and Cletus Franklin without my asking. It was almost as if he were taunting me.

If the prosecution established that there was no reasonable hypothesis other than Reverend Clay was the murderer, a jury could convict him. If we could provide a reasonable theory that another person could have killed Sarita Jo, Clay might walk free. I questioned whether Clay could get a fair trial in this isolated universe where Sheriff Leo Staunton was the arbiter of justice. To find Clay not guilty, twelve citizens, tried and true, would have to accept Clay's version of the case. The jurors would have to accept that not only would Clay leave Chambers County with Sarita Jo's fortune, but they would remain in Sheriff Staunton's world, subject to his fury for the rest of their lives.

I wanted to be proactive in offering a defense, but there was a real possibility that Clay might never testify. The prosecution's case might not be strong enough to get to the jury. That was not likely in a town where everybody knew everybody, but I held out faint hope. What if we didn't think the state had proved a *prima facie* case? We could be put to the test of not providing evidence and betting that the jury would understand. The defendant has no obligation to provide evidence in the trial. That said, the jury would want to hear his story. If he were just some ordinary local man, his defense would be simple. But he was not only not a local, he was a mystery man of the cloth who appeared from nowhere and was looking to leave town with Sarita Jo's fortune.

Randall Clay was an uncontrollable client. He was dead sure of his faith and cocksure that God was directing this case, not me. There was hardly a story to keep straight. Clay was in the shower and heard an argument downstairs. He was naked, then dressed before he went to see about the disturbance. The Medical Examiner's report said Sarita Jo bled out from multiple internal organs. I was disappointed that Sarita Jo's fingernails held no tissue from scratching her assailant. Apparently, she had reached for the gun and was shot.

There was a critical flaw in the state's case. Inexplicably, they had not tested Clay's hands to determine if he had fired a weapon. It had been a very haphazard investigation. There were two possible explanations for their lack of effort. Either they had focused on the only person at the scene and were sure they had their man, or they didn't want to find any exculpatory evidence that might point to someone else. Sheriff Staunton was a hometown hero, a retired Texas Ranger who'd come home to bask in the town's adulation. It didn't add up that he would do a half-assed investigation because he was lazy.

"Do you want to go to Anahuac and talk to Clay with me tomorrow?" I asked Aurora.

"Are you doing a final prep on his testimony?"

"Among other things—I want to explore what he thinks he's going to say. I haven't been able to corral him so far. I know he will preach a sermon. That seems like all he does."

"Sure, this might be fun. I did a year on a master's program in theology at Yale," Aurora said, smiling.

"What?"

"I dabbled in the occult for a while. A year of divinity school was enough to explode my head. I fled to safety."

"It was enough to send you to the dark side?"

"I'm partially back," she said.

"Who are you?" I said to this mystery woman whose past was obscured in a cloudy mist.

"That was what I was trying to find out."

"Well I'm glad you're on board. I need someone who can talk religion to the Reverend. I can't put him on the stand and have him kill his case with some goofy religious view I don't understand."

The next morning, we drove by the front of the Chambers County Courthouse at 8:30 in the morning. Several pickup trucks were parked in front of the café across the street. It was the only other place that showed signs of life on the square.

152

"Let's go down to the park and check in with Marrow before we talk to Clay," I said. I knew he had been busy working with several of the local preachers to minister to the congregation in Clay's absence.

"You don't want to take your eyes off this guy for very long. He is slippery," Aurora said.

The population of New Jerusalem had soared. The park had become a small town. There was a clearly defined residential area where most of the congregation had set up tents. There was little separation between the black and white settlements. Some of the more affluent pilgrims had campers on the back of pickup trucks. There was a revival tent in the center of the park. Marrow, who was either the rabbinical leader or the Pope of a new religion, had rented a long line of portable outhouses. Portable showers were erected on each side of the park, one side for men and the other for women.

Marrow's RV had taken on a look of permanence with the erection of a small white picket fence in front. Inside the fence, there was a table where he was meeting with a small group of men. I could see that it was most of the group of men who were debating who should be an elder in Reverend Clay's ministry the first time I visited. The group was discussing sanitation.

"We need to increase the number of portable toilets. We need at least one for every ten residents," one of the men said.

"Can we get some help from the local churches?" another asked.

"Don't worry about money," Marrow answered. "Our contributions are flowing in from the radio broadcasts. We don't want to tap these folks."

Marrow saw us and terminated the meeting.

"Welcome to New Jerusalem," Marrow said as the men left.

I shook my head in disbelief. I was surprised that the sheriff had not tried to stop this before it got so out of hand. He probably would have, except for a combination of factors restraining him. The press had continued reporting on the congregation over the past weeks. The flock had become an oddity that people were drawn to see. A few local residents had even joined in on Clay's vigil. More importantly, the local preachers were spreading the word in their churches that these were good people just like them who needed their support. Sheriff Staunton might have been able to run them off, but for the first time he had the local spotlight on him, not to mention the Houston media.

"We're here to prepare Clay's testimony. Any thoughts on how we keep him under control?" I said.

"His testimony in court would be a perfect opportunity if we could get Reverend Clay to give out the telephone number and address of the ministry. If we can get the press to repeat it we might double our contributions," Marrow said.

"I'm talking about his defense. This trial isn't a fund raiser," I said, shaking my head. "I need him to stay focused on the facts of the case. If he gets off on a ranting sermon, he may give the prosecution some ammunition that he is some kind of religious nut. We need to win this case, not souls."

"Good luck on that," Marrow said. "But there is hope. The other day I went to the jail and he told me that God has revealed a vision to him. He's calling it the Gospel of Prosperity. He says God told him that most preachers have got it all wrong. God told him the Bible makes it clear that God is a good father who will provide anything your heart desires if you ask him. Reverend Clay is still working on the concept, but I think it may be a winner."

"It looks like we have a lot to discuss. I guess we better get over to jail and get started. You guys seem so calm about this. I'm serious, this isn't a publicity stunt," I warned.

"Don't worry, God and I will provide everything you could need," Marrow said.

"That's what Reverend Clay says too. God help us if he doesn't."

"Right," I heard Aurora whisper to herself as we walked away. It was her usual answer for everything strange.

Reverend Clay stood at the door waiting to be let into the consultation room. At least he was unshackled. His broad smile preceded him into the cage. His mental state seemed unchanged, but his incarceration had taken a physical toll. He had lost at least fifteen pounds. His orange prison suit was now draped on his body. His once-tanned face had assumed the pasty, sallow look of one alienated from the sun. His formerly stylish razor-cut hair was now short. Yet, he greeted us warmly.

"Jim, Mrs. Wilson, it's so good to see you."

His greeting could have just as easily been delivered on a street in downtown Houston as it was in this dungeon. I studied his face closely for signs that he might have misgivings. Could his acceptance of his fate be real? I saw no pleas to his God to take this cup of suffering from him. He seemed to relish it. The more I accepted that his faith was legitimate, the more I wondered if we should have asked for a psychiatric exam. Who willingly accepts a God who throws him in jail for something he didn't do? What the hell was this "message from God about prosperity?"

"We're here to prepare you for your trial testimony," Aurora explained. "This is very important because once you are on the stand we can't control what happens if you get confused."

I was surprised that she took the lead without talking to me, but it seemed natural and I sat quietly.

"God will provide for us all," Clay said in his calm manner.

Aurora's next statement was even more surprising.

"We are God's instruments here on earth. We have been appointed by him to save you. You have to listen to what we say."

Clay's head snapped back as if he was disturbed that God had not let him in on this important information.

"God moves on the face of this earth in so many diverse ways. I suppose you could be right. You have my attention," Clay said, although his answer sounded as if he believed that God only worked through him.

Aurora tried to speak again, but Clay cut her off. "One more thing before you begin. I know God brought me to this cell for his greater glory. Before I entered this cell, I believed that God wanted us to suffer on this earth. I didn't understand why, but that was what I'd been preaching. But it didn't seem right that a loving God created this world to be a place to suffer and things only got better when you died. I'd misread scripture. I was reading Psalm 37 a few days ago. Some of the verses tell us that God wants those who *truly* believe, to have what they want to glorify God's name. He will give you what you need to glorify his name if you ask. It's a contract between God and his true believers."

"What verses are those?" Aurora asked.

Clay opened his worn Bible that never left his side and read:
Trust in the Lord and do good;
> *dwell in the land and enjoy safe pasture.*
Take delight in the Lord,
> *and he will give you the desires of your heart.*
Commit your way to the Lord; trust in him and he will do this:
He will make your righteous reward shine like the dawn,
> *your vindication like the noonday sun.*

"That verse opened my eyes to the benefits of being one of God's chosen. Jesus died to take away our sin and suffering. You don't have to wait for His blessings until you are with God in heaven." Clay said with a rising inflection full of the spirit.

155

"So prayer is just God's post office box where you send your Christmas list?" Aurora said with a tone that bordered on hard cross-examination.

"Not for just anybody."

"Just the *chosen* ones?" Aurora said as she leaned closer to Clay's face.

I had studied predestination in hopes that it would explain the horrible drowning of those two little girls in Kansas when I was a boy. I knew her use of the word chosen was not accidental. I couldn't wait to hear Clay's response.

"John: 14-15 gives us that answer," Clay said as he thumbed through his Bible and began reading.

And whatever you ask in My name, that will I do, that the Father may be glorified in the Son.

If you abide in Me, and My words abide in you, ask whatever you wish, and it shall be done for you. Until now you have asked for nothing in My name; ask, and you will receive, that your joy may be made full.

"That relates to spiritual fulfillment. That's what they taught me at Yale. It couldn't mean God will make you materially richer," Aurora said.

"Where does it say this verse doesn't include monetary and physical wealth? The difference between me and those professors at all these divinity schools is that I read my Bible literally. I listen to God. I don't try to make up theology based on some Godless liberal theory. The Bible says God will grant whatever I ask for in His name. Jesus said these words three times in the gospel. They are not my words. I prayed hard that God would give me the resources to spread his word and he sent me Mr. Marrow. I prayed we could expand the radio broadcast, and in his wisdom, he multiplied my fortune so that I might start a television station. My faith has been rewarded. God revealed this to me so that I could spread the word to those people out there that it wasn't their destiny to be poor in spirit, health or in material things."

I could see that Aurora now had the picture but she stayed after him. "Paul suffered throughout his life of evangelism. How do you square that up with your Gospel?"

"Paul was a narcissist who misunderstood what God was telling him. People need to hear that God wants them happy. I can help them see the light. It is God's gospel, not mine."

Clay was going to preach a sermon on the stand. We needed to make sure that his sermon didn't include a slip that got him convicted.

156

"I want you to stay with the facts of what happened the morning of the murder." Aurora said.

Reverend Clay put both hands together in a prayerful mode and said, "Don't you see that it is as important that the people in the courtroom see that Sarita Jo's fortune has been passed to me so it can be put to the most important work on earth—saving souls? Her death, while tragic, will mean that thousands of souls can be saved. I don't know who killed Sarita Jo, but the murderer will be destroyed. Psalm 37: 21-23 says that.

The wicked borrow and do not repay,
but the righteous give generously;
those the Lord blesses will inherit the land,
but those he curses will be destroyed.

Did we have a mad man for a client or was he talking directly to God? There was no need to bring in a psychiatrist because he knew the difference between right or wrong.

"For right now, let's stick to the facts that are relevant to the case, okay? This gospel thing will just confuse the jury," Aurora said. Clay took a deep breath so that he could patronize us.

"I awoke and heard Miss Franklin walking around downstairs. The house is ancient and everything creaks. I got into the shower and when I got out I heard her say 'No!' There was a noise like a struggle, very brief, and then a gunshot. I was standing naked and dripping wet. I dried off and dressed quickly. By the time I got downstairs she was lying on the floor and I heard a car or a truck driving away. I could see blood on her blouse and she looked dead. I called the sheriff and then I tried to help her, but I just got blood all over me and she didn't get better. When the deputy arrived he said, 'Get away from her, she's dead.'"

"Jim tells me that the deputy asked you why you did it."

"Yes, and I told him about the intruder."

"Did you tell him about the letter?" Aurora asked.

"I was too upset. It never entered my mind. I knew I didn't kill her. It didn't occur to me that they actually thought *I* did it."

"You signed no statements. You have no copy of the letter that Sarita Jo sent you and you don't know who killed Sarita Jo?"

"All true, as God is my witness."

"Can you do this for us? Can you answer only the questions that are asked and not embellish? People try to say too much on the stand and it makes them not believable. Can you do this?" Aurora asked.

157

"God's will for me is to make sure that his glory is magnified. I will try to stay on the script, but he may lead me elsewhere," Clay answered.

"It's not a script; it's the truth," I said.

I had a burning desire to test Clay's 'Prosperity Gospel.' "I've got a question for you. Is God just here to please us? Does he have authority over us? Did he predestine our lives?"

"God's will is paramount. God's will is for his people to be full of life and abundance. His will is for them to serve him. Those who don't serve his will never enjoy the life he desires for them. God loves his people and will give them abundance if they serve his will." I didn't think he had answered my question. Before I could follow up, Aurora was on him again.

"He's sort of a big sugar daddy for those who mind him?" Aurora laughed disdainfully.

"No, but I haven't studied all of this fully. God is providing me the knowledge as I have capacity to understand it."

"So this Gospel you have been given is a work in progress?" I asked.

"The Gospel is fully known to God; it is the messenger who struggles to understand it all. I have no question that it will be revealed in due time. I only know that it is true," Reverend Randall Clay said.

I had listened to as much of this as I could. If this was what went on in divinity school, I understood why Aurora had bailed.

I wanted to put a wrapper around his testimony. "Look, we are going to take your story from the top when you are on the stand. We'll start with you getting the letter and coming to Texas. Here's how I want the story to come in. I got a letter inviting me to Texas. I went to Texas to talk to the lady who wrote it. She gave me her estate. She was killed before I went home. I didn't do it. This glory of God crap, pardon my French, needs to be for your next broadcast. You clear on that?"

"I hear what you want, Jim, but God wants me to do something different," he said.

Aurora stepped in to back me up. "Fine, you've been advised. I'm going to write you a letter to that effect. If you don't want to follow our advice, it's your funeral," The way she said it, the unspoken epithet "asshole" could have finished her sentence.

"I understand." Clay said.

"Mr. Ward and I don't have to go to jail. It is *you* that will be in jail for the rest of your life if you get this wrong. It sounds to me that your God wants you to be in the money, not in jail," she hammered home. "Got it?"

"Got it," Clay said and we were don

CHAPTER THIRTY

The 13th of November broke with drizzle, light fog, and anxiety. Coffee was all that I needed or could stomach. I did have one piece of good news. It had seemed reasonable that if my life was controlled by a fate predetermined by God before the earth was formed, perhaps he might give me a road map to ease my journey. I was 15 when I first got hooked on reading the newspaper to see what was on tap for my life. I was hyper-vigilant about surprises. My horoscope in the Baytown paper was perfect. It was as if God had given me a sign as to how it would go.

Gemini, your brilliance will be at its brightest today. Legal, business and investment ventures are favored. Take charge, it's your day.

I smiled and tore out the horoscope. It was in my pocket as I opened the *Houston Post*. I couldn't wait to see if it would confirm my good luck. Cooper took the editorial page and I hungrily raced back to the horoscope section before even looking at the sports page. The daily horoscope was wedged between Ann Landers's advice and a car dealer's ad for the end of season distressed sale of all of the remaining 1972 Chevrolets. The horoscope was identical to the one from the *Baytown Sun*. I was elated. I needed some confidence. This was the first criminal case I had ever tried from the defendant's side. I was nervous.

"Wow, I am going to knock them dead today. My horoscope is off the chart!" I said to the back of the editorial page.

She peered at me over the top of her newspaper.

"That's great, honey. I don't think you need a horoscope to tell you that, though. You'll do fine."

Now I was full of confidence. It wasn't because of my substantial experience in the courtroom, but of the promise of planetary good luck. Cooper's newspaper suddenly dropped and her eyes appeared over the top of her paper.

"Let me see that." She said. It looked as if she had a grin on her face.

I handed my passport to victory to her and she gave it a cursory glance.

"Jim, I hate to tell you this but the syndicated guy who does these for us and the Post died two days ago. The horoscope we ran is the one from last year. Looks like the Post did the same thing."

The horoscope had given me the idea that I could know my fate in advance. Now I felt alone in an infinite universe without a roadmap.

Surprisingly there was something that brought me back quickly. I was not alone. Aurora was going to help me try the case. I would never admit it to her, but I needed and wanted her help.

I had begun to settle my nerves by the time I met Aurora at the office. Aurora was in her office when I walked in the door.

"You ready to go kick ass and take names?" I said. It was one of those inane things that people say when they are tense.

"I think we are in good shape if we can rein in the Reverend. I figured out that he is used to being adored by the flock. He can't imagine that a jury is going to be any different. Marrow has always been the filter that keeps him on course. He's not with Marrow every day."

"Maybe it's all been preordained. No need to worry if that's the case," I said, not sure if I was kidding or not. "Either way we have to go do it now."

"Oh, there is a bit of bad news. Harrison Chambers called me back about whether he remembered a discussion of the letter. He says there is nothing in his notes."

"Well, there is nothing I can do about it," I said. "It doesn't matter, really. It would all be hearsay. It would have taken a miracle to get the testimony in."

Aurora and I drove by New Jerusalem around 7:45. The city was alive with activity. A small group was singing a gospel hymn as they were preparing breakfast. There was nothing for us to do there, so we went to the courthouse. The streets were otherwise empty, but the Fort Anahuac Café across the street from the courthouse was full. Ten or twelve large pickup trucks were parked on the street in front of the café. The trucks were muddy, well-worn and outfitted with gun racks adorned with various assortments of shotguns, rifles and cattle prods. Three of the truck racks contained baseball bats. It seemed routine to me, but Aurora couldn't fathom the weaponry.

"Are they expecting a war or a baseball game to break out?" she asked.

"Welcome to rural Texas."

"Oh no it's not just here; I see it all over Houston. What is it with you people?"

"We're a people that don't take kindly to irritation."

"Ah, Texans," she said, shaking her head slowly. "¿Quien es mas macho?"

"Bloodthirsty colonists, mainly. We came by it honestly. We've been pitching tyrants off this continent since 1776."

Aurora eyed me for a moment. "Let's go into the café and examine these potential jurors. I need to hear them speak, if they can."

"Careful, this ain't Manhattan. Don't piss anybody off."

Her smile made it clear she was enjoying her latest visit into no-pantsuit territory. "Well sure, partner," she said in her fractured impression of a Texas accent. She touched two fingers to her forehead as a salute to confirm her understanding.

We opened the door to the café and surveyed the scene. The conversations of the locals were free-ranging across the whole of the dining room. It was as if everyone in the place was involved in one conversation. At first we weren't noticed, then one customer shouted, "So you think that preacher man is guilty?" to no one in particular as we stood in the doorway.

The communal conversation ended abruptly as the locals noticed the six-foot blond in an expensive custom-made English suit. I had tried to tell her to dress down. She had done the best she could. At least she'd left her new pantsuit at home. An unseen diner said, "Oh me, oh my." I had no doubt it wasn't for me.

The cafe had no more than seven or eight tables. The smell of coffee and frying bacon filled the room. Ads for area merchants adorned the tables under a laminated top. All of the tables were taken. There were open seats at the counter and we plowed through the locals and sat down. The communal conversation remained muted. A man, maybe 50, with a grease-stained apron was behind the counter. He seemed in charge of the waitress who was going from table to table refilling coffee cups. He eyed us warily.

"In for the trial?" he said, more to the collective room than to us.

"We are," Aurora answered before I could speak.

The British accent caused the owner's head to draw back abruptly.

"We're lawyers for Reverend Clay," I said before she could speak again.

"Where you folks from?"

"La Porte."

"Long way from home."

"Not as the crow flies."

"What can I get you?"

"Black coffee for me."

"What kind of teas do you have?" Aurora asked.

"Sweet and unsweet."

"Coffee, please, with cream and two lumps."

"Sugar packets are on the counter. Take all you like."

With that he was gone to pick up an order of eggs and bacon from the fry cook.

Aurora looked at me with a grin that threatened to explode into a howling laugh. I frowned and she nodded her understanding. I had never before felt like an outsider in Texas. I talked Texan. People were always friendly when they heard my Texan twang. Aurora's presence marked us both as outsiders. It all seemed strange to be an outsider in my own land.

The coffees arrived and we drank them quickly, without conversation. As I reached for my wallet to pay for the coffee, the owner took off his dirty apron. He addressed the room as if he were their leader. "Well, boys, sheriff says we're supposed to be in the courtroom by 8:15 to get some instructions."

With that, nine of the diners rose in unison and walked out to cross the street. Small town justice was way more personal than in Houston. I never had a case in six years where one potential juror knew another.

I looked at Aurora and said, "I guess *voir dire* has begun. Let's let them get inside the courthouse before we walk over." I wondered what kind of instructions the sheriff was going to give them.

The café was mostly empty after the prospective jury panel members left. The waitress who was now the only server offered us a refill of our coffees.

"I think we're done." I said and offered her a five-dollar bill to pay our tab.

"No charge, mister. I hope you get him off. Be careful of that Sheriff Staunton. He's been politicking pretty heavy around town that your client's a phony who's just out to steal the Franklin fortune. I heard him tell my boss that those people down at the Fort are just hippies waiting to kill us, like Manson did." Then she leaned her face in close to Aurora's and mine and whispered. "Personally, I think it was Clete that done it. He's sorry as dog shit."

"Thanks for the heads up," I said and left the five dollars on the counter. Nobody in their right mind would pay five dollars for two ten cent cups of coffee, but the news about Sheriff Staunton's shenanigans was worth its weight in gold.

We were crossing the street when one of the Reverend's flock intercepted us.

"We've been praying all night for you. We've been praying that it's God's will that you prevail over these Philistines," he said with a fervor that startled me.

162

"We'll do our best," I said as the man first pumped my hand and then Aurora's.

"Godspeed," he shouted after us as we continued across the street.

I always used that line as the conclusion to my jury arguments. I never really knew what it meant, but juries seemed to like it. I thought for a moment I should go back and ask him its meaning, but there was no time.

As we walked up the limestone stairs to the courthouse entrance, I felt uneasy. We were "not from around these parts," as Texans were fond of saying about outsiders. I had never tried a case outside of the Harris County Courthouse and it had always been as a prosecutor. I had been dealt a high-profile case to launch my defense career. My mind wandered off to Taylor's repeated admonition to not get involved with all this criminal defense crap. There was money to be made in representing Taylor's interests. Money and prestige were there for me on the civil side of my law practice. Yet, I loved the competition and adrenaline rush of a criminal trial.

My mind was awash in career choices when I realized that I was trying to escape the anxiety I felt about this trial. "Get focused!" I said in a whisper to jar myself back to the task at hand.

"What?" Aurora said.

"Nothing, I'm just getting my game face on."

"Right."

No one was on the first floor as we walked into the courthouse. It was quiet except for the staccato click of Aurora's four-inch Ferragamo heels striking the marble floor. The echoed sound filled the empty hall and it heightened the feeling that we were all alone in this defense of Reverend Clay. Sure, I hoped that the prayers of the flock would bring God's powers to help us save the good Reverend Clay. Truth was, I'd looked for his help in that pond in Kansas so many years ago. He'd taken a vacation day just when I needed him most. Two little girls died that day. I wanted nothing more than to save Reverend Clay, but I wasn't looking for help from the heavens.

The second-floor hallway was crowded with what I assumed was the jury pool. It made me uneasy to be in the middle of them. In Houston, the jury panel was isolated from the courtroom. A deputy sheriff was attempting to take roll of those called to serve and to seat them in the courtroom for *voir dire*.

We had argued all of the pre-trial motions the Friday before. Lindell II referred to Reverend Clay as 'that charlatan from Arkansas' every time we talked. It had a certain ring to it and I admired his persistence. That's why I filed a Motion in Limine to prevent him from saying it during the testimony.

The judge had granted my motion. That meant he couldn't call him a charlatan except in final argument.

At 9 o'clock sharp, we were starting trial. One departure from my experience in Houston was that the deputy knew most of the jurors. "Bob, you next and then Joe, no Joe Jenson, not Joe Baker, Mrs. Nelson, you next, then Leonard, there we go," he said, satisfied he'd gotten them in the right order. It seemed more like they were setting up a group picture at a family reunion than seating a random jury. Chambers County was long on bayous, alligators, migratory birds, lakes, creeks, cattle and rice farms. It was decidedly short on prospective jurors.

Aurora and I made it through the hallway into the courtroom. We needed to check in with Reverend Clay who was being held in the small cell behind the courtroom. The bailiff seemed perturbed that he had to stop reading his newspaper to take us back to our client. One thing I never understood was the attitude of bailiffs. With few exceptions, most seemed professionally grouchy. I suppose if my job were to sit and listen to lawyers all day I would have been grouchy too.

The transformation of Reverend Clay from prisoner-in-jail back into the man who enthralled his flock was magical. I had grown used to seeing him in his garish jail jump suit. During his incarceration, his hair had begun to gray slightly. One thing that never changed was his smile and enthusiasm. I had to hand it to him, if it was an act, it was a damned good one.

Mr. Marrow had his tailor fit the Reverend with a new suit. This suit was dark brown light wool with a conservative cut. We had decided that the sharkskin suits the Reverend favored, while stylish for the day, weren't appropriate for the image we wanted to portray. Reverend Clay had lost fifteen pounds while sitting in the jail, losing weight on the chicken fried steak diet told me he wasn't eating. My personal barber had come from the barbershop in the basement of the Rice Hotel in Houston to cut his hair. He looked ready to preach or testify, whichever was the case.

Our client met us with an enthusiastic greeting. "Mrs. Wilson! Mr. Ward!" I was astonished at his energy. He seemed to welcome what was to come. I longed to believe, like Clay, that acquittal was his fate. Reverend Clay was in the business of selling faith. From all appearances, he had bought into his own product.

We had something in common. Clay wasn't at that tomb almost 2000 years ago and I wasn't in Sarita Jo's mansion the morning she died. I believed Clay's story because I had faith in him. If Clay's faith in the product he was selling was justified, he would have eternal life. Right now, I was only interested in saving his earthly hide.

This was a circumstantial case. Only Sarita Jo and the person who murdered her knew what happened. My job was to convince a jury that they should accept our story on faith. It wasn't farfetched to say Clay and I were in similar lines of work.

The fateful hour had arrived for the jury selection to begin. The defendant and his lawyers—us—were at counsel table. The prosecutor was cutting up with the court reporter when the bailiff cried, "All rise, the District Court of Chambers County, Texas is now in session." Judge Hope was on the bench and we were ready to go. There was a wrinkle that I had never experienced before. The court reporter was a masked reporter. Masked reporters are not trained in stenography. They repeat the testimony into a mask that looks like an oxygen mask borrowed from a World War II fighter pilot. The testimony is transcribed by a stenographer later. I had never seen one before.

"Good morning," said the judge. "The case of the State of Texas versus Randall Clay is called. Are the parties ready?" I watched as the reporter repeated the words into her mask.

"State's ready."

"Defense is ready."

"All right then—Ladies and gentlemen of the jury panel, this is a serious case that will require your undivided attention. As I look at the prospective jurors I see many of you are rice farmers. Thank God we all got second cuttings this year. I know it has been bountiful. I also know that most of you take vacations at this time of year and that a trial is an inconvenience." Then Judge Hope stood up and walked down from the bench to the American flag. "I know that you want to get away before you have to get ready for next planting season. But think of this…" As he spoke he wrapped himself in the flag. "There are boys, our boys lying in the fields of Europe and the Pacific Islands who gave their lives for this country so that you would have the right to be here today." The judge stared directly at the prospective jurors for a moment before he unwrapped himself and climbed back behind the bench and sat down. "Now if any of you have business so pressing that you must ask to be excused from this duty, please come forward."

As it became clear that no one was moving, Aurora whispered, "Oh my God, they'd have laughed him out of a Manhattan courtroom."

"Yep," I said, "but this ain't Manhattan."

165

The judge said, "Now the lawyers in this case are Lindell Washington II for the prosecution and Jim Ward and Aurora Wilson for the defense. Do any of you know Lindell II? The entire jury panel raised its hands. "Now would knowing Lindell II cause any of you to be unable to be fair to the defendant?" No one said it would.

"What about the defense lawyers or Randall Clay the defendant?"

One hand went up from the jury panel. It was the owner of the Fort Anahuac Café. "I met Mr. Ward and that *woman* lawyer over at the café this morning," he said. The mention of a woman lawyer brought a snicker from the panel. "But I don't really know 'em, 'cause they aren't from here, but I can be fair."

"Right," Aurora whispered.

"All right, then," the judge said, "let's get cracking. Mr. Washington, begin your *voir dire* of the jury."

Lindell II stood up and walked to the rail that separated the lawyers from the jury panel. "Good morning, y'all. How y'all doing?"

The jury panel, being friendly Texas folk, responded as if it were a personal question directed to them. If Aurora needed any further proof we were not in midtown Manhattan, it was now clear. Hell, we weren't even in downtown Houston.

For the next twenty minutes, Lindell II proceeded to outline his case while he addressed jurors by their first names. He asked specific personal questions about their kids and every other kind of thing he could do to become their newest best friend. Cases can be won or lost in this preliminary stage. Lindell II clearly had home field advantage.

"Well, your honor, this looks like a real fair bunch to me. Probably be happy to have any of them on *my* jury." He was crafty. He had just made it look like anyone who was cut was being cut by the defense. I would have objected, but I didn't know what I could say.

"Mr. Ward, you're up." the judge said and I was on my feet. Aurora and I were looking at the small amount of jury panel information that they had all provided. It was hard to get any sense of who might be a problem and who might be a friendly juror.

"Talk Texan," Aurora whispered and gave me a wink.

"Right," I mouthed and turned to face my first jury panel as a defense lawyer. Over the years, my inflection had moderated from a hard Texas accent of the 1950s to more of a Midwest intonation. Part of my accent was beaten out of me by a speech professor from Ohio, and part of my accent had disappeared after national television had flooded our homes with Midwest-sounding voices. One look at the jury and there was nothing Midwest about them. They were dressed in their everyday work clothes with the exception of one man. I glanced down at his jury information card and saw that he was the undertaker. I then figured he was in his work clothes too.

"Hey, y'all," I said and it surprised me. My ear had grown so used to not hearing the real Texas dialect that I was afraid I sounded like Gabby Hayes. My fears were allayed when most of the panel said "Hey" right back.

"I'm sorry that this trial comes at an inconvenient time, but the judge is right. It's our duty and honor to be here. Now I know you said that you knew all of the local witnesses when Mr. Washington was reading you his witness list. I know you all said that it wouldn't make you lean their way, but I want you to think about it again. If you're embarrassed to say your mind in front of the panel, we can go up to the bench and talk to the judge about it."

A few panel members looked around at each other to see if anyone was taking the bait. Nobody moved, and I said, "No? Just look into your heart and be fair to the defendant whom you are going to judge. Would you be happy if someone like you were judging you?" Still no one moved, and I knew that Sheriff Staunton and the smallness of the community weren't going to let me knock anyone off "for cause." I had picked a bunch of juries, and in a way, this was just one more, yet it wasn't. I had to live for the rest of my life with what this one decided. I had never thought that way as a prosecutor. After twenty minutes of my prodding, the jury was getting antsy. I had asked every question I could think of, to ferret out anyone who might harbor a secret ambition of convicting Reverend Clay. It was time to cut the jury.

We adjourned into the jury room to make our cuts. Lindell II simply sat at counsel table smiling at the jury panel before he struck the folks he thought might be soft on crime.

"What do you think?" I asked Aurora.

Before she could answer Reverend Clay said, "Cut three, five, seven, ten, eleven and fourteen."

"Why?" I asked.

"God spoke to me."

I looked at my notes and with the exception of fourteen the rest were on my cut list. "Good enough for me," I said. We struck those potential jurors and I wondered, if my horoscope from last year was still valid.

CHAPTER THIRTY-ONE

"Gentlemen, as I call your names, please go into the jury box," the judge said.

It was my first hint that Lindell II had struck the three women who were in the front end of the panel. I wondered what his worry was.

The twelve whose names were called filed into the box. "The rest of you can get back to your farms and businesses. You ladies can cook those hard-working men in your lives a good dinner tonight." The judge spoke naturally and without derision.

The twelve in the box were all white. The small black population of the county hadn't produced a single black juror. The local undertaker was the only juror wearing a suit.

"Please stand and raise your right hands and swear after me," the clerk said.

After they had all sworn before God to follow the law and were seated, the judge said, "Mr. Washington, please read the indictment."

Lindell II stood before the jury box and read the grand jury indictment that alleged that Randall Allen Clay had murdered Sarita Jo Franklin "with malice aforethought against the peace and dignity of the state."

The "malice aforethought" allegation simply meant he hadn't done it in a fit of passion and that he meant to do it. Arcane words from an earlier time still defined the crime. After Lindell finished reading the indictment, the Judge said, "How does the defendant plead?"

Clay, Aurora and I rose and Clay said in his best holy voice, "Not guilty, your honor, as God is my witness." He stared earnestly at the jury as he said the words the way we had instructed him. Knowing Clay's way with people I suspected he didn't need our help.

"Call your first witness, Mr. Washington," Judge Hope said with a sing-song weariness of a man who'd rather be fishing.

"State calls Sheriff Staunton, your honor."

I had invoked the "rule" which meant that all of the witnesses had to stay outside so they couldn't hear each other's testimony. The bailiff lifted himself from his chair as if he had been inconvenienced, and slowly walked to the swinging wooden gate that that separated the bar from the gallery. The free-swinging gate continued to swish to and fro in his wake. The courtroom grew deadly quiet. The hard-soled heels of the bailiff's boots struck the marble floor with a cadence that echoed off the light oaken walls. Every eye in the courtroom followed the bailiff to the dark green leather covered padded doors at the back of the courtroom. He carefully pushed one of the doors slightly ajar. It was as if there were wild beasts resting behind the door ready to pounce. The bailiff peered through the crack and said softly, "Sheriff."

The bailiff stepped back from the door and it slid shut. For a moment, the entire courtroom sat motionless, filled with a suffocating sense of anticipation. When the door did not immediately open, there was a subtle stirring in the room, but not one whisper was heard.

I'm not sure, but I think the sheriff had someone open the doors for him. Both doors swung open simultaneously and there was the ramrod straight Sheriff Leonard Staunton standing at attention. He stood in the door for no more than a second before he began to march at double time toward the witness stand. His crisply starched brown khaki uniform was adorned only with a highly polished silver five-pointed star pinned to his chest and patches at the top of each sleeve that said *Sheriff Chambers County Texas*. There were no fancy epaulets or other folderol to distract from his professional appearance. He was wearing military-looking aviator sunglasses. As he approached the wooden gate he stopped and dramatically removed the glasses with his left hand and adeptly hooked them over a button on his shirt. I doubted that it was the first time he'd performed that maneuver. As he marched through the gate I noticed he was carrying his large white Stetson cowboy hat in his right hand. His gait increased as he marched directly in front of the Judge's bench.

"The clerk will swear the witness," Judge Hope commanded.

The sheriff raised his right hand higher than any witness I'd ever seen. It looked like he was reaching into heaven to make sure God was watching. He answered the clerk's inquiry with a solid baritone. "I do." After he swore his oath he stepped into the witness box and Judge Hope said, "Be seated." I was hopeful that the performance was over, but the sheriff had one more move. After he sat down he balanced his white Stetson hat on its crown on the front of the witness box, in case anyone had failed to understand who the good guys were.

Aurora leaned over to me and whispered, "My God, where did they get this guy, central casting?"

"John Wayne wasn't available today," I whispered back. I could only hope that the sheriff was all hat and no cattle.

Lindell II began his direct examination and it was quickly clear that the sheriff was no hillbilly. He answered only what he was asked with a clipped, emotionless expression. "I retired from the Texas Rangers in 1965 to come home and raise cattle. The sheriff at that time died and I saw that this county needed a professional law man. I have served Chambers County ever since."

"Have you testified in court in murder cases few or many times?"

"Over 100 times."

I knew all of the Sheriff's background, yet I hadn't taken him seriously until he testified. Assumptions about opposing counsel or witnesses in a case are always dangerous and sometime fatal. When a trial starts, it is like being in a serious fist fight. You can't ask for a time out. It was too late then to get prepared. When I was a prosecutor, I had laughed at busy defense lawyers who underestimated me. Now the shoe was fitting uncomfortably on the other foot. Managing a law office, your life and a trial was serious business.

Lindell II did a smart thing. He asked the sheriff to describe what he found when he arrived at the crime scene. The sheriff took over and Lindell hardly asked another question. The sheriff's testimony was orderly and short. He came to the scene and found Sarita Jo dead. He found Reverend Clay highly excited and covered in blood. The sheriff pointed at Reverend Clay in response to Lindell II's question about whether the man who was at the ranch covered in blood was in the courtroom. He continued that there was no one else at the ranch and no evidence anyone else had been there. No weapon was ever recovered and Reverend Clay had told them he was to inherit the ranch.

It was as if there was no need to go further with the trial. I had used the same technique many times with professional lawmen. They didn't like to be interrupted with questions. I didn't want to object too much. The jury might think we were trying to hide something. I would remedy it on cross.

"Did the defendant confess to you that he murdered Sarita Jo Franklin?"

"Well, I thought he was about to when Mr. Ward broke into our office."

I was on my feet. "Objection, your honor. The answer is speculative and there is no evidence in this record that I broke into the sheriff's office."

Before Lindell II could respond, Judge Hope said, "Sustained."

"I'd ask for an instruction to the jury that they disregard this inflammatory testimony that's only purpose is to prejudice the jury."

Judge Hope looked bored as he said, "Gents, please don't pay any attention to the sheriff's last answer."

The difficulty with a surprise attack like this is that your only real remedy would be to ask for a mistrial. The jury can never really get the words or images out of their collective mind. I didn't want a mistrial with a client who was in jail. "I'd ask that counsel be reprimanded for soliciting this scurrilous and outrageous testimony."

"Both counsels come up here!" the judge said, now fully engaged.

As we stood before the bench, I looked at Lindell II and shook my head. The judge wasted no time. He whispered, "I won't have a trial conducted on this basis. Lindell, you quit this crap now or I'll declare a mistrial. You know better than this. Ward, you tone it down. We're all gentlemen here and I want this trial conducted accordingly."

We hadn't been in trial twenty minutes and there had been a major dust up. Lindell had tainted the jury's perception of me and my client. I wasn't toning anything down if this kept up. This wasn't my first rodeo. Unfortunately, it wasn't Lindell II's or the sheriff's either.

Lindell had one more question. "Sheriff, did you receive any communication from the defendant as to how he came to be in Sarita Jo Franklin's ranch house?"

"The defendant told us that he got a letter that invited him to her house to discuss Sarita Jo giving him all of her property. He said..."

"Objection, your honor, the witness is testifying to oral admissions of a defendant who was in custody. There is no showing that his rights had been read to him," I said.

"What about it, Mr. Washington?" Judge Hope demanded.

"Was he under arrest, sheriff? Was he free to go when you were talking to him at the ranch house?" Lindell asked.

"We needed to find out what had happened. He didn't ask to leave and we didn't tell him he couldn't. We didn't have enough evidence to arrest him yet. He said she sent him a letter, but I never read any such letter."

The last thing I wanted to do was make the jury think I was trying to spring the Reverend on some nitpicking technicality. Nothing the sheriff had said had really hurt us. The possibility of a letter was in the case. My fear was that some other false statements might be attributed to Clay, and it would be his word against the sheriff's. If I didn't object, it could be deemed that Clay waived his constitutional rights. If I did object, I was taking a chance with the jury. I did the next best thing.

"Any other testimony from the sheriff or any other of your witnesses that's going to include conversations with the defendant?" I asked Lindell II.

"I'm through with direct of this witness."

"No objection, your honor."

I sat down and Lindell II said, "Pass the witness."

I smiled at Aurora and stood up. The sheriff was smirking at me, full of pride that they had Pearl Harbored me with his testimony. I was fully engaged. This prick was going down.

CHAPTER THIRTY-TWO

The crazy part about the case was that there was only one thing for certain. Sarita Jo Franklin had been shot by someone. All I needed to do was to foul the pond of evidence enough to give the jury another reasonable hypothesis than it was Clay.

"You fancy yourself as a superior law enforcement officer, do you not?" I said calmly to Sheriff Staunton.

"I have nearly forty years of experience. I was in the Texas Rangers, which in my opinion is the most elite police force in the world and I have been sheriff in this county for seven years."

"Solved a lot of cases during that time?"

"Too many to count."

"You're one of the top law men in Texas?"

Staunton had testified too many times to be led too far down the primrose path. He smelled a rat. "I am qualified to investigate a murder," he said modestly.

"Assume with me all the facts that you know in this case. Assume that someone asked you to judge the competence of a brother law officer. Assume that brother law officer didn't test the one person he arrested to see if they had fired a gun. Would you think him competent?"

"Objection, your honor, this isn't relevant to this trial," Lindell II said as he jumped to his feet.

I tried to keep the pressure on and asked, "Did you test the defendant to see if he had fired a gun?"

"There wasn't any reason; he was the only one that could have done it."

"I've objected, your honor. He has to stop asking questions. I move this whole line of questions be struck," Lindell insisted.

Judge Hope was late to the party. I could have sworn he was reading a book in his lap like some seventh-grade boy in a math class. "Uh, what is the objection?

"Relevance, your honor," Lindell said, clearly annoyed. He gave me a glance that said, "Do you believe this?"

I couldn't help but laugh. You either love being a judge or you hate every minute of it. Judge Hope clearly fell into the latter category.

"Well, it's cross examination, I'll allow it," the judge said as he glanced into his lap. "But let's get it tied up quickly, Mr. Ward."

"I think I already have, your honor." I said.

Lindell sat down and his frustration showed as he slammed a yellow pad on the counsel table. It was never fun to find these things out while in trial. He had not recognized an important misstep by the Sheriff.

"I don't think I heard your answer, Sheriff. Would you give your fellow officer a passing grade if he forgot to test the defendant's hands to see if he had recently fired a gun?"

"If it was as obvious to him as it was to me that that charlatan from Arkansas sitting next to you did it, I would say it was done well."

"Are you familiar with any modern crime manual that would agree that once you've made up your mind, there is no need to do a routine test to confirm your opinion?"

"He was the only one there. It is seven miles to another house." The sheriff was defiant.

"But that doesn't answer my question, does it?" I taunted.

"Okay, Mr. Ward, you've made your point. Let's move on to another topic," Judge Hope said. He had to live with Sheriff Staunton. He wasn't going to let me destroy him.

"Yes, your honor." I looked at the jury to see what they were doing.

The jury saw me looking and I looked away. There were no telltale signs that they were impressed or bored. It was early, but I always kept my eyes on jurors for clues. One thing I did have to watch was time management. The last thing I wanted was to take too long with the sheriff. Juries and lunch are dangerous. If they are hungry, they lose focus. After lunch, they may not be awake.

"Let's get back to your statement that Reverend Clay was about to confess, but I broke into your office. Is asking to see my client the same as breaking into your office?" I asked.

"We had him ready…"

"No, sir, my question requires only a yes or no answer."

"Well…"

"Yes or no?" I said firmly.

"He's badgering this witness, objection," Lindell II interjected.

"Yes or no?" Judge Hope said, looking down at the sheriff without ruling on the objection.

"No!" Sheriff Staunton said loudly.

"No, it's not breaking in?" I continued.

"It's not breaking in. I just meant that …"

"You've answered the question. The prosecutor can ask you more if he likes. Let's move on to another subject," I said. "You said you never read a letter. Was there a letter, but you just didn't read it?"

"I never saw a letter."

"So, you can't say that Reverend Clay was not an invited guest at Sarita Jo Franklin's house, can you?"

"No, but..."

"Thank you, Sheriff you've answered the question." I cut him off. "Was there evidence that Reverend Clay was staying at Sarita Jo Franklin's house?"

"My deputy looked around and brought down a suitcase with his things in it."

"But you didn't go upstairs?"

"No, I sent Zeke—his full name is Deputy Ezekiel Fontenot—up to look around. I was busy talking to the defendant. I don't remember anything about a letter."

"Did you ever interview any other person before you filed a murder charge on the defendant?"

"I talked to Clete Franklin, the deceased's nephew. Someone had to notify the family that Miss Franklin was dead."

"Did you ask him where he was that morning about the time his only living relative, the deceased, was killed?"

"Good God, no, the man had just lost his aunt."

"So his feelings were more important than doing a thorough investigation?"

"I know Clete. He loved his aunt."

"So your investigation into the death of Sarita Jo Franklin was essentially to pick the only person at the scene who wasn't a local from Chambers County?"

Lindell II was on his feet, "Objection, argumentative."

"Sustained."

I could have cared less. The facts spoke for themselves. A decorated law man had conducted a careless, or was it an intentionally sloppy, investigation. I just had to make the jury care about it. For now, it was a piece of evidence that opened the door to reasonable questions about how Sarita Jo ended up dead on her kitchen floor.

"Pass the witness."

Lindell II's head popped up. He clearly thought I was going to take longer to cross the sheriff. He seemed confused by my brevity.

175

"Any further questions?" Judge Hope asked after fifteen seconds had elapsed.

"No, your honor, subject to recalling the witness later."

"Sheriff, you are excused, but subject to being recalled."

The sheriff stood up in the witness box and put on his sunglasses. He picked up his white hat and walked out of the courtroom. I didn't know how the Chambers County jury had received the testimony, but I was elated.

"Let's take a break for lunch now. It's 11:25, let's be back here at 1:30. Gentlemen of the jury, please don't discuss the case during lunch. What is the special today, R.C.?" the judge said to the juror who ran the only café in town.

"Chicken fried steak with two sides."

"Perfect," the judge said. "We're adjourned."

CHAPTER THIRTY-THREE

We let the jury walk across the street to the Fort Anahuac Café first. They were having lunch in a side alcove of the dining room where the Lion's Club met each Tuesday for lunch. As Aurora and I stood at the top of the courthouse stairs watching the jury walk across the street, we could see the Red Rover was parked on the side of the building. Chinky was lurking somewhere. There was a surprise visitor at the bottom of the steps. Cooper had joined us for lunch.

"How's it going?" she said.

"Jim did a good job on the sheriff," Aurora said as she looked around to assure that the sheriff or the DA weren't nearby.

"Why are you here?" I asked.

"I've never seen you try a case."

"You're not here as a reporter?"

"I took a vacation day," she said with an impish smile.

"We're just going for lunch across the street," I said. "Just be careful. The jury is in there and probably the judge, the court reporter, and half the courthouse employees."

As we walked to the café, Taylor's car rounded the corner and pulled into a spot in front. I was full of adrenaline from the courtroom. His sudden appearance sent my mind into turmoil.

He spotted us and waited beside his car.

"Daddy, what are you doing here?" Cooper said.

"I had a meeting over here this morning and the fella I was meeting with told me that Jim was in trial. I thought it might be interesting to watch."

"I'm going to watch, too," Cooper said.

Taylor never met "with a fella" unless it was business. He was not about wasted motion. He hadn't told me about any deals in Chambers County, but I'd been distracted by the trial.

We found the last four-top table that was empty and sat down. I could see into the alcove, and the jury was already fully involved with their chicken fried steaks. The cream gravy alone would assure that the next witness would be facing a group of twelve men more ready to nap than hear testimony.

"What'll y'all have?" the waitress asked. She was the sympathetic young woman from breakfast. She seemed glad to see us.

"Do you have a vegetable plate?" Aurora asked.

"I could make you up the special without the chicken fried steak. You could have another side."

"What vegetable do you have?"

"We have them all, corn, mashed potatoes, hush puppies, French fries, rice and fried okra. Personally, I like the okra best. You could get two portions."

Trials were hard on my stomach. I never ate during them. The food smells of the café had me on the verge of nausea. On a regular day, I would have been happy with sampling the special.

"I'll just have the special," Taylor said.

"Me, too," Cooper said.

"Iced tea for me," I said.

Aurora was pondering the one page menu. Clearly the delicacies of the Fort Anahuac Café were new to her. "Get the catfish," I said with a grin.

She looked at me as if I had lost my mind. "Could you bring me an egg white omelet, with spinach?"

The waitress looked amused and said, "I think I saw a can of spinach in the kitchen. Let me see what I can do."

After the waitress left, I noticed Chinky and her cameraman sitting in the corner of the room. She nodded at me and I nodded back. After I nodded, I turned back to the table to find Cooper staring at me. Her head was shaking slowly from side to side. "Amazing how Chinky thinks this is the trial of the century," she said with an edge that made me wince.

"It's had some play on the other stations in Houston. I even got a call from Beaumont about an interview," I said. "This preacher thing and the vigil is news."

"Taylor, why are you here again?" I said. I wanted to change the subject.

"Just a little oil deal."

"Did you want me to draft some paper on it?"

"It's just a routine deal. I used the Producers 88 form. That Producers 88 is just fine. I've used that printed form for years and never had a problem."

"I know you're used to doing your own leases, but there is a lot of new case law that you probably don't know about. I'm happy to help."

"Naw, I got this. You're in trial. You need to stay focused on that preacher man. There is a lot of money at stake," Taylor said.

He was right. Clete had filed a will contest to challenge Sarita Jo's will and the ranch deed to Reverend Clay. If her will and the deed were declared invalid she would die intestate. That meant that Clete, her only living heir, would inherit it all under state law. The will contest case was on hold pending resolution of our criminal trial. If Clay was found guilty, he could not inherit from Sarita Jo and her will would become invalid. None of that worried me. I had whatever was left of Clay's life in my hands. Money wasn't my concern.

The judge and his clerk walked in to the café while we waited for our food. A table had cleared next to us and they sat down.

Taylor stood and held out his right hand. "Judge Hope, Taylor Faircloth, it's good to see you again."

"Mr. Faircloth, I know who you are and appreciate your past support. I'm glad to see you. Your son-in-law is doing a fine job."

I knew that Taylor put money into every district court race in East Texas. Lawsuits could be painful for a fellow who hadn't been politically involved in the election process. I was happy to see that Judge Hope knew we were all friends.

I surveyed the room and noticed that pretty much my whole universe was here, wife, former lover, father-in-law, law partner, judge and jury. It was hard to imagine something less comfortable. Conversation was restricted to the weather, the recent reelection of Richard Nixon, and the question of whether the Dow Jones Industrial would crack 1000. About the only person of importance in my life not there was Wells. I was staring at my ice tea thinking about the sheriff's testimony when I heard Aurora say, "Wells, what are you doing here?"

"I wanted to be here when Little Harry testifies. I wanted to make that little prick…"

"Wells, have you met Judge Hope?" Aurora interrupted.

"I'm sorry, Judge, I didn't see you sitting there. Are you coming out to the hunting camp this year? You know it's about that time again."

"I wouldn't miss it for the world. Are you going to have all of the Harris County judges out this year?"

"The fun ones, anyway. It'll be a big time. I'll call you and let you know when the birds start flying."

"You do that."

Wells pulled up a chair and sat down. I'd had enough excitement for one lunch. "Can you wrap up a piece of pie for me?" I asked the waitress.

"You taking it over to the preacher?"

"I am."

"You wish him good luck from me. We sent apple pie to the jail for lunch today. You want a piece of black bottom? It's real good."

"That'll do," I said. I looked at Cooper and said, "I'll see y'all over there."

As luck would have it, Chinky and her cameraman were headed toward the door at the same time. I froze at the table until they were out the door. Cooper eyed her all the way across the room. The pie arrived and I deemed it safe to leave.

"Don't get lost," Cooper said.

After lunch, the cast of courtroom characters had reassembled. Judge Hope entered the courtroom as the bailiff said, "All rise."

"Call your next, Mr. Washington," the judge said.

"The State calls Carolyn Fisk, M.D."

The bailiff began his languid stroll to the hallway door. This time he stepped out into the hall and returned with Dr. Fisk in tow.

After she was sworn, Lindell II began asking the questions to predicate the witness being admitted as an expert witness. After his second question I rose and said, "Your honor, we stipulate that Carolyn Fisk, M.D. is an expert in the field of medical autopsies. I have offered Dr. Fisk as an expert myself on several occasions."

"She will be so admitted," the judge said.

Lindell II looked at me and said, "Thank you Mr. Ward. Now Dr. Fisk did you perform an autopsy on Sarita Jo Franklin on or about September 5, 1972."

"I did."

"I'll hand you what is marked as State's Exhibit 10. Is this a written report of your findings from that autopsy?"

"It is."

"Can you summarize your findings?"

"Miss Franklin was a 61-year old woman in declining health. I found evidence of significant coronary artery disease and liver damage, perhaps caused by alcohol consumption, as well as almost crippling arthritis in her lower extremities. Her medical records reflect she was injured in a significant accident with a horse. She had been shot once just above the medial line of her chest. The entry wound was remarkable in that there were significant powder burns at the point of entry."

"So she had been shot at close range."

"Apparently, she also had powder burns on her right hand."

"As if she had grabbed the weapon?"

"Yes."

"Go on."

"The small caliber bullet entered on a significantly downward trajectory first striking her in her Xiphoid, or lower sternum. The projectile then traveled downward striking the coastal cartilage of her rib severing the coastal artery. The projectile was then deflected into the decedent's liver and traveled out into her retroperitoneal space. In lay terms, it made a mess of her liver. I found a .22 caliber bullet fragment located immediately anterior to her liver."

"I'll show you a photograph that has been marked as State's Exhibit Number 11. Have you seen this photo before?"

"Yes, it is the bullet fragment that I removed from the deceased's body."

"Does it fairly and accurately depict the bullet that you removed from the deceased?"

"It does."

"Did you determine the cause of death of Sarita Jo Franklin?"

"I did. She died from a single gunshot wound that caused internal bleeding in her retroperitoneal cavity. She might have survived a gunshot from a bigger weapon. The bullet I recovered is from a type of weapon that is commonly referred to as a 'Saturday Night Special' on the streets of Houston. The low velocity of the bullet allowed it to deflect inside her body leading to catastrophic hemorrhage."

"In lay terms, she bled to death."

"Yes."

"Pass the witness."

As I rose to begin my cross of the medical examiner, I caught a glimpse of Chinky, Cooper, Wells, and Taylor. It was disconcerting. The people whose opinion mattered the most sat in the audience ready to judge me. It was as if two juries were in the room. I fought to regain focus.

"Dr. Fisk, it's good to see you again," I said cheerily.

"Thank you, Mr. Ward, you too."

"Now, Dr. Fisk given your vast experience in doing autopsies, is it possible for you to determine the height of the assailant?"

"Based on the powder burns on her right hand and the steep angle of descent of the bullet I can say that the gunman was taller than Miss Franklin or at least was standing at a higher level than she, but I can't speculate on height, per se."

"But assuming that the assailant must have been standing directly in front of the deceased at the moment the shot was fired because Miss Franklin's right hand was burned, could you offer an opinion then?"

"Objection, calls for speculation," Lindell II said loudly.

"That's what expert witnesses do, Mr. Washington," Judge Hope said. "Assuming it's in her area of expertise. Is it Dr. Fisk?"

"Yes, your honor, to a point."

"I'll let it in. She's your witness, Mr. Washington. You can try to clear up what she says on redirect. You may answer the question, Dr. Fisk."

"Assuming that the assailant was standing directly in front of the deceased, the shooter would have likely been at least two or three inches taller than Miss Franklin, taking the angle of descent into consideration. I suspect she grabbed the gun and pulled it down before it was fired," Dr. Fisk answered.

"If that's the case, is it possible the shooter could have been even taller than two or three inches taller than the deceased."

"Yes."

"Do you know how tall the defendant is?"

"No."

"Please stand up, Reverend Clay." Clay rose from his chair. "Can you estimate how tall Reverend Clay is?"

"He looks under six feet."

"If I told you that he is five feet nine, would you think that is true?"

"That appears about right."

"How tall was Sarita Jo Franklin?"

"I need to refresh my memory from my report."

"Please, go ahead."

Dr. Fisk looked through her report for a moment and then said, "She was approximately one hundred-eighty-nine centimeters. So she was close to five foot eleven or six feet tall at the time of her death."

"What position would an assailant no more than five feet ten have to be in in order to shoot the deceased at the angle the bullet entered her chest?"

"If he were standing directly in front of her his hand would have to be over his head."

"That seem likely?" I asked.

"Objection, your honor."

"Sustained. Even for opinion, I think we're outside the witness's expertise."

"Pass the witness."

Lindell II was in front of his witness like a shot. "Now what if she was sitting down? Then a shorter person could have shot her, right?" he asked.

"It's possible that it could have happened that way."

"Pass the witness."

"Would a person sitting down present their body in a way that it was more or less likely that the trajectory of the bullet would have been the one you examined?"

"That's a good question. My instinct tells me no, but I haven't studied it."

"Pass the witness."

"So, you're only guessing?"

"It's an informed guess."

"But a guess, nevertheless?"

"Yes."

"Pass the witness."

"No more questions, your honor." I said, satisfied with the outcome. My job was to muddy the water. I might not have won it with this testimony, but the water was getting cloudy.

"You're excused, Dr. Fisk." Judge Hope said. "Call your next, Mr. Washington."

"State calls Harrison Chambers," Lindell II said.

Once again, the bailiff began the arduous journey to the back of the courtroom. He opened one of the doors and said, "Mr. Chambers, you're up."

Harrison Chambers moved quickly to the front of the bench.

"No need to swear you, Mr. Chambers, you are an officer of the court."

"Thank you, your honor."

"State your name to the court and jury," Lindell II said.

"Harrison Franklin Chambers."

"Any kin to the deceased in this case?"

"No, just a coincidence."

"How did you know the deceased in this case?"

"I was her lawyer for many years."

"When was the last time you saw Sarita Jo Franklin?"

"When she came to my office with that fellow over there."

"You mean the defendant, Randall Clay?"

"Yes, sir."

"What did she come to see you about?"

At that moment, something occurred to me that I should have thought of earlier. "Objection, your honor. We have a significant issue to discuss with the court and would ask that the jury be taken out at this time," I said.

"Approach the bench," Judge Hope said.

When Lindell II and I arrived at the bench, Judge Hope said, "What's your objection?"

"Attorney-client privilege, your honor. Sarita Jo Franklin consulted with her lawyer and received legal advice. Without a waiver of the privilege, we don't believe that Mr. Chambers can testify without breaching the privilege."

"Who's the independent executor? Wouldn't the independent executor be able to waive the privilege?" the judge responded.

"Reverend Clay has filed an application for probate, and the will he has submitted names him the independent executor. Clete Franklin has filed a contest of the will claiming fraud, and also that Reverend Clay murdered Sarita Jo Franklin and is therefore disqualified to serve as executor or inherit her estate. The county judge has stayed that hearing, pending the outcome of this case," I said.

"So there is not even a temporary executor managing the estate?" the judge said.

"We advised the county judge that there must be someone appointed, but he has said he isn't going to try this case twice. I may be able to solve the issue. I request that I...or Mrs. Wilson be allowed to take the witness on *voir dire* outside the jury's hearing to determine what he is going to say. If we are satisfied, we'll waive our objection as to this case." I said.

"What if Mr. Chambers won't testify?" the judge said. "He may not want to be in a position of taking a chance of waiving the privilege and getting sued by whomever is ultimately appointed the independent executor."

Harrison Chambers was a cocky little man. He sat in the witness chair hearing the discussion and it was pretty clear that he wished he'd never heard of Sarita Jo or the Reverend.

"What say you, Lindell?" the judge said.

Before he could answer, I said, "It looks to me like you can take him off the stand if you won't agree to the *voir dire*. There is nobody to waive the privilege. You're going to have to give us a peek at his testimony or put him in real jeopardy."

"I don't want to testify," Harrison Chambers said in the deepest voice he could muster.

"Wait a minute!" Lindell II said. "If these are all documents of public record, then they can be admitted into evidence. He can just agree that he drew them up and they can stand for themselves."

"Ward, I think he's got a point," the judge said.

"Well, we are going to continue our objection," I said, fairly sure that we were screwed. Sometimes brilliant ideas in trial go awry.

"Bring back the jury," the judge said to the bailiff.

"I don't want to testify," Chambers said again.

"Can't help you, Harry," the judge said as the jury filed back in the courtroom. "You may proceed, Mr. Washington."

"Mr. Chambers, I'm going to show you two documents that have been filed for public record in the deed and probate records of Chambers County, Texas. Do you recognize these documents?"

Harry looked around for an escape from the courtroom, but there was none. "I drafted them."

"And who was your client?"

"Sarita Jo Franklin was my client."

"Before you met him in your office, you hadn't ever seen hide nor hair of Randall Clay, had you? Miss Franklin had never mentioned him to you, isn't that right?"

I was holding on to my chair trying to keep from objecting to the question. The second question called for a hearsay answer, but I didn't want the jury thinking we were hiding anything. Besides I was pretty sure the whole adventure of Sarita Jo and Reverend Clay was common knowledge on the streets of Anahuac.

"Nope, never seen him before," Chambers said.

"Was your client getting senile?"

"Not that I knew about. I mean she was getting old, but I thought she knew what she was doing, even if I thought what she wanted to do was kind of crazy."

"Did the defendant appear to have some unnatural sway over Sarita Jo?"

"No."

"No further questions."

I had assumed from the beginning that Aurora would cross-examine Little Harry. Now there was a real question of whether we should just let it go.

"Let him go," Aurora said, and we did. He hadn't hurt us and if we kept him on the stand, he might.

"No questions, your honor," Aurora said.

"Call your next, Mr. Washington." the judge said.

"Your honor, we hadn't expected to get so far in this case in one day. We request a recess until tomorrow morning at nine a.m."

"No objection," I said.

"Gentlemen of the jury we will stand in recess until nine o'clock in the morning. Now don't go talking with your family, friends or neighbors about this case, you hear?"

The jury all nodded their heads yes, but they couldn't wait to get home to tell everybody about their day in court.

"Only one more witness to go for the state," I said.

No one was listening because Reverend Clay and Aurora were in a serious whisper conversation. After the deputy led our client back to the jail I said, "What was that about?"

"I'm not sure if it's important or just more of Clay's preaching. 'Expect a miracle, tomorrow' is all he said.

I really didn't care. I felt great. Surely there was nothing I'd done today that wasn't good enough.

"Good job," Cooper said. "Chinky wants to interview you on the courthouse steps in the morning."

"I think I'll tell her no. Things have been going too well. I don't want to jinx them."

"I'll talk to her. No need for her to bother you," Cooper said.

"Tell her legal ethics prevent me from commenting. I'm happy to talk to her after the trial."

"How do you think it's going?" Taylor asked Aurora.

"Jim's doing fine. This is a screwy murder case. I've never seen one move so fast," Aurora said.

"Yeah, but you're going to get him off, right?" Taylor continued.

His interest in my winning seemed unusual, but I humored him. "Have him back on the street converting souls by tomorrow night," I said. After I said it, I wished I hadn't. Not that I was superstitious or anything.

CHAPTER THIRTY-FOUR

The anticipation of cross-examining Clete Franklin was building as Aurora, Wells and I barreled toward Chambers County. Wells was so taken with the trial that he got up early to ride with us.

"What do you think Lindell II is going to try to do with him?" Wells asked.

"Lindell is in a tight spot. As a prosecutor, I sometimes got left with bits and pieces of what I thought I could prove. You have a theory that sounds good until you realize that all you have is wish and innuendo rather than real proof. The problem for us is the local people may be looking at this through the sheriff's prism. I don't know that Lindell has a case that will survive a motion for instructed verdict unless Clete says he saw Clay shoot her. Of course the judge doesn't want to grant our motion and take the heat for possibly letting a murderer go free. It's easier for him to deny the motion and see if the jury will do it for him. If they don't, he can always reconsider and grant a new trial. I only wish I didn't have to put Clay on the stand. He could blow the whole thing if he starts a sermon on the Prosperity Gospel," I said.

"Just take it slow and easy with Clete. I think he is a powder keg ready to blow," Aurora said.

"Keep me under control. I don't want to get into a fight with him that makes him look good. Drop your pen on the table if you see it happening. That'll be my cue to slow down."

"Let me take him. I will intimidate him. He isn't going to like being questioned by a woman. You can drop a pen if I'm going at him too hard."

I drove the Lincoln for a mile while I considered her offer.

"She's so smooth when she crosses me at home that I never know where she's going until she's tied me in a knot," Wells said. I could tell he wasn't kidding. I looked to see what she was wearing. She'd wisely put on a tailored suit that included a skirt. I tried to think of a single time I'd seen a woman handle a significant part of a trial. No lawyer in his right mind would allow this woman near this cross.

"O.K." I said, "but don't fuck this up." I wanted to take it back immediately, but it was done.

"Don't worry; I've dealt with bullies before," she said, and I prayed she was right.

"I have to ask the client," I added.

"He'll be fine. I talked to him about it yesterday."

"You should have asked me first."

"He brought it up. He says God told him to do it."

"So now God is running our partnership?"

"It could be worse," Wells said with a laugh.

At 9 o'clock, the cast of characters was assembled. Judge Hope ascended to the bench and said, "Be seated. Mr. Washington, call your next."

"State calls Cletus Franklin, Your Honor."

The bailiff ambled to the back of the courtroom. He opened the door into the hall and said, "Mr. Franklin, you're up."

Clete Franklin burst through the door into the courtroom with his eyes darting around as if he was looking for the fellow who had stolen his horse. His starched blue jeans were creased. His coat was a western-cut sports jacket that was made of brown suede-looking material. A string tie with sparkling silver tabs adorned his white western-cut shirt. He sauntered through the swinging gate into the bar area of the court with the assurance that he felt comfortable to be there. Clete Franklin had gotten what he wanted throughout most of his life. After he was sworn, he didn't sit down in the witness chair quickly like most do. He looked around the room with a defiant, tightlipped arrogance that caused most to look away. Finally, he turned his gaze to me and made it clear that he wished this was a fist fight.

"Have a seat and state your name to the court and this jury," Lindell II said to stop Clete's performance.

"Cletus A. Franklin."

"Tell the jury about yourself."

"Well most of them know me personally, but I own the Circle C Ranch over at High Island. I've lived around here all my life. I was the captain of the 1958 state champion 1A football team here in Anahuac."

"So you've lived around here all your life?"

"So far!" he said with a broad smile on his face. There was a ripple of nervous laughter that washed over the courtroom. Judge Hope sat up straight in his chair, but said nothing.

"You kin to Sarita Jo Franklin?"

"My dear aunt, may she rest in peace," he said and he made an exaggerated glance to the heavens.

"Had you seen your aunt close to the time she was killed?"

"I had, indeed. I went by her place, as I often did, to check on her right before Labor Day. It was clear to me she was crazy."

188

All six feet of Aurora was out of her chair quickly. "Objection, Your Honor, the witness is not qualified to offer such an opinion." Her British accent sounded elegant as it floated through the courtroom. Clete's jaw dropped and his face screwed up in a knot. He continued looking at her as the judge said, "Sustained, the jury will disregard."

Lindell II continued. "Well, Mr. Franklin, can you describe your aunt's behavior that caused you to be concerned about her?"

"I asked if I could take care of her place for her and she got mad. Now she and I always had a good relationship. She used to take me to town to the movie house when it was open."

"But now she was not friendly and loving, as she had been in the past?"

"No, I was real worried about her."

"Had she ever mentioned the defendant to you on your many visits to see her?"

"Never, that fellow came out of Arkansas like a thief in the night."

"Objection," Aurora said calmly.

"Sustained. Mr. Franklin, just answer the question that is asked. The jury will disregard the answer," the judge said in a monotone.

"Had you always helped your aunt at her place, particularly after her accident?"

"Why, yes, she'd have had to go to a nursing home if it weren't for everything I did for her. I was all she had."

"You are aware that she wrote a will only a few days before she was killed, giving Palmetto Ranch, which has been in the Franklin family since 1856, to the defendant?"

"Yes I am. Far as I know, it's the first will she ever did."

The more I heard Clete talk, the more it sounded like he was drunk. The bravado he exhibited was the work of alcohol, not confidence.

"Have you filed a will contest in Chambers County Court to set the new will aside?"

"Objection, not relevant," Aurora said. Every time she spoke she became the center of attention in the room.

"Sustained, the jury will not consider any civil proceedings that are pending between these parties. Jury will disregard."

Lindell knew what he was doing. Every question was designed to put inadmissible information in the jurors' minds that would not be disregarded. If the jury convicted Clay, it would be hard to reverse unless a juror would admit they used the excluded information to make the decision.

"Now, Mr. Franklin, did you ever receive a copy of a letter from Sarita Jo Franklin in which she advised you that she was writing this will?"

"Never."

"So to sum up your testimony, is it fair to say you were surprised by your aunt's actions regarding her estate after all you had done for her?"

I looked at Aurora and she was gauging whether to object to the question as leading the witness. She sat, still focused on Clete's face.

"Yes, I loved my aunt and she loved me. She was like a second mother to me. There had to be something wrong with her if she did what she did. It just makes me so mad."

"Pass the witness."

Aurora rose slowly from her chair and walked around in front of the counsel table. "It made you so mad you killed her, didn't you?"

Simultaneously, Lindell II and Clete were yelling.

"Objection, Your Honor, there is no evidence in the record to support such an outrageous question."

Clete was absolutely red-faced. He stood up as if he was coming to strike Aurora but his pugilistic tendencies were hobbled by the witness box. He shouted, "Goddamn your sorry ass, you bitch."

"Bailiff, take the jury to the jury room. I want to see counsel in my chambers." The judge left the bench.

I looked at Aurora and she was calm. The whole macho physical scene had me ready to fight. Putting Aurora up had been a good decision. She didn't have to prove her manhood.

"He's drunk, at least that's what I think," I said to her.

"So do I, and Lindell has to know it now. He's going to ask for a recess to sober him up."

When we were all in chambers, the judge said, "We're going to cut this off right now. If you have some evidence that Clete killed his aunt, then put it on. If not then don't ask these inflammatory questions."

"I'm certainly ready to explore his role in the murder, Your Honor," Aurora said. She was the only calm person in the room.

"My witness is so upset, Your Honor, that I think we should take a recess," Lindell II said.

"Your Honor, his witness is drunk. That's why he wants a recess. If he's not drunk, let's get this finished up," Aurora said.

"Is he drunk, Lindell? He usually is," Judge Hope said.

"Of course not, Your Honor."

"Then let's get this done. Bailiff, bring the jury back."

"Well, maybe we should give him an hour to recover his composure," Lindell II said.

"I move the court find him in contempt of court," I said helpfully.

The judge looked at me with a frown and said, "Don't be a smart ass." I took it as a compliment.

"I'll give you an hour to, as you put it, 'let him gain his composure,'" the judge said. "You tell that witness of yours to clean up his mouth or he can spend the night in jail."

"There won't be any more of it, Your Honor," Lindell said.

Aurora and I followed Lindell II out of the judge's chambers. "Hot black coffee will probably help his composure," she taunted.

Lindell II looked over his shoulder at a woman at least an inch taller than he and shook his head with a look of disgust. A woman in the courtroom was proving tough on everyone.

Clay was sitting at the counsel table when we returned. He had a tight-lipped smile on his face that I'd not seen before.

"Gather around close," he said conspiratorially.

The three of us stood together in a small huddle. "I knew God would provide," Clay whispered. "Deputy Zeke has the letter. He has seen the light of redemption. God be praised."

"Where is he?" I said.

"He's gone to New Jerusalem. He's waiting for you there. He's hiding at Marrow's RV." Clay said.

Aurora looked at me grinning ear to ear. "Let's get going, we've got an hour."

The letter wouldn't prove that Clay was innocent, but it would make it clear that he was invited to visit Palmetto Ranch, and it would cast reasonable suspicion on Clete. The best part was that it would embarrass the sheriff and weaken his testimony about the investigation.

191

CHAPTER THIRTY-FIVE

Our frequent visits to the camp in our lawyer clothes had diminished their anxiety. We made our way through the trucks with campers, tents and campfires to the back of the encampment where Marrow's luxurious RV was parked. He was meeting with the Elders at the picnic table in front of his RV. He abruptly stood as he saw us.

"We'll take this up in the morning," he said to the assembly.

We greeted the Elders as they left the table. They eyed Aurora curiously as they always did. We sat at the picnic table after they were gone. "Is he here?" Aurora said hopefully.

"Well, not *here*," Marrow said. "I hid him in the remnants of the old brick kiln over there." He pointed at the ruined brick kiln near where the old fort had stood.

"How's his pulse beating?" I said.

Neither Aurora nor Marrow had any idea what I was asking. They looked puzzled. "Is he going to help?" I interpreted.

"He's scared silly. I don't think he will testify."

"I really need him to testify. Let's get down there before he runs off. We don't want to let him get cold feet," I said. There was something about a man hiding in a kiln getting cold feet that made me laugh.

Aurora ignored the distraction and said, "We need to maintain a chain of custody with him for evidence purposes. I assume he's had the letter exclusively since he found it. I'd like to take possession of the letter, but then we would have to take the stand to prove it is the letter he gave us."

"I agree, but I don't like the idea of any delay. Should we tell Lindell we have the letter?"

"What's the fun in that? Don't you want to make a splash when we call him? Put Clay on first. Lindell is going to mock his testimony about the letter. When the sheriff's own deputy puts it in evidence, it will be a show stopper," Aurora said, smiling wickedly.

"We could recall Clay to confirm that the letter that Zeke found is the one Clay received from Sarita Jo. I know that would really frost Lindell II's ass. Clete is known to these people as a bully. Let's pass him when we get back in court. They'll rest and we'll put on our case if we can't get a motion for an instructed verdict of not guilty."

"Let's get over to the kiln," Aurora said.

Zeke was nowhere in sight when we approached the kiln. This was the historic ruin where William B. Travis, martyred at the Alamo, had been held by the Mexican army in 1832.

"Zeke?" Marrow said quietly. There was no sign of him. "Zeke?" Marrow called out again. "It's us. Everything is okay. Are you here?" Silence.

Panicked that Zeke had fled, we stared into the darkness of the large fireplace at the back of the ruin. There was a movement. Zeke stepped from the shadows. "Are you alone?"

"I told you we would protect you," Marrow said.

"You don't know how vindictive he is. I won't testify. I'll leave and never come back if that's your plan," Zeke said.

"Do you have the letter?" Aurora asked.

"Yes, God help me."

"May I read it?" I said.

Zeke inhaled deeply and said, "Yes, but I'm scared to death."

"We have the press interested in this case. The sheriff wouldn't dare to do anything to you. He might get indicted if he isn't careful," Aurora said.

Zeke handed me the letter and said, "You don't know how it works here in Chambers Country." It was in its original opened envelope. It was neatly typed on Palmetto Ranch stationary. There was a postscript in what had to be Sarita's handwriting.

I sent a copy of this letter to my nephew who may kill me. He wants to put me in a nursing home. If he kills me please let the sheriff know. SJF

Sarita's cold dead finger pointed at Clete from the grave. It was exactly the alternate theory I needed to raise reasonable doubt. "Zeke, how did you get this letter?" I said.

"I searched the bedroom where the Reverend's things were at Palmetto. I found the letter on the dresser. I took it downstairs to show it to the Sheriff, but he said he was fixin' to interrogate Reverend Clay. I took it back upstairs and put it in my briefcase. I guess I forgot it was there until I heard that you were asking questions about it in the trial. I guess the sheriff must have forgotten about it too."

This was a dilemma without an easy solution. Zeke's story defied logic. In a different universe, I would have jumped at the chance to cross-examine him. But discrediting the far-fetched story of a man who would now be my witness was not why I was in Anahuac. As his lawyer, walking Reverend Clay out the front door of the Chambers County Courthouse was my only job. How could I get the letter in without Zeke? I needed time to think.

193

"You hold on to this letter for now. I wish I could make a copy, but the only place in town with a Xerox machine is the county clerk's office. I don't want anybody to know what we have," I said. "Stay here in the kiln until we send for you."

He put the letter back in its envelope and nodded. I watched him recede into the darkness of the ruin and I pitied him his plight even though his story stunk. Aurora, Marrow and I walked about fifty yards away from the kiln to talk privately.

"Watch him like a hawk," I said to Marrow.

"I think he's good. The Reverend has been working on him for weeks. He is solid, washed in the blood. He isn't going anywhere." Marrow said.

"Hallelujah," Aurora murmured.

I wasn't so sure. I stared out over the park that had once been a Mexican fort desperately looking for a gambit that would get the letter into evidence without Zeke taking the stand. Clay's case hung in the balance. I don't know if it was desperation, inspiration or insanity, but a thoroughly risky plan lit up my brain.

"Aurora, change of plan. Go back to the kiln and get Zeke. Take him back to the holding cell. Tell him to give the letter to Clay, and tell Clay not to worry. I have a plan. I'll meet you in the courtroom. Marrow, you can get back to the flock."

I wasn't laughing at Clay's rants anymore. He seemed to always know what was going to happen. I didn't have time to let him in on my plan, although I was beginning to think he already knew.

I needed to clear my head and prepare for a final battle. I walked over to the edge of the bluff and stared out at Trinity Bay. This was the same bay that William Travis had looked at as he was incarcerated in the kiln. I wondered if he'd been scared and unsure of himself as he waited to see what his fate would be. At this moment, I was in need of the courage that sustained this Texas hero through his tribulations. This plan of mine could end up being a holy mess. A gentle breeze blew in from the bay and it calmed me. It was silly to think it was a message from Travis, but deep in my soul I wanted to believe it. Murder trials do funny things to your head.

Aurora was sitting at the counsel table when I came back to the courtroom.

"Zeke in the courthouse?" I asked.

194

"He was hiding in an office next to the holding cell the last time I saw him. He was going into the holding cell to drop off the letter when the coast was clear."

"All rise," the bailiff said.

"Gentlemen, are we ready to proceed?" Judge Hope said. He realized his error and said, "And lady." We all nodded agreement. "Bailiff, bring in the defendant."

The bailiff disappeared into the holding cell area and returned with the Reverend. Zeke was nowhere in sight.

The judge looked down at Clete sitting in the witness box. "You composed?" he asked sternly.

Clete looked like a small boy who had been chastised by his mother. "Yes sir, sorry about my outburst." Lindell had obviously been feeding Clete more than black coffee during the break.

"Proceed," the judge said.

"Pass the witness," Aurora said.

Lindell looked at me as if I'd done something wrong. I smiled at him and shrugged my shoulders. He frowned back. "Nothing further, Your Honor. The State rests," Lindell II said as he continued to frown at me.

Judge Hope sat upright in his chair and addressed the jury. "Gentlemen of the jury, the State has rested its case."

This was a critical moment in the case. The State has the burden of proof in a criminal case. A jury has nothing to decide if the judge finds that the State has not proved a *prima facie* case. In a circumstantial case like this one, a prosecutor is always haunted by a dread that he has missed an element of the offense or not sufficiently tied the defendant to the crime. It hardly ever happens.

"You want me to handle the motion for instructed verdict?" Aurora said.

"Really?"

"I'm really good at these kinds of arguments."

It all made me nervous. I could see headlines: *"Girl Lawyer Springs Reverend."*

"No, I got this," I replied. I would have just as soon let her do the argument, but the specter of having to explain to the world that I needed a woman lawyer to win my first case on the defense side wouldn't let me take the chance.

"Mr. Ward, are you ready to proceed?"

"Yes, Your Honor."

195

"How many witnesses, do you have?"

"I have a motion first, Your Honor."

"You and Lindell II approach the bench. We'll handle this from here." Clearly the judge didn't want anything I said to get back to the jury. The gallery was packed with friends, relatives and neighbors of members of the jury.

Lindell II and I stood before the bench. The masked court reporter joined us. She brought her little reel-to-reel tape recorder that captured her comments and plugged it in next to the bench. She was standing beside me with her steno mask tightly strapped to her face. Her reporting was not so noticeable when we were at counsel table. Now we were standing 18 inches apart.

"Judge," I began.

There was a soft but unmistakable echo in my ear. "Judge," the reporter repeated into her mask. I struggled to continue.

"Judge," I began again.

Once again, the reporter repeated, "Judge." It sounded as if she was mumbling under water.

I decided that I had to get it out quickly. I blurted, in rapid-fire fashion, "We request that this honorable court instruct the jury to find the defendant not guilty. The State has failed to establish a *prima facie* case. There is no evidence that Reverend Randall Clay played any role in the death of Sarita Jo Franklin, never mind killed her. There is nothing in the record that would sustain a finding of guilt." It was not my finest hour of oratory. The masked reporter dutifully repeated each of my words a second or two behind me. For some reason, it all just left me breathless.

"It's a circumstantial case. It's a jury question. I overrule the motion," Judge Hope said without delay. To make it worse, each word of his ruling was repeated from under water in my ear.

I turned to go back to counsel table and my eyes met Aurora's. Suddenly I wished I'd let her argue the motion. I trudged back to the table, defeated and nervous. It was time for the Reverend Randall Clay show. I hoped he was ready. We hadn't had an opportunity to talk about my plan. The judge's voice brought me back into focus.

"Call your first, Mr. Ward."

CHAPTER THIRTY-SIX

This moment in the trial had been on my mind since the first day I met the Reverend Randall Clay. In a perfect world, I would have molded his testimony into a tight, coherent and understandable denial of his guilt of this baseless charge. But Clay would never give in to my idea of a perfect world. He was going to deny his guilt, but in the way he perceived that God had preordained. If Zeke had given Clay the letter we were in business.

"The defense calls the Reverend Randall Clay."

Before Clay could walk away to be sworn, I whispered, "Did Zeke get the letter to you?"

Clay stared straight ahead and said nothing. His right hand slowly rose to his chest and he gently patted his coat. He turned his head toward me slightly. His face showed no sign of anxiety.

Judge Hope turned to the jury and said, "Gentlemen of the jury, the State has rested its case. The defense will now present their case."

Clay began his walk to the witness box. He stopped before the jury box, bowed slightly to the jury, and said, "Good afternoon." Most of the jury members smiled and nodded back. At least two said "Reverend" as a greeting. It was totally unheard of, but Clay had an understanding of people. He had made contact with them on a personal level before he even made it to the witness stand. I wished I had thought of it. It was brilliant.

Judge Hope sat up in his chair and gazed down on the moment but said nothing. Lindell II had risen about halfway out of his chair to object, but slumped back down without a word. Clay stood before the judge.

"Please raise your right hand. The clerk will swear the witness."

After the clerk read the oath, Clay turned to the jury and said, "So help me Gaaawd."

The jury was alert and showed no signs of lethargy from whatever gastronomical concoction the Fort Anahuac Café had fed them at lunch. They watched Clay closely as he sat in the witness chair.

"State your name to the court," I said.

"Reverend Randall Allan Clay."

"I assume by your title that you are a man of the cloth."

"I am an ordained minister."

"Do you serve a church?"

"My church is not a physical place. I bring God's word to the people through their radios."

"How long have you so done?"

197

"Three years."

"Do you have many listeners?"

"The latest number of souls we routinely reach is approximately 4,000."

"How do you know that?"

"The radio station subscribes to a service that measures listenership."

"When does your radio program air?"

"It's on every night for thirty minutes on a station from Little Rock."

"But you yourself live in Hope, Arkansas?"

"I do."

"And your program is recorded?"

"It has been while I have been confined here in Anahuac. I do the show live, normally."

"What denomination are you?"

"My ministry is not affiliated with a denomination."

"Why is that?"

"I believe that God has commanded me to follow his will. That will is not predicated on the church of man. My ministry is based on God's will as written in the words of the Bible."

"Was it God's plan that you end up in jail?"

"It was, and originally when I was wrongly placed in a cell, I cried out to God and asked him why he had forsaken me. I forgot that as a Christian, I was ordained to accept his will for me on this earth. Sometimes when things aren't going the way we think they should, we think we're in charge of our lives. That's just ego talking, Mr. Ward. I got the answer when I prayed to God. He told me why I had to suffer in this way."

"And what did he tell you?"

"He revealed his wisdom for my life, to help me understand his word. He rebuked me for not trusting that he was a good God. God has no need for us to suffer. Jesus did that on the cross to redeem our sins. God asked me, 'Randall, have you not read the words of James? Look up James 4:1-3: 'You do not have because you do not ask. You ask and do not receive because you ask with wrong motives so that you may spend it on your pleasures.' After God came to me, I saw that we will prosper if we do his will. I wasn't wrongly accused in order to punish me. I was accused so I might understand God's word and preach it here today. Big blessings sometimes come with big troubles. We just *have* to trust God's will."

Lindell II rose slowly and said in a labored tone, "Are we going to be singing the Doxology fairly soon? I thought we were trying this man for murder. Objection, relevance."

"Mr. Ward, what say you?" Judge Hope said with an aggravation not concealed.

"I believe we are through with the sermon, Your Honor. I'll move it along. Reverend Clay, did you come in contact with a woman named Sarita Jo Franklin in connection with one of your broadcasts?" I asked.

The jury visibly leaned in toward Reverend Clay. One of the jurors on the front row had cupped his right hand behind his ear to make sure he heard it all.

"I did."

"And how do you know that she heard one of your broadcasts?"

"She sent me a letter and asked me to come to Anahuac after she heard me preach."

"What did the letter say?"

Lindell was one his feet. "Objection, hearsay, Your Honor. The best evidence rule provides that the letter, itself, is the best evidence of what it says. May I take the witness on *voir dire?*"

"No objection, Your Honor," I said, secretly laughing that Lindell II had stepped into the snare I had set.

"Now, Reverend, you say there was a letter, but the only testimony in this case is that no letter was found at the scene of the murder. Are you planning on testifying about the contents of the letter?"

"I am."

"We'd renew our objection, Your Honor. The best evidence rule would require that the original letter be in court."

"Mr. Ward?" the judge queried.

"May I continue my questioning? He won't testify to the contents of the letter until a proper foundation is laid."

"Proceed."

"Do you have the letter you received from Sarita Jo Franklin?"

Lindell II looked at me suspiciously.

"I do."

"Please show it to the court."

Clay took the letter from the breast pocket of his coat. He removed the letter from the envelope and held it up for all to see.

"Is this the letter that you received from Sarita Jo Franklin?"

"It is."

"Did you know her before you received this letter?"

"No, but God led me to pick her letter out of a large number we had received that day. I opened it personally."

"May I take the witness on *voir dire* again, Your Honor? This letter has not been authenticated."

"No objection," I said. I sat down with my heart in my throat. Would this ploy really work?

"Have you had this letter the entire time you have been in jail?" Lindell asked.

"No sir."

"Then pray tell, when did you obtain it?"

"Ten minutes ago in the holding cell."

"Who gave you the letter?"

"A member of the sheriff's department."

Lindell II was stopped in his tracks. He didn't know what to do. The sheriff had testified there was no letter. If he went further, he might be putting the sheriff in the penitentiary for perjury. He vacillated, and his lengthy silence grew heavy on the room.

"You done?" Judge Hope finally asked.

"Yes, Your Honor."

"Continue, Mr. Ward."

"What did you do as a result of reading her letter? Please don't go into the contents of the letter at this time."

"I got in my car and drove to Anahuac to meet with Miss Franklin."

"As a result of that meeting with Miss Franklin, did anything happen?"

"We met with Mr. Harrison Chambers to have documents drawn up."

"Did you see the documents that Mr. Chambers brought to court that were admitted as State's Exhibit 15?"

"I did."

"Were those the documents that Sarita Jo Franklin asked Mr. Chambers to prepare?"

"Yes."

"Did you in any way threaten or coerce Miss Franklin to sign those papers?"

"I only knew Miss Franklin for a short time. In that time, I came to believe that no man or woman could have made her do anything she didn't want to do."

I saw the jury looking at each other, nodding their heads in agreement.

"Did you in any way threaten or coerce her?"

"As God as my witness, no!"

"Where were you when Miss Franklin was shot?"

"It was about 6:30 in the morning and I had just gotten out of the shower. I was drying off. I heard Miss Franklin say, 'No!' and then I heard what sounded like a gunshot. I had to put on clothes. By the time I got get dressed and went downstairs, Miss Franklin was lying on the floor with blood all over her. There was no one else there, but I heard what sounded like a big truck driving away. I had to tend to her, so I didn't go see what kind of truck it was."

"What'd you do next?"

"I called the sheriff's office. She had the sheriff's business card taped right next to the telephone. I asked for an ambulance and told them what had happened."

"What'd you do next?"

"I prayed for her recovery and then I started putting pressure on the place where the blood was coming out. That's where I was when Deputy Zeke came in and told me she was dead. The sheriff came and they took me away to this courthouse. I thought they just needed to get a statement, but they threatened to beat me if I didn't confess. I had nothing to confess. I didn't harm that woman."

"What do you believe would happen to you if you lied under your oath to God about this?" I asked. Lindell II was already standing to object, but Clay got there first.

"I would rot in the everlasting flames of Hell. I'd rather rot in jail than rot in hell."

"Pass the witness," I said.

Lindell II tried to lodge his objection, but the testimony was in. "Oh, never mind," he said, throwing up his hands.

CHAPTER THIRTY-SEVEN

"Tell me again how this religion of yours works," Lindell II said. His voice had taken on an edge and his questions sounded as if he were scolding a third grader who had acted out in school.

"God wants us to be successful. He gives us the tools to have abundance. If we come to God with honest hearts and confess what we want, he will give it to us."

Lindell II interrupted Clay. "Let me make sure I'm following you, Reverend Clay. So if you just make up your mind that you want to walk out of this courtroom, you only have to wish it and God makes it so?"

"I would have to pray, not wish. God has made a contract with his people. If we believe in him sufficiently, we have no need to suffer. Jesus did that for us on the cross. Our confession of faith in God is the first step. Once we've got our business straight with God we are on a path to claim what is ours—peace and prosperity. To answer your question, God sent me here today for a purpose. His purpose is not for me to walk away from this trial. His purpose is for me to illuminate the great power of His glory to those who have not seen it."

"So you haven't prayed to walk away, but you could save yourself if you wanted to?"

"I'm following God's will."

Lindell II looked skyward with a skeptical expression and asked, "But if you wished for something different, God has to grant it?"

"The Bible lays out the contract we believers have with God. We were created in his image. Like any contract, God is a party to the agreement. This contract is God's will for his people."

"You and God are equal parties, in other words. God's sovereignty is limited by this contract?"

"God has given his people a gift to change the world by their faith in him."

"You believe that?"

"With all my heart and soul."

"You sort of a God yourself, preacher? Do anything your heart desires?"

"I have faith in God."

"You want to explain to me how your religious teachings jive with Matthew 6:24? 'You cannot serve both God and money.'" Lindell II was practically strutting as he shot what he thought was the final arrow into Clay's argument.

I was an avid observer of this theological scuffle. Reverend Clay was counterpunching with vigor. My conversations with him had led me to wish his gospel was true. I longed to be in control of my life. Positive thinking might open the door to all that I craved.

Aurora's sharp elbow in my side brought me back to my role as Clay's lawyer. "Objection, relevancy," she hissed in my ear. This wasn't a theological debate, it was trial for murder. Lindell II was conducting a withering cross on a topic designed to make Clay and his theology look foolish. His lawyer was getting pummeled and was so deep in his own head he was missing the show.

"Objection, relevancy!" I said as I leaped to my feet.

Judge Hope was rocked back in his chair. Now he was sitting straight up. I wasn't sure that he was going to sustain my objection. Neither was Lindell II. He came out swinging.

"It goes to the State's position that the defendant is a charlatan from Arkansas who came to Chambers County to prey on an aging and defenseless woman. We think his preaching is just a cover for his thievery."

"Your Honor, I object to the statement of counsel as not based in any fact."

"Sustained!" Judge Hope said forcefully.

"The prosecution has so prejudiced the trial that no instruction to the jury can erase these unfounded and scurrilous statements," I shouted.

Judge Hope once again called us to the bench. He leaned forward and whispered, "Enough of this bullshit. Lindell, we've had enough of this theology class. Quit making final arguments to the jury in the middle of trial. Ward, if you have a motion for mistrial you make it outside the jury's presence. You want me to send the jury out? We all clear how this is going down?"

Lindell II and I exchanged angry glances and then grudgingly said, "Yes, Your Honor" in unison. I looked back at the counsel table and Aurora was mouthing broadly, "*No mistrial.*" Like two scolded schoolboys, we retreated back to our desks. I was satisfied that the line of questioning would cease. I suspected that Lindell II thought he'd discredited Clay.

"We don't want a mistrial. We have this thing under control. Our guy will have to sit in jail waiting for months for another trial," Aurora reminded me.

"I know. I was just trying to rattle Lindell's cage."

The trip to the judge's bench had caused Lindell II to lose his rhythm. He was sorting through the notes he'd made on his yellow pad. I looked up at Clay and he and the jury were alternating looks at Lindell II and each other.

Finally, Lindell stood up and walked over to the witness box. He turned his back to Clay and faced the jury. "Let me see if I've got your story about how you showed up here one day and the next day you're named the heir to one of the largest fortunes in Chambers County. You got a letter out of the blue inviting you to come to Chambers County and take a family's wealth that has been in Chambers County since shortly after the Texas Revolution. The letter came from an old woman out in the country and nobody even knows why she would send such a letter. Then she writes a will that cut her nephew, her only living relative out of her estate. Is that about right?"

"I know why she sent the letter."

During all of this testimony Clay sat with the letter in his hand. I'd never marked it as an exhibit. Even a first-year litigator knows better than to ask the next question that Lindell II asked. Whether it was the pressure of trying to protect the sheriff or God knows what else, he asked it. It was just as I'd planned.

"How do you know that?"

"The letter told me I had to get there quickly. It said…"

"Objection, Your Honor, the letter isn't in evidence." Lindell was desperate.

"He opened the door, Your Honor. The witness is entitled to answer," I shouted.

"Sorry, Lindell, he's right. Reverend Clay, you may answer."

Lindell II had opened the door to testimony about a letter that I would have had difficulty getting into evidence without his question. He stood looking around the room. He was either looking for a hole to crawl in or someone to come to his rescue. Either way we were in business.

"The handwritten part on the bottom of the letter is why I had to come quickly. It says, *'I sent a copy of this letter to my nephew who may kill me. He wants to put me in a nursing home. If he kills me please let the sheriff know. SJF'.*"

There was a collective gasp from the courtroom. I felt like Perry Mason, but I had no faith that this jury was going to let Clay walk free. Lindell II had compounded his error by not looking at Clay's letter. Call it what you will, it was a damned miracle.

"So you got a letter from a lady you didn't know, saying her nephew was going to kill her. So your first thought was, I better get down to Texas and collect her fortune before he kills her?" Lindell said.

Clay sat in stony silence. It was that deadly moment of hesitation that has convicted many a defendant.

Lindell sensed redemption and continued. "Did it ever occur to you to call the sheriff *before* you saw Sarita Jo Franklin dead on the floor? You say that God tells you what to do. Did he say, 'Oh, don't worry about Sarita Jo Franklin; just get down to Texas and collect your fortune?'"

I needed to give the Reverend a moment to get his answer straight. "Objection, that makes about four or five questions the prosecutor has asked. He has to ask them one at a time."

"I'll rephrase," Lindell said quickly. He was fully aware of what I was doing.

"After you got Sarita Jo's letter that says her nephew had threatened to kill her, did you call the sheriff??"

"I did not call the sheriff."

"Some might say that you'd be guilty of helping to murder her even if you didn't pull the trigger. You had millions of reasons why you'd want her dead."

"I did not want her dead before her time. It was all a surprise to me," Clay said in a more subdued voice than before.

Lindell II looked pleased as he said, "Pass the witness."

I took a slow, deliberate breath. The turn of events had been so sudden that I had to be careful. What had seemed so clear had been muddled by Lindell's Hail Mary question.

"Just to be clear, Reverend Clay, did you have anything to do with the death of Sarita Jo Franklin?"

"No. I wish now I'd called the sheriff, but I assumed she had done so."

"We'd ask that the letter in Reverend Clay's hand be marked as Defense Exhibit 1 and admitted into evidence."

"Objection, Your Honor. It's hearsay," Lindell complained.

"Part of the document is in evidence through testimony. I'm entitled to have the whole document admitted," I said.

"It's admitted," Judge Hope said without hesitation.

"Pass the witness," I said.

Lindell II looked at his notes for a moment and said, "No questions."

"Defense rests, Your Honor."

It was Lindell's time to put on any rebuttal evidence he had to disprove our case. I could tell he was agonizing about whether there was more he needed to do. If he did not offer more testimony and rested, the evidence part of the case was through.

"You're up, Mr. Washington," the judge said.

"State rests."

"All right, gentlemen of the jury, the State and the defense have rested their cases. I am going to let you go home now, but my instructions are still in place. Do not talk about the facts in this case with anyone. Be here at 10 in the morning. I will prepare a charge now that will instruct you on the law about how you are to arrive at your verdict. You will have no other guide as to how you conduct your deliberations. Good night."

The jury filed out of the room and the gallery exploded with talk of the day's testimony. Lindell II sat in his chair scribbling notes on his yellow pad. Aurora and I talked to Clay about the final argument to come. He acted as if the outcome were assured. The sheriff showed up to take Clay back into the jail. Zeke was nowhere in sight.

"Tomorrow," I said as Clay walked away. The sheriff gave me a dirty look.

Aurora and I were about to go outside when Lindell II said, "Ward, talk to me a second." He looked grim.

I walked over to him. He was still in this chair. It had been a grueling day. He did not look up.

"I'm going to offer you the deal of a lifetime. Two-year probation and I'll reduce it to negligent homicide. I suspect it was an accident."

"But he loses any right to inherit her estate," I said.

"He's looking at life. Is money all your client is interested in? It will be better than being the new meat on cell block ten at the Walls."

"I have to talk to him."

"Get back to me before final arguments. I don't want to argue the case if we have a deal."

Clay was still in the holding tank next to the courtroom. "They've offered two-year probation on negligent homicide. You can walk out of here tonight if you want to take it. As you know, you would likely lose any right to the estate."

"God told me that there would be temptations. I studied the men of the jury. They know I didn't do anything wrong," Clay said.

"You can cut your losses and get out of town in one piece."

206

"What do you think I should do? Ultimately, God put me in your hands. Give me your advice. Know that *I* did not kill her."

"I don't have to tell Lindell your answer until in the morning. You pray on it and I'll talk to you in the morning."

I was in anguish. If Clay didn't take the deal and we lost big time, it wasn't going to help our firm's reputation. There was the matter of our contingent fee worth millions that was riding on our defeating the will contest also in play. We couldn't take a plea unless I could get him to say he was guilty. My client's interests were paramount to the firm's interests. It was a violation of the canons of ethics for me to allow him to plead guilty if he weren't guilty. Either way, if Clay ended up in the penitentiary for life, I would have to live with it forever. Clay in jail and millions out the window; it was the worst position I could imagine. I didn't want to make a decision like this. What if I was wrong? Why was I in this position? I was nearly frantic when gentle melodic soothing thought flowed through my head. I can't describe it other than to say it sounded like a Gregorian chant. I didn't hear any actual words, but it felt like, "Trust me, it's not about you. It's not about you."

I looked at Aurora to see if she had heard it, but she and Clay were talking about Zeke. "He's with my flock."

The words were repeating over and over in my head, and I suspected that I had become dehydrated by my lack of food and water. I wasn't going to tell anyone about my hallucination, but I needed to get out of this cell.

"We'll see you tomorrow morning," I said abruptly.

"Don't fret about it Jim," Clay said. "In the end, God's will is all that is important. Don't try to be God."

"Sometimes it's easy to get confused about that when you're a lawyer," I said.

Aurora and I walked to the car and we could hear gospel music drifting gently on the gulf breeze from the encampment. I wondered about the lives the flock lived. They ate, they prayed, and they trusted that there was a merciful God that was watching over them. I fought hard each day to maintain the illusion of control. Taylor hoarded more and more money to stave off remembrances of hunger as a child. Cooper fought each day to show Taylor that she was just as good as the son Taylor never had. My need to somehow right the now-mythical childhood disaster at the Kansas farm pond drove me to prove I wasn't a failure. None of us trusted anyone but ourselves. Clay had called me out in his testimony. He'd said my need for my will was only ego. I wanted to believe that God was responsible for it all, but a voice in me said, "Be a man, and take responsibility."

I sat for a moment, lost in thought. Finally, I realized that I hadn't started the car. My mind had been awash in contradiction.

"I envy those people and their simple lives," I said.

"You aren't going down there to join them, are you?" Aurora laughed.

"Might," I said. "I just might."

CHAPTER THIRTY-EIGHT

I don't know if was God's will or not, but final arguments were my best trial skill. At 3 o'clock in the morning I was giving my finest of arguments to the Anahuac jury when I realized that I had forgotten to put on pants. The adrenaline rush from that dream cost me my sleep for the rest of the night. The most difficult kind of courage is 3 o'clock courage. At three when you are lying in bed in the dark, trying to control the uncontrollable world, you are alone with your fears. Clay's admonition about not being God had not stopped me from trying to be one.

I drifted back to sleep only a few minutes before the clock radio was broadcasting KTRH's morning news. As I tried to shake off the drowse of my momentary return to sleep, I heard, "In Anahuac today, the trial of Reverend Randall Clay is expected to wrap up. Clay, charged with killing wealthy rancher Sarita Jo Franklin, is represented by Jim Ward, a former Harris County assistant district attorney. Millions of dollars of property are involved in a related matter. Clay is the beneficiary of a disputed will that made him the sole beneficiary of Franklin's entire estate. In other news…"

"Turn that goddamn thing off," Cooper groaned. "You were all over the bed all night long. I just want thirty minutes more sleep."

As if I needed any more pressure, KTRH's newscast had hurled my brain into trial mode. Once dressed and downstairs Jerome urged me to eat, "It'll give you energy," he said.

"You want me to throw up into the jury box?"

"I don't know how you do it," he said.

"Do what?"

"Talk in front of all those people."

"You're good at it too. I remember how you handled folks when you worked at the Petroleum Club."

"That was different. I was working for my tips."

"That's all I'm doing. I'm just *Mister Bojangles.*"

For a moment, the trial was gone and it was just Jerome and me bantering about life, as we often did. He knew what he was doing.

"More coffee?" he said.

"I got to get to the office."

At that moment, Cooper appeared at the door in what I called her reporter suit. She looked all Lois Lane in it.

"I need a to-go cup of black coffee. Mr. Famous Lawyer here kept me up all night," she said.

"Where are you going?" I asked.

"With you. I wouldn't miss it."

"Great, I can fall on my ass in front of my wife."

"Stop it. You know you're just getting hyped up and you'll be fine. I've seen you do this act before."

"Let's go if you're riding with me," I said.

"Coffee!" she pleaded as Jerome put a fresh cup in her hand.

When we got to the office, Aurora and Wells were waiting for us. "Are we going on a double-date?" Wells asked.

"Something like that," I said, "except we may be coming back in body bags if we don't win this damn thing."

"Nothing to it, you've got this," Aurora said. "How about letting me argue one point?"

"Which one?"

"That Clete did it. He called me a bitch."

"So I start with the no evidence produced by the State that proves Clay did it, and you give them the answer to who did?"

"Yep." She said it in a new-found Texas drawl.

"I love it. Short and simple: You heard no evidence that Clay did anything except answer a request to come to Texas, and the bully did it?"

"Yep."

In the euphoria of the moment, I had forgotten that there was two-year probation on the table. It came back to me as we arrived at the courthouse.

"One last thing, you make sure there is a circumstantial evidence provision in the charge," I said to Aurora.

"Juries think it means that the evidence is weak. It's really indirect evidence rather than direct. Use the word circumstantial over and over in your argument," Aurora said.

"Good idea. Let's get this conversation with Clay about the probation offer over with," I said.

"Can I come?" Wells said.

"You're his civil lawyer. Of course," I said.

"Can I come too?" Cooper said.

"Of course not, you're not his lawyer. You'd blow up the attorney-client privilege. You're a newshound looking for a story," I jested. Cooper looked like she was left off of the invitation list for an exclusive party.

Clay looked like he'd gotten a good night's sleep. I was envious. "What do you want to do?" I asked.

"What do you advise?"

"Are you guilty of *accidentally* killing Sarita Jo?"

"No"

"Then you've answered your own question. We have to turn down the offer. God help us if we're wrong," I said.

"He will help us to be right if it's His will. Either way, I'm at peace with your decision," Clay said.

"I don't have to go to jail if we're wrong. Besides it's God's decision, right?" I didn't want Clay claiming incompetence of counsel later if this all blew up.

"It'll be fine," Clay said.

"I talked to the lawyer representing Clete yesterday after the news of the letter got out. He says he is dismissing their challenge to Sarita's will if you are found not guilty," Wells said.

"Praise be the Lord." Clay said.

"We still get our fee under the contingent fee contract," Wells said.

"We have no problem with that," Clay responded.

"Let's go see what the judge's charge looks like," I said.

"We'll see you in the courtroom, Reverend," Aurora said. "You look nice in your suit."

"The Lord be with you."

We sat in the judge's chambers reading the charge he'd written to give to the jury. The judge had already included the circumstantial evidence provision.

"I guess you are rejecting my offer," Lindell II said.

"Yes."

"Your funeral. You know that jury must just hate this charlatan taking all this wealth out of this poor county."

"The answer is still no," I said.

He started to say something else, but the judge broke in. "Any objection to the charge?"

"No, Your Honor," I said.

"None," Lindell said.

"We'll start the arguments at 10."

"We'd like to split our argument," I said.

Judge Hope looked over at Aurora. "Well she's got a skirt on. I suppose it'll work to let a woman loose on the jury. It's never been done before in this county. How about 30 minutes a side?"

"We'll probably give some of it back to the court. There isn't much to argue about," I said to prick Lindell.

The judge looked at Lindell. "You good with 30?"

"Sure, thirty is fine. We'll see how you smart alecks feel when we haul your client off to Huntsville in a couple of hours."

The thought was chilling, but this was just lawyer talk. "We'll see about that."

The twenty citizens of New Jerusalem selected by Mr. Marrow to represent the congregation had lined up early to pack the courtroom. Surprisingly, there was a large group of locals standing around talking with the outsiders. The outsiders had more in common with the locals than I did. They had almost become locals during their stay. Any initial paranoia from either side had largely evaporated as the two groups got to know each other. Even the blacks were welcomed after it was clear they were not there to cause harm. Aurora and I waded through them to get into the courtroom. The bailiff had already brought Reverend Clay into the courtroom.

We had a few minutes before the argument and we sat quietly. At five minutes before the hour, the bailiff opened the courtroom to the gallery and it filled in less than a minute.

At 10 sharp, the door opened from the judge's chambers and the bailiff said, "All rise." My heart was slowing down in preparation for the argument. I was in my world and this was what I did. I looked at Aurora, and saw she was smiling, although I didn't know why.

"Bring the jury in," the judge said to the bailiff.

The twelve looked like they had slept the night before. I stifled a yawn that wanted to escape my mouth. I was at peace as the judge read the charge to the jury. It was mostly boilerplate language that was designed to keep a jury from straying away from their task. The defendant is presumed innocent. The indictment is not evidence of guilt. The state's burden is to prove guilt beyond a "reasonable doubt," not all doubt. The jury is the judge of the credibility of the witnesses. The key words were in the circumstantial evidence paragraph.

In considering the evidence, you are permitted to draw such reasonable inferences from the testimony and exhibits as you feel are justified in the light of common experience.

In other words, you may make deductions and reach conclusions that reason and common sense lead you to draw from the facts which have been established by the evidence. Do not be concerned about whether evidence is "direct evidence" or "circumstantial evidence." You should consider and weigh all of the evidence that was presented to you.

"Direct evidence" is the testimony of one who asserts actual knowledge of a fact, such as an eye witness.

"Circumstantial evidence" is proof of a chain of events and circumstances indicating that something is or is not a fact.

The law makes no distinction between the weight you may give to either direct or circumstantial evidence. But the law requires that you, after weighing all of the evidence, whether direct or circumstantial, be convinced of the guilt of the defendant beyond a reasonable doubt before you can find him guilty.

The charge was read and Lindell II was on his feet. He had the burden of proof so he would open and close the argument. His Texas accent had broadened to new heights. He was one with the jury and he praised them for their service.

"You are the conscience of Chambers County. Today, you are the law. Your duty is to protect us from vermin from the outside that come among us to murder and maim. You'll recall that the judge wrapped himself in this flag and reminded you about the war dead that gave you this right to live free. Don't soil their memory by letting the Charlatan of Arkansas walk free." He turned, pointed directly at Clay and sneered, "Charlatan" again.

Then he sat down. He had not argued one point of fact or testimony. He had the right to close the argument. He wasn't going to tip his hand as to how he would argue the case.

It was now our turn to address the jury. I stood and looked around the room for dramatic effect. The jury followed my gaze. When I had their attention, I walked directly in front of the jury box. I could have reached across the rail and touched them.

"This room is a cathedral of truth. Those boys dying on the beaches of Normandy didn't die to protect those who have wrongly accused others. Read the judge's charge. The prosecutor is asking you to leave your common sense at home and blindly follow what is as close to a lynching as I've ever seen. When does the State intend to put on evidence that this man has done one thing to harm Sarita Jo Franklin? When the prosecutor gets back up here in a minute to conclude his argument, make him show you his proof beyond a reasonable doubt that Reverend Randall Clay committed a crime. The State's whole case is circumstantial and that means you have to assume some things to get to a guilty verdict. Those so-called facts you have to *just* assume aren't in the record. So the State wants you to fill in the gaps where they had no evidence for them. I know this jury is going to hold the State to the standard that the law expects and you swore to follow when you entered that jury box."

I stood directly in front of the jury box and looked slowly at each juror directly in the face. Some squirmed in their seats. I was purposefully introducing them to the uncomfortable truth that they should follow the law.

"Randall Clay is a man of God. He told you on the stand that he made an assumption that Miss Franklin had called the sheriff about her nephew, Clete. He didn't know that Sarita Jo hadn't taken care of that business. She made a courageous decision when she sent Reverend Clay a letter. A letter that remained hidden from the defense until yesterday, by someone in the Sheriff's department. My partner, Aurora Wilson, asked Clete Franklin a simple question and he called her a bitch. I'm going to sit down in a minute or two and let her talk to you. I've lived in Texas all of my life. Now you men know she doesn't talk like us, but she's a Texan now. God knows every once in a while she says something that I can't understand. I try to get her to speak English, but, well you know."

The jury had begun to laugh and a couple of them gently elbowed their neighbor. They were looking at Aurora and then back to me.

"I grew up in a Texas that didn't countenance bad behavior like calling a lady a bitch in public. When we look at Clete's behavior and read the note that a strong woman wrote about his threat, I think we know who killed Sarita Jo. The State's case is circumstantial and points to a man, but it's not this man, the Reverend Randall Clay. If you had a chance to pick between Clete and Reverend Clay, who do you think is the most likely to have killed her? Circumstantial evidence, that's all you have to work with. All you can do is *guess* who killed Sarita Jo Franklin. That's not the way it works. You can't convict a man for murder when the facts show that Sarita Jo Franklin tells you in her own handwriting that it's likely Clete Franklin did it."

As I sat down Aurora stayed seated for a moment. She rose slowly to her full height and walked around behind her chair. Unlike the way I argued, right in front of their faces, she was respecting their space. I suppose some might say she was in her place, and in a way, they would be right. She was my partner now and she belonged here. She rested both hands on the back of the leather chair and stood quietly for a moment. When she began to speak it was calm and soothing.

"Sarita Jo Franklin was killed. That's about the only thing we know for sure in this record. The State has presented a case so weak that it is laughable. I don't know if the prosecution thinks you gentlemen don't have common sense or what. Maybe we could just have a town lottery and pick someone to convict. If you convict Reverend Clay, it would be about the same.

"The way that Clete Franklin responded to a simple question tells me he has something to hide. Now I've been called worse than a bitch."

The jury alternated between squirming uncomfortably in their chairs and giggling like schoolboys.

"Maybe I am a bitch."

"Objection, Your Honor. This kind of talk has no place in this courtroom," Lindell II said. His face showed he regretted his objection the moment he made it.

"I think that's her point, Mr. Washington, overruled."

Aurora stood calmly for a moment to let the judge's words filter through the jury box.

"Maybe I am a bitch, but just like Miss Franklin, I have a job to do. You men know that a ranch is no place for sissies. Sarita was hard, like men and women have always had to be to survive out here. It is a reasonable interpretation that she stood up to a bully and he killed her. You know the evidence. You know the man she wrote about. There is no reason for me to even say his name."

"The prosecution and law enforcement raced to an easy conclusion and charged the wrong man. The uncontested testimony in this record is that somebody in the sheriff's office had this letter in their hands and chose to do nothing with it. Don't compound their mistake by making one of your own. Acquit this man of God so that he can get on with his Father's business and Godspeed in your verdict."

Aurora had used my final sentence in her argument. I would have been mad, but I had forgotten to use it. I was glad she was here. Maybe she'd know what Godspeed meant.

"Mr. Washington?" the judge said.

"Thank you, Your Honor."

I was mentally patting Aurora on the back. She had crushed it. For the first time, I was beginning to feel like we had won. Lawyers should never allow that emotion in the door.

"Well, ain't that cute. Pretty lady waltzes into town and tries to sell you men a story. Don't let your heads be turned by her little slander of a local man. There's no evidence that Clete done anything."

Lindell II was dangerous. He was a wounded prosecutor. He spoke in the vernacular of his people. It was frightening because his appeal to the men could work and we had argued our last. He had the burden of proof. He had the last word.

"You all saw it yesterday with your own eyes. This so-called preacher man sat quietly when I asked him why he didn't call the sheriff if he knew Sarita Jo was really in danger. It took him a long time to come up with his story. Who benefited from Sarita's death? Not Clete; he was out of the will. Reverend Clay was too greedy to wait until she died to inherit what wasn't his. Who gives away the family ranch to strangers? I think you'll agree that common sense tells us it is an old woman who has lost her senses. I bet she got paranoid and the preacher just took advantage of her."

"Objection, there is no evidence in the record to support such a theory," I said.

"Sustained, the jury will disregard."

Lindell II was now introducing a new theory for which there was no evidence. The problem was that the jury had heard it and we'd probably never know if that was why they convicted Clay.

"Well, you boys know what I mean. Just use your common sense. Just like the judge told you to do. In the end, I know you'll do right by the memory of Sarita Jo and what's right is not to let that charlatan sitting right there in his fancy suit get away with it."

If I could have argued more, I would have said, "He means Clete." But we had to sit quietly. The State got the last word.

"The jury will now retire to deliberate. Bailiff, give the jury their copy of the charge and take them to the jury room," the judge instructed.

We stood as the jury left the courtroom. When the door to the jury room closed we were at *their* mercy. There was nothing left to do but await Clay's fate.

CHAPTER THIRTY-NINE

Three hours passed and the locals who had come to watch the trial had largely drifted away. Every few minutes, two or three of the congregation from the tented city would appear to monitor the jury's progress. The communications between the emissaries and me were no longer vocal. The flock members would give me a hopeful glance and the solemn negative shake of my head was all that was necessary. There were a few print reporters standing in the hall outside the courtroom. Aurora and Wells had walked the short distance to the Fort Anahuac State Park. Someone had reported that several of the park's resident alligators were sunning themselves on the banks of the tidal river.

My mind was filled with a tangle of apprehensions about my decision to turn down Lindell II's offer. Would I ever forgive myself if I had misjudged the jury? A quick verdict is usually good for the defendant. Now three hours had passed. It would be suppertime soon and a verdict might be delayed until tomorrow. I had no confidence that the sheriff's shadowy influence wouldn't creep through the doors of the jurors' homes after the reporters were gone. The jurors were a part of Staunton's flock. He gathered them not by love, Jesus or hope of redemption. His flock stayed behind him out of fear of his retribution.

The passage of time fueled a wild thought that perhaps I should ask Lindell II if his offer was still open. He was only a few feet away in his office. He had to be worried if he had made the offer in the first place. But again, what if I was hasty and the jury was going to find the Reverend not guilty? They only had to believe that there was not enough evidence to convict.

I glanced out the window and caught sight of Chinky and her cameraman filming location shots around historical statues on the courthouse lawn. Chinky was the last person I could afford to think about. The middle of a murder trial was no place for my mind to wander away to what had been or might have been.

Total dread washed over me. This high-profile case might be my last if it fell apart so publicly. If Reverend Clay got a life sentence, and it got out that I had turned down a manslaughter plea, I would be a public laughing stock. My mind and my pulse were spinning out of control. I stood in the hallway without hearing or feeling. I felt only a low buzzing inside my head. It was a feeling I had experienced before. The buzzing was more a sensation than a sound. It helped to take me away from those things I could not stand to experience. I vainly struggled for control. Was I losing my mind or having a heart attack? As my heart raced and I struggled to breathe, a distant voice broke through the fog.

"They have a verdict."

My focus was slowly returning, but the quick walk from the hall to counsel table was a blur. It was as if one moment I was in the hall and the next, back in the courtroom. The bailiff opened the door from the holding cell and the beneficent countenance of Reverend Randall Clay emerged with not a care in the world. I was dying and he was nodding confidently to his flock who had rushed upstairs to reclaim their seats in the gallery. The Reverend patted me gently on the back, comforting me. I needed to be comforted although I wasn't going to be in jail for the rest of my life if we lost. Judge Hope reappeared from his chambers as the bailiff voice boomed, "All rise."

Lindell II looked over at me with a smug look that said it all. "Ward, you fucked up."

"I'm advised that the jury has reached a verdict," the judge said solemnly. "Now ladies and gentlemen, I don't know how they do things in Arkansas, but we in Texas don't put up with shows of emotion after a jury's verdict. Win or lose, you will maintain the dignity of this court. Any outbursts are going to get you a night in Sheriff Staunton's jail." With that he turned to the bailiff and said, "Bring the jury in."

The bailiff disappeared through the door that led to the jury room and returned with the twelve panel members. I watched the jurors' intently as they filed to their seats. A hint was all I was after. Not one of the jurors looked at Reverend Clay. I had seen jurors so anxious to let the defendant know that everything was all right; they smiled and nodded to them. My heart sank. The courtroom was totally silent, but charged with electricity. I felt a rainstorm of perspiration flooding my armpits.

"Gentlemen, have you reached a verdict?"

The foreman of the jury turned out to be the local undertaker. With a consoling tone that only a man who is used to dealing with bereavement possesses, he soothingly said, "Yes we have, Your Honor."

"Please pass the verdict to the bailiff," the judge said, his demeanor formal as befitted the moment.

The bailiff ambled over to the foreman, took the verdict and strolled back to the bench. I swear he did it to heighten the drama. He handed the folded verdict to the judge. The judge opened the verdict and spent at least ten seconds looking at it. A man's future hung in the balance. A man coughed and Reverend Clay whispered, "Thy will, not mine."

My heart was pounding. I wondered if I was the only one who could hear it. The judge stared down at the verdict for another moment and then looked over at the jury without expression. Then he looked down at the verdict again. I knew by now the sound of my heart was audible to all. Then the judge's gaze was directed at Reverend Clay.

"The defendant will please rise." The judge's voice was commanding.

The Most Reverend Randall Allen Clay, Aurora and I stood up and faced the jury. My legs were wobbly and my throat had lost all hope of moisture.

Without looking back down at the verdict the judge said, "We the jury find the defendant Randall Clay…" He stopped for either half a second or eternity. They both felt the same.

"Not guilty."

There was dead quiet and then the flock let out a collective exhale in unison. My legs had partially given way at the verdict, and now I was busy adopting the air of a lawyer who never had a doubt about the outcome. Reverend Clay and I exchanged a handshake and then an all-enveloping hug. The courtroom was buzzing quietly, but persistently when Lindell II stood and said, "I request that the jury be polled."

I didn't know if it was out of spite or if he hoped that a juror would recant his vote for acquittal. I didn't like it one bit, but it was his right to require each juror to rise and acknowledge that he had voted for acquittal.

The courtroom was quiet for a moment. There was confusion amongst the flock as to what was happening and the noise level escalated. I turned and signaled with my hand for them to settle down before the judge slapped somebody in jail.

Judge Hope turned to the jury and said, "Gentlemen, the State has requested that the jury be polled. When your name is called, please stand and acknowledge that not guilty is your verdict."

I looked back at the flock and could see Sheriff Staunton standing in the back of the courtroom. Inexplicably, he had put on his mirrored sun glasses. He stood ramrod straight. His eyes were now hidden, but his tightlipped expression left no question that he was pissed as he eyed the twelve men.

The judge called the names of the first six jurors and they each answered in the affirmative. The seventh juror rose hesitantly. I saw him glance at Sheriff Leonard Staunton and then look down at the floor. "Well, you see judge…"

"No sir!" Judge Hope said quickly. "Yes or no. Is not guilty your verdict?"

The seventh juror continued to look down at the floor and I turned to look at Sheriff Staunton's menacing face. He had removed the dark glasses, and his gaze never deviated from juror seven. The juror was R.C., the local café owner who provided meals to the jailed prisoners under a contract with the county. Juror seven looked back at Sheriff Staunton and then the judge. This was a man who had incurred the wrath of one of his financial benefactors. As a member of the jury he had a small bit of anonymity. Now singled out to confirm his vote the spotlight shone brightly upon him.

"Yes, Your Honor." He said in voice that was between a gag and a whisper.

"Yes, what, R.C.?" the judge said, breaking with decorum and calling the juror by his first name.

The terror-stricken man's eyes darted back to the menace of the sheriff and then back to the judge. "Not guilty" escaped from his mouth like air out of a balloon. After he confirmed his vote, the café owner-turned-juror slumped back into his chair with such force that it rocked back precipitously. His eyes fixed firmly on the worn marble floor, no doubt wondering if a large part of his monthly income had just vanished. It was one thing to tithe at the church. It was quite a different matter to donate three times his church tithe at the altar of justice.

The next five jurors promptly answered that their verdict was not guilty. The judge looked at the jury and said, "Thank you for your service. Gentlemen, you are excused. Please see the clerk of the court to get your checks." There was the matter of the six dollars a day juror fee payment. In the cash-strapped rural economy, the payment would be appreciated.

There was little in my life that could replace winning a jury trial. The glow usually lasted for at least a week. Then there was a need for another fix. The opposite of that high was the low I felt when I lost. Lindell II sat by himself at counsel table straightening up his papers and putting them in the file. I walked to him and held out my right hand.

"Congratulations," he said as he shook my hand.

"I've been on both sides of these deals. I know how it feels," I said.

"Aw, this was a bullshit case. I had to do something with it. I'm glad it's over. Enjoy your millions. I knew Sarita Jo. She was as tough and ornery as they come, but she didn't deserve killing. Who do you think really did it?"

"Clete, I guess."

"Well you might want to take a long look at that Jew boy down there in his fancy RV."

"I think he's converted," I said with a laugh.

"What, to the Church of the Holy Shekel your preacher boy is peddling?"

"I guess we'll never know," I said.

"I don't give a shit anymore. I've got a file cabinet full of cases to try."

"I would hope one of them is going to be against your sheriff. Withholding evidence is a pretty serious crime."

Lindell II just blinked.

"Good luck," I said and we shook hands again.

Aurora and I held our ecstasy until we could get to the ground floor. We looked at each other as we walked out into a cool afternoon and let out a small whoop. Fall was finally making an appearance. We hopped around in a crazy dance that made no sense but felt great. Clay was being processed out and we would have him on the street for the first time in months.

Cooper who was standing next to us said, "I get the first interview."

Chinky was racing over to talk to us. She was trailed by several other TV crews.

"You've got me all the way home. Let me get rid of these folks," I begged.

Cooper gave me a look that I interpreted to be permission.

"Aurora," I called, "get over here."

She was talking to Wells and some of the flock. It felt like my days in the DA's office when I won big cases. It was a feeding frenzy.

I had not spoken to Chinky since the last interview. This meeting was strictly business. I couldn't deny that part of me was glad she had been here to see my victory. After my interview, she asked Aurora twice as many questions. When they were finished, she said to Aurora, "See you next week."

Chinky was focused on promoting women, but I knew she would always be somewhere in my life. Her cryptic comment that her son neither looked like the boy's father or her was still with me. Sometime, I needed to meet that son.

A few of the exultant congregation had gathered outside the courthouse at the foot of the stairs to escort the innocent one, Reverend Randall Clay, back to New Jerusalem. All six stood in a circle repeating the Lord's Prayer over and over. A small group of the locals stood quietly a few feet away. The news crews from Houston and Beaumont had strategically positioned their cameras on the lawn to record Reverend Clay's exit from the courthouse. Aurora, Cooper, and I stood halfway up the stairs. I wanted to try to manage our client's exit. Wells was mingling with some of the citizens of New Jerusalem at the bottom of the stairs.

The small crowd buzzed with anticipation. I stood watching as a few of them continued to pray on their knees. Then they all erupted into shouts of joy and moved toward the bottom of the stairs. Reverend Clay stood at the front door, a free man. I tried to get his attention, but the Reverend Randall Clay was in his element. He clasped his hands high over his head in a victory salute, but his beneficent smile radiated calm. Standing above us, he was now in command. The newshounds rushed up the stairs and surrounded him. Aurora and I were superfluous to the proceeding. The Reverend listened without comment to the flurry of questions thrown from all directions. Slowly, palms open he raised his arms above his head to silence the hounds and they were silent.

"My friends, I have no grudge against anyone responsible for my incarceration. Forgiveness is the key to Christian love. Instead of recrimination, we say love thy neighbor. The Reverend Randall Clay Prayer Hour will be moving to a new headquarters in Dallas to spread the word of God. We have plans to build a 5,000-seat arena for God. Even more importantly, we have acquired the rights to a television station that will become the Franklin Broadcasting Company to spread the word of God that Sarita Jo Franklin had so long embraced. Now it is time for me to go to God's chosen people, my congregation. I bid you goodbye until we meet again in Dallas."

Aurora and I stood watching the television reporters as they milled around the acquitted one again shouting questions before he started his triumphant walk back toward New Jerusalem. I gazed out over the scene and saw Clete standing by his truck. He took a quick drink from a flask and put it back in his jacket.

Chinky yelled, "Can you get me an exclusive?" I shook my head no. I wasn't in charge of any of this anymore. I didn't see the sheriff until his face was directly in front of mine. His sunglasses glimmered in the fading light. He was so close I felt his breath on my face.

"Get back in the courthouse," he said. "Someone says Clete's going to shoot somebody."

I didn't hesitate. I grabbed Cooper and Aurora's hands and pulled them back up the stairs. Reverend Clay and the throng were walking up the sidewalk toward Clete. The sheriff pushed through the crowd of reporters and news crews and put his arm around the Reverend. He leaned over to say something to the man he had accused of murder. Clay nodded calmly and kept walking.

I saw Clete walking toward the throng as they headed to Fort Anahuac. The sheriff suddenly peeled away from the procession and walked directly toward Clete. Clete's right hand was concealed inside his jacket. The sheriff casually held out his right hand to Clete as if to shake hands. Clete pulled his right hand out of his jacket and a silver pistol flashed in the autumn sunlight.

The sheriff grabbed Clete's hand and the sound of a large caliber gun exploded on the square. Before Clete could fire again, the pistol fell to the pavement. The sheriff spun the younger man around and slammed him to the ground. In a single motion, he put handcuffs on him and pulled him to his feet.

The reporters had all fallen to the ground at the sight of the gun. Only Reverend Clay was standing on the courthouse sidewalk. He staggered backward slightly. For a moment, he stood perfectly still. Then he began marching briskly toward New Jerusalem, apparently unharmed. Once again, I had underestimated the showmanship of the clever Randall Clay.

The sheriff marched Clete by us in the lobby of the courthouse and Clete shouted, "You bitch! You bitch!" at Aurora as he was marched by us.

"Shut up, you stupid son-of-a bitch," Sheriff Staunton said.

I went back outside to see the entire population of New Jerusalem surrounding Reverend Clay. Their shouts of praise to God for his acquittal filled the square. Not one of them was praising his lawyers.

He held up his hands and the courthouse square was silent. He shouted, "Children of God, there is a new gospel upon us. It is a wonderful thing to behold. God wants you to have riches and life abundant. He has told me, 'No more crying, no more want.' Prosperity is ours for the asking!" The crowd roared and then they followed him off to what I assumed was going to be a celebration of praise like Anahuac had never seen.

Our job was done here It was time for the WW&W trial team to simply exit and fade away back to Bay Villa. I was exhausted, but thrilled that we had not taken Lindell II's bad deal. A lawyer should never have to decide such a thing for his client.

The television crews following the Reverend had been right in the middle of it when Clete was arrested. One station had its remote crew on live television when the shot was fired. The story would run for a week in news outlets all over the United States and abroad. Wilson, Wilson and Ward was handed a million dollars' worth of publicity. Aurora and I grew tired of giving interviews, but it was much better than being dead.

CHAPTER FORTY

The news media across the country were fascinated with the take down of Clete Franklin. The East Coast press had a field day talking about how Texas was still the Wild West. The dramatic acquittal of the Reverend Randall Clay might not have had sex, but it had the two next best things— greed and violence. I sat in my office two days later basking in my own radiated glory. The partnership of Wilson, Wilson and Ward had accomplished something that no one could have ever imagined.

Clay's revelation of God's promise of prosperity had electrified New Jerusalem. The Reverend would tell you it was all simply God's plan, but was it possible that the Reverend Clay and the shadowy Mr. Marrow had orchestrated the greatest fraud committed in history of the courts of the great state of Texas? If it had been a fraud, was I a part of the fraud?

Who knew who killed Sarita Jo? I didn't know and the good news was it wasn't my job to find out. We had done what lawyers are required to do. We gave our client a defense. I wasn't in the crime-solving business anymore. That was for the sheriff and Lindell II to do. Praise was raining down on Aurora and me as the new high-profile defense team in Texas. It was a good day.

My telephone rang and Alice Ann's pleasant voice brought a call that I dreaded. "Mr. Faircloth is on the telephone for you."

For a solid month, I had avoided his calls while I prepared for the trial. He had been at the trial for the verdict, but we didn't talk. I steeled myself for a thrashing. I sat up straight in my chair. Now composed, I said "Dad!" It was the first time I had ever called him that.

"Well, Perry Mason, I guess you showed them who's boss. Congratulations on being the slickest lawyer in the state."

"I might have had some help."

"Oh, no question Aurora was right there big time, but you know nobody's ever going to want a woman lawyer representing them when their life's on the line. I am, however, worried that you are forgetting why I put you in private practice."

I began to protest, but Taylor was on a roll.

"But that's O.K., because I've wanted to drill that Franklin dome for twenty-five years. I talked to Sarita Jo years ago, but she said she didn't want any dirty wells on the property. She had a fortune. The woman sat out there figuring out which stocks to buy and which to sell like some kind of fortune teller. Now I guess God's messenger has got it all."

"Franklin dome?"

"Well sure, Jim, that house sits on top of the prettiest oil play that's left on Smith's Point. It hasn't been a secret. Everybody in the oil business including Ross Sterling back in the old days has made a run at it."

"It's a salt dome?"

"Of course. I finalized the deal with Marrow this morning. He said he was going to hire you to write the deal up. I told him you represent me too so it would be easy. Son-of-a-bitch wants a seventy-five percent lease. You gotta be careful of these religious types. These preachers always got their hands out."

"So that means that the working interest would be responsible for 100 percent of the costs and only get seventy-five percent of the income. You must be sure of this."

"Hell yes I am. I already had a deal with Clete Franklin for an 85 percent lease. You winning that case cost me money. I've walked all over that ranch. My doodle-bug damn near broke my wrist."

"Why didn't you tell me about it? It would have been a perfect way to show motive in Clete Franklin."

"I guess you didn't ask."

"But he's in jail now and about to be indicted for attempted murder."

"Do you think they're going to indict one of their own?"

"He took a shot at Reverend Clay."

"I suspect some clever lawyer will just say it was an accident. Clete Franklin gives a lot of money to all the politicians over there. I don't think Lindell II is going to do anything."

"Well, what about murdering Sarita Jo?"

"They got nothing on him there. He told me that he was home with his wife when Sarita Jo was killed, so they won't get him for that. Besides, he lost out on the ranch and the Franklin Dome play. That's pretty good punishment."

"Does that disturb you?"

"I've seen worse. Sarita was a hard case. I barely knew her, but from what I heard it was just like her to stand strong against a bully to give the family inheritance away to some radio preacher. No reason I shouldn't make a buck on her salt dome. She should have leased it years ago. Hell, I don't know why it would bother you. Your firm has a piece of the deal now. You'll do all right. Do you have a problem with making the money?"

"I don't know how I feel about it."

"Well, Hell's bells, give it to your preacher man's church if it bothers you."

"I don't see how that helps."

"Neither do I. You've done well, Jim. Quit worrying about dead people. Enjoy the money."

"Thanks, I'll try," I said. I'd spent my life trying to overcome the death of two little girls that I couldn't save. Now I'd saved Reverend Clay and I had no idea if he and his shady business manager had murdered Sarita Jo Franklin. I would have a large check, courtesy of her estate each month, for probably the rest of my life to remind me of the mystery. One thing I knew for sure, I wasn't giving any of it to the Reverend Randall Clay Prayer Hour.

CHAPTER FORTY-ONE

A festive mood lingered at Bay Villa the Saturday after the verdict. Cooper and I sat on the portico bathed in the warmth of the mid-November sun. Thanksgiving was less than a week away, yet fall was barely in sight.

"Would you like more coffee?" Jerome asked.

"I'm good," I said. I had no desire to kill the effects of a three-mimosa buzz.

Cooper placed her hand over her coffee cup. She was so engrossed in an article about the second term plans of the recently-reelected Richard Nixon that she did not look up.

"I don't want to bother you, but I found some boxes in the basement. I stacked them in the ballroom. I thought you might want to look at them before I threw them away," Jerome said.

The intrigue of found boxes made Cooper look up from her newspaper. "What's in them?"

"Old-timey Christmas decorations; they must have been Ross Sterling's. From the looks of them I assume they might be from the '30s. Some of them are in good condition."

"It couldn't hurt to look at them. They might be historical," Cooper said.

When we arrived in the ballroom, the trove of decorations held in heavy wooden boxes covered most of the dance floor.

"My God!" Cooper said as she clapped her hands. "Look at this. We can deck the house out like it was in the old days. Daddy's coming out next week for Thanksgiving dinner. I think he'd get a kick out of seeing the house decorated."

Our initial enthusiasm was blunted as we searched through the contents of the ancient boxes. Even in tightly sealed containers, the humidity and bugs had taken their toll. In the end, there were enough useable wooden reindeer, metal angels and candle holders to decorate the dining room.

"Daddy's family was never able celebrate the holidays much when he was a boy. I'm sure he'll enjoy this."

Thanksgiving broke gray and foggy, but still warm. The Texas sun burned off the haze, and by turkey time, it was beautiful. Jerome had prepared two large turkeys that would have fed twenty-five people. We stood looking at the feast laid out in the main dining room, now reminiscent of what it might have been like in the mid-'30s. The oak-paneled dining room was cavernous. The dramatic dining room table, fully set, could seat 20 for such a meal.

A gentle breeze blew through doors and windows that opened onto the bay. The recent victory in Anahuac and Taylor's coup of leasing the Franklin dome made life seem like it could be no better.

"Do you like it, Daddy?" Cooper said excitedly as we stood looking at what could only be described as the best of life's material bounty.

"It's great, but it could use a couple of things more," Taylor said.

"What Daddy, what do we need?" Cooper said anxiously.

"I miss your mother so much. She always put so much sparkle in the holidays. She loved them so. I…I thought we could save her."

Taylor's tough façade cracked ever so slightly. Neither his wealth nor the finest physicians his wealth could hire could save Electra. Was I seeing a different, more human Taylor?

"Jim and I miss her too," Cooper said with a voice full of emotion.

I had never witnessed such open emotion from either of them. Yet here they stood. A father and a daughter, vulnerable and freely expressing their shared loss.

"But what else, Daddy? I think Jerome has cooked everything we could think of."

"Such a big house and just the three of us for Thanksgiving. We have so much. Before she took sick your mother talked about how much fun it would be to fill this house with grandchildren. It would be nice if we had some little ones running around this table. It would make me more thankful."

The silence of the 20,000 square feet of mansion was deafening. There it was. Taylor had it all and he had sounded as if he had nothing. His lament was either an honest confession of his humanness or a ploy so calculated he might be the devil incarnate. It was Thanksgiving and I chose to believe the former.

"Children…" She began and stopped. "Mom was the best mother. She was always at home for me. She did make the holidays so special. I wish she was here."

The conversation stopped as Jerome appeared with two bottles of white wine.

"Which should I pour first?"

I was not confused about which wine I preferred. It was the rest of life that had me wondering. I was sure that wealth and fame could wipe out all of my doubts and fears about my adequacy as a man. Here I sat with a father-in-law who probably blamed me for being unable to accomplish a manly task that I stood ready to accomplish if given the chance. I was feeling sorry for myself until my eyes met Cooper's and I saw her uneasiness. This was her father. The man she wanted to please at all costs. Pleasing him could jeopardize her role as the publisher of newspapers. I knew her passion for her work was as much for herself as it was for Taylor's approval. It was an unpleasant conundrum at best and I could see it pained her.

Jerome had filled our wine glasses with a Puligny-Montrachet, a world class grand cru. I didn't want Thanksgiving spoiled.

"I want to propose a toast," I said holding my wine glass high. Cooper and Taylor raised their glasses. "Here is to Electra. We give thanks for her and the sacrifices she made to raise the best newspaper woman in the world, Cooper Faircloth."

"Hear, hear," Cooper and Taylor said. Then Taylor said, "To Electra."

"And Cooper." I repeated, lest anyone forget she was a strong woman making her own sacrifices in this new world of the 1970s.

"To Cooper," Taylor said. "To Cooper," I repeated and the mood was festive even if all I had done was restate the problem that was on the floor. Professional success or motherhood or both each required a sacrifice; was the choice between professional success and motherhood mutually exclusive? Taylor had fired Electra from his newspaper so she could go home and raise their baby. Cooper had more options than Electra, but would she ever have the desire to be a mother? I really didn't know.

When the mood had lightened, there were more toasts to our good fortunes. Finally, I made one last toast. "To the twelve jurors of Chambers County whose verdict has sent a good man off to do God's work!" At least I hoped that's what they'd done.

Christmas came and there were parties and celebrations to attend all over Houston. The new year brought the likelihood of a steady stream of high-dollar cases for WW&W. There was another exciting aspect to the New Year. I don't know if it was the cold weather or what, but Cooper and I began having sex more often than ever before. Cooper and I were in love and life at Bay Villa seemed to be the best it had ever been for us.

On January 22, 1973, the Supreme Court of the United States issued a decision that shook the fabric of the country. Roe v. Wade, a case from Texas, announced to the world that a woman had a right to control her body. The controversy over legalizing abortion was hailed and damned equally throughout the country. Cooper threw herself into the story with a vengeance. She and Taylor clashed over editorial policy and their relationship was frosty for a time.

Finally, springtime reigned supreme over the bay. Life had settled into a pattern and I was happy to see its predictableness. It was Easter morning and Jerome had prepared a breakfast feast. I was reading the paper.

"Your fondest wish has come true." She said it all the time.

"Well sure, I married you." It was a sliver of the liturgy of our marriage contract. A rote responsive reaffirmation of our marriage vows routinely said. I didn't even look up from the newspaper.

She sat quietly and I realized that she had not said 'and I love you", that completed her part of the affirmation. She'd always said it before.

The sense that something was missing slowly alerted my brain. I looked up from my newspaper to see Cooper's serious face.

"I'm pregnant," she said, almost in a whisper.

Elation filled me and then apprehension replaced the joy. I assumed it must have been an accident. Were those pills not foolproof? Now fully engaged, I said, "What are you going to do about it?"

Her expression clouded and she stared down at the breakfast table. "I was sure when I stopped taking the pill, and I'm still sure."

I realized that a legal abortion was hers for the asking and yet she was apparently ready to have my baby. It was a miracle. The woman sitting across from me was carrying *my* baby inside of *her*. The enormity of the moment would never let our lives be the same.

Cooper sat composed and she was smiling.

"Why didn't you warn me you were off the pill?" I said.

"If I changed my mind, I didn't want to disappoint you."

"You mean you would have had an abortion and not told me?"

She looked hurt and I recognized I'd said it in anger.

"I wasn't sure I'd get pregnant. I wanted to wait to tell you when I was sure I was."

Her answer pleased and shamed me. "Have you told your father?"

"I'm going to tell him later today."

"I'm so happy," I said. "Don't worry, we'll hire a nanny and you'll never miss a beat at work."

"We'll see. Maybe I won't go back to work."

"I can't imagine that. Are you conflicted by any of this? Is it what you want?"

"I want what you have. I want it all," she said softly. "I can *do* it all," she rephrased.

I got out of my seat and walked behind her chair. I wrapped my arms around her as she sat. "I know, I know, I know," I said. It was almost as a lullaby. We were turning a corner that could never be undone.

"Should we tell Jerome now?" she asked.

"Of course, his life is changing too. You should tell him now."

She walked to the kitchen and I didn't hear what she said to him, but his shouts of "Praise Jesus! Praise Jesus!" filled the halls of Bay Villa with hope and excitement on this Easter morning.

"Thy will be done?" I inquired to no one in particular. Taylor, Cooper, and I were willful people. I had no idea if God had played a role in this moment. I was sure that Reverend Randall Clay could enlighten me about the prosperity that was mine to claim. No matter, there was a child coming to Bay Villa and I rejoiced.

Cooper came back from the kitchen with Jerome in tow. "I couldn't be happier," he said as we shook hands. Then Cooper, Jerome and I hugged each other. Yes, the world was changing at Bay Villa and I could tell it was for the good.

"My God!" Cooper said.

"What?" I asked in terror that something had already gone wrong with the pregnancy.

"We'll have to join a church," she said with a look of bewilderment.

"Why?" I said with an equal dose of surprise.

"Our child has to be baptized," Cooper replied.

Under my breath I repeated, "Thy will be done?"

SELAH

Acknowledgements

The author thanks Al & Mimi Lodge, Peter Kindrachuk, Dale Laine, Cindy Boldebuck, Maud Hamovit, Patricia Nuhn and Lynn Bradley whose support and guidance made this book possible.

Special thanks to my wife Kathy, whose enthusiasm for this project never wavered.

Made in the USA
Coppell, TX
12 May 2021